TurnRight at the
WaterBuffalo

Turn Right at the Water Buffalo

by Jeannie Barroga

REGENT PRESS
Berkeley, California
2021

— *A Caveat Lector Book* —

[paperback]
ISBN 13: 978-1-58790-591-9
ISBN 10: 1-58790-591-4

[e-book]
ISBN 13 :978-1-58790-592-6
ISBN 10: 1-58790-592-2

Library of Congress Control Number: 2021951122

COVER CREDIT: Image ID: 223161967
Copyright Mstjahanara903 | Dreamstime.com
https://www.dreamstime.com/mstjahanara903_info

Manufactured in the U.S.A.
REGENT PRESS
Berkeley, CA 94705
www.regentpress.net

DEDICATION

TO

Tony Williams, my husband of a mere twenty years and theater bud for forty years. His talent and "good eye" and candidness have buoyed me through many (many) peaks and valleys throughout my theater career, now through two books, and throughout our married adventure together. He performed in my first television theatre project "Reaching for Stars" to his portrayal as Jan Scruggs in 'Walls" and is usually the first test case to read every new writing project over the past two decades, patiently so. A partner, friend, and lover, he brings me morning tea and hugs; a post-work day's report, an evening meal when I forget, a carpet for my studio, and provides not only a haven for us all but also unquestioning love, just what a writer needs without asking. Even my cats, Chanz, Duster, Buck, Angel, Des, and Sarah had accepted him. That, too, is good enough for me. Thanks, Tony, for your Endurance of this artist's career.

ENDORSEMENT

I've known Jeannie Barroga for several years now. Besides being a joy to work with, Jeannie is a prolific writer. Her shows have been performed in countless theaters and her work chronicled at Stanford University.

I have been a fan of Jeannie's work for three decades and throughout this time I have witnessed her work consistently grow, sharpening her voice, narrative, and composition. Jeannie's work as an actor has undoubtedly informed her as a storyteller whose work has increased in its breadth and in its depth each time she creates and discovers a good story.

In addition to her extraordinary talent, she just happens to be an overall good person with a great heart and a keen eye for compelling stories.

It is with enthusiasm that I recommend Jeannie Barroga for any award for which she qualifies, and I welcome any publications of her works.

— Ron Simons
Founder and CEO
SimonSays Entertainment Inc.
4-time Tony Award winner,
4 premieres at Sundance

ACKNOWLEDGMENTS

I must mention a few other supporters particularly through this journey to "Turn Right at the Water Buffalo" since July 2017: my mother, Restituta with whom a similar trip changed my writing focus; Ron Simons of SimonSays Entertainment, Inc.; Christopher Bernard, poet and cohort in our mid-1980s S.F. Playwrights Center writers' group; Cindy Knoebel, Sausalito Writers Circle; Mike Dorado, illuminating me on body guards; Jamie Morris, editor; and particularly, Kathy Sieja, fellow writer from our Stowell Avenue writers' group, Dem Women soccer team, and steady soul bud; Wendy Werner Zupke, first grade friend and Turn Right's dreamer; and my most urgent prodder to finish this book, Bill Broder, Sausalito fiction novelist. His range of subjects and foresight resound and influence my work. Thank you all for your unflagging belief in me over time and distance.

Salamat to: my parents' root islands, Leyte and Luzon, their barrios/barangays, its welcoming kababayans, those designated as the "Mays" and all revelers at their own ongoing reunions.

Thanks to readers: Francis Tanglao Aguas; Ken Barroga; Bill Broder; Christopher Bernard; Mike Dorado; Frances Gulland; Cindy Knoebel; Jan Komoll; Victoria Barroga Link; Maria Luisa Penaranda; Myrna Barroga Schultz; Kathy Sieja; Ron Simons; Deenie Tagudin; Stephen Williams; Tony Williams; Wendy Werner Zupke; Kathy Zeinemann; to Mark Weiman, Regent Press publisher; and to the Stockton FANHS Museum inviting me to present the book's early chapters in 2019: Letty Perez; Terri Torres; Val and Ben Acoba, Elena Mangahas; and Emil Guillermo.

To siblings, their families I hope will read TRWB: Ken, Norie, Mike, Monty, Peter.

Maraming Salamat Po.

WITHIN OTHER EDITORS' BOOKS:

UNBROKEN THREAD: An Anthology of Plays by Asian American Women ("WALLS") Roberta Uno, editor (1993) University of Massachusetts-Amherst Press, publisher

TWO PLAYS by Jeannie Barroga ("KENNY WAS A SHORTSTOP"; "THE REVERED MISS NEWTON") Luz DeLeon, editor (1994) CrossCurrents, publisher

MULTICULTURAL THEATRE: Scenes and Monologues from New Hispanic, Asian and African-American Plays ("WALLS") Roger Ellis, editor (1996) Meriwether Publishing, Colorado Springs, CO

REFLECTIONS OF DIVERSITY: A Scenebook for Student Actors Gough, editors (1996) Jennifer King and Thomas A. University of California-Davis publisher

BUT STILL, LIKE AIR, I'LL RISE: New Asian American Plays ("TALK-STORY") Velina Hasu Houston, editor (1999) Temple Press, Philadelphia

WOMEN PLAYWRIGHTS OF DIVERSITY Suzanne Bennett, editor (1994) Jane T. Peterson and Rutgers University/Greenwood Press, publisher

PERFORMING ASIAN AMERICA: Josephine Lee, editor (1999) Temple Press, publisher (dissertation on "TALK-STORY")

FIL-AM ("One Fil-Am's Experience in American Theatre") Alfred Yuson, editor (1999) Philippine National Bank, publisher

MONOLOGUES FOR ACTORS OF COLOR ("TALK-STORY")
Roberta Uno, editor (1999) Routledge Press, publisher

BOLD WORDS ("EYE OF THE COCONUT") Rajini Srikanth
and Esther Iwanaga, co-editors (2001) Rutgers University Press,
publisher

ASIAN AMERICAN PLAYWRIGHTS: A Bio-Bibliographical
Critical Sourcebook (p.6-13) publisher Miles T. Liu, editor (2002)
University of Massachusetts-Amherst Press

NATIONAL ABJECTION - Asian American Body Onstage ("TALK
STORY") Karen Shimakawa, editor (2002) Duke University Press

BEYOND LUMPIA ("Haunted") Vangie Buell (plus), editors
(2015) Eastwind Books of Berkeley

Theater Productions by the Author

A Good Face
Banyan
Buffalo'ed
Eye of the Coconut
Gadgets
Lorenzo, Love
Rita's Resources
Sistersoul
Talk-Story
Walls

Also Available for Production

Aurora
Gadgets
"M"
Mattie Mae's
Tracking Kilroy

For rights to productions, contact:
Jeannie Barroga
415-717-6905
jeannie@jeanniebarroga.com
www.jeanniebarroga.com

CHAPTERS

I

The trip wasn't about boxes or mules but more about the first grand steps of Lainie's mother, Reena, re-entering her hometown of Ormoc City, Leyte. She would just first regally arrive – without Lainie.

Lainie loved travel. She'd pack and fly the next red-eye flight at the drop of a kerchief. Reena knew that. She knew Lainie knew. Lainie hated that.

But Lainie should have known to heed the signs.

Reena took on 1870s Shanghai Kelly's ruse. He instead had spiked drinks of unsuspecting saloon patrons, who by morning, had been hijacked. On ships miles from shore, captive deck hands, sailors and landlubbers alike had succumbed to the shenanigans Kelly perfected. The bar right across from Lainie's sway-backed redwood cottage on Broadway Avenue and Polk Street was a testimony to Kelly's notoriety. Reena spiked her ruse enticing Lainie with the lure of "roots" – theirs.

The timing of Reena's call, the roar of honks in the nearby clogged Broadway tunnel, the simultaneous clang of the cable car, the dissonant foghorns bellowing across the Bay warning ships of sloped land encroaching their paths, and that evening's sudden thump of faults shifting the earth underfoot into second gear, all orchestrated to alert Lainie: *heed*, they all called, *heed*.

But none were so resonant a warning or so red a flag as Reena's offer to pay Lainie's fare to the Homeland, the Philippines – *pay*, aka, FREE. Reena had dangled the invitation; Lainie had bitten.

She thought to look deeper behind Reena's gesture, to pay her way, but only for a second. Lainie had been sedentary lately, and bored, drugged into near slavishness, and her travel bug was thirsty.

Hearing the word: *free*, Lainie, lured, dared, destined, had heeded none of the signs.

Carry her mother's *balikbayan* boxes? Decipher an unknown tongue? Consult any map?

How could she be a mule or a translator when she was born to be an explorer?

This trip wouldn't be about boxes. Yet once again, Lainie would not heed.

II

Reena was groomed for heat. Packing sundries for her trip, she was distracted, planning.

In her mid-sixties, she pushed at a strand of hair, shiny black-white. This way, her good eye, could dart to far-off points beyond her window. Her idea had been launched. All day, more sparks of genius would illuminate her features like a Midwestern firefly in flight at dusk.

Flashing forward, she had envisioned almost to the hour Week 1 around her hometown and then Week 2, Ormoc. She squatted among gifts and tiny boxes. This was her go-to position, the Filipino chair. She could have perched in this position for hours. Her cockatiel screeched. She swiped her hand in its general direction within its cage. "*Na!* Quiet!" Her house, her rules.

The Wisconsin humidity pushed rivulets of sweat from her brow. Shelled bugs twanged against the screen door sounding much like her deceased husband Geraldo's broken guitar strings during nights of his exuberant strumming with the band. Years ago, neighbors had draped themselves over fences, bobbing their heads in rhythm to his free music. Reena now relished her silence and her plan.

Suburbia's mauve and beige, one- or two-storied tract homes like hers lined her street. Reena had fronted her house with flowers and trellises. Geraldo's touch was gone, like his arty painted triangles on the gate, faded and indistinguishable. He had shown them off to Lainie weeks before he died.

For years since Geraldo's death, Reena's kids and grandkids stopped in for visits, which sloughed off. Backyard music was all that had lured them, now nonexistent, and maybe the food and maybe Reena. Indian autumn baked suburbs and sizzled moods. Kids had moved nearer to Lake Michigan's cool shores.

One neighboring couple would check on Reena, the lone widow. Sharp heat radiating from cement would seep through their shoes. Till she answered, they'd dance on one foot, then the other, not invited to enter, bleating her name and hooding their foreheads. She used to wave, her signal that she was still kicking. Last July, she ignored them. They hadn't been back since.

Geraldo was the draw for them and his spontaneous gigs, not his "China-doll" wife.

To Reena, they were so unlike neighbors (*silingans*) back "home". Here, streets were maintained and paved but empty. At "home", languorous couples paced in slow promenades on trails jammed with chaperones at a decent distance behind the lovers. Here, no nearby mountains gave Reena a sense of scale. No heady aromas of roasted chicken or dinuguan filled her nostrils. No fellow Ormocanons of Ormoc, Leyte, called to her in Cebuano.

Once "home", Reena determined that she would show off her English after forty-two years in America. Vi, Reena's best friend had visited "home" many times whereas Reena hadn't ever, yet. Vi always stuffed her *balikbayans.* "Ormoc love American goods, cuz. *Sigé,* Americans are our saviors!" Vi paid no mind to their history reflecting only American successes, including decimating Ormoc.

Their island had been strategic during World War II Japanese occupation and made famous with General Douglas MacArthur's vow: "I shall return". In 1944, he did. American planes strafed and sliced the crap out of the Bay of Ormoc, most of its buildings, citizens, and scurrying Japanese soldiers. The U.S. had leveled Ormoc after Reena had turned seventeen. She had been crowned Queen of Agriculture. For Ormocanons in WWII, theirs was an era of landmarks.

Now in 1989, Vi would join Reena on her trip home. Clueless Lainie would follow.

On flight day, Reena would haul loaded *balikbayan* boxes, squirreled from behind stores, to check them in at Milwaukee's Billy Mitchell Airport. Reena decided enduring hardships for travel was like a Catholic thing, similar to the annual Lenten season depriving oneself of comforts. Anyone like Reena desiring redemption must suffer continually and serve penance for leaving the homeland and, in her case, representing her wooden cross, cart boxes with American goods.

But penance for her would be two boxes, no more, no less, and protests from her kids:

"What about kidnappers? What about bathrooms?" One sibling had her priorities.

In 1989 Philippines, the P.I., citizens were still crawling out from under Ferdinand Marcos's dictatorship. Nationalists, labeled insurgents, ran rampant, and emotions steamed between them and leftover Marcos loyalists. The young Filipinos whom Lainie taught were actually self-exiled League of Filipino Students and active in the highly publicized 1986 Manila Revolution that "surprised the world". Reena received the students' warning through Lainie.

"Tell your mother that travel's easy going to the P.I., just not so easy coming back. With only a visa," they added, "Your mother may not be allowed to return." Unknown to Lainie, Reena ruminated on returning at all to beautiful downtown Mukwonago. After all, two years had passed since Geraldo's death.

Widow of a naturalized citizen, Reena had believed she sat pretty till her kids left pamphlets on Reena's table: "U.S. Deportation Removal Proceedings." Her alien status meant deportation. Even hushed, the term, Immigration and Naturalization Service, set Reena on edge.

So she had crammed for the exam. Now, with her liberating passport Reena could disperse iconic American goodies and to all of Ormoc, show movies and photos of her U.S. Christmases.

Vi, as ever, had let a comment slip watching Reena pack albums and cartridges and labeling them with dates. "Oy, no *BHS* players, *sigé na*, only BETA, did you not know?" Vi lorded over the moment.

Reena swore. "*Tangina!*" Hell with VHS. She had more tangible proof of success.

She had snagged Lainie who would show how milk and orange cheese fattened children who would fill out crinoline dresses and sequined tops, not just viewed in photos.

Reena's Ormoc cousin Luis's family basked in wealth and privilege. Arriving with just one of her kids, grown and nourished, would place both herself and her brood alongside that category. Yes.

Already withholding some minor travel details from Lainie, Reena had also swept to the side a slight family land issue, a simple repossession, possible through one sibling signing papers for all her siblings as the closest kin beyond Reena, hence, the proffered airfare. She had to be steps ahead of Lainie who might avoid such a trip and accountability, unless it was free. Besides, the others already said no . . .

No matter: get her on the plane. Upon landing, Lainie would descend the rollaway staircase and shine as a prime example of U.S. acculturation, daughter of the Agriculture Queen.

Reena pushed the hair covering her eye recalling cousin Nita luring her with letters about the land to "regain what's ours." Nita had enclosed a legal notice of the final three-month deadline to respond in person, only forty-some years overdue. Nita was always dependable. Reena felt smug, confident.

Hell with home movies. Ormoc: meet a real, live Filipino American.

Otherwise, Reena's escape from Ormoc years earlier held no weight; hearsay, they'd say, *leaving "home" and for what, better lives? Aiie, look: proof of success! May insurgents not take her, talaga!* Ha! Reena would still have her worthier American legacies safely stateside vs last-choice Lainie. Insurgents would not dare take her. Reena had talked up the others more. Besides: Reena could get her back. Yes.

Either way, Reena would gain favor again, though Lainie would rail a bit. Alienation between Reena and all her kids was already steeped in resentment like thickened tea, clouded and cold. She reminded herself: I'm doing this for them. Her bird squawked. Reena smiled, reappraised one gift she had been packing, a de la Renta silk top. She should keep this luxury for herself. Plans were coming together.

III

Lainie was probably a product of an alien encounter. Her culture clashed with Reena's culture.

Perhaps, she thought, that's why they had altercations, each growing much like an irritating pustule blocking reconciliation and, having run its course, morphed into a stony pimple.

Yet here she was, Lainie the Other, about to join Mom in the homeland.

Lainie fantasized her alien conception: the band's pit stop, Route 66, Kansas, Geraldo, on the music circuit, newly married, blinded by light, sucked out of the Buick, balls injected with alien sperm, returning for nookies with Reena, his reward for that year's highest-paying gig. Lainie was conceived, no matter that the other musicians saw no light nor had more babies conceived at the same time.

How could she be a part of her family, a group already visibly unlike their neighborhood, namely, white? Hardheaded, belligerent, deserving swats, even orchestrated reasons for them, Lainie would stand ramrod stiff against Reena's blows as only an alien could, with no tear ducts. Yeah, and, and why would anyone treat her own kid like Reena treated her? Why, even when the other sibs had said no, would Reena still invite her – *her*? Antsy, she needed a walk, no, a ride.

Lainie threw on her caftan and caught the Powell/Hyde Street cable car a block from her cottage. She had a seat all the way – perhaps a sign? She had carried no map, priding herself on getting around, testing her travel skills and imagining herself in Ormoc, alone.

For a simple Midwestern gal, she was exhilarated stepping onto the legendary clanking, windy car on a daily basis, marveled still by the grip man working gear handles half his height. The rails still protested and squeaked uphill while passengers endured each other's proximity. Singed air tasted like nickels in her mouth. The route skirted Chinatown, a cathedral, a mansion, hoity-toity hotels, a church, and the beefy, hormonal male grill, which reeked with agéd meats and old cigars. At Market Street, laconic cops directed muddled traffic.

Lainie had educated herself around towns, known or new, around modes of transportation deciphering languages she barely spoke, with charts and their keys, like with men, but with tattered maps to their secret caves and leaving few crumbs marking paths to her own heart.

And this trip, she already felt, would challenge her to use or discard her alien ways. Lainie, informed that she was mom's last choice, headed to a hotel bar to salve her smarting, otherworldly ego.

Lainie, right up till the second Tuesday in October weighed plusses and minuses: go or stay. Only last spring Lainie had severed ties when Reena accused her wrongfully of pocketing change after buying her dried mangoes, rare in Mukwonago. So had one sister, for mocking Bette Davis, and her brother who had peeled an orange for her without permission, for Christ's sake. All events ended in absences and then in acquiescence.

Reena, triumphant, only uttered, "Oy, see? God punishes. Feel better now?"

Lainie had wished for a map to Reena's interior: God, a queendom for that map. She signaled a Hyatt Regency waiter. Funneling from point A to B through the City, she thought, had proved she was San Francisco's girl, not Mukwonago's or Manila's or Ormoc's.

Each successive floor with its puzzling walls slanted inward in the Hyatt Regency lobby creating a tottering, dizzying effect for Lainie, like for Jimmy Stewart in "Vertigo." She nursed her very expensive Glen Livet. Just the thought of travel with mom provoked her to drink Scotch, little ice. Even mom's friend, Vi, had threatened to stay home three times in two months.

"You don't need a guardian. I don't." Vi had complained over lunch at Ming's Szechuan Delight. "What are you up to?"

Reena sniffed. "Hmph, I tell you anything and it's splattered everywhere, like shit."

"Aiee, you are a shit! You go by yourself, see if I care!" Vi paused. "Oy, you still going?"

"Why wouldn't I? I'm not helpless. I'll pay baggage clerks to carry boxes."

"Pay me!" Vi had to whine. "Oh, just keep your secret and go to hell!"

Patient Chinese waiters brushed off white napkins nearby, rolling their eyes heavenward.

Stubborn Reena won out. Their flight day arrived. Vi ate humble pie and tagged along.

Once in the P.I., both created havoc particularly Reena with her *grande dame* entrance: "Oy, I held up the plane. A *balik-bayan* box broke. Vi forgot she hid her passport inside the barf bag. Stewardesses found it. Four porters carried my boxes to the curb. I paid them four quarters."

Over the phone, Lainie had asked. "So no creature comforts or heating pad or ice cubes?"

"We have ice cubes, for five minutes. Just drink fast."

Lainie related her warning from some P.I. students. "A lot of NPA's kidnap tourists, the New People's Army."

Reena snorted.

Lainie backed off. "That's probably not every island."

Still, she quoted one young woman wearing her familial tribal neck scarf: "Leyte's between Cebu and Samar, places that are really active." Lainie had nodded sagely.

The woman had added. "You should know this."

To that, Lainie had just blushed: *dang know-it-all, radical, Ateneo-now-S.F. State University student.* Yet Lainie had invited rebukes earlier quipping that hybrid Fil-Ams were *upgrades.* Ooh.

Their reaction had whittled her to her knees in embarrassment with a cutting, "Ay, colonial mentality!"

This phrase sliced through most of the lively discussions between Fil-Fils and Fil-Ams, the Philippines-born versus the American born. These students were at least the third generation whose local history had been peppered with the United States white-savior antics after the P.I. had quashed their first oppressors for over five hundred years, Spain. The same scarfed woman had spouted. "We revised our history. It reflects us more now.

23

Your history books gloss over all the histories of the countries the U.S. conquered." She clipped this line: "You should know this."

Maybe Lainie didn't deserve the Hyatt's over-priced warm, watered-down Scotch. She drained it and headed out, still undecided and less informed. What *was* she flying into?

Outside, she swerved south toward Market Street. An older, all silvery, white-haired woman caught Lainie's eye. She wore a kimono, bedangled hoop earrings, glittery bracelets, beaded necklaces and was draped in a long hippie-style, pattern-swirled skirt. She stood cawing and jangling her jewelry. Men in suits and women in designer outfits took great pains not to look but had to peer over a hotel's lidded refuse cart blighting their views. The matron herself blocked a city bus.

"Garbage! All garbage! You eat garbage, you live in garbage!" the old woman blared. "This ain't it! This ain't it!"

Her clarion message declared that they, the suits, the purses, the shoes, and the snubs *were not* It. Everyone hearing her gaped as the silvery woman trudged off, mumbling and waving the air in front of her. Lainie boarded the bus, stalled by the woman's rant.

On the ride home, Lainie thought, the woman, like a town crier, trumpeted about something larger, something that *was* It. Why is mom returning now? Why did Lainie have students from the P.I. *now*, as if any sign was meant for her, or both of them, to heed – *heed*.

The woman's rant made Lainie view her ride back through the city's richest and poorest areas seem as illusionary as a trek through trees dripping vines, heady with intrigue yet belying any true safety.

Marking her own bus stop, Lainie's neighborhood was just as contradictory: upbeat, affluent, depressed, and unaffordable.

But in her cottage among her bills spilt from her mail slot, she found a check, overdue but fated to be her passage to the unknown. This was finally the full seven hundred fifty dollars for the travel article on Puerto Vallarta. Her luck four months earlier included a week in canceled yet paid timeshare complete with luxurious accommodations and a tour to Los Cabos, despite a spiked drink, Shanghai Kelly style.

Signs, more signs: the Universe had granted Lainie permission to go, to sally forth.

She was heading to the Philippines.

She could tell those students on her return: I know more things now. *I've been there, nyah.*

Plans: for her three jobs, she would call in sick or cite "limited availability". She would pack, again and again. Paltry chores done, she dragged on a joint. Curling up, an oven-like bun, Lainie lay among the pillows and drifted in and out of sleep. Traffic, shouts in Chinese, lilting Italian opera, and thumping hip-hop music called from nearby North Beach. Did she imagine the steely smell of century-old gears, its friction against wood, then a sharp, reeling, exotic aroma of cloves, spices, fishy-ness, and salty bays with turbaned men in pantaloons as if they were from an another place, tattooed by time?

Still dreaming, she saw a shiny woman with hoop earrings hold up a barf bag, remove papers, and wave them. She huffed in a kind of crazed, ominous chuckle, scaring Lainie. Her nightmare prompted her to kick at sheets. As if glued, she could only crawl or claw forward. Streaming nowhere by car, train, plane, she was then braced against a battering din of noise and touched ancient crypts baked by heat.

She awoke from a similar dream a week later, her neck cranked and her temple flat against her portal window on Philippine Airlines. Reena's fledgling had arrived at their *home.*

IV

A thud had banged under Reena's feet. Outside her own port-hole window a week earlier, Philippine Airlines workers had zipped around haphazardly parked, open-air train carts. They hauled unmatched luggage and boxes onto the conveyor belt under her cabin seat. Finally they drove off in a line, leaning into the turn, laying rubber, their carts lightened of loads, like her *balikbayans*.

Hours earlier at Milwaukee's Billy Mitchell Airport check-in, she had whined to her son-in-law who had driven her. "You can load and unload the boxes, yes? And you can lug them to check-in, eh? Oh, and give me American quarters so I can pay the porters in Manila, okay? Good son, good son."

Dutifully, he had waited till both boxes he had hoisted onto the conveyor rode out of sight, smooched Reena's head and left. Charmingly, she wiggled through Customs and followed Vi in the B queue line, found her row, and spun three times before backing into the far seat. Travel was so hard, Reena sighed, and – because she could – had directed an attendant to dig for her own seatbelt tucked within reach between the seat cushions, a queen re-training minions.

On cue Vi timed her freak-out, synched to flare up whenever Reena got too much attention.

The plane taxied. Ah, *home* would be just like before when she and Geraldo married, Reena added: *God willing*. She was ready. She had lingered on possibly her last view of America, that flat Midwestern horizon beyond the tarmac. She even made herself feel abject loss.

She had ignored Vi beside her, maneuvering for more space than her center seat allowed.

She thought of one daughter's goodbye kiss, the other's worry, another's inward silence, and her gadget-obsessed grandkids. Neighbors had marveled at her abundant, nurtured flowers; she knew few of them detected how she thinned the patience of her own children.

Lainie would arrive in a week. Reena recalled her daughter Calista's misgiving. "Lainie? *Your* guard? Who'll be hers?" The other four kids were professionals in their fields, a doctor, two investors, and a realtor. They touted actual pay stubs, houses, and children. Lainie's forté promoted fantasy, travel writing, painting with words pictures of poor countries with big hotels, visions hardly based in reality. If surrounded, she'd probably be glued to a notebook while Reena batted off insurgents with a slipper.

So Reena had set up a type of guard for Lainie, paid not directly by her but by covering airfare for Lainie, who in turn would pay for the guard. Maybe Lainie would not get that at first, but fantasy also ruled Reena: Lainie accepting travel–guarded travel–free travel was the tradeoff.

By now, Reena reasoned, Lainie should have grown out of misadventures, at five getting lost while Reena shopped; joyriding at fifteen with boys touting misdemeanors; graduating in five years, encountering a shady shaman, an aged painter, and almost marrying a Mykonos fisherman. Lainie had been noticeably reticent re-telling that incident. "No worries," she had said. However, if in Ormoc, Lainie erred that way again, Reena's plans might not unfold as simply as she had thought.

Reena touched her large purse with Nita's letters collected over the years, with clippings from the Ormoc's Eastern Visayan News. She had memorized the key letter: "This is it, cuz: three months notice. We can file our final response together. Come soon. We miss you."

Ignoring Vi's streaming monolog next to her, Reena took out her stiff, official-looking, blue passport. In her picture, she faced left, one earlobe visible. Compared to her town mates' photos, her skin was still starkly white and her chin still firm. Yet she had aged. Her Bette Davis eyes, maybe they bulged a bit more. But friends, she believed, would recognize her. After all, a mother will show some exhaustion after birthing five abundant children. Abundant, was that what she meant? Or were they full-bodied, stocky? Jesus, they definitely were not rich or they'd pay *her* way. Prosperous! She'd report that they were *"well off and prospered"*. How original of her.

Perhaps she should at least warn Lainie about "rebels" still contesting American takeover. Or maybe the nationalists finally buckled under U.S. rule.

She decided to bypass politics with Lainie.

Americans run their country. Americans still dominate, Reena determined. It's a given.

She removed the article from Nita's aerogram envelope and read again – "Extrajudicial Settlement of Estate with Sale of a Portion of Real Property." Reena had grouped the notice with a clipping: "Petition for Declaration of Absence Presumptive Death", namely, their granduncle.

So many letters had been sent over so many years. Once, young Lainie had sped into the house with an aerogram from the mailbox. "Read it to me." So Reena half-translated the slanted Cebuano handwriting, re-phrasing, skipping, and even fabricating sections. Otherwise she mumbled. "You won't understand . . .some kin you don't even know." She had then hid the letters.

In Ormoc, Lainie could uncover things for herself if she wanted.

Reena wanted only to keep her secrets smoky and to bury what she had been.

Would anyone miss Reena, at home, in Mukwonago, besides her cockatiel, cared for now by her grandniece? What would *she* miss: the young ones, her flowers, and the house. That's all.

Doctors – she may miss doctors and other conveniences. Still, how silly to even keep a list.

Way problema. Soundly, she slept most of the flight, endured Vi's wig-out misplacing her passport, cried alligator tears meeting friends, posed for Kodak snapshots, inscrutably listened to forgotten Cebuano during the ride to Ormoc, ate, ate more, and began to mumble back her language which she had not mouthed in years. Reena was satisfied she had covered all the bases, except for the decision if she would return or not. Prodigal Reena had re-entered the fold.

V

Greeting Lainie's arrival, the sun had flooded the cabin of the plane, waking her. She made her way past seated passengers and stumbled into the can with her handy travel cup, with which she'd wash her hair, pouring cup after cup over her head. Back in her seat after the fifteen-hour flight, Lainie braced for the landing at Manila's Ninoy Aquino Airport. Gripping the armrests, she gazed at the small puzzle of *hectares*, plantations, all askew and lush. Then she was shocked by corrugated, tin-topped structures, ragtag and one-storied. People lived like this?

Farther ahead, a steaming pile of hills with more slap-shod dwellings signaled one edge of the international city of Manila. Infamous Smokey Mountain was a dumpsite, home to thirty thousand people, sorting garbage for a living. Why not, thought Lainie, why not just remove it?

The pilot skirted haphazard huts blanketing the runway's edge. He taxied to the gate. Lainie had tensed till the seatbelt light winked out. Rising to stand mid-aisle, passengers began hauling their over-sized luggage from above and below their seats. Foot traffic lurched. Bodies flattened against her and crushing everyone forward through the narrow aisle and spilled down the ramp. Far from the terminal, Lainie gasped and then inhaled heat, a smothered intake. The humid heat of high noon baked her. What else hadn't Reena mentioned in her phone call a week earlier?

VI

Resting in her mother Billina's former room in Ormoc, Reena dreamt about flies, flight, and leafy hideaways. She had been lounging, queen-like, biding her time when cousin Nita entered and sniffled remembering this as Billina's nest. Nita had housed Billina here till her death. Wiping off her tears, Nita left. Now, in 1989, alone in Nita's spare room, Reena allowed herself to review her own final moment in 1947 with Billina.

That final moment was not at all weepy or showy. In fact, Reena was cool, detached. Billina had tried to hug her daughter as she headed out. Instead, serving as her farewell, Reena swatted at flies. Three years earlier, Leyte's 1944 Liberation, had soured her.

Reena, by age 20 had graduated, took summer classes in Cebu honing office skills, English, her hair, hygiene, and fashion. Swarms of American soldiers, one named Geraldo, had remained stationed in strategic Ormoc harbor. She sewed. Her couture drew envy from town mates. She laundered an older officer's clothes. She had money. She just needed an opportunity.

Reena, since the bombing of Ormoc, had made time-sensitive plans. She bought every eye-catching color movie magazine that flooded Ormoc heralding the need for American goods. She borrowed pesos from Vi to purchase bolts from Hong Kong, to sew and sell outfits, and to reimburse Vi with a free dress. She upgraded herself and lost more of the former Reena, childlike and wide-eyed, before the bombs. By 1947 she held her chin higher, locked her stares, quipped saucy retorts, stood her ground and never gave a millimeter of herself. The newly re-vamped Reena led her gang into town, collecting sighs and shy boys. Her goals were either to be an overseas worker or a war bride. Show the wares; snag the man. Gain status. Live abroad.

She had laundered well, catching the attention of the officer. She ignored how he gauged her other assets. The officer had children and needed a governess back in the States.

"Why don't you come work for me in Texas?" the captain had asked one day.

She did not hesitate. "Okay."

She took the job. She did not have to marry or take the lesser-paid overseas housemaid job. For the captain's offer, she had to submit foreign travel papers in the capital of Manila. But even for this short trip, at their door Billina had reached for Reena, who had avoided her.

She never returned from Manila. Only one swat in the air had served as Reena's farewell to her mother. A war had proven home had no safety. Why stay? She polled more reasons. Geraldo, her fiancé, hadn't written as promised. Forget his stolen moments and kisses.

Hell with him, too.

But, through scheming friends, Geraldo had found her in Manila filing travel papers.

"I can go to the States!" she had glared at Geraldo. "I need to go to the States!"

"I'll take you, if you want to go. I'll marry you. Your officer won't. He'll take advantage. Reena, *carinosa*, you are too young to know what men really want," Geraldo was pleading.

Reena had snubbed him, his hand reaching for hers. The next day she had married him.

VII

At Customs, Lainie swung her backpack onto the long chrome counter, expectant.

"Is this all you have, ma'am?" Customs saw her blue passport and spoke English.

"Yes, that's it."

"No other checked bags, boxes?" he slowly patted down the sides of the pack.

"No, I just have this."

He spoke to his co-worker in Tagalog. His partner said aloud, "Plebiña Cortez."

"A Plebiña came through here last week." He was keeping his delivery too casual.

"Yes, I'm catching up to my mother."

Lainie reviewed Reena's conversation about Vi's passport in the barf bag and torn boxes. Oh my God, Lainie blanched, they remember her mother!

"Where, ma'am?" Ah, the Test, the queries, faster.

"Ormoc."

"Ormoc City, yes, I remember now."

With Lainie's arrival, even baggage clerks joked over the incident, the havoc.

"Usually, Filipinos bring gifts to the islands, in the, uh, the . . ."

"*Balikbayan* boxes, yes." Lainie finished. She did know something after all.

"Yes," he still had not looked at Lainie. "Presents for their countrymen."

Lainie got it. She, in contrast, had brought nothing with her, nothing to share from the richest country in the world. To Customs, she was one more privileged, stingy American-born piker, in other words, thoughtless.

She maneuvered through the obstacle course after braving

32

Customs, ignoring the catcalls from behind the cyclone fence. The homing call sizzled in the muggy air: *Sss-ssst*, those distinctive hisses heeded by blood relatives, drilled since toddler age to hone in and dash toward the Call.

"*Oy, ssst-sst,* 'Merican, come here, oy, babee-babee-babee . . ." was not a family Call. Whatever defined her as American, she wondered, aware of her blousy outfit.

She hugged herself, a habit since puberty. The heat and stares made her face burn.

She reached the large exit, which put passengers smack on the street. Eager and hopeful welcome parties displayed signs with names. Then Lainie saw her name . . . and her relatives.

The tallest man, large-featured, held the sign high. Another man with a buzz cut and in shorts grinned nearby. A woman waved in her light floral dress and fanny pack strapped to her waist. Three children waited, knees turned inward. She could see any of them resembling her.

Lainie approached them and smiled shyly. Amazingly, they descended on her, hugging, patting her on the back. But the first to tear up was the lanky tall man. Lainie also started crying. She didn't know why. She did not know how they were related to her at all.

The woman wore no makeup. Lainie thought of Reena's used lipstick cases packed in those *balikbayan* boxes. When Reena had asked Lainie for hers, she begged off: she had no leftovers. Sorry.

The woman prodded Juan, buzz-cut. He could face Lainie directly; his toothy grin, and grizzled gray buzz hair belied his age. He moved like a teen. In his mid-fifties, he and the taller man, Primo, were brothers. The woman and the boys were Primo's family. Their names eluded Lainie. The Taglish mix of their language tested Lainie.

During the four-hour layover, they mimed or spoke short English words while Lainie struggled with hastily gleaned Tagalog before reverting to her more comfortable English.

"So you know Nita? My mother, Reena, she arrived with Vi?"

Their hands flew about, they talked over each other, they pointed, and they jabbed her to listen. Lainie felt bruised. Primo pointed to himself and Juan. His forefinger cut the air above himself and his brother. "Nita, sister, our sister. One." Ah, Nita was Primo and Juan's only sister.

Lainie felt the hunger pangs while they hand-signaled in the grueling sun. When they lapsed into silence again, Lainie made a gesture to her mouth. Everyone knows the sign for EAT.

To Lainie's surprise, they all piled into an actual cab. Juan was a seasoned Manila cab driver. He maneuvered through the Makati streets between the airport and Metro Manila, made a short stop where he jumped out, ran up some stairs and returned with a bag. Barreling on in his jeepney, Juan squeezed through the narrower throughways, past brick buildings, and crowded, wood-framed hovel like storefronts with handmade signs or boarded windows.

The city's beat pummeled Lainie, a rhythm to which the cab hummed and warm, guttural talk harmonized. The family pointed past her face to the sights on either side of the cab. Juan sped by the weeping grayed cream fortification of the ominous Walled City. Fort Santiago had protected churches, *illustrado* (upper class) houses, stores, government edifices, and a seventeenth-century university. Luneta Park marked where poet/novelist Jose Rizal was executed. He penned romance and rebellion. After five hundred plus years under Spain, his death catapulted Filipino resistance. Within fifty years, the U.S. had bought the Islands and then finally had granted native Filipinos their own independence. Lainie knew some history. Beyond language, though, within an hour (she had timed it), she would show her butt on cultural nuances.

Lainie stepped from the jeepney. Before entering gritty San Agustin Church, Primo's wife plopped a limp, lacy circular mantilla onto Lainie's head. Reena had managed to warn her during her phone call that upon arrival, street urchins would surround her. "So watch your bags."

The children, barefoot, thin but eagle-eyed, frightened Lainie with their targeted unblinking eyes, gauging her size as if she were edible. They brushed fingers against her waist and back. She knew her valuables were inaccessible, but she recoiled at their pawing. Riding the wave of crowds, Lainie spilled into the narthex of the church leading to the center nave. The beggars backed off from a priest who forbade them any entry or more likely, any sinful behavior within sacred walls.

Soon, Lainie was whisked back into the cab and the lacy mantilla was swiped off her head. Aromas teased her stomach, which grumbled. The group asked. "Filipino food. You like?"

They showed surprise when Lainie said, "Chinese?" In her mind, she figured a meal near the airport saved someone from cooking and she would catch the last leg into Tacloban, Leyte.

Besides, that way everyone would actually see each other face-to-face and not just passing traffic.

What *was* she thinking?

Primo's wife chose the restaurant. They scurried into their seats around a rectangular plastic covered table, children close to their parents, and Juan close to Lainie. She noted the lack of knives, valued especially in the provinces. Instead, customized World War II blades from bayonets replaced any cutting utensils. On string belts, men would secure their makeshift, thick-bladed machetes, also former G.I. leftovers, handy to hack at stalks and pineapples and ward off jealous husbands. Like in her childhood, here in the motherland, Lainie would use forks and spoons only.

Once Primo's wife started ordering, Lainie was shocked. Had she ordered the whole menu? *Budget*, Lainie became stressed. She had a budget! With the table stacked, they gestured at her to fill her dish. Then they descended on the food. She had to play this out, for her budget.

The bill arrived, nearly a quarter of her purse. She waited. They waited. With hand signs, she demonstrated. "Half. Split. Whole table." Karate chop. They stared. She stared. Finally, the woman unzipped her fanny pack revealing bills of pesos, much more than what Lainie carried, that were beautifully printed paper pesos with their first president Aguinaldo's portrait.

The group had covered their large lunch bill fare evenly. Lainie managed a creaky, "Salamat (*thank you*)." Only Juan stared but looked away whenever she caught his eye.

Lainie figured suggesting Chinese food and negotiating payment were big *faux pas*.

Then Lainie handed out gifts at Ninoy Aquino Airport. To Primo, Juan's taciturn older brother with a rather large mouth, Lainie presented a wrapped American t-shirt. Once Primo opened it, they all saw the Rolling Stones logo, the one with very large lips! Lainie was mortified. While packing, she had just grabbed clothes, any clothes, unworn, over-sized, and free.

Everyone was silent. Then they mumbled low and were secretive. Juan paced around and past everyone. His high-pitched hum sounded like a warning. Lainie had screwed up. They hated her. She should have checked the shirts. She should have held off on any thoughtless gifts.

Lainie caught a phrase about a bodyguard. The woman projected Juan at her. He had picked up her backpack when they met and had been hauling it ever since. Lainie smiled. "Um, how nice, but I don't need a bodyguard. I'm only here another hour, so, um, *salamat*."

They looked puzzled. "Escort," someone stated. "Ormoc". She still smiled but got it.

"Sigé, no one needs to join me, *salamat*, it's all right, um, I travel alone just fine."

The group shuffled, undirected. Lainie deduced that it was not all right.

Primo's wife pointed to Lainie's waist, then to Juan, and then at Lainie. She crossed her arms defiantly. Lainie wilted. Here only three hours, she had angered them. She felt glum.

Juan stared, unblinking. Wait, she thought, did he, did

THEY think she would pay for Juan's flight? That despite whatever she said, somehow it was a given that he would be her escort while she was in Ormoc? The woman seemed demanding; Juan's hurt expression tugged at Lainie.

Primo's wife stated briefly, in English, "Your mother."

Ahh. Lainie's mother had proposed the idea. Lainie was painted as the rich daughter from America, someone who could afford this trip and a guard: Lainie can pay, *way problema*. She sighed.

Biting her lip, she looked around for a ticket counter. They all eagerly turned her in that direction. Lainie chided herself. Reena had withheld more details. Reena was duplicitous – again.

For Juan, his job started immediately. He trailed her closely to the ticket counter. The cost was 900p (pesos), or thirty-two American dollars. Juan watched, eagle-eyed. Somehow, if he had again looked away, Lainie would have said, "No go, sorry." But his gaze was steady, bearing whatever fate was left for him: *You decide. I am in your debt, or I stay here.*

She could almost hear that thought. One Manila lunch, one bodyguard: *ka-ching.*

"Two for Tacloban, round trip," she stated to the counter clerk.

Juan watched over her shoulder. Lainie parted with her dwindling pesos. He relaxed.

Bodyguard, she sighed, a free ride, in her book. Within four hours, she felt sucker-punched with an age-old hustle. Damn it.

From then on at her heels, Juan really did become amazingly attentive, grabbing her backpack plus his and guiding her along in an efficient, professional manner. The group, not lingering on Primo's inappropriate t-shirt, showered Lainie with tearful farewells and clingy hugs. The older woman sniffed each cheek: *Okay, we're done here, thanks for nothing. Juan's ticket is the least you could pay, Ms. Rich American. Have a good life, sellout.* Lainie felt deflated with illogical fears, the one looming largest: what other promises had Reena made to strangers on Lainie's behalf? She was drained. On board, Juan followed her carrying both bags and even tried to brush off their seats before plopping onto them. His servitude surprised her.

"Have you flown before? Ever?" She mimed wings but then hid her hands.

Juan shook his head. He remained edgy when the attendant tried to rearrange their bags in the overhead compartment. He uttered quick words and blocked the nonchalant stewardess.

Lainie pointed to the window seat. "Okay?" As if shell-shocked, he took the far seat. The aisle passenger settled in and immediately flounced into a sleep mode. Lainie, center, yearned to do the same. Juan remained agitated staring at the tarmac and at the far-off dusk carpeting other airplanes. They now were two strangers from different towns headed for one place together.

She asked, "So you sailed by boat? Ferry?" Juan raised his eyebrows and lower lip: a yes. Here, no one pointed; they jut out their lips. Lainie then prodded him. "How long ago?"

He kept looking through the port window and replied simply, "Thirty-two years, ma'am."

Lainie stared – first, shocked that he spoke English, and second, amazed that this must be his very first trip back to Ormoc. She figured both of Nita's brothers had never been back. Good paying jobs generally meant leaving the poorer provinces for Manila or elsewhere, sometimes forever. Over thirty-two years, Lainie figured, Juan's cost of living somehow could not cover any interisland flights.

Turning to Juan, she found him crying! Oh, screw me, she panicked, did she do or say something to offend Juan? What could she do? Helpless, she pushed a tissue at him.

She faltered badly. "Um, Juan, I-I didn't . . .I hope nothing I said . . ."

He dabbed at his eyes. "My wife."

"What? What about your wife?" Lainie mentally set aside

more bills for airfare.

"She doesn't know I'm gone." He looked longingly out the small window. He. Just. Left.

Lainie ran through the sequence in her mind. On arrival, mom must have solicited his service then. Would he not commit at first? Yet he packed a bag to have handy, goaded by the relatives, pushing and prodding him till they all stood by the ticket counter. Probably at the time, mom didn't know his decision. He let them all wait and see. Even Lainie and Juan's wife hadn't known. Lainie thought, this man makes up his own mind, and then, he's all in. She kind of liked that.

She needed to sleep but then saw another bag Juan hoarded: food, from the lunch. She tried to say, that flights provide food. But he was diligent. Without fanfare while she slept, she'd be monitored. He explained, "When you're hungry, you'll have food."

He added, "You'll be protected." She believed him and dozed off.

In her dream, a knight in armor held aloft – flight food. Gesticulating, the knight mimed carrying her hair band into battle, She Who Has Paid My Fare, She Who Has Made It Possible To Return. He would defend her against vendors eager to separate She Who Paid My Fare from her many American dollars. Yes, this, he vowed, I Will Do!

Lainie awoke sitting next to Juan, cradling two flight food boxes, one for home. To help him save his "souvenir", Lainie shared her box with him. When they descended off the plane, Juan, full-on vigilante, with her backpack and his bag, maneuvered them through the travel-weary crowd and seemed to gauge that an arm's distance would be near enough to snag Lainie from cars, curbs, and rebels.

His supreme charge was to keep her safe.

She pointed, forward as if to say, *my guardian, explorers that we are – Forward.*

VIII

Cool flight air spoiled her. Lainie now stepped smack dab into a bath towel-like mugginess.

Juan and Lainie had descended from the small inter-island plane onto the tarmac with luggage and leftover food. He had "stared out the window all the way!" He erupted spotting the welcome party and waved excitedly. Like in Manila, a large man held up high a hand-made sign, *Plebiña Cortez*. Lainie had hurried toward her mother, Reena, and tears welling up, grabbed her in a big hug. Reena, receptive at first, was the first to push away as usual. Lainie was relieved to hook up at all. She whirled like a dancer to the giggling faces peering into hers and to the new names overlapping all the chatter: Nita's daughter, Bonita, and granddaughters, Teri-Teri and Sari-Sari, in the moment, indistinguishable from each other. They rattled off similar names of ancestors. Their double nicknames amused Lainie. The large man stood by.

Nita, built like Reena, was placid-faced and stood straight with little exertion conserving her sweat in the dank humidity. Hers was a calming presence. Wordlessly, she bent her neck. Juan approached. They touched foreheads. Lainie felt the day's stress leave her. Nita's eyes sparkled with tears. Without warning, Lainie, too, became teary-eyed seeing family she had never known, watching them re-connect.

Nita had been 28 when her brothers Primo and Juan left Ormoc. Now, reunited siblings mumbled endearing phrases to each other, her gentle touch on his neck, petting his buzz cut head close to hers. Lainie saw a sister again, at age 28, her brother, at 19, reliving a moment years earlier. No time had passed nor had they aged. Lainie, wistful, suppressed rocks in her throat.

In soft, choked Cebuano, Nita and Juan hummed their sing-song welcome to each other. Lainie could still detect a translation both joyous and woeful:

I missed you, oh, how long, too long, Até Nita. Tama na,

you are still my baby boy, manghud. I'm home, Até, don't cry. I hid them too long, let my tears drop . . .

Reena's welcome was less warm. "If we are stopped, say you are American."

Lainie recalled dark jungles. She turned slightly toward the very stoic, large man.

Another hint at danger – should she heed this? And why couldn't *she* pass as Filipino? Nita smoothed any alarm. "No, Rinang, we won't be stopped. This is not wartime."

"Rinang," chortled Lainie, banding up her hair. "Cute nickname, mom," Lainie remarked. She zapped a targeted dig at her mom. "Got to upgrade your forty-year-old memory banks."

A silence, but someone coughed, and one girl giggled. I'm a Hollander, Lainie shrunk. Some Wisconsinites termed Hollander for the predominantly Dutch Northern Wisconsinites, the rubes and spazzes. Showing her butt again, Lainie was equally snarky, *American* – alien.

"The enemy stopped us!" Reena was adamant. "Especially teen girls they wanted to . . ."

"*Tama na*, Reena," Nita said calmly. "They hurt some of us that way, not us. Ssshh now."

Reena veered, bringing up her home movies. Secretly, Lainie collected questions. She listened to Reena stumbling in Cebuano, mistaking times and landmarks, and again bellyaching that Ormoc just had Betamax and that she could not correctly launch her Ormoc film premiere.

"How will you all see our Christmases? Lainie, tell them. We decorated good. I made clothes. You remember my sewing. *Shiminy*, good thing I only packed four VHS cassettes."

Nita deflected Reena's repetitive complaints. " Cuz: we've seen your many pictures."

Using home movies, broken phrases, and clips of her parading, coiffed children, Reena delighted in being producer, director, emcee, and star of her saga, unknown in Ormoc. Lainie recalled her parents' faded honeymoon photos. She had always wondered what young Reena was like. This Nita: she called Reena out and deftly put her in her place. Lainie liked her.

The crowd of passengers jabbered in the jeep, jocular and peppery at first and who then turned reflective during the nearly two-hour drive into Ormoc at break-neck speed. Nita cautioned the driver. She had addressed him as Mike but still had not introduced him.

Reena announced. "This was a dirt road. It takes five hours to reach Ormoc."

Again, countering Reena's war memories, Nita added. "Back in 1947, cuz."

Reena just nodded, a familiar response that Lainie recognized. Her mom absorbed corrections but never copped to errors. She recounted her memories as if through a Mylar sheet, cloudy and dated. That sheet was now scratched and spotty and those memories, altered.

Lainie tipping out the passenger side window, allowed air-streams to cool her neck. Jungle, heavily vine-draped, thick and impenetrable, wrapped the road on both sides. Squinting for minutes into the dark void a few feet away, Lainie finally turned to view the road ahead.

"Whoa." Lainie jumped.

Flanking the road, some tousle-headed figures in shorts squatted in their "Filipino chair," unmoving. They looked sleepily into the headlights, seemingly confident that they would not be run over. Scattered along tar roads, they actually moved closer as the Jeep passed. Nita explained. "When cars race by, the air cools them. Otherwise, the air is still, and beds are hot."

" NPA's hide in the jungle's *darkest cavities*." Lainie was sure young Sari-Sari quoted something. "You know, the insurrectos." Lainie felt the nine-year-old twin was testing Lainie's fear factor.

"They ransom tourists, Americans, too." Reena cautioned. "Don't go into jungles alone. More than three trees *is jungle*. You are lost. No one can see you past two trees."

"KFR," said Bonita, "to pay for their larders." She explained. "Kidnap For Ransom."

Lainie shrugged. She had a litany of other questions: How many big towns are there? How many square miles is this island? Juan corrected her: hectares. *Are we there yet?* The girls giggled.

Though riding over potholes had rattled Lainie, on the road near Nita's house, two round, red eyes popped out of the darkness had startled her. The eyes bobbed behind a makeshift corral, lightweight enough for some monster to pummel its way toward her. Then she saw a set of draped horns and a glint of nostrils. The Jeep lit a dull-eyed beast, no, a cow, no, a bull, no, a . . .

Nita announced. "We turn right here."

"Is that a water buffalo??" Lainie gasped. Everyone nodded.

"*Carabao,*" stated Teri-Teri, also testing Lainie. "Their horns toss you high in the air!"

Lainie had expected a buffalo with no mane, but not this hefty cow-like steer. Its horns swerved upward, a stiff wave of rippled bone sweeping over its ears. Its massive skull ducked below its neck. This was nothing like an American buffalo even with wool and a beard. The beast was just rather plain.

"Ugly," Reena commented. "Good workers, though."

The animal regarded them, content, as if unfazed by its own unremarkable features.

After the turn, Nita gave the girls a key to the two red gates. "Our 'compound.' *Diba*?" Bonita joked. Everyone guffawed. Passing the gates under a moonless light, Lainie could still see mismatched chairs under a leafy arbor and a comfortably wild yard. Bulbous mangoes, gourd sized, hung like bats from low branches, a short distance from the door. Well-used, cushioned chairs faced the exterior's focal point, a low tile-topped table. A small, whitish dog trotted from its hideaway wagging its tail and plopped at her feet for a pat on its head.

Before entering the house, Lainie ruffled the dog. "Careful, cutie: you may be dinner."

Word was, *Filipinos ate dogs*, a mean joke Lainie endured in grade school from other kids. Of all the foreign nuances, heard from their soldier dads who fought in the Pacific, the phrase, *Filipinos eat dogs,* is what sticks? Recalling that period, Lainie jostled Sari-Sari playfully at the door. Did these girls even "get" her dinner joke?

Nita's "compound" was a cement building with glass block windows. A plastic wavy roof and arbor shaded the setting. Inside, sedate furniture, framed holy pictures, portraits, and a calendar lined the soundproof walls. On the cool tile were rugs (*banigs*), and on a compact table were fresh fruit and wrapped *pandesal*. A twinge touched Lainie: home. Home.

Front room and dining room served as one living space. Retrieving her gate key from the girls and depositing her purse on a round table, Nita offered. "Ade? Coca-Cola, tea, juice?"

Lainie breathed, exhausted. "Orange juice, please."

Silence. Lainie rephrased. "Or pineapple?" Nita passed Lainie a glass and explained. The local Pineapple was beginning to be a profit for Leyte; the Hawai'ian import, the Orange, cost them.

Lainie, worn out, sighed. She would shut up, drink anything and sleep. She had arrived.

Bonita sent the girls to bed. They protested but soon acquiesced and their whines faded.

"Everyone's eager to meet you," Teri-Teri yawned, rubbing her eyes, and Sari-Sari signed off with, "Good night, *Até*."

Wow, Lainie was an *Até* for a change, someone older to whom anyone younger would pay respect. "Yes," she stifled her own yawn, "In the morning, I'll meet them."

"Tonight." Nita exchanged glances with Juan who nodded. "Now."

Lainie blinked and blurted. "Really? Now?"

From the room where both girls had entered, a man emerged, coiffed and clean-shaven. Bonita introduced her husband, Nate, a businessman. He was neatly dressed in long trousers, for four o'clock in the morning.

"My husband works here when we visit. But he will take us around when he's free."

Lainie caught Bonita's look at the big driver for a nanosecond. But still, no one would introduce him. Lainie noted that everyone, noticeably attentive, also ignored him.

"Mike!" the mountain-like man barked the single syllable like a gunshot.

Everyone, properly introduced except him, halted. Mike had been carting all of them for a couple hours in his souped-up Jeep with barely a nod from them. They froze till he pronounced: "I drive."

Nita wouldn't look at Mike but drilled her eyes into Reena– a glare, thought Lainie.

"So," was all Reena said. "This is it, hon. This is home."

IX

When the oldest woman (*manang*) climbed through the window into Nita's kitchen, Lainie knew then she was not dreaming. Within seconds, more faces surrounded her, wrinkled and smiling.

Initially, Lainie had just noticed two fingers testing the window ledge and then a hand, which then disappeared. She figured she had imagined that. No one had hailed the May Family. Bodies kept spilling in using that one window. Another veiny hand groped for the ledge. "Oy," a man called. Nate leaned out and offered his helping hand. Once inside, both Nate and the visitor pulled the woman to the ledge and easily lifted her into the room. Eight, Lainie counted, had climbed into the house in thin cotton coverings or shirts. Exhausted, Lainie bobbed her head.

Apparently, no one considered using the front door.

Graciously, half of the visitors catered to the *manang* and even brushed off her flowered dress. The room buzzed as they pushed a chair toward her back. The woman, beaming, toothless, was enthralled to be involved, like a girl, swinging her bare feet.

Nita, and in a fawning way, Reena, introduced Lainie to the barely dressed, tousle-headed neighbors, none of whom Lainie would remember at first after her fifteen-hour red-eye flight and four-hour layover in Manila preceding the redder-eye flight into Tacloban, and drive to Ormoc.

The similarity in names, Lainie realized, would confuse her: Nita, Bonita, Juan, Jun, etc.

Visitors spoke to and over each other as Lainie nodded, eyes heavy. She smiled at their giddiness and her own awkwardness. She shook out her jet lag and then turned to her mother. Thirsty, Lainie cleared her throat and held up an empty glass. She searched for the word water.

But Juan scrambled to fetch the water pitcher and asked a quick Cebuano question. Nita nodded. "Ay, *sigé*!" He poured the water for Lainie. "It's boiled. Otherwise . . ." He shrugged.

Reportedly, there was no potable water on the Islands, maybe rain-filled pools on rocks. Statistics included rocks as some of the seven thousand islands. Fresh water was scarce. Traveler's diarrhea could result. People boiled then refrigerated water before washing vegetables. Juan added. "Sometimes."

A man wearing only shorts actually stated in English. "She is big in the, you know."

Lainie clipped. "*Soo-soo's*, right, thanks."

Reena jabbed her. "Don't be rude."

Come on, Lainie thought. A stranger comments on her tits,

46

and *she's* being rude?

Soo-soo's are tits. Even relocated, U.S. Midwestern Gen 2 Filipino kids knew that.

"How old is she? Is she married? Where's her brother, the male in the family?"

Lainie curled. She might as well be invisible, like a reference to a stool.

"How much does she weigh? She is big, *sigé there,* in the . . ."

She sighed. By Ormoc standards, Lainie's breasts were triple the size of these women.

Reena was in her element, the center of attention. She was royalty, the young, beaming seventeen-year old "Queen of Agriculture" like the photograph she showed her children numerous times. She rattled along with the visitors in her version of Cebuano. Lainie noted silence and stares. Like Lainie herself, the visitors had no clue. What was she saying? But respectfully, they listened. "Ay, *sigé, sigé*, yes."

Nita, a perfect hostess, patted Reena's hand and offered a slightly corrected translation to the room, to which a number of heads bobbed and grunted agreement. One man eyed Lainie and lifted his chin, protruding his lower lip at her. *"Maka istorya ka ug Binisaya?"*

"Aiie, Jun," someone said. Everyone she had just met in the last ten minutes turned to Lainie, expectant, till her mother sniffed. "No, she doesn't speak the language, Visayan or Cebuano. None of them do." She broadcast this like a scarlet letter for Lainie to wear: "A" – I am American instead of "B" – I'm bilingual.

In recognizable English to Reena, Jun probed. "So why did you not titch them?"

A soft murmur went through the crowd. Lainie herself turned to Reena. "Mo-m-m?"

"They'd get mixed up. Their father was Ilocano." Reena, no kid of hers in sight, spoke not to Lainie but to the house and shut off the conversation.

Instead, a flurry of protestations filled the room. Visitors leaned into Reena, imploring her to reconsider, that she should have "titched" her own kids, that kids are like sponges and soak up whatever influences lay in front of them, that's how kids learn.

That's what Lainie detected they were all saying. Undeterred for now, Jun turned to Lainie but urged the room to hear him speak. They all nodded except their *manang*, still beaming tooth-lessly, palms on her knees. Jun cleared his throat. Lainie's eyes widened. He sang:

"Welcome into da jungle we got da fun and da games . . ."
He was close, but not very.

Everyone laughed openly and raucously. Un-ashamed, Jun raised his head and held up his hand. The laughs faded away. He opened his mouth, stopped, and again everyone blew out deep belly laughs and clapped him on the back. He reverted to his more comfortable Cebuano.

The attention had veered away from Reena. So she an-nounced, "Lainie can listen to *you* now. Speak Cebuano to *her*! She'll have to learn."

Lainie had learned itty-bitty words from the young Filipino expats. They spoke Taglish, that distinctive mix of English and Tagalog that generally got across just enough of any idea.

So very tired, she imagined she went up to each neighbor in the room, some of them wearing scapulars or rosaries. She shook hands and said hello, to which they would echo their hel-lo to her. Or maybe she didn't do that. Maybe the mental trans-lation became too much. She was staring at the dimly lit corner of the brick-walled interior and saw the inquisitive gecko, green-backed, unblinking, gripping the rough texture, and eyeballing her upside-down.

Animism, an earlier religion, Lainie was told, still loomed here and had once dominated the P.I. Animists would tag the liz-ard an ancestor. Lainie tagged this one as a household pet, Pickle.

Dreaming, she thought, I'm in Ormoc with my mother, her

cousin/girlhood friend nearby, in the house where grandma died. Lainie smarted at her own recognizable family traits in these relatives: correcting, baiting, testing, teasing, inscrutable, transparent, and appraising, just like her.

"Sunday?" her mother sounded interested.

"What's on Sunday?" Lainie tensed her nostrils suppressing a yawn.

"Day dreaming." Reena clicked her tongue. "We just said we will have a family reunion in the school pavilion on the hill, God willing." For a non-church goer, she said this term often.

Lainie calculated. "People will get the word? In five days?" Lainie looked around. No one knew what the heck she was asking, even her mother.

God forbid Lainie bring up anything like a phone tree to pass on any announcement.

Reena turned to Mike bent over the table. "You tell her. Look, he's already writing."

"RaidJOE." Mike scribbled away, while another man pointed at the sheet, commenting in a low voice. "This will go out twice Wednesday and Thursday, and once Friday and Saturday."

Lainie had to wake up a bit more. Mike was such a hulking bulk compared to all the petite bodies around him. But till now, he may as well have been invisible. He drove in silence, but once out of the jeep, ebullient, he dominated everyone. Massive, barrel-chested, arms spaced from his sides, and his neck dripping sweat like spring rain, Mike was a Herculean presence.

Reena poked Lainie who re–focused on the bricked interior of Nita's crowded house.

"Oy, all this is for you." her mother hissed softly.

Because only a smidgen of this is about the returning Crown of Ormoc, Lainie sighed.

Mike grunted as others nearby approved his radio copy for the town's only radio station.

"Where IS the raidjoe station?" Lainie now used that phrase herself.

Visitors pointed in different directions with their lower lips. "Town," Mike said.

"How far will the announcement go, the whole island?" Lainie now was quite curious.

"Far across the mountains."

Mike turned as someone chirped. "Lunao. North."

"Lunao!" announced Mike as if he owned the identified town.

"By Sunday?"

Whoever was still awake just regarded Lainie, perplexed.

Someone else uttered, *way problema*, which he echoed. "*Way problema!*"

The eldest *manang* snored leaning to one side. Bodies were propped up or stretched on the bamboo-strip *banigs* (rugs) blanketing the floor. Juan had already snagged his little tiled patch near the couch. Please go home, Lainie thought, please.

Lainie openly yawned. "It must be about 4:30." Mike checked. "Five." He spoke louder, rousing everyone. "I will be back in the morning and escort you wherever you want to go."

"Oh, okay, thank you. What time?" Lainie asked.

"Ten," proclaimed Mike then saw Lainie's look. "No? Nine? Earlier?"

Nita pointed her lip at Mike. "We'll call you, *sigé?*"

Sigé, sigé, thought Lainie, was a noncommittal phrase to sprinkle like mom's ay 'sus.

Visitors stumbled out the window to their own homes, all of which surrounded a common plaza of sorts. Lainie gauged the height from the ledge as each person dropped to the ground, about four feet high, she decided, an exit even she could handle. She waved. Climbers hailed: *maayong gabii* (good night).

Once Mike left, Nita stood at the bedroom door where Lainie and Reena would sleep in bunk beds. There were no sinks. She showed Lainie the large, deep bowl of water and thin cloths nearby. After toweling off the day's sweat, Lainie climbed up to the top bunk. The two massive *balikbayan* boxes took up the rest of the room. Lainie thought she saw again the green-backed *Toka* lizard, clinging to the wall by her mattress, but she didn't care. Pickle dashed across the room. Nita patted Reena who was focused on boxes and nuzzled Lainie's cheek. Unlike the woman in Manila, Nita's gesture was loving and sincere. Lainie gave a deep sigh when Nita closed the door.

Reena busied herself reviewing items in the boxes and moving one to the other. Outside their room, Nita and Juan continued their soft talk. She heard a strange male voice, Nita's husband, Horatio, or *Tito* to Lainie. She'd been told he was once a professor and that he'd rise early for his dawn run. Family members were conked out around this cemented "compound".

"Why do they all just look at me when I ask something?" Lainie murmured.

"Maybe the English, maybe how you ask, maybe why you ask, I don't know." Reena dismissed Lainie's inquisitiveness. Lainie snorted. Reena, she swore, would answer questions, all of them.

Both Nita and Juan would talk into the remaining early hours before he drifted into sleep.

Lainie dozed and finally descended into a deep doze after deciding to write key phrases she learned each day: *sigé*, raidjoe, and *way problema* . . . no problema . . .no problem.

X

PUBLIC SERVICE ANNOUNCEMENT – ORMOC CITY
RADIO
    CONTACT:Nita Plebiña May
    PSA START:October 10, 1989
    PSA STOP:October 13, 1989
    LENGTH:30 seconds
    The Plebiña Family will hold its Reunion to welcome back
Reena Plebiña Cortez and her daughter, Lainie on Sunday,
October 13.

    The May Family at the Barangay 35 pavilion, Ormoc City will
hold a reception from 10:00 a.m. to 4:00 p.m. Our local daughter
does good and returns after forty-two years in America. Food will
be served, and a lottery will be held.

    More information is available at (*Jun wrote and crossed out
many names and numbers*)

    With Lainie snoring above her in the bunk bed, Reena read
the radio copy thinking, Lainie would never do this, fly with gifts
across an ocean; none of her kids would. None of them would understand her town except Lainie, maybe.

    Outside, a sharp crack popped – a .38? No, a motorcycle's
backfire, she decided. Reena's town mates driven into darkness
by escaping the mugginess of their huts had agitated the millions
of crickets owning the night, roundly protesting any human presence. The din could pass for buzz saws.

    She would need to tell Lainie about the crop and the land and
family and eventually *before* five days from now, Sunday, at the
Plebiña Family Reunion. Magnetism and manipulation, Reena's
tools as a teen, would need some brush-up.

    She knew family had compared the teenaged Reena to Bette
Davis, her petite figure, her challenging posture, even her ears
and her eyes, coy, teasing, tossing crumbs of promise, yet like her
translations, misunderstood. *Why would G.I. Geraldo read in her*

frank eyes anything else?

Now, Reena had watched Bonita's girls fascinated with her makeup, marveling at their transformations in a mirror, like she had as a teen, with Revlon tubes or Max Factor gloss pots. She, Reena, had begun her transformation at their age, the deserter and prodigal daughter of Barangay 35 still paying penance. Only days earlier, she had been pretending she cared about land. Now, by actively pursuing property she would quash any *tsismis* that the land was not hers, after dismissing Billina years ago. The land was Plebiña's. Reena almost canceled the trip. But she heard the song "Bette Davis Eyes" on the radio: a sure sign to return to Ormoc, directly from Bette. She reviewed her mantra: "I will not forfeit my Philippines. I will not forsake my homeland." Yet she had: by relinquishing her citizenship and earning an American passport. And above everything, for the land, she would have to meet Luis.

Born the same month, both Reena and Luis suckled at her mother Billina's breasts. They had faced each other. He poked Reena's eye, which still wandered sideways. He cheated her, stole her pesos, Billina's legacy. Because they were both light-skinned, he spread *tsismis* that Reena was illegitimate, not him. Reena balked. Nita had pulled her away. "Everyone knows what's true."

Still, Reena would get Nita to call Luis. With luck, maybe she'll even see Antonio, an old schoolmate, more sedate than Geraldo, actually boring, and another reason she had left Ormoc.

XI

"You should not go into town by yourself." Nate, Bonita's coiffed husband, warned Lainie.

"Or go." He contradicted himself. "Go *with* someone. Maybe." He was confusing her.

Lainie had awoken to Pickle staring from a ceiling corner. She shimmied down from the bunk bed. Reena snored as Lainie dressed, slipped out the door with a simple floppy purse and her journal and tiptoed over Juan conked out on a thin banig. Who'd miss her for a short while?

To her surprise, Nate was in his jeep and had waved that palm-down come-hither gesture, like scratching a pet, and warned her. But Lainie had announced that she would "go". *She was not afraid here or in Mexico or in Europe or in New York City*. She hadn't said that but Nate blinked, never broke a sweat, ever, and drove her close to the bay and over Anilao River right into town to the post office. Lainie admitted, "Heh-heh, this would have been a long walk. Um, *salamat*, Nate."

After counting pesos, she paid a postmistress who was avoiding direct contact peeking behind bars and who gingerly moved postcards at her. Lainie began her stroll by stores with wavy tin awning roofs. Streets were dirt-packed or tarred. Some men wore thin tops, striped shorts and flip-flops. They stared. The day's popular American music fought the air for volume and focus. Jeepneys zipped across her path and those of somnambulant pedestrians. The heat blanketed what little oxygen anyone could gulp. The town's routines seemed fated: move only between house and market.

Across one street, Lainie recognized Horatio from pictures, casually walking, arms empty, only a pager stuck in his back pocket, seemingly not there to shop. She called out.

"Mr. May? Um, *Tito*?" He didn't turn. She called again. "Over here! Reena's daughter!" At that, Horatio saw her, alarmed. He pawed the air, frantic, and barked. "*Tama na!*"

54

Something happened behind her, a rush of bodies. She had even ducked. But no one had touched her. She turned to the crowd's foreboding stillness and caught sight of a thin, nimble man slipping through the crowds. Another man had even lunged to grab his shirt but missed. People turned to face Lainie, as if she were guilty and the one to watch now. She was puzzled and took a step. But the crowds dispersed, uneasy, till the street cleared, and she stood alone.

"Go home!" The voice startled her. Horatio, farther now, scowled and paced a bit. Then he disappeared into the crowd at too easy a clip, dismissing her. A smattering of strangers stared.

Had she been too demanding when she had first called to him, too brazen? Was she like a bellowing "hospitality girl", a term Reena labeled women soliciting their "johns?" Believing that, red-faced Lainie receded. No hole could swallow her, already knee-deep in fuck-ups.

Suddenly above her, the skies opened: a cloudburst.

People lined up under store awnings and froze like statues cradling their brown-wrapped packages and lolling in daydreams. Smarting after Horatio's dismissal, Lainie also assumed a casual stance under an overhang. One man lit up a cigarette, a sure sign of a long wait. A bit dispirited, she tried to recall the other nuances of Filipiniana literature or culture. She did not recall anything about a fire drill-like siesta under awnings during full-minute downpours.

That downpour just started and stopped. Dazed, people cranked up and continued on their ways. Lainie stepped out onto the furrowed dirt street. Rainwater had filled the tire tracks yet drained as she watched. She caught an audible gurgle of water above her. The store's awning was like a soup ladle filled with gallons of water. She took note and stepped aside: *good to know.*

Lainie wanted to shop for that one thing proving she even took a trip, not for shirts, cups, or caps. But nothing struck her to buy at all. She had to get back. She decided to flag a *tuk-tuk*!

The post office had a taxi stand for *tuk-tuks* or jeepneys, the G.I. castoffs left after WWII tricked out with cassette players blaring American music. Some drivers draped their vehicles with streamers and amusing paraphernalia. From rearview mirrors, a driver would dangle rosaries or beads. On dashboards, he would pose Jesus statues, plastic hula dancers, and amulets.

When one driver nodded, Lainie took the back seat and spelled the vague "Bgy. 35." The driver just uttered. "Nita's?" Numb, Lainie nodded. Now how did he know that?

Again, the skies opened. The driver lit a cigarette. The deluge poured lasting a bit longer.

She hesitated but then pointed a finger. "Um, drive? Go? Or, like . . .go?"

He ignored her finger, inhaling, waiting. The lip, she reminded herself, use the lip (pout). That didn't work, either. She thought, we could at least drive in the rain, right? His wait meant no. When the rain stopped, he still remained. She left the *tuk-tuk* and headed back further into town.

Only an hour in town alone, Lainie decided to catch up in her journal. She found and sat by the pier. Men loaded a large trawler. She absorbed a slew of tongues and revelry from the open-air market to her right that housed the daily vendors in colorful trucks and stalls. Not yet acrid, fish on the docks gave off a briny morning odor. Wharf workers were swarthy, lean, and a bit bow-legged, skein-like veins bulging from their thighs. Their oak-colored skin glistened. She imagined rebels on the run, hacking dense fronds with bolo knives, and compared them to these workers. What would distinguish them from one another; what outward sign marked them as passionate, driven *insurrectos*? How could she tell, if she wanted to, well, talk to one of them?

How could dockworkers or fishermen have any time for revolutions or jungle warfare? They had families to feed. She jotted her sage questions in her journal. One bold fisherman stared defiantly at Lainie. Document *them*, will she?? He scowled when she focused her camera on them. More of them catcalled, loud, frightening the market vendors. Lainie did not move. Baleful, the men swung crates, a busy foreground to the powder blue skies beyond them and lapping teal-tinted waves below. Their "nets", not those catching *tilapia*, would not ensnare her.

Inspired, Lainie heaved a sigh, wishing for a palette of watercolors to use for a quick gesture drawing. She wanted to scoop up for one sketch all the views, foods, catcallers, and singers. She had stroked the goods, woven, pearlized, shimmering, asymmetric, intricate, earthy, delicate, organic, whimsical, beaded, appliquéd, luxuriant, and exotic. She memorized features of Ormoc faces, some like hers, the vendors, wharf workers, and perhaps among them, one rebel.

Once she'd actually rubbed shoulders with Ormocanons, she'd see what they see. Still writing, she scratched through that nonsense and re-wrote: *she would see how Ormoc regarded her mom.* She drew lines through that thought, too. The odd, uncomfortable truth was Lainie might actually earn Reena her redemption showing off Lainie to Ormoc as prosperous, and that Reena's departure in 1947 was justified. But Lainie knew. She herself did not, in any way, prosper.

Maybe Reena's town mates would forgive whatever venial sin Lainie and her siblings had committed embracing America and forgive Reena her mortal sin, forsaking Ormoc. *Two generations slouch toward forgiveness*, Lainie wrote in a margin, *and cross an ocean for absolution.* Hmm.

Reena was . . . complicated. Lainie suspected which of her traits she also carried. She tagged the ones she would hopefully never nurture, the defiance, the targeted digs . . . the rage.

Siblings Anne-Marie, Adam, and Lainie as toddlers had tried eluding Reena's sudden boiling wrath usually brought on by nothing at all. She would just stomp up and swat them. If they hid, she'd find them under beds or squeezed behind couches tight and furtive, like a mouse. If not a hand or a shoe, she'd use her pine yardstick to poke under chairs till they yelped.

Just as suddenly, she would howl and crumple to the floor. Hiccupping, the kids would huddle in one place wordlessly. One day, years later, Lainie, who was dealt the most blows, lunged for the stick. Reena swung high and broke it on Lainie's shoulder. Headstrong Reena's daughter shed no tears.

Neighbors heard. The woman next door in her perennial apron would ring the bell obsequiously offering a dish of cookies. Reena blared. "Mind your own business!" People called the police who did nothing. Geraldo would return home from work and see his children trying to hide their bruises. Reena retorted. "Then you discipline them!" To pacify her, Geraldo would swipe a hand across them once, lined up like boot camp recruits. Grateful, they cried on cue.

As toddlers they would sniffle away these memories. As youths, they no doubt dreamed them, maybe; and as teens, they had dismissed the myths altogether. Perhaps, Lainie thought, Reena took too many prescribed pills for the pain of births too close together, or perhaps not.

All she knew now was she would hold eyes with workers, hardened, having been trained to handle confrontations worse than this, and not cry. They soon stopped taunting and slunk off, much like Reena had when her oldest daughter halted the years-long abuse: Anne-Marie had quickly pushed Reena's hand wielding a vacuum tube inches from Lainie's head, saving her. Reena shrunk back and released the weapon. She crumpled and barked that she had to hit *something*. She said. "This life, these walls! YOU!"

Leaving the pier, Lainie realized she had not written any of this and instead had held the pen recognizing the wrathful glare of the fishermen, who bore their own unfair lots in life.

She had earned glares before, all to perfect her escapes and again be furtive, like a mouse, invisible – unaccountable. Danger sought her out, she convinced herself. She just dodged.

XII

Juan slept. But by nine a.m., everyone in the May compound realized Lainie was gone.

Reena was listening from her bottom bunk as the family had awakened. She had detected Bonita shuffling from her room bypassing Juan on the cool tile floor. She heard the girls giggle, swirling like otters in the big bed vacated by their parents. Bonita in the kitchen shushed them. Reena yawned. Lainie must still be asleep in the upper bunk. But when Nate returned and the girls bounced out to greet him, Reena heard him comment, "I dropped Lainie off downtown."

'*Ay sus*," Reena swore. The volume ramped up, Juan scrambling off his banig, Bonita interrogating Nate, and the girls jumping around. "Let's go, let's go get her!"

A silence fell. Nita must have put a finger to her lips, Reena thought, time to get up, emerge from her room, and level Juan with her stink eye, which always delivered judgment. She knew he was anxious over his impulsive flight. He carried his wife's disapproving features on his brain like a helmet. Reena counted on, but would never take any blame that he, again, like others back in the forties, had fallen under her spell in Manila a week earlier.

She had snuck into his sense of honor and had wheedled him to be Lainie's bodyguard.

"It's not hard, just watch her," Reena told him. "Make sure she's not cheated. She doesn't know the exchange, or our tongue, or anything. Make sure she's not kidnapped. She will cover your flight. I paid hers, she can pay yours!" Juan then would guard Lainie, Reena's ace card.

Reena orchestrated that. She hadn't forced Juan or Lainie. She just skimmed some details.

Reena was right, as usual: insurgents ransomed hapless tourists, even American tourists, even Filipino ones. They were hardy, intense groups since Marcos was run off. They defied unguarded loyalists and corrupt officials. To Reena, Juan was responsible for Lainie's solo escapade into town.

A flurry has stirred among the Mays. Reena urged Juan, now off the floor. "Go! Go, *sigé!*"

At certain times, Reena reasoned here again in Ormoc, she must again be manipulative, just like she was in the States. She would layer admonitions on others with guilt, like she had on her kids. And then as now, she skirted past memories like these, ignoring that she had ever treated anyone poorly, like undesirable aliens in her world.

Reena slammed the silk top into the box but then smoothed it. Why damage silk?

Let her get lost, Reena sniffed. Her own ulterior plan was set in motion. Reena would sidestep this issue, worrying over the family renegade among the other frustrating kids. Instead as if she were incensed, she barreled Juan through the red gate as Nate followed. "I will get her back, *Ate,*" mumbled Juan.

Except for Nita's mid-1980s letters, in this manner Reena faced uneasy issues, buried decades earlier. Coming home meant confronting some of them head on, like when she translated one letter to young Lainie. Still, she fabricated its contents written in a language her kids didn't know.

Nate's jeep revved up. Juan's an adult, Reena vexed. Why can't he just watch his charge?

In the Plebiña household, devoid of island cultures and acceptably American, Reena's kids had not bonded with any Filipino kids – in Mukwonago? Only now did Lainie herself work with some Fil students. She had zinged Rita with, "They already educate me, like you should have."

Reena fumed, "Why do you have to tell everyone our business, even your students, just because they're Filipino? They are children. Why do you care what they think? We are American."

"Wow, ageism and classism," Lainie had remarked, "All in one fell swoop."

Till that forty-second year when Reena returned home, she blanketed her hidden mysteries within old, thin, one-page aerograms. She would deal with the land issue with more artistry than the reticent, young Reena would have. She believed that now, she was much more patient.

She will coerce strangers and loved ones to smooth her path toward regaining a legacy.

She will spend the money and the energy to make her barrio love her again.

She will look the bastard Luis in the eye.

And Lainie will help that all happen.

Reena stubbornly kept her own barrier hinged and guarded.

But Lainie wanted to scale her mother's "fence".

This, and her wandering off, will cost Lainie a toll.

Lainie's writing hand hurt. She had sat on the pier penning journal entries for an hour.

Memories of escapades, domestic and foreign nagged at her: *do not repeat. Do not repeat.* But Lainie overstuffed with questions all her life rose to challenges. Who was this prodigal daughter of this island, her mother, before she and her siblings were born? What dictated her ornery moods back then that defined her now, and why was she so vague about her past? What entrancing assets, both charming and aloof, made the mix she called mom?

And why return now? Could Lainie even dig for information that could explain everything?

Why did Reena hate her?

Lainie swiped at her wet eyes, still protecting and covering her journal.

She stood and decided she would draw information from perfect strangers. She would mirror Reena whenever she coveted something. Lainie wanted something, too: answers.

"*Sigé na*, come here." Fishermen catcalled, petting the air at her. Lainie took a step.

Opposite at the end of the pier, market vendors were pawing the air. "Na! *Ssss-ssst!*"

Both groups wanted her: one signaling retreat from danger, the other, that danger.

Defiantly, Lainie took five more steps. With each move, women at the market chirped frantically. She looked at them. Frenzied, they tread their hands in the air as if swimming in water. Yet they stayed glued to the pier's edge, their bodies urgently leaning forward. Lainie grinned, as if she, of course, knew that teasing the workers was silly. But accommodating the women, she headed back. A woman screamed at her, palms to her mouth, her eyes registering horror as a swish of air brushed against the back of Lainie's head. She quickened her step. Reaching the crowd who effusively fanned their chests with slim, oak-brown hands, Lainie risked a glance at the men. Two of them were hauling a third man to the trawler. The women cooed at Lainie, re-enacting the man's swipe that had just missed her skull. Each woman repeated the gesture. Some of them would pet Lainie's arm. Murmuring, some of them soothed her wrist. She had not been harmed at all nor had any part of her. For them, a missed swipe was harm enough.

For all their bravado these sinewy, sulky, fisherman, only one flipped her off, third finger upward. One woman whispered in Lainie's ear. "Take you, rape you. Sell you."

Another woman harrumphed. "Aiee, one eloped with your sister instead of you. *Krush kinya.*"

Lainie browsed her brain for a key word: *krush*, crush. The first woman had had a crush on a fisherman. Yeah. He preferred her sister, and, and they ran off, yeah, and jealous, the second woman gossiped about those who might ransom, to frighten Lainie, actually all fodder for her article. Yeah.

She gaped at the armpit-high female vendors surrounding her, those close to her face. For other reasons, they would avoid the men; these women would warn Lainie, not scare her. Their features were warm, concerned, faces work-worn, lined. They had flat, distinctive noses, welcoming smiles, some with no teeth. They meant well. Scarves covered their wispy, thin hair or heavy braids. They maneuvered her toward their open-aired market away from trouble. Probably, because of them, she had dodged danger – again.

She shook herself, now aware that she had been silly and embarrassingly naïve. Briefly, she recalled key memories of other imminently dangerous scenarios, equally silly and conveniently dismissed. She always smiled. "I'm safe, though, right? No worries."

The vendors clucked their tongues. Like the memories she removed, Lainie pulled one of three elasticized cloth hair bands from her wrist. She bunched and lifted the swath of hair from her sweaty neck, cooing back to them, "Okay, okay." Mischievously, she attempted her newly acquired words, "*Sigé na, sapé now, manang.*" Relieved, the women laughed. Then she was caught up by the view of a nearby high-rise behind them. The hotel's sign read: Don Padre.

She must go there. She would sip a tonic and review the pier and her silly encounter.

Maneuvered toward their stalls under the covered market, Lainie fielded the women's questions, none of which were about introductions.

"*Sáan?*"

"Where? I'm at, um, Nita's? Um, Barangay 35?"

Nodding, they pushed closer. "Oh-oh, no. You, YOU – *sa'an?*"

She replied, "Um, America."

They bobbed their heads in answer. "Oh-oh, *sigé*, Calipornia!"

They knew, of course. Who would have not heard about a visiting single American Filipino and where she was housed in town, traveling with her mother from the United States?

Lainie knew how word-of-mouth spread rapidly based on how U.S. Filipinos in the U.S. knew about meriendas and parties. Mind readers, she figured. An impromptu visit, an exchange of *tsismis*, a phone call or ten, and within hours, delicacies and families would descend on the cheery hosts.

Without preamble, the vendors ladened Lainie with strange, oversized fruits, gourds large as elephant tusks and tubular green ones like her father Geraldo's *ampalaya*. She recalled other fruit she vowed she would try. She asked, "Um, jackfruit?" They shook their heads: all gone.

Other vendors rushed toward her with more unknown vegetables. She tried to explain that she couldn't carry all of these items or even pay for them. But they shook their heads. "No, no, take, take, to Nita, take." For some equitable exchange, Lainie removed her remaining hair bands from her wrist and randomly handed them out. The women grinned, each of them either binding up her hair or slipping the band onto her wrist like Lainie had. Awed, open-mouthed, they displayed wide smiles, looking like a keyboard of black and white spaces.

Someone beeped and actually leaned on the horn careening his jeep right up to their group. His entrance raised more dust and shouts from the women. Nate, and a sorrowful Juan, leaned out.

"Look what they're giving to Nita." Lainie beamed showing her collection.

Nate nodded, urging her nearer. "Come. They're waiting for you at home."

She climbed into Nate's red, tricked-out jeep, music reverberating the interior, and draped her hand on the door. The women stroked the thickness of Lainie's forearms and pushed more produce at her. She touched each of them, smiling, and repeating *salamat, salamat*. A few cried. Not knowing why, her own tears formed. Brushing one away, she wondered if she'd have time to come back and recapture this moment, just one more time.

Once Nate screeched off, Lainie asked, "How did you know where I was?"

Nate kept his eyes on the road switching radio channels. "When you left the post office, you headed either for the harbor or the market."

Lainie blinked. "Oh. Well, before the market I huddled under an awning during a downpour. The driver never left, so I went to explore." He nodded. "Mm."

Nate rounded the corner heading back to Barangay 35. "You get a jeepney stuck in a ditch, you need four men to get you out. For the market, a woman alone must be careful."

"I was okay. I sat at the breakwater." Silence. "Writing, at the stone wall by the pier."

"A long time," he said calmly. Again, he knew. They all knew, all the time.

"I have to keep up on my journal," Lainie explained.

"Ah, like last night." Nate clicked his tongue. "Some men at the pier are *malo*. Bad."

Refusing to feel reprimanded for side trips or writing, she remarked, "I dodge them."

Nate drove past the corral housing the water buffalo. The animal posed sideways, head directed at her, outside the far palm trees. In daylight, the carabao was muscle-bound and keenly outlined against the lush green background, picturesque. He judged nothing.

Nita, Reena, Bonita, the girls, and Juan were all waiting as Lainie got out of the jeep and Nate drove off to park in the shade. Quietly, Nita hugged Lainie, saying once, "You should go into town *with* someone. NPAs are everywhere, watching. They are not like your students."

Reena hovered, swiping hair out of Lainie's eyes. "'*Sus*, where did you go? Why didn't you tell anyone? You know you could be taken, no one would know! Always something."

Lainie deposited all the produce on the exterior table. "The market ladies wouldn't let me pay. It's for you." She avoided eye contact. She hoped they would stop any more lectures.

"The women told us where you were. Why are you always writing? Write at home!" Reena would not let the incident go. "Jun's cousin biked over to Jun's who came to tell us."

Their string-and-tin-can pipeline reigned supreme. Lainie changed the subject. "Oh, the downpour! I saw Horatio. I thought maybe Nate could wait and then drive us all back together."

Juan and Nita shuffled. Even humid, the air chilled with the mention of grandpa Horatio. Nita busied herself with the vegetables.

Bonita ushered her daughters into the house. "Daddy usually returns late."

Lainie paused but went on. "There was . . . mud."

Nita mumbled, "Let's eat."

Okay, then, Lainie thought. She checked the house's interior. Nita had decorated one wall with familiar flat, polished monkey pod-sculpted dancers poised in the Tinikling stance between long bamboo sticks. On a shelf out of reach was the Barrel Man. Anyone curious could lift the wooden figure from its wood barrel, and its erect penis would twang at the viewer – surprise. Another common wall hanging was a shield with miniature weaponry of southern Philippines Mindanoan Moro tribes. Most every Filipino house had these items, but not in Mukwonago, WI.

Beside the entrance, a window with smoky Venetian blinds filled the wall. Bodyguard Juan had rolled up his thin banig rug in a corner on tile. He would be sleeping on the floor every night. Lainie ran her hand over the inner cement wall, still cool from the night's air. She peered over the window ledge measuring again what the height was to the ground: only one leg down. On the plain round table, Nita had set a bowl of bananas, mangoes, a papaya and individually wrapped bread rolls (*pandesal*). A table nearly blocked the entrance to the kitchen and to the comfort room. Shortened to C.R., the windowed room had a ceramic commode and at its base, a two-inch resident insect, stationary but intimidating. Each visitor would need a bucket of water and for proper pressure, pour it – from a good height – into the bowl. Another bucket might be required.

"Juan, *sigé na*! Ay, American now, ano, bathroom,

bathroom," Nate had joked.

Juan had earned C.R. jokes having spent ponderous hours behind the closed door.

Nita had lined the main room shelves with family photos, those of Bonita's daughters as babies, then as toddlers, then finally with Nate and Bonita at their current age. Lainie knocked on Bonita's door. The whole family of four had been packed into one bedroom. Reena and Lainie had taken up the last bedroom with bunk beds. Older by five minutes, Sari-Sari and her slightly adolescent sister, Teri-Teri, both lay sleepily on the bed, with their lovely, even-teethed, dental-cared smiles. They were shy in Lainie's presence.

"You girls, you see everything, don't you?" Not waiting for a reply, Lainie tickled them till they all were giggling, high-pitched. At the peak of screams, Bonita burst in. "Sari-Sari, Teri-Teri, *sigé na*!" From the kitchen, someone clanged a pan, a signal for the family to come eat. Double first nicknames were common and sometimes kept as adults, baby-ish as they sounded.

Breakfast included *siligong* (thick bacon), abnormally orange eggs, Lipton teabags with canned condensed milk, and ever-present sugar. Chickens, she noted, were scarce which in turn meant so were the odd orange eggs. American fare breakfasts were rare then in the provinces.

Lainie noted the dinner leftovers of heady bay leaves, pepper, garlic, vinegar, and cloves over rice. Nate pointed to those dishes. "Oy, more breakfast here."

Both Juan and Nita, the last to sit, were conspiratorial and secretive. Juan emitted that high-pitched whine and argued, "I don't think so, I don't agree, Nope, nope." Nita uttered Lainie's name and other things, and Juan shut up. Brother and sister disagreements never age, Lainie decided, cutting the tiny, fried-hard egg with her fork. Her big soupspoon doubled as a sharp edge. But giving up, Lainie reached for the table's communal knife. Although riveted, the knife was hand-made.

Bonnie pointed with her spoon and reminded Lainie. *"Ay, sige'*, did we tell you these kind of knives are made from the blades of bayonets?" What Lainie didn't know was what Bonnie added. "We still find these in the tall grasses. Eat, eat."

XIII

A motorcycle engine died down in front of the house. The girls ran to the window and gestured, palms down, to both Bonita and Nita.

"Oy, do you know who this is?" Nita beckoned Nate.

He left the table and peered outside. "No. Who is this?"

Reena's Bette eye widened. "Oy, it's him, my uncle, no, my, my . . ."

Nate went out first and then the women. Reena and Lainie were called out to meet the young stranger. He sat just outside the red gate on his Kawasaki Enduro 350. Slim and *gwapo* (good-looking), the man looked at Reena. *"Maayong buntag*, I'm Fausto. Jovita sent me to . . ."

Reena exclaimed, *"Ay 'susmarjosep*, I thought you, oh, oh! Oh, how did you get here, by bike?? Oy, Lainie, this is your cousin, Fausto, my sister Ynez's son." Fausto blinked once, that family trait.

Lainie noticed. Nate coughed. Bonita elbowed him. Sister? Aunt? Aunt's son?

Lainie faltered. "Um, my cousin?"

Reena frowned. "Who else? Yes, your cousin, or half-cousin, just cousin!"

As he seemed her age, Lainie bypassed the *mano* and hugged Fausto, her aunt Ynez's son. Lainie thought, "An actual blood cousin, not someone's friend, not distant."

"Ynez died after years in Subic Bay." Reena was blunt. Lainie watched Fausto.

"I was in the States already," Reena continued. "She and I weren't close, anyway."

Nita stepped toward him. "Please, come sit." Fausto was determined to remain on his bike as Reena trilled, "Oy, you're here, same time as me. How many are you, your half-siblings?"

A nanosecond flare flashed in his eyes. "Many."

Reena grimaced at Nita. "Because you know, Ynez was with many men, but anyway. Are you married, do you have kids, you staying with, you staying near the Anilao? The river?"

With her run-on question, Reena had already revealed she knew where he stayed.

Unflappable, Fausto spoke evenly. "Yes, I'm married. I have a daughter. When I'm here," he emphasized, "I'm with *my mom*, Jovita. MY family lives by the Anilao." He paused. "I see now why my mom wanted me to pay my respects to the Americans for her."

The veil parted behind Lainie's first day's *tsismis (gossip)*: Lainie's aunt, Reena's sister, Ynez, abandoned her children, like Fausto. Lainie and her siblings never had a blood aunt in the States. Oh, God, Lainie thought, how Fausto must feel, to learn now, in this manner, who he is.

"Well," Reena shrugged her signature shrug, "Now you know. Anilao, eh?"

The dilapidated area of closely built huts near the city-dividing waterway was the least desirable location. Fausto sounded clipped. "It's usually flooded from the mountain's wash off."

Nita explained. "Illegal lumbering shaves trees off the hills. The Anilao River turns into mud during monsoons, near where Jovita, Fausto's mom, raised him."

Tension eased, now that Fausto knew. Was Jovita also

wounded? Lainie smarted.

She felt Fausto watching her as she touched his bike. "I, um, I've ridden a Kawasaki and a couple Hondas, one Yamaha but not over 250-horse power."

He shifted. "Maybe, I will take you for a ride if I'm still in town."

"Are you leaving?" she asked.

"I split my time here and in Arabia," he replied. "I'm an OSF, overseas Filipino. My wife and daughter live here, and I send them money."

She had to ask. "Does that give you enough time with them?"

"For a couple months every three or four years."

Lainie marveled at the agelessness of Filipinos. At twenty-eight, Fausto appeared so young to be an absent father working in a foreign country. He added, "We have time."

"So you have real siblings?"

His question surprised Lainie, thinking how hungry and hurt he must be.

"I believe," he began, "I'm thinking you really are my cousin. You know bikes."

He promised to stop by again, perhaps for the Reunion, depending on his wife's job. Did he miss his wife, Lainie wondered, could they remain married and still live so far apart? He revved up and departed on his Kawasaki in a cloud of dust and along with him, any answer.

Reena spoke. "He looks a lot like his namesake, Lainie's uncle-in-law. Too bad Ynez left him."

Nita was short. "Rinang, she's your sister. Respect the dead. You know how she died."

Reena tossed that off. "Of course, I know! She's my sister! Everyone said she . . ."

Nita brushed at her apron. "What they say is not what you should believe."

Reena, unfazed, was already planning. "What to give them

from the boxes – 'sus – family."

Behind the closed bedroom door, Lainie found Reena puttering again with the *balikbayan* boxes. "Aiie, what is something special for Fausto and his family. Help me here."

"You never really mentioned your sister, Ynez, or any of her kids." Lainie sat nearby and picked at the items vacantly. Reena stayed intent on her search.

"Are there any pictures of them when they were children? Or any of your sister?"

Reena shook her head and pulled a face. "No, we never kept in touch after Ynez left for Subic Bay. Anyway, Jovita raised him. She just told Fausto the truth, knowing I'd be here. Hmph, why would I admit to anyone, 'Ynez worked in Subic Bay!' "

Reena shook out a cotton top. "Fifty percent cotton, that's good. I thought, maybe give his wife the silk." She returned to her boxes. "But what if I want it . . .oy, I'll keep it aside."

Lainie regarded Reena. She left her sister when Ynez was fifteen. She just met Ynez's son. Nothing really affected Reena, reflected Lainie, neither accidents nor deaths. Indifference gated up Reena like a wall tight around her, heavily bricked, insurmountable, and familiar.

"You told Jovita to tell him he's a bastard, because you're here?" Lainie had to ask.

"No! 'Sus, no one uses that word to his face. But everyone knows what Subic Bay is: G.I.'s and easy women. That's where poor women earn money, the, the . . . prostitutes. That's what Ynez was. Jovita tells him first so no one slips up before he knows. It's not my fault. He's grown, he should take it like a man, no matter who tells him, Jovita or someone else . . . or me."

Lainie blinked twice. "Did *you* just tell him, or did Jovita earlier? I'm confused."

Reena's Bette eyes were trained on the silk. "Maybe Jovita didn't get around to it yet."

Lainie's heart sank. "You mean, he may have just heard

about it . . . now? Here? Doesn't he know that his grandma lived here, nearby, when he was still young?"

Reena kept holding the two tops not looking at Lainie before she finally spoke.

"Maybe, maybe not. Maybe that's why Nita was cross with me, who knows."

Lainie looked around the room, gauging its size and her mother in it. Never was Reena small in rooms or tight spots, not even now. They would have more room to move if those dang boxes were gone, she thought. Sunlight caught dancing dust orbs swirling and winking each time Reena pulled out items as if to wake them from a folded slumber. Even the bunk bed was a spare and utilitarian amenity. Pickle watched, unblinking, then dashed to the floor, as if pursuing Fausto. Shrill birds and abrupt shrieks from children outside startled Lainie. She began again.

"So Ynez had Fausto . . ."

"She had many children, many husbands." Reena flicked at Pickle too near a box. Seeing Lainie's face, she heaved a sigh. "She raised the older ones, then died, and then the younger ones were left with friends, like Jovita. That was after the knife fight between a couple of her johns."

"Mom, please."

"Who else could they be, huh, in Subic? Anyway, Ynez got in the way of the knife, that's all I know. Now let it go. You don't know the ways here. These are kin you don't know and things you don't understand. Why are you crying?"

"I'm not." Lainie lied, brushing at her cheek. "Don't you jab at Pickle, either."

Lainie allowed lingering aromas of breakfast to distract her. Maybe she'd nosh on a *pandesal.* Meanwhile, Reena scolded items in front of her as if chiding them as choices of gifts.

Lainie left the room to stand outside the house. Juan lingered nearby behind her, holding a travel-size package of tissues in his palm. She waved him away, then changed her mind and pawed the air between them. He held out the package and said nothing. She took a tissue.

Visitors drove up. Voices rose from the house and out dashed the family. Lainie saw a young boy driving an older woman, seated, whose head could barely top the dashboard.

Descending on them was infamous Deling from the Anilao River.

XIV

"Ah, *kummusta ca*. We pay our respects. Ay, beezeetors, so big, *talaga*, in the chest! Oy, com-ports here, not like my house. Horatio gone again?"

The very short, old woman, with wisps of salt-grey hair, stood inside the house, her umbrella held open by the young boy. Deling, Lainie was told, was the barrio's main manang, a *doyen* of sorts, and an elder of substantial influence in Barangay 35. Her opening sentences both complimented and denigrated everyone present or not, intentionally.

Deling blared, "So tomorrow is my special dinner with the guests of honor!"

"Ah, Deling." Nita was blockading. "We can schedule sometime after the Reunion. Till then, we have to get the food and the people to help. Mike may get the *lechon*. But now we go to see the sights. Sorree-ah, we must go before it's too late."

Lechon, one term Lainie knew, is roasted pig. An eighty-pound piglet could feed sixty to eighty guests. Feeds like a Reunion would, of course, be laden with twenty plus dishes, and the gathering would still be labeled *lechon*. Lainie had this feeling that *silingans* (neighbors) like Deling would offer what help they could to justify an invitation to a kin-only Reunion, one not theirs. But leftovers, if any, would be added to breakfast *siligong*. Precious food was conserved.

Lainie was now satisfied that Mike drove to and from the airport and delivered pigs.

"I will send people. I will organize the whole Reunion," Deling pronounced, obviously not offering money but a need just as valuable: staff. Lainie believed her.

"The radio ad goes out today. We'll let you know the number of people who respond, *sigé*?" Nita *mano*'ed Deling. Lainie had dispensed with that tradition as a flouncing teen but recently re-instated it, respectfully taking an elder's hand thrust under her nose and with it, touching her own forehead. With best wishes, Nita sent Deling and the boy on their way.

"Deling is very well respected," Bonita explained. "But she is very insistent. She wants something. You'll see. She spreads things, about mom, she . . ." but Nita *sss-ssst*'ed her.

"She's a hoot," Lainie mused. "So a dinner after the Reunion?"

Nita smiled. "You have two *lechons* to attend plus the Reunion and meriendas."

Reena had already clued in Lainie that guests of honor would be stuffed with food throughout a whole vacation. They would witness local talent. Why, right next door, Jun could blast his CD player the song he already played all day and night, despite its uneven quality.

"We go into town together," Bonita remarked. "We order the *lechon* ourselves, and Mike can deliver here Friday. That's what he can do."

Nate offered to drive. Juan, alert, stayed close to Lainie for the family's first trip out. But without knocking, Mike burst through the door. He announced, "Swimming today!"

Lainie looked to Nita to gauge her reaction: nothing. Who

was he? Mike ignored their travel plans. As he was prone to do over the next few days, he'd changed them.

"You can go to town another time."

Too loud, Lainie stated, "I thought you just drive and deliver pigs." Bonita coughed.

Mike already needed to rinse off, thoroughly drenched just standing, glistening with oil and sweat. The man could ooze by simply batting his eyes. Rivulets also dropped off Lainie like cool beetles, deliberate and slow, not any she'd bother to wipe away. But, whispered Bonita, this was not a poolside hotel but a waterfall. Adolescent and teenage divers flew down into a mud pond the size of a bathtub. Maybe Lainie could convince the girls to turn a hose on them instead.

She sighed, not really disappointed. "Oh, I didn't bring a swimsuit."

She learned at this point to never mention aloud what she didn't have. Listeners with less than what she had, rather than listeners with more, will always try to provide that item, any item.

A scramble ensued. Nita and Bonita scoured the drawers. They found outfits saggy, old, and far too small. Lainie would not, could not beg off. However, she would go along for the drive, close her eyes in the jeep, enjoy a cool ride, and just not go in the water.

In the back of the jeep, one girl sat on Bonita's, Reena's, and Nita's laps with Juan squeezed a bit forward. Sari-Sari sat on Lainie's lap, "shotgun," the passenger seat next to Mike.

Reena had urged Lainie. "Sit up there, hon. you'll see better. Yes, next to Mike."

Mike cranked up the radio. Lainie sighed. Not all Americans loved constant, loud music.

Pointing where places used to be, they stopped at a street sign: Plebiña. Lainie gasped: proof of family. Reena, though, no longer recognized the town. "It's not like before the war."

The road up the western coast of Leyte rose higher. They stopped again at a turnout to gaze back at Ormoc Bay, the site of the 1944 autumn bombardment that shuddered and popped past November 27 till the end of that year. Nita pointed to landmarks. Reena said nothing.

Lainie snapped a photo, Ormoc in the background, a sharply defined ballooning cloud overhead parked in the unreal, azurite sky with an alert water buffalo grazing deep in the grasses. But to her shock, the owner, in a three-cornered, woven banana frond hat feathering his hollow-cheeked face, viciously kicked the animal, which fell to its knees, bellowing.

As if enraged by her camera, the man raised his switch as if to strike again, daring anyone to stop him. Whatever had angered him eluded Lainie. "Hard life," quipped Mike. "Farmer."

Gazing at a handful of the seven thousand rocklike islands that rose from the seas, they lingered on one jagged pinnacle mid-ocean termed uninhabitable. Admittedly Reena had never seen this view cleared by bombs. When she had gotten separated from her family during the invasion, she had headed away from water toward Madawawing Mountains. All she could do now was gesture at the horizons and identify one island. "Cebu," she chortled. "I went to school there."

Reena seemed oblivious. The Reunion would proceed, though the island had changed. She yakked aimlessly in her own type of Taglish amusing people in the jeep. She no longer knew any structures or stone landmarks to point out. Nita corrected her, which began to annoy Reena.

Mike veered inland up towards the waterfall. Late in the day, most everyone was already wilting from the humidity. They trudged toward the trickling waters as Lainie sweat profusely. She vowed she would not get under the waterfall, not with Mike, whose eyes constantly roamed over her body. She fell back in step with Juan nearby. A father and son, staring, called back to Mike's hail, something about no swimming today, no pond, too dry.

Mike just motioned the women back to the jeep. Lainie was thoroughly puzzled. Why did he act more than some local chauffeur? He never discussed his work except for a strange phrase. "The fields lie fallow when the soo-gar's not sweet." Bonita alluded that he supervised a sugar plantation. He was a *Luna*, no doubt, a stern position. *Way problema*, thought Lainie, just don't crash us.

At Reena's insistence, they stopped at a small, dilapidated village along the Anilao River.

"Cousin Vi lives here. She said she had a merienda for me, I mean, us." Reena aimed straight for a narrow walkway flanked by flaking walls. All but Mike joined while the others puffed stepping at a clip to catch up. Reena waved at them to hurry and join the feast. Flanking shacks along the route were made of cardboard or thin wood. Faces peered at them behind newspapered openings. Vi's abode was slightly better. They all entered her cement block building, smaller than Nita's.

Inside on a broad table, a roasted pig lay among many other dishes. Above, a couple of scoop lamps lit revelers leaning their backs against cement walls. Some surfaces were adorned with holy cards, crosses, and curled family photos. Lainie had no idea who these people were.

On a toy table, men played pool games, smoked, and drank. The women receded. Their thin clothes hung on their tiny frames. They pointed lips at the dishes. Lainie stood amazed, too long. They hid toothy smiles. They tried, without luck, not to stare, and then looked away, blushing. No one spoke directly to Lainie, although she tried to look accessible. Only knee-high kids fell against her, grinning, making pretzels of their arms and legs among hers, squealing. Lainie detected behind the women's shyness something distant. Nita came to Lainie's rescue.

"Who are they? What should I call them?" Lainie begged for any know-how. She was at sea in this setting. "Why won't they talk to me?"

Nita whispered, "They know English but will not speak until Vi brings you up to them."

Nita uttered a short phrase to the women who nodded, speaking a full Cebuano sentence back to her. Lainie nodded. They nodded back, pleased. They were Vi's relatives not allowed to connect because Vi was noticeably absent. Vi must be pouting again, Lainie thought.

Lainie asked, "Mom, what is up, what are we doing here, standing around?"

Reena shrugged. "They haven't been properly introduced. Only Vi knows their names."

Lainie blinked. Nita's frozen smile never wavered. Bonita looked for Vi. Reena wouldn't.

Juan had already left to join Mike. Lainie imagined them leaning against the jeep, like chauffeurs. Lainie wondered if Bonita, looking terse, would light into Vi for her bad manners. Bonita had made her daughters linger with her till finally, they swept past Lainie. Bonita remarked, "Make my mother wait, *ay 'sus.*" Nita, Reena, and Lainie moved outside, again doused by the squalid heat of mid-afternoon.

Mike held open the house gate for Lainie. He forgot to do the same for the other women.

Lainie nearly barked. "Oy! Please open the door for my aunt and my mother."

Nearby, children with large abdomens and big-eyed women pushed against Lainie all the way down the path between huts, like the Manila orphans, looking haunted. Nearby, mothers bathed babies. Boys defecated in the river. Lainie was repelled by the squalor. These villagers lived in and accepted it. Would they, like Reena, replace this life with a better one elsewhere?

XV

Reena, before entering the jeep, stood staring at the river, eyes blank and distant. She recalled being that child once, splashing in the same waters. How could she only identify the waters and none of the newer buildings? Vi's house was nothing like Nita's, and for a reason: not enough American dollars from U.S. relatives had been sent "home".

She also knew why Vi was absent. Reena had failed to tell Vi that Nita had room for Reena and Lainie, after Vi announced the two would stay at her own house. Seeing Nita's compound, Vi held her embarrassed tears in check until she was alone with Reena. Then Vi ranted at her for her endless better luck, her choice of husband, her house, and her hostess's house. Reena's homecoming had more fanfare than Vi had ever received. And Vi had always returned. Reena, on the other hand, visited this one time. Vi stung Reena saying, "I love my Philippines more than you ever did! I came back!"

Well, she hadn't, really, but Vi could say, she knew Ormoc, before and after the war.

The town Reena showed to Lainie held no anecdotes to share, not one.

In the jeep, Bonita clucked her tongue. "Vi is rude." Nita patted her hand. "Those people were Jovita's neighbors and watched Fausto grow up. They thought they'd see drama. They knew, everyone knew: Reena told him whose son he was."

Reena just flounced, scrunching closer to the window and echoed Bonita. "Vi is rude."

But family mysteries would not affect Reena's months-long plan. The barrio would have their drama once she revealed the hidden papers, decades old, aerograms, gossip-drenched, aerograms – just circuitous truths and secreted legal notices.

XVI

Mike pulled into the small town of Lunao showcasing one white but ornate church across from a windowless pavilion, usually the center of activity for most towns. A crowd of about a dozen women was waiting, eager to hug and greet the Ormoc group all of whom were surprisingly similar in build with their endomorphic apple shapes and hunched shoulders. Here, Lainie really matched the height and weight and body muscle of this side of the family. Reality set in.

Any kind of strenuous workout or weight loss for Lainie would always be a losing battle. This bloodline had hearty, ingrained genes. She, too, would always remain stocky – abundant.

The townspeople knew Lainie wrote about trips. The most active woman, second half-cousin Evie, who was typing up last-minute copy to run off the vintage mimeograph machine, plied Lainie with her own recent issues, books, and pamphlets. Glancing over them, Lainie detected a rather leftist slant, which relaxed her in a way. Amazing that there was no fear here, she decided. Evie was a truthsayer, and for her, writing also stamped a family trait.

Everyone ate a light lunch sitting around a long table, one that bore the signs of many, many gatherings. This was not only a visit; this was a meeting. Evie continued to type her newsletter. Locals spoke in casual Waray-Waray, Nita explained, and English. Reena took center. Mike and Juan hovered outside in the shade and did not join at all.

Lainie noted that some copies were ink-smeared from the typewriter's ribbon caking on the pages. This nagged at her. She asked about a printer.

"Oh, I wish I had a printer!" Evie exclaimed. She was an older woman, her exuberance contagious. "I could type once and then print as many copies as possible if we didn't have our usual brownouts. For now, though, God permits, the manual typewriter works just fine."

When Evie rose from her chair, Lainie asked if she would mind if she tried typing a bit to test if the typewriter kept sticking. Evie openly welcomed her. "Oh, yes, yes, please type!"

The rat-a-tat of Lainie's rapid typing hammered the air like a machine gun. She stopped. The whole room was looking at her. She blushed. "Sorry, I-I just thought . . ."

In half-English, the occupants exploded with amazement about how anyone could type so fast, that she must be a writer after all, and that the clippings Reena sent were true. Reena herself sat, smug. She spoke above the crowd, "I told you so. Show them, hon. Type some more."

Lainie was quizzical. "Mom, you wrote them when? I only knew I'd join you last week."

But Reena had turned away to engage a woman louder than she was. Lainie took Evie aside, still apologizing but asking if she had a sewing kit or toothpick. "Please, please allow me to clean your keys. Please, if I can help at all, I could do that. Please." Evie excitedly produced a needle. Lainie picked out chunky ribbon ink inside selected keys and typed again. Grateful for the break, Evie sat with the women at the table.

"Oh, this is rare for me," Evie sighed. "I turn out a four-page weekly."

The group accepted Lainie working, something not ill timed or even rude. She took the tiny stiff brush, scrubbed the keys, and once more typed a high-school practice line:

Now is the time for all good men to come to the aid of their country.

Children had gathered at the foot of the hill below the pavilion. Evie explained, "The town hears you. They want to see who you are." Some of the women walked with Lainie to meet them till Lainie asked, "Are they relatives, too? Should I know their names?"

But Evie, too, demonstrated the yes-but-no contradiction and nodded. "Oh, no."

Lainie, now on to this routine, also nodded back, saying,

"Okay – no."

Lainie was only a head taller than the children who walked close touching her, pointing to houses Lainie didn't know. They were especially proud of the oddly ornate church. Only at the door did anyone tell her it was closed. She, a tourist, viewed a lone landmark on a day no one could tour the place. Only then did Lainie realize she saw just these women and children in town. She saw not one man, except Juan and Mike. Evie quipped, "Harvest time even past sundown."

Mike made noises about heading back before dark. "*Sigé, sigé,* because of all the NPAs."

"New People's Army," Lainie spoke too loud. Town mates and children were silent.

Everyone piled back into the jeep, waving at the Lunao townspeople. Evie pushed her written address and phone number at Lainie. Lainie had liked her immediately.

Evie promised to print her own review of Lainie and Reena's celebrity visit including the American who knew exiled students present in Manila in 1986. Lainie now got it. This empty town in the north sent militant newsletters to preach to the converted, the overworked farmers.

During the ride back to Nita's house, Lainie reviewed Day One. Mike sped off while Lainie sagged, realizing how little she knew. Nita strode by Horatio at the door. Reena groaned, her bare feet on cool tiles. The girls echoed her. Strange women cooked food on the very large black iron stove, at least five feet wide with many burners and a huge stovepipe. Lainie felt she had worn blinders till now. The Mays kept a well-maintained and stocked household.

These strange women ruled Nita's kitchen. They served. None ate. What were they doing here? After eating, the men moved to smoke outdoors with other men who hadn't eaten. Women, maids, served them beer bottles and emptied ashtrays. Then the maids cleaned the kitchen.

If one were not family, that person stayed outside until they were invited. Hosts might share leftovers. Still, the guest waited till granted permission to join, and would usually demur. The host then insisted. The guest sat. Then family filled their plates before any guest scooped up food.

Lainie never saw any of the maids eating at the table or in the kitchen. She wondered what were they paid for daylong services. She recalled her Filipino-born students who filled her in on distinctive class differences in the Philippines.

Classism was rampant, and the two classes lived uneasily together, the Rich – not Lainie's family – and the Poor. The latter cleaned, cooked, or held jobs in maintenance or construction. They were not introduced. They were limited to abject invisibility. Class, not race, defined their status.

Actually, if anyone had pesos to spare, that person could pay for a maid. Nita's many guests required maids. Even a timid maid, deferring all day to her employer, who could have a guest like Reena, could also treat her own one-time maid as she had been treated: invisible. A gardener could own a bicycle and shuttle a maid; she could pay the gardener bike money, and the cycle went on.

Still reviewing, Lainie recalling the issue over Juan's ticket and so, confronted Reena.

Mother and daughter had also cut off contact till just before Reena offered airfare. Reena's continual assumptions, blithe and thoughtless, had irked all her children who had also vowed at times never to speak to her again. Lainie, like the others, gave in. And Reena, as she had with the others, tested the resilience of each renewed bond.

"Mom," Lainie began as Reena again checked her *balikbayan* boxes who knows what for, "Mom, did you promise anything else to anyone about my trip here?"

Reena frowned. "What? What do you mean, promise? I didn't promise anyone anything."

Lainie leaned closer, "Juan's ticket. You told people I'd pay for it. What else did you promise? You mailed clippings to Lunao. You hinted I'm rich."

"I said, prosperous! And why shouldn't I? Americans are prosperous, everyone is . . ."

"Mom, Juan's ticket. What if I couldn't have paid for it? I'd be so embarrassed."

Reena insisted, "I didn't say you'd buy his ticket. I said she needs – that you need – a guard on the city streets for the thieves and, and the NPAs, that's all."

"Mom, I know what big, bad cities are like."

Reena snuffled. "You don't know the ways here."

Hers was not so much an apology as an oblique admission. Reena had convinced the Manila family that Lainie might need protection in Ormoc and someone could pay someone, someone they all knew, like Juan. Not yet giving up, Lainie intoned. "O-kayy, let me synopsize."

Reena snuffled. "Hmph, you and your big words."

"You hinted someone should escort me, like Juan, who could finally visit after thirty-two years by flying there and back with me, right? I shell out; everything stays family, right? Mom?"

Reena was silent, fiddling with a child's pajama set. "Nita was missing him, and he was nice driving me around Manila. This way, I pay him back. We make good. We do that here."

"I'm poor, Mom. You're paying him back with my money and didn't tell me."

"We both paid: me, for your fare, you, for his. Did you forget?" Mom made sense.

As Lainie headed for the door, her mother's final zing was, "If you made money at your travel writing, you would be rich by now."

Lainie mustered up some pride and left the room.

Under the patio's shadows, the men were talking low and laughing but shushed when Lainie sat nearby. With a deprecating grin, she opened her journal and read over her last entry.

Soon enough, the men again revved up their conversation. Horatio mentioned his morning jog. Lainie made a note. She would jog with him. As she began to write, Juan in increments edged over to her and finally asked. "What are you writing?"

Lainie said, "Just some thoughts, about what each day is like while I'm here."

Juan nodded swinging his knees slightly left to right and then asked. "Why?"

Lainie thought a moment. "So I don't forget."

Juan waited. "You're here now. Maybe be here. Now."

Lainie closed her journal. At the pier people had approached her yet strolled off – because she was writing, inaccessible. Drat, she thought. Juan had a point.

Lainie admitted, "I speak pretty bad Cebuano or Waray-Waray, don't I?" Juan blinked. She bit her lip and asked, "Can we, would you teach me some words? Tell me what people mean, what they're really saying. And, and I promise: I be here."

Juan began to smile but then covered his mouth. He had few front teeth. He nodded.

Lainie felt exhausted. Horatio fetched more beer for all the men except Juan who was not drinking. She patted Juan's shoulder, followed Horatio into the house, and rushed through a thank-you at him for their stay at his house. Horatio smiled. "Family. We're all family." But as he moved away, she added. "I jog a bit, too. I could join you sometime."

Horatio halted, mid-step. She had already decided when. He couldn't really stop her.

"Five-thirty's a good time. You can show me the barrio, yes?"

Horatio started to shake his head, so she went on. "Sorry if I startled you in town 'cause we hadn't really met yet. I must've looked lost in a big place, but this area's smaller, so here I won't get lost. It's safer for someone like me to jog with someone like you who knows the area."

He remained frozen. Kitchen clanging stopped. She thought,

"God forbid I boo-boo'ed."

But Horatio grunted. "Um, okay." Someone banged pots and pans in the kitchen.

Lainie, bidding all good night, entered the bedroom. Reena looked up. "What happened?"

"Nothing. I'm turning in early to catch up on some sleep. Go ahead. Stay up a bit. Don't mind me." Lainie climbed to the top bunk, watched closely by Pickle on the far wall.

"Something happened, I don't know what." Reena added. "Always, it's you."

"I told Tito Horatio I'll jog with him in the morning. Wanna join us?"

Reena just snorted. "Tomorrow and no more. He has things men have to do."

Lainie, arched, spoke. "We'll talk and run. You can't talk when someone runs away."

"Of course not! What are you talking about?" Reena flapped open a girl's top.

"'Night, mom," called Lainie with her face deep in her pillow.

After reviewing her day, Lainie's eyes fluttered but managed a secret grin. Annoyed, Reena flounced out and joined Nita. They both could be heard boning up on the recent gossip.

Trilling night insects and lilting streams of rattled-off sentences punctuated by musical chortles and guffaws dampened far-off songs. The din melded into indistinct hums. The last she heard, lulling her was the crackling tune from Jun's CD player: " ... *Then we'll be to-* (crackle) *some where out there out* (crackle) *dreams* (crackle) *-rue...*"

XVII

"And (crackle) *night wind starts* (crackle) (crackle) *some lulla* (crackle) *helps to think we're* (crackle) (crackle) *underneath* (crackle) (crackle) *-ky . . ."*

Morning: Jun had cranked his CD player's volume till his daily song was broadcast to the far reaches of Barangay 35. Lainie stretched sleepily. Why no one bellowed to turn that CD player down puzzled her. She figured on her first night, not even thirty hours earlier, the *silingans* looked up to Jun, not just because he was tall. He was a personage, an icon, and one who could blast the same song all day long without worry. *Way problema.*

Lainie yawned and then slid down from her top bunk, slipped on her sandals, dropped a fresh, cotton top over her head, and pulled on her shorts. Someone shuffled outside her door headed past, opened and closed the front door softly. She dashed out, again noticing Juan without a blanket on the banig spread out on the tepid tile floor snoring.

Outside, she saw Horatio loping up the road nearing the water buffalo's corral, so she sped up to him. "Good morning!" she called about ten feet behind him. He turned. He could not avoid her this time like he had in town. If Horatio showed dismay, she ignored that. She would get him to acknowledge her. So what if she was a bold "American". She really didn't care.

Maybe her friendship with the Fil expats made him wary. Maybe he avoided those Filipinos who disagreed that Americans, through their takeover after World War II, saved their islands.

"Sorry if I scared you again. So this is your route? Cool." She jogged in place as if warming up.

"You know, yesterday?" she puffed. "I hope you didn't think I was going to rob you."

He drew himself up a bit. "No, no, not at all, I-I just, I was in a hurry."

"You made it, though, right?" She stretched, making a pretzel of her arms.

He regarded her. "You should be told about the NPAs, about the kidnappings. You must be careful on the streets alone, even public ones. I shooed you when I saw no one with you."

She frowned. "But with you, I wouldn't be alone. I'd go back with you." He coughed. She said, "But no problem—*way problema.*" Lainie jogged, hardly moving. "This road?"

So they jogged, older man, younger woman 5:30 at sunrise warming the hazy dawn peeking over Madawawing Mountains. A sherbet light brightened Horatio's features.

Last night, his wife and daughter had bumbled over his absence, adding to yet another mysterious discussion, also untouchable. What kind of host would be so uninvolved?

The previous day, he made her feel like a street urchin, a beggar, worse yet, a whore. He dismissed and maddened her. Lainie had rallied today: payback. Horatio did repeat the NPA warning, which she had dismissed. Still, she vowed she'd bring Juan shopping next time.

Lainie tread next to Horatio along semi-dark, palm tree-lined paths, and jogged in silence, puffing. A sizzle, an odor, fishy, an abrupt curse – sounds and smells loomed and faded as they passed leaning huts and stalwart houses. Once her night vision set in, she commented on his pristine outfit, flat seams, spotless Adidas, plus that familiar sinewy, green alligator on his three-button shirt. Horatio straightened, chest out, and took the compliment. Lainie remarked that she had brought only two pairs of shoes and that neither pair was that great for jogging.

"What size?" he asked, looking straight ahead. She told him.

Her feet thumped soft earth as she looked beyond the overgrown fronds and stumps hiding rickety rows of nipa huts. "The water buffalo, I like him. Already he signals home."

Horatio glanced at her. "Yes. Yes, he does . . .you're a writer, yes? Reena sent clippings. Your brother and sisters, all accomplished, *sigé*?"

So Reena shared clippings. What a surprise that Reena actually promoted Lainie. She had never mentioned receiving Lainie's printed articles and when asked, had never read them.

Horatio pointed to some huts beyond his cement house. "That looks like my family's place years ago. We had to share one C.R. with four other huts. Our old house was made with our leftover bricks. But no running water like us." Horatio laughed. "Soon, though, soon. Pumps work for now, God permits." She smiled secretly. These God refs dotted every conversation.

Lainie continued. "From outside, I didn't know your house could hold so many people. Who are they, these women cleaning, cooking, washing, and more of them every day?"

"Some are neighbors. Some are maids." Horatio leaned into the corner they turned and waved at a man in shorts. A cigarette hung out of his mouth, a wavering line of smoke in the air, his hair awry, his face lined and unsmiling. He tipped a rusted coffee can watering a lush, darkish tree. Lainie was struck that more care went into that tree than into the care of the man himself. But his mood lifted seeing Horatio. The man tipped up his chin, now less sleepy, eyes twinkling.

"Big houses, many maids. Yours is big, yes?" Lainie dodged a rock on the path.

Horatio explained, "Jobs help our countrymen, and this week Nita needs maids."

Like strummed washboards, a kind of sawing of birds and insects built up and added to the soft pounding of their feet on dirt paths. An acrid aroma of a distinct *bagoong* (fermented fish paste) for breakfast again punched the air and whisked away as they ran past the loneliest hut. A dipping, lean dog wagged its tail and followed them for a short distance before scampering back to its house. Nearby, a church bell rang. She heard low, monotonous chanting.

Lainie asked. "Where's the church, where is Mass held?"

Horatio pointed off. "No, no church. They're observing, uh,

matins, I think."

Lainie stopped. Horatio took this opportunity to sprint away. Chanters marching, somber, carried lit candles. A priest held up a crucifix of a tortured Jesus. A glint of the gold-cast body held aloft flickered in the rising sun. Horatio turned into the parade, running parallel against their current. He was eluding Lainie. Her eye drifted left, pulsing. She caught up to him.

"That's the rosary," she corrected, as if a prayer, matins, or a rosary made a difference to her. Worshippers, decked out and transfixed, lumbered past. No one hailed the heathen Horatio.

"You can join them," Horatio suggested. She refused and peered into the faces of mostly women, heads draped with lace mantillas and some men actually wearing the traditional *barong tagalog* shirts, made of stiff *piña* (pineapple) material. This early in the day, chanters were sleep-deprived but devout Catholics. They cast their eyes downward, as they stroked at the beads between their fingers. Their mouths moved in unison, and their repetitive drone buzzed. They mumbled through the familiar prayer: *HailMary FullofGrace theLordisWithThee.*

"Wow, pretty devoted, like running."

Horatio was distant except to some men. He pushed his lip toward them. This irked her.

"Does the Catholic religion really define everybody's lives here, day and night like this? Not you, of course, otherwise you'd join them yourself, but most everybody else, let's say, in this barrio? They drag out of bed every morning, save their souls another day by chanting the rosary? Then gallivant about gathering new sins?" What a mouthful. What irked her about him?

That did it. He definitely was uncomfortable. But he replied. "This is a Catholic country. And commandments, you know, thou shalt not kill, all those other things, are set in stone here. Some of them, some of the people, disregard them. You do not practice? Mass? Confession?"

Lainie shook her head. "No, not much since sixth grade.

What does a sixth grader need to confess? Adultery?"

Horatio pumped up his pace a bit as they neared the house. The sun was bright enough to distinguish muted flowers planted inside the red gates, none of which Lainie noticed before. Patio chairs were rounded chrome curved tubes for legs with riveted Naugahyde seats. Plastic woven strips adjoined to aluminum frames passed for worn-out loungers. A pup panted under an awning. Thin chickens clucked quietly pecking at dirt. A cock crowed.

Lainie's senses were heightened by the run. She pumped, and vision cleared. Adrenalin gushed through her. One-upping Horatio had settled her. She followed Horatio into the house.

Inside, Nita sat at the table, her palm supporting her chin as she gazed at Horatio, his back to her as he drank a large glass of juice. Compared to everyone else, he really was immersed in health and exercise. Nita asked her quietly. "Did you have a nice run?"

Lainie felt flushed, drippy. "Yes, and we talked, and I got to know the neighborhood, the rosary crowd." At that, Horatio turned and nodded, still gulping. "And now he'll know me, right, *Tito*, whenever we see each other, wherever that is."

Horatio was cool, finishing his drink, and nodded before heading off.

Standing by Nita's chair, Lainie touched her shoulder, and Nita smiled sadly. Juan in the shadows by the couch issued his familiar *tch-tch* of disappointment. Nita chided him softly. He steamed, small, looking baleful.

Lainie got it. Their short, nonverbal exchange was about Horatio, not about Lainie's second disappearance.

Perhaps he racked up more *faux pas* than she had.

XVIII

"Camarones," Bonita read. "Big shrimp. Giant shrimp."

"Then that's what I'll have. " Lainie had convinced the Ormoc group to eat in town. Mike chauffeured again, this time driving his jeep near the stands a few feet away while they browsed and then slowly motoring a little farther till they caught up.

After strolling half the town square with its little shops and a growing trail of townspeople, they had chosen an open-air eatery. Lainie waved to Mike to join them, but Nita poised her hand on Lainie's arm and shook her head. A very shiny-eyed, bowing, waitress seated them at the corner table under awning that sagged. Lainie backed off, peered over the top of the plastic sheet, and saw the surface was relatively dry and somewhat securely fastened. The waitress brought a tray of glasses with water. Lainie paused, "Umm."

The waitress looked at her like everyone else did. Lainie gave back her glass. "Could you please, I just prefer boiled water?" The waitress agreed eagerly that yes, of course, yes, we can boil your water and not waiting for the others, she left quickly with one glass.

"You, uh, all want yours boiled, too, right?" Lainie looked at them but they all shook their heads and shifted. "We'll just have sodas." Lainie blanched. In preserving herself from stomach problems, she again demonstrated how American she acted.

The skies, again, opened. A burst of rain began to fill the sagging awning.

"Should we move?" Lainie backed under the awning. The others nodded but didn't move.

The torrent that splashed down and bounced high on an unoccupied table flushed the surface clean and abruptly ceased. The waitress, apologizing, stood by Bonita's chair easing her away a bit and, with a broom handle, pushed up into the corner of the awning forcing a few gallons of water to gush down. Fawning, she backed out. "Boiled water coming right up."

Nita quipped. "'*Sus*, she could've served that instead."

The whole table full of people laughed, especially Juan who kept covering his mouth.

As usual, utensils were only forks and large spoons, the edges of which cut food. Nita noted the camarones were old. Bonita added, "And hard." Everyone was quiet. They poked and pried open helmet-hard shells and pulled out shredded meat. Lainie sagged. She wanted to cover one meal. When Nita glanced at her watch, they shuffled in their seats. Lainie called. "Check?"

On the street, they browsed a bit more among the growing crowd. Radios blared from stores and revved-up vehicles pummeled Lainie's ears.

A gaggle of girls, followed, and one of them catcalled. "American! American!"

"What are all these people looking at? Are we that odd?" Lainie asked Nita. When she asked Bonita, she would get shrugs and no answers. Nita, after ten seconds, replied. "Your hair."

"My hair??" Lainie echoed.

"Your shoes, skin, your bigger body," Nita continued. "Your hair shines like on TV. Your shoes are foreign (Birkenstocks). Your skin is better. And you're well fed."

That answered that. Hers was a body nurtured.

"Oy, the bank!" Reena had banking to do and signaled Nita to accompany her. Lainie and Juan would catch up to them after checking out the remaining stores. Bonita and the girls would meet them later at Mike's jeep. The entourage of pre-teen teen girls squishing together, shoulders touching, alternately high-pitched and whispering, began to get on Lainie's nerves. They pointed to her hair, eyes, and lips from afar. They held up their own fingernails and compared profiles. One raucous, unguarded guffaw made Lainie turn. A thin girl parodied a belly. Lainie knew the rail-thin girl referred to Lainie's weight. She still hadn't bought a thing. The stores carried the same junk that U.S. dollar stores carried: fake nails, purses, nail files, lipstick, barrettes, luggage, and Japanese toys. What was unusual?

Lainie fixed on a simple, flat *piña*-woven bag, cloth-lined, double-handled. The whimsical twist was a palm tree woven onto the surface sewn with a thinly embroidered *Ormoc City*: the right size, packable, and inexpensive. Juan haggled for a price with the saleswoman.

"Twenty pesos, sir."

"Aiiee, five," Juan stated simply. She stared. Sighing, Juan displayed eight pesos.

The merchant removed the purse from its hook.

"Ten," the merchant offered, noncommittal.

Juan pocketed his pesos, walking off. The merchant called. "Sir. Sir. *Sigé*, eight."

She swiped her palm against his, sealing the deal. Through Juan, Lainie had bought the bag.

When the merchant handed over the purchase, the coterie of teens burst into laughter. Lainie whirled on them. They pretended innocence but revved up again when she turned away.

"Why are they laughing?" Lainie asked Juan. She reimbursed him eight pesos. He protested. He would negotiate her purchases. He waved the girls off. "Ay, young." Lainie still held out the money. "*Siguro*, take it, Juan. Otherwise, you just paid for the purse for me."

He shrugged. The girls' laughter echoed farther away. They had dismissed Lainie, the poor American who shopped for bland items. She imagined they'd say they could buy better.

Lainie asked again what was so funny about the bag. "I think it's cute."

Juan explained. "Is not a purse, not best purse, more like, like a refuse to them, like throwaway, like a, a 'garbage bag' – hey, oy, stop now. Never mind, they're just girls, it's a good bag, to carry things, *tama na*, don't cry." Lainie turned away and headed for the bank.

She wiped her eyes at the door. Juan waited outside, like a bodyguard. The brick building inside looked very much like an actual bank. Both Reena and Nita stood in front of the only open barred window. No one slouched, including the clerk behind the bars. Things seemed tense.

"What, uh, what's going on?" Lainie edged in beside them. Reena had four piles of bills spread before her. Shifting from one pile to another, she saw Lainie and sighed. "Oh, hon, what are these denominations now."

Reena was trying to divvy up what would pay for the Reunion, for Nita's costs so far, for her remaining vacation, and Miscellaneous. She looked alarmed, vulnerable. Lainie stepped up.

"Okay, Mom," Lainie spoke quietly. "These are all the receipts here, right?" Nita nodded slowly. Lainie clarified for everybody. "Your nod means yes, right?" Nita nodded confidently.

Lainie watched Reena bunch some bills together, eyes darting to a point in the air. "And what's left should be Miscellaneous, right?" Lainie felt Reena's anguish – until she spoke.

Drama-heavy, she posed the back of her hand onto her forehead, exclaiming, "Ah, it's just too much. Nita, count my money for me. I'm so tired!"

Lainie froze. The top of her head tingled. The teller shuffled. Nita looked down but then lifted her chin and held out her hand. Reena gave her the last pile. As mortified as Lainie felt, she did not show that or her rising anger, for Nita's sake. The proud woman silently counted Reena's bank notes. Lainie and Nita both were aware the notes were, and had been, easily countable. Both knew first hand that Reena, homeowner, investor, bill payer, could sight-count and call out any error. Lainie, chest heaving, witnessed Reena pulling class over her own cousin.

Nita turned to Lainie, indicating to re-count the bills herself, if Reena still couldn't. Lainie just quietly and slowly shook her head. Reena, *grande dame*, put all her money in the large purse, held close to her right side.

Lainie settled her chest. Heave only to breathe. Say nothing. Blurt out nothing.

Everyone met up at Mike's jeep, and the eight of them headed to the edge of Ormoc City where pineapples grew close to the ground. The women wanted to visit the sugar plantations. But Mike, being the driver, said pineapples were ripest now and ready just over this ridge. The women, odd to Lainie, sat stoically while Mike waxed poetic to Lainie about the healing benefits of pineapple.

"Constipation! Indigestion, even arthritis, wounds, and, and constipa- . . ." He faded off nearing a field. A boy, long strands of black hair shading his eyes, waited by the road. The boy, cocoa-colored, in a thin shirt and shorts, looked down as Mike approached.

Mike barked, "Oy, you Hernando's son?" The boy slouched. Mike instructed him to fetch a pineapple. Mike acted more like a boss than someone requesting some fruit. The girls giggled. The boy was cute. Barefoot, he bounded over a field looking like an artichoke field. He carried a bolo knife half his height. He bounded back and with his foot placed near the base of the fruit, he thwacked once and presented the football-sized gourd like an offering to Mike, and backed away, head down. Mike, in this setting, was one bowed to.

Lainie was startled. The first night neighbors deferred to Mike. No relatives introduced him as family at all. Without knocking, he entered Nita's house. He changed their plans. He was never invited for meals. But here, he decreed no one would visit any sugar plantation today, and given his obstinate manner, they probably never would.

Mike barked for the boy to approach and slice up the pineapple. Brandishing his very sharp bolo knife, the boy chopped it vertically into hand-size pieces and then held up the juicy bulk of fruit for Mike to present. The girls, very close to Lainie now, hung nearby her, sucking on the liquidly slices, grinning, humming, and oohing over the flavorful fruit. Mike grinned, holding aloft a slice, like a scepter, and chortled, "Ormoc's gold!"

Lainie was momentarily puzzled. What was his mantra: *The soo-gar's not sweet.* Yet, pineapple was gold?

The boy and Mike pointed above them at the palms.

Reena breathed, "Ah, coconut!" And the boy began to climb. But Juan protested. Mike debated him. Juan emitted a high-pitched warning. Nita sniffed. Bonita heaved a long sigh. "Whose trip is this?" Mike and Juan both raised their voices on who knew coconuts the best.

"Good nuts are farther down the road. Coconuts here are too green."

"No, they're good here." Juan insisted. Mike argued. "Too young! We go to the ridge." Even Bonita was frustrated. She and Nita had accommodated Mike's presence till now.

Mike drove over the ridge with the boy hanging onto the back of the jeep. They stopped and still barefoot, the boy clenched the bolo knife in his teeth and climbed a shorter tree with a slanted trunk. He hooked the arched parts of his feet onto each side and pulled himself heavenward. Then he caterpillared his body pushing with his arches. The girls held their hands to their mouths, eyes wide. So did Lainie. She had never witnessed this feat before, as if he performed for her the first acrobat she had ever seen. Unseen above the thick, leafy fronds, the boy called sharply, thwacked coconuts, tossed them down, and both Mike and Reena katonked the fruit of the palms, flicking at them with their forefingers and heard a resounding thunk. These nuts were hefty and full of milk.

Mike called up for more. He had no bolo knife of his own. The boy whose tiny face peeked out above the branches tossed down more coconuts yet paused at the last one. Mike glared. There was a standoff. The boy held the orb like a football, but then let it drop. He slid down slower than his ascent. Mike moved to cut the nuts, but the boy hacked at them and doled them out to the girls like cups. He would not let Mike touch his bolo knife. Mike scowled. Juan grinned and clapped the boy's back.

Reena slurped down her shell and scooped out the innards with her fingers. Lainie followed suit. Liquid dripped down her chin, like a waterfall, cool, and sensuous. The half-eaten coconuts were thrown to the roadside. Lainie saw the girls giggling when the boy mumbled, "*Ibagsak ang lunas, talaga?*"

Nita translated in a low voice to Lainie: "Down with lunas." She indicated Mike with a nod.

Reena cautioned, "Careful. Too much will give you the runs." Boiled water kept any loose bowels in check. Alas, coconut milk would not. Both good to know, thought Lainie.

The boy stood on the road with his knife as Mike pulled away from him, the jeep again packed with only Juan and the six females, the two girls sighing deeply, a bit lovesick.

"How will he get home?" Lainie asked.

Mike shrugged. "Hernando can get his son."

Lainie shifted. Why was everything so testy today?

Mike grumbled. "Thinks he can buck me like some young cockerel, hmph."

"That's a rooster, *talaga*?" Lainie meant to lighten the mood. " I never saw a . . ."

"You will." Mike cranked the wheel to turn left. "Now that's a fight to the end."

About five kilometers from the house, Mike's front right tire blew.

Lainie turned to everyone in the back seat. Nita's eyes twinkled. Both of them burst out into laughter relieving the built-up tension. Somehow Mike's blown tire let out all the gas of his big-plantation-supervisor show. All the gas was let out of the whole day. Even Reena's melodramatic bank moment and the young field hand's recalcitrant glare now seemed comic. Nita and Lainie held their stomachs and spilt wheezy tears. Juan tried to shush them. Mike stomped about, kicking the spare tire and cursed. "*PUUU-tang-ina-mo gahdamsommama bitz!*"

Lainie howled, high-pitched, swiping at her eyes. Both young girls and even Reena were puzzled, Mouths open, they didn't understand Lainie and Nita's outburst.

"Idontevenknowwhathessaid - it's the longest-ass cussword I ever heard!" Lainie guffawed even more. The girls giggled. Juan covered his mouth. "'*Susmarjosep*," Reena mumbled.

Sputtering to a stop, Nita and Lainie toned themselves down, exhausted. Mike refused to acknowledge any silliness. He carried the tire a few feet away to one of the ever-present makeshift vulcanization sheds, the term for tire repair. Reena tried to get Nita to tell her what was so funny. Nita waved her off. Mike rolled the tire back, and he and Juan installed it in grim silence. Back in the jeep, Mike mumbled. "De-playTEd, ano." Nita and Lainie burst out again, hooting without abandon. "Deflated!" Mike blared above them, "Like de RUBBER!"

Everyone, even the clueless girls howled till they coughed hiccupping and laughing.

They were uncontrollable all the way through Nita's red gates.

XIX

The butcher was tall, very stringy, and dark. His mass of streaky-gray hair bowed out, framing his narrow, glistening face. Stalwart, commanding, he looked like abolitionist John Brown, Lainie decided. He was her image of an NPA. Like Brown's image, he posed with unblinking focus, patient, like the official Filipino eagle five times the mass of any American predator. The cigarette never left the side of his mouth. He wore a threadbare short-sleeve faded shirt, long pants, and flip-flops, the breadth of him like dusted pecan, head to foot. He never blinked as he was introduced to everyone who had just arrived in Mike's jeep. Mike, impatient to leave, drove off. Road dust masked his exit. Lainie mused, not staying even for a frosty beer after a very public dressing down?

Dom, or Domingo, tall like the neighbor, Jun who blared his endless CD player, had been the island's pig butcher for decades and for hundreds of *lechon* meals for anyone rich or poor. His pay was free board, beer, and talk-story. He was their traveling minstrel dispensing poetic meat cuts. He knew everything that was happening from Biliran Island down to Panaon Island, both flanking Leyte north to south. No one could tell Lainie how old he was.

Reena shook his hand, but Dom said, "I remember you. The White Sister."

Reena gave that rosebud smile, eyes sparkling. "You do? What do you remember?"

"Boys, many boys following you. You caused trouble." Dom was easy and affable, delivering his blunt remark lightly. Lainie straightened her mouth. Reena paused, seeming to be unsure if he were joking or not. Men eased past Reena to be closer to Dom. Lainie sensed he was like a Pied Piper to them. He radiated Freedom. Lainie wondered, would they, urban-bound husbands, sons, or fathers, ever live, bowed-out hair in the wind, like Dom?

Lainie, too, was awed. Dom kept that damn cigarette in his mouth never dropping an ash.

"Do you want to see the piglets?" Bonita's youngest, Sari-Sari, asked shyly.

The piglets were penned up near the water buffalo, and were considerably small (forty kilograms or ninety pounds) pale, doe-eyed, with curly tails, high-pitched squeals, and winning personalities. Lainie compared: the two *lechon* gatherings so far presented dead pigs. How can anyone coo over something one day and barbecue pets like pigs the next? And then there were their dogs.

Returning to the house, Lainie glanced at the clumsy, wiry

also whitish puppy. Two maids, both rather taciturn squatted nearby, petting the animal, their looks inferring, it's just another dog. Lainie would not touch the shivering animal. On this trip she vowed she would not bond with any house pet living only to be a meal. This trip, she swore, no attachments.

Inside, Nita was reading a delivered phone message not glancing at Lainie – a clue.

"Mike will be back to drive you to a cock fight," Nita said, crushing the message.

"O-kay-y-y-y," Lainie drawled, and noticed Juan pacing. "When are we going?"

"You," Nita began setting the table. "He said, just you."

Juan protested with his high whine. Nita added, "Juan must go with you. You tell that to Mike." Reena, wide-eyed, added, "You don't go alone!"

Lainie nibbled at her food but eyed the people around the table. Why could this Mike just order them about especially for someone else's visit? Juan stuffed his mouth and dashed to the C.R. Lainie guessed, Juan as the bodyguard now on duty would forego further potty breaks.

She sighed. Mike had now determined they would catch a cockfight. Mike would regain some dignity, unearned, she decided, judging by his treatment of Hernando's boy.

Mike arrived in his customary, blustery manner, and only slightly glanced Juan's way when Lainie petted the air, hand down toward Juan. She now used the distinctive Filipino invitation. As usual, Juan positioned himself in the back seat as Lainie sat up front riding shotgun. Night wrapped them. Mike cranked up Guns N' Roses' ditty, *Welcome to the (crackle)*.

Lainie caught a whiff. Mike had been drinking. Since leaving Nita's, he bellowed. She figured he had downed a few frosty beers since he had driven off in a huff two hours earlier. She inexplicably hugged her shoulders. Watching her, Mike began to broadcast vociferously.

"I know you all look at me. I come from a big family Big means you are seen, and strong means you are feared. I make lots of money on fights. When I win tonight, I will share the winnings. You will be my good luck. You will blow on my hand!"

Lainie felt queasy. Unlike the day, she felt, he would not be made the butt of jokes.

Barreling through the jungle beyond the main road, his paw-like hands dwarfing the steering wheel, Mike twisted onto unpaved roads down a nearly undetectable path as desiccated, needling fronds raked the vehicle. Lainie pulled closer to center of the open-air jeep to avoid any possible sharp cuts from the leaves. Their arms touched. Mike rumbled a deep, sensual laugh.

They burst onto a cleared-out opening where jeepneys, bicycles, discarded pens, and dented animal carriage littered the ground. Muffled shouts, cheers, and curses leaked from a round, primitive covered coliseum with large billboards and signs of rural advertising. Hopping from the jeep, Lainie hugged her purse. Mike paid the entrance fee. The interior was packed.

"Seasoned owners," Mike slurred, "use their premium birds. *Sigé*, maybe half of the roosters fight already! Half of those may be already dead."

He pointed. "Those men hawk their bets. People match them. And the *kristos*, see the fluorescent vests, they memorize all house bets, no pen or paper, all memorized. In the center ring, that man sweeps away bloody feathers, and that man splashes water on the bloody surface, and that man pulls a toothy broom making it all nice again. Him there, the *sentensyador* is like a referee, even if he has no marking. We'll sit close to the pen but don't worry. We won't get any blood on ourselves."

Mike and Lainie sat in the third row. Juan took a seat behind them.

Facing each other, the owners were billing their birds, hovering them over each other, revving up the blood match. They would fight to the end. Lainie reasoned that even surviving birds are not winners, never ever bred to be bodyguards to a yard of hens. Their combs and wattled red throats had been removed before training. During their short lives, they only fight.

Mike had blasted sound bites of information on the *sabong*, or cockfight, above the din of men betting their meager wages, fight after fight. Lainie was aware that she was one of maybe three females in the crowd, one was an old, bored woman, and another was a mirror image of the male beside her, both heads shaved from their necks to above their ears, their tops still capped with sleek, bowlike strands. Cock fighting did not lure native women, Lainie guessed, and slumped a bit. Mike's thigh touched Lainie's. She moved.

Lainie blinked. The first fight was over in five seconds. The loser lay limp where he had dropped, probably gut-sliced by the other cockerel's curved and officially applied razor on one leg. The referee urged a peck out of the battered bird – no go. If the survivor won't fight the near-dead bird, the fight is a tie. For the owner, either bird would make a hearty, if tearful, meal.

Mike kept urging Lainie, "Bet! Go on, I will front you. Bet." As she held back, he held up his hand. "Okay, I bet for you. Blow." He held out his palm. Mouth set, Lainie puffed once.

A vested *kristo* ignored Mike's hail for a marker. Mike swore. " '*Putang ani mo*" (son of a whore) and signaled another hawker. The next fight's result was the same, bloody birds and no winners. The crowd wanted wins. Mike chortled, his throat liquid. Again, he bumped Lainie.

Action sped up. Lainie couldn't even see which part of the body lost feathers, only a very shell-shocked bird, past crowing, defenseless against the other bird's surprise flank attack.

The referee shook the dying bird at his opponent and dropped them both. Neither once-proud rooster initiated a peck. Lainie, submerged behind men in the front rows, compared the birds to movie anti-heroes. They defied the odds of sure death, withholding jabs or counter-attacks. In resisting the inevitable, they were magnificently sublime, steady, and doomed.

Lainie had been an avid adolescent boxing fan. Her goal, back then was to howl and scream at the TV. Pummeling empty air, her dad, Geraldo, and friends on couches performed their armchair athletics while she bellowed at the screen. But like the rooster, lilting sideways in the circle, she, too, swallowed her howls. Family drama had its day and would not play out here.

After a half dozen beers, Mike was very drunk. Lainie had been tipping her bottle through the floor slats. She turned to Juan, who was also lost in the battles. She begged the air, somebody, please, win. Or somebody lose, so Mike would recoup his losses. The crowd groaned, shouted, and swore. Mike finally won. Juan, also relieved, lifted his chin at Lainie: we will get out of here. Juan whispered in Mike's ear. He awoke from his slurry posture, weaving slightly as he counted his bills and pesos. "Oy, we go now? When we're winning?"

Lainie patted her stomach and frowned. "C.R.", she said.

They rose from their seats and squeezed past yawning bettors. Mike roared, "Ay, you'll lose a week's pay if you stay the night and through tomorrow!" He never did share any winnings.

Once they were on the road again and through the inky-est part of the jungle, Lainie gasped at the brilliant pinpoints, sprinkled, as if airbrushed onto the sky. Familiar celestial patterns seen at home now looked awry, tilted. She felt for her camera. Gone – her camera was missing. Juan was daydreaming. She would not bother him. Mike hummed, a rumbling snore.

Lainie fingered her temple plucking for a memory: the jeep, the pineapple, and the bank! She had placed the camera on the bank counter to divide Reena's bills and witness her mother's diva act.

Aiiee, let it go. For the price of her camera, she, Lainie Cortez, saw an actual cockfight in the provinces of the Philippines. With that, she had earned one invisible "medal" enduring blood and bets on birds, a known Filipino tradition, just with no visible proof. *Way problema.*

At Nita's, she slid from the jeep avoiding any expected good-night kiss. Juan whisked her toward the dark house, thanking and bowing to Mike who weaved in his seat and screeched off.

The night was oddly silent, no sound even from the neighbor's relentlessly blasting CD player. Juan stomped ahead of her in the darkness. Not even a porch light was on.

"Thank you," Lainie began but Juan did not answer.

XX

While Lainie lingers in the patio, Juan fills in the May family, which Reena half-hears.

"She had curled up so small in the third row, like a cowed child." Reena notices that he tosses a cloth, damp from his neck, onto a chair. *Tama na*, why is he so upset? She sighs.

"Too close to the ring, I should've said something. What guard am I that I cannot say to Mike, sit us farther from the fights?"

"She should not see the pigs killed." Juan beat himself up about things required for this job and how he doesn't fit the position. He sighs. "Ay, she knows so little about things here." He clicks his tongue. "In Lunao, she types. She makes herself too visible. Her actions are too American. She does not know . . ." he pauses. Reena thinks, drama, drama. He ends his remark in Reena's direction, "who these people are to her." Reena avoids making eye contact with Juan.

But his next remark makes her perk up. "She is just so, so

fragile, so, so beat down."

Horatio pulls a chair out for Juan to sit. "So American, *ano?*" He thinks it's funny.

"Men here are not all like Dom and go anywhere they please!" Juan shakes his head.

" ' . . . *pelting like a monsoon rainstorm, battering forest-green sentinels.*' " Horatio quoted someone. No one asks whom. Instead, Nita pats Juan's arm.

"She has what Reena has, as a girl, diba, even more."

Reena sends Nita the stink eye, which Nita ignores and adds, "Lainie has The Eye. God willing, she knows what to do with it."

Reena is about to say what she believes Lainie will do. The door to the patio opens. Speak of the devil, thinks Reena. Juan looks for another chair.

XXI

Lainie sauntered, lagging behind Juan, wispy breezes brushing her face. Before entering the house, sudden shrieks and caws sharply slice the air and shred Lainie's reverie. Then she heard a scream, and another, then giggles, and again, blessed silence. She concocted girls testing their lungs on how to sound when lovers rescued them from imaginary captors. Night with no lights does that, Lainie mused, but not to her. She welcomed this sedentary cave of darkness. She missed neither nocturnal San Francisco's sirens, nasal and irritating, or the city's gunshots. Here she could shed the urban cloak of paranoia.

Gazing at Nita's cement bricked house, she imagined herself back in time, eavesdropping on Reena as a bride seated with Lainie's *lola*, Billina, at their old house. This would be years before Reena would join Geraldo arriving to take her to his hometown north of Manila while he finished his military tour. Completing her mental picture, Lainie could even hear a guitarist's serenade. She fantasized.

"What did you and grandma say in those last moments?" Lainie had asked earlier. Reena had minced her version warning her own daughters about marital duties, like Billina had. A barely educated bride, Reena had prodded Billina. "*Nanay*, what more do husbands do to wives?"

"You must submit to your husband but you might still not get pregnant, "Billina hinted, who, when standing, was even shorter than Reena. "Oh, my God, sometimes you could submit many times in one night." Reena only smiled, Mona-Lisa like, and stopped Billina cold.

"Mommy clicked her tongue." Reena recalled for Lainie, her own too-eager daughter.

"Mommy said, 'You must be planning.' But I said, 'Just imagining.' She told me, 'Do not plan. God wants women pregnant.'"

But Billina had whispered. "If you don't really want it for babies, tell your husband to give you a sign, like a tap on your hip, for that other type." She pointed behind her.

Reena was perched to ask. "What's that?" Billina shushed her. "To defy God's plan is a sin, *anak* (child). It's less of a sin if you defy the plan but just not say it out loud."

Reena had recounted for Lainie that even the clarion birds after dusk quieted down to eavesdrop. Wide-eyed, Reena leaned into her as Billina whispered, "He . . . he may get crazy, and loud. Do not clench up or you'll hurt, just, just breathe in, and out. Relax. Oh, my God, how I tell this to you: Sex is good for men but not for women. Sex hurts. Having babies hurts. If you're a married woman, you hurt."

And that was the extent of last words between them about the birds, bees, or sex.

Reena hadn't returned. Billina's house was leveled by 1955. Billina moved in with Nita.

Reena would stay for a couple months with Geraldo's family. There she perfected Tagalog more than Ilocano, the dialect of his Ilocos Sur region. She had honed phrases with a local student she met, Antonio. That was his name. Of all her connections she made over that time, Lainie noted his was the one name Reena repeated often, unlike family, unlike Ynez, who ran off at age sixteen.

Lainie shook herself out of the imagined scene on the patio from the 1940s and entered the dark May house. Around the table faces eerily lit by Coleman lanterns looked expectant.

XXII

Reena, Nita, Nate, and Bonita sat around the Formica table lit only by lanterns. "Van Gogh's painting *Potato Eaters*," Lainie thought. Like the image, here, too, words hung unsaid under ashen lights dabbed onto worn faces over a somber meal.

Nate answered her unasked question. "Brownout."

Reena spoke up. "Ever since you left. Maybe it's a sign. How was the cock fight?"

"They died." Lainie summed up. "Um, do you mean, blackout?" They shook their heads vigorously. Nate spoke. "Only if the whole island is out. There's lights in Tacloban."

The other side of the Leyte, great, thought Lainie. "Seems like a sign from on high, almost ominous." She noticed the group smiled.

Nita loosely held a cigarette. "Maybe it is."

Nate added, "We could be in the dark for a few nights."

Lainie regarded all their secret smiles. Juan, brows knit, jutted his lower lip at her.

"*Cuz* (cousin), torch or lamp?" He had read her mind. She felt sheepish.

Nate retrieved another flashlight and some beers. Nita struck a match for her cigarette. The flame briefly illuminated her features. The match blinked out just as Nita's eye fluttered.

Lainie remarked, "I didn't know you smoked."

"For brownouts, it's okay." Nita shrugged, usually unflappable. She drank little, yet to calm herself she smoked.

"So, Reena," she tapped off loose ash onto a dish, "About Luis. We'll call him when? Our half-cousin about what we'll say to him about the land."

Reena cleared her throat.

Lainie blinked. "Luis? Land?"

Bonita said, "Family land from years back, early 1900s and before. You might as well tell her, *Até*." The use of the term of respect at this moment made everyone shift.

Lainie perked up – a secret? Could this be the family mystery, one with passion, and angst, and drama, like some epic television series? Around the table, people shuffled in their seats or reached to fill drinks in half-drained glasses.

Reena started. "The family street sign, that's where the land starts and goes north through . . ." she now looked to Nita. "Well, hundreds of hectares maybe even a thousand."

"Past Lunao, and east to the mountains." Nita pointed with her lip. "*Soo-gar* plantations."

Soo-gar, Mike's pronunciation, was also his bread and butter, as a kind of plantation supervisor, called locally a *luna*. Huge companies split their fields into so many hectares, each monitored by men on whom Mike cracked the whip, like the boy who climbed palm trees.

Lainie blurted, "Weren't we just in that area, where we ate pineapples and coconuts?"

"Today we were given the run-around. Mike drove along the edges. But we know. We know what Luis knows. Whoever owns the soo-gar, owns Mike."

Lainie tried summing up. "And Luis doesn't want anyone to see his land?"

Everyone shifted. Reena sat ramrod straight, uncharacteristically stoic. Nita sighed.

"Luis doesn't want anyone else to own his land."

"Squatters, field hands, like Hernando's boy." Bonita then added, "The lower class."

"Oy, *sigé*." Murmurs of agreement rumbled around the table.

Nita tapped the Formica. "Our mothers are half-sisters. Billina was the direct line to our grandfather. With no brothers who are interested, Reena's first in line to the inheritance."

Lainie was blinking rapidly. "Which is, not the land but . . . or it is the land, but . . ."

Bonita interjected. "I told mama to write Reena and get her to come back and get what she's due, now that your daddy went to heaven. Together, they could pursue the property."

"Luis owns your, your," Lainie swiveled to face Reena, "He, he . . . your cousin . . ."

"The land was fallow from the 1900s because grandfather was in the mountains." Nita pushed her cigarette into the ashtray. "You know about that. Grandma died, rest her soul, then Luis's father died, which leaves Reena. Years passed. No one said anything. Squatters won't muddy the waters, *sigé*? So no one kicked them off. They stayed."

No one in the room contested her rendition, which made sense. Reena smoothed her top.

"Say it," urged Nita softly. "Say it out loud, Reena. Just tell her."

Reena reached for a folder, avoiding Lainie's look. "Luis took over my mother's land."

In this far off country, Lainie discovered family, Reena's, hers, had a legacy of worth.

Lainie uttered, "So, we're like gentry, rich, like *Dynasty*?" Mentally she did the math. To that, everyone guffawed and reached for their drinks. Blushing, Lainie switched up. "But why now? If Luis ran the works since grandma died, what's stopping him now? Why didn't anyone contest him? Is he lining up his ducks for something?"

Nate held up one hand and briefly interpreted Lainie's slangy lingo. They nodded.

"Yes, yes! Nita's been watching. Luis has kids in college, and last year 1988 one of them graduated in Law. Her brother studies Agriculture and soil and cane work . . . and pineapples."

Lainie was wide-eyed. For her mom, Nita had been busy tracking the pursuit of this land Lainie had never heard about before this night. She realized what Luis had been waiting for – testing soils and yields, expecting legal updates, and wondering if any Plebiñas would contest.

Nita was on a roll. "Anyone could contest within ninety days, a direct descendant, not in-laws, but actual siblings, even half-siblings, illegitimate half-cousins, like Luis and . . ."

"Wait, wait. Mom," Lainie turned to her. "If Luis is only a half-brother, then he can't just waltz in and take over. So you must've filed, or someone for you like . . .?"

Reena announced, "Nita did while I filled up boxes for a Reunion. Might as well, eh?"

Lainie blinked. Whatever precious time Nita could buy for Reena was used to plan this trip over the last year. Lainie knew from a temp job with a sneering lawyer that legal motions to delay could hold off lawsuits indefinitely.

She ventured a guess. "Did you file a motion to delay, like, more than one motion?"

Nita nodded. "Nearly a year's worth. Bonita helped me." Nate looked proud of them. She was not the timid cousin Lainie figured her to be.

Lainie asked Reena directly, "So together you'll both take on this half-uncle Luis?"

The group now looked at Reena, who feigned innocence, maddeningly uninvolved.

Nita was softly accusatory. "Oy. You didn't tell her? Even *that? Cuz . . .* cousin."

For the first time Lainie heard Nita address Reena with that term, truly as her full first cousin and not just as an accommodating, servile hostess. This was a night of many firsts.

Reena mumbled and shrugged. "It's not necessary to tell that part. They don't want to know, anyway, you know kids. Anytime I told them, I get this." She rolled her eyes heavenward.

"Mom, we asked. In increments, we asked, till the others gave up. You and Dad never wanted to tell us anything about your time here, except for Father Smile and the church."

"Aiiee, Father Smile?" Nita brightened. The talk about land ownership swerved away.

Reena said, "How her dad and I met, that's all, post-war, the movies, the projector . . ."

Nita said, "And the *aswang* and cigar-smoking *kaprés* in the trees, the Japanese . . ."

Reena said, "Of course, all of that. See? I told her things!"

Lainie stopped them. "Actually, Dad did. Please, back to the land, great-grandfather, and the mountains. Primo in Manila . . ." Lainie turned to Juan. "And you, Juan, you're both male descendants. How come neither of you took over . . .?"

Nate spoke up. "Primo and Juan do not want the land. They won't contest that side of the family. Spanish Serrañaos are now in our line, like illegitimate Luis, the one with the Midas touch. Everyone defers to him in everything especially this land. Now do you understand?"

Obviously, from Lainie's look, she didn't, so Bonita continued. "Bastard son of philandering Spaniard is too big and unscrupulous. Luis now owns Ormoc City."

Oh my God, oh my God, oh my God, thought Lainie. She could hear Reena blurting out, spilling her real intentions. "That's why I came, hon, just to see, not that I know what to do, Nita said they're all lawyers and own restaurants and have all the best jobs, so we just wanted to see the land, but Mike does what he's told and he's told to not show us our own land, and today we learned that we must find ways to go see for ourselves."

Lainie flopped back. "I'm all mixed up. Three generations of descendants do nothing until my illegitimate half-uncle, second cousin, who knows what he is. No one filed counter-claims, just motions. I don't get it. Why now? I mean, do you even want the land, mom?"

Everyone looked at Reena. She darted looks around the table, the briefest glance was at Lainie. Then she shrugged. Lainie figured Nita had filed papers on Reena's behalf and probably scheduled a visit to a City Planning department or Reena would now take the reins or . . .

Or did Reena think . . .of course. She paid Lainie's fare. Lainie would do the job. Not Anne-Marie or Adam.

Lainie who had already vaulted barriers to join her mother in Ormoc would, of course, willingly jump through the biggest hoop of all, of course. Lainie would take on this sticky family obligation. The granddaughter of Billina, of direct lineage, would run the gauntlet and wave a banner for justice for the forty-some-year-old absentee descendant.

Lainie's neck prickled. This was a sign, the one to heed when another point is not mentioned. Her mother, with land procured, might not even return to the U.S.

Rather than introduce the thought as one of her own, Lainie shut up.

The Coleman lantern sizzled, its sign to refill the fuel tank.

Reena lapsed into her bilingual double-talk. "*Ay 'sus*, too many ay whatchacallit hoops talaga '*susmarjosep.*"

Nita scooped wayward ashes toward her into her opposite hand. Juan kept looking at the floor, and Bonita, tapping her fingers, finally caught Nate's eye to rise, say good night, and head for their bedroom. Lainie, too, got up and said good night. Reena now held out the manila folder like an offering, which no one touched. Nita rose from her seat. "I'll blow out the lantern, *sigé?*"

In their bedroom, Lainie was already in her top bunk. Reena began. "So, hon, our Plebiña property. If we contest Luis, it's mine, and then yours, for all of you, if . . ."

"I'm tired, Mom. Good night."

Internally, she raged. First, that Reena's guilt-tripping had worked on her again to join her not-so gullible mother on this already expensive trip, to have paid for a complacent bodyguard, and now to tackle powerfully rich quasi-blood relatives.

She was sucker-punched again.

XXIII

November 27, 1944

Devastation: Reena watched from the side of the mountain, with Japanese airplane debris falling around her and on her hometown below. Japanese pilots, pitted against U.S. dogfighters, were losing. Incendiary bombs from the battleships shot right at her but missed. She was alone. She deserted her family left in their hideaway constructed of bamboo walls roofed with coconut leaves far from their barrio home. Reena's family had run a few miles with no lantern. Hundreds of P-38 fighter warplanes and bombers careened overhead dropping bombs. Dark smoke hid the day. Streaks of bullet trails from the planes briefly lit areas. This was a true brownout.

She had panicked scrunched up in that hut with her parents and Ynez. Hearing a fighter plane roar overhead, she scrambled toward a far grove of coconut trees, clawing dirt. Ancestors would protect her, yes, they must. Reena repeated this mantra puffing erratically. Nothing scared Reena this much, ever, not even Japanese soldiers who barked when she peered into the church where they stockpiled bombs. So they leered. She evaded them. After all, how could soldiers hurt her, a mere young curious villager? Billina, her mother, warned they'd "take advantage". She doused both daughters in pig's blood. But now Reena knew how the enemy would use them: by bombing them mercilessly.

Reena had dashed behind one tree and then another, hoping to avoid any stray bullets raining on her hiding place. She scurried too far away. No hut was in sight. She stepped down and slipped. Removing her foot from the mushy earth, she recognized the Japanese cap on a body, rotting from the late fall's oppressive heat, slurpy within the crevice. An odor seeped into her bare feet. Her senses reeled. Gagging, reviled, Reena swiped at flies, flies, so many flies. Horrified, she screamed. Her screeches hammered and echoed in those hills, with strafes pelting like a monsoon rainstorm, battering forest-green sentinels, dissecting Leyte except that, above her, roaring engines and aerial dogfights drowned her out.

Scrambling out of the ditch, Reena lunged for a large trunk of a coconut tree just as a series of bullets chiseled the area inches above her head. She prayed," I'm too young to die I'm too young to die!" She kept chanting in her head. "Please, oh, please, dear God, let me live, let me find someone, let me have children, let me live longer and happier and better, please, please, please! I'll take care of mommy, and raise my family, and show them. I'll show them all

I deserve to live, just let me get through this day!"

The strafing continued for hours. A month earlier, the worst bombings begins, an unrelenting battering of missiles at storage areas for Japanese munitions and housing. There are weeks of erratic bombs, and torn bodies and smashed huts. Today, the barrage never stopped. Yipping, wracked with hiccups, she was exhausted. But her drifting eye aligned with the other one, and she became steely and heard a menacing growl, hers. She swallowed, moistening her constricted throat and strained more, willing the growl to fill her head. Tiresome explosions angered Reena. Prayers weren't helping her. Angels weren't guarding her. Only her own stealth and almost intuitive moves saved her, dashing from spots smattered by bullets only seconds later. That discovery was like, like an epiphany. She howled, unchained.

"You are no god!" she bellowed beyond the sweeping dogfighters above her. "A God would stop this, why can't you stop this? You are not here! You just curse us! I defy you! I dare you! Kill me now or let me live, and I swear I will repay you! I will live how I want! I will not do good in your world! I will live without stupid rules till I have done it all! Or kill me, and I will come back, goddamn you! I will be worse! That is my vow to you! You have deserted me! I have no god!"

The bombing, as if answering, ceased.

Uneasy stillness followed. Wobbly from her outburst, she waited for the bolt that would strike her dead. Instead, silence was god's response.

Only at dusk did she find her family safe. Billina wept and held out her arms. Reena slipped past. She also extracted herself from her from sister, sobbing and relieved. She knew she appeared wooden and shell-shocked. She used that façade and, unlike her family, bypassed any show of gratitude to an aloof god, especially on her knees. She didn't care if she deprived herself of connections. "Reena," Ynez's voice cracked. "Daddy . . ." She cried, "He-he could not find you. He is no more."

Reena didn't move. She stared down Billina who soon broke down. Her father was dead. Billina expected a prayer. Reena would not lead one. This was god's loss, too. And she would not thank Mommy for reinforcing the lie that a religious crutch would save them. God would pay.

"There is no church," Reena stated as they returned to town.

Actually, the church hiding Japanese munitions really was gone. The Japanese soldiers figured that as irreverent as Americans could be, they would never desecrate a church. A Filipino gave them that plan. Reena decided godless American liberators were like her, blasphemous, blatantly dismissing God, his edifices, and his intervention.

But in fact, both Japanese AND American forces had decimated the whole town of wartime Ormoc. The conquered and the liberated could label the Americans utterly blasphemous, should anyone emphasize that fact. Few did.

Flaming bombs had strafed Reena's hideaway as if Lucifer's demons had fallen from heaven.

Reena, full of wrath, the Lord was not with her.

On that very day's final bomb, Reena dismissed any god from her life. Connections were discarded like old harvests and left, thin and dry. She would never, ever love anything.

She was seventeen.

XXIV

Lainie had hand-washed some laundry in the designated bucket before she realized the hand pump would have been easier. She had written in her journal, too, all before Reena was awake. More strange women were scrubbing down, for the last time, the piglets that grunted and squealed in mock protest. If only they knew their true fate. The kitchen hummed a dirge.

The electricity was still out judging from Jun's silent CD player. Cooks splayed chicken carcasses, like lean, pale loaves, on the counter near the stove. A sign – swarms were gathering.

On her way to the C.R. by their door, she had seen but ignored a box near their bedroom door on the chair. Seated inside the C.R., she could look out the square hole blocked by leaves that was head height. She saw Jun's hut. Insects shrilled in protest. Another hot day, she decided.

Outside, Lainie wandered. Today was the first time since she arrived that she got the lay of Nita's property within the red gates. To even have a gate meant Nita was someone with "things". Nate parked his shiny, red Jeep inside the gate. Throngs of strangers milled about. Half a dozen men had installed a type of swing set on the packed dirt. The deep trough under it was lined with kindling and human-sized leaves. She saw and approached Dom, hacking at a long branch, shaving its outer skin. Measuring the branch with outstretched arms, he then, with his bolo knife sharpened one end of the branch. She was close enough to block a flying sliver.

Dom never looked at her, intent on his work, his ever-present cigarette dangling from his mouth, daring the long ash at its tip to fall off. Lainie guessed he was testing his own steadiness and the patience of viewers. She had heard him speak English, and well, too.

"May I?" she asked. Laconically, he tapped his cigarette allowing the ash to drop before reaching for another pack in his front pocket. His eyes were jaundiced, the color of pale limes. He

118

shook and tipped the pack toward her. She took one cigarette. He lit hers and his own on one match. She squatted, like others she had seen in the ever-ready chair pose.

Dom would not begin a discussion. She started. "Where do you go? From here, *sa'an*?"

Lainie had learned that some Filipinos pause before speaking, for a very, very long time. Dom's was probably one of the longest. He pointed with his lip. "There."

North, she figured, the direction to the land.

"Do you really remember my mom? She went by another name back then."

Dom interjected. "I know it." And he said it without a pause.

Lainie was impressed. His memory was legendary, still sharp and quick.

"She was white, her sister was dark, her father, younger than her mother. *Mapang*, you know." He flipped at the end of his nose, looking far off at the mountains.

"She was stuck up?" Lainie tried again, "Snooty? Um, full of herself?"

He looked down over his nose and pointed with his lip, and then nodded. He clearly indicated that Reena thought herself above others. That sounded right, figured Lainie, still . . .

Should she defend her own mother to this new stranger who perhaps knew Reena better than Lainie did and for a longer time? Lainie drew on her cigarette, deciding. Dom continued to sharpen one of his many knives spread on the ground on a heavy skin cloth. She got up.

"Don't go into jungles alone." Dom suddenly called to her back. "You don't know the ways here. Use your escort."

Men filled in the spaces around Dom when she left. They waited for instructions.

For that day's trip, Bonita and the girls would stay home. Nita announced, "We go to the family plot and pay our respects to ancestral bones. Nate drives today. Wear these shoes." She held out a pair of Adidas from the box. "I opened it. Horatio reminded me you'd need them."

Lainie recalled the morning jog. "But I didn't ask for them, I swear."

Juan perked up at her tone. Nita said, "It's just a gift, to replace his presence, in a way." She pointed to her shelves. Whimsical knickknacks next to the Barrel Man lined the surfaces.

Lainie changed into her new shoes that did not go with her long skirt. She winced. The Adidas were very tight. She put her regular shoes in a bag in case her feet began to hurt. Lainie noted to keep her mouth shut about cockfights, shoes, or anything ending up as presents by their door.

Nate drove pell mell in his Jeep to the market. Nita trekked off with Reena. Strolling with Juan, Lainie, feet throbbing, remarked, "Why did Horatio buy this? How does he earn money?"

"Ma'am." Juan began, and she corrected him. "Lainie."

"Lainie, you ask a lot of questions."

She turned to him. "I'm just curious. For my journal."

Juan scratched his head. "Sometimes is just questions to ask questions, how far, how long, what time, tch, tch. Is just as long as driving takes, as far as a road goes, talaga?"

They stood in front of the camarones eatery. Lainie ducked inside. The waitress recalled her visit, left, and returned with a glass of water. "I boiled the water for you. I remembered."

The glass held ice. Lainie drank quickly and left, meeting up with Reena, Nita, and Juan at Nate's Jeep. Juan's comment nagged at her. Be in the moment, she scolded herself. Shut. Up.

A few miles away Nate passed under a twelve-foot gate with die-cut letters that read, Ormoc Cemetery. Nearby under a makeshift awning, a merchant sat under his hand-printed sign, Candles. Next to him was another tire repair shop with its sign, Vulcanization. Nate drove them up to a very large, sheening mausoleum in an inviting landscaped setting. The mausoleum sported letters engraved in gold atop the marbled, templed facade:

SERRAÑAO

"Ours??" Lainie burst out but then bit her lip. No questions!
Both Nita and Reena laughed. "Of course, not ours. Theirs!"

They looked around at all the plaques with different first
names, an occasional Plebiña, and the constant surname Serrañao.
Were they like the Carringtons in *Dynasty*? Was Reena's return
like the delayed entrance of Alexis/Joan Collins, minus the many
costume changes? Was Lainie some surprise money-grubbing offspring? So many eyes were on them – her. So many reports of their
whereabouts spread rapidly throughout the barrio. Was Nita the
ever-patient, placid Krystle/Linda Gray? Lainie wiped her finger
on the most prominent, centrally visual plaque on a marble horizontal tomb. Her print left a darkened spot. The surface was gold-
toned. Reena was enthralled with the marble and magnificence.

Lainie sighed. "Can we go? This isn't for us."

"Yes," said Nita. "Let's go see our side of the family." Signaling
Nate that they would walk, she knew he would wait by the Jeep.
They would find Billina's grave, death date: 1965.

They walked toward an overgrown, unkempt part of the cemetery with overturned tombs. Lainie's feet screamed. These tombs
were crypts above ground, like in New Orleans, the typhoons and
floods overtook land that was not ideal for burials. With such
prestigious materials, notably the Serrañao Mausoleum could
withstand any kind of maelstrom.

A man poked his head up above a tall growth and scrambled
off. Juan sharply cursed, looking down at his flip-flops, morose
and mumbling. Nita laughed. "He stepped in some shit."

Around a bend, the plot's area balanced surplus coffins for
future burials. Nita said bodies had been piled up for centuries.
Not all names could be seen. Lainie's stomach talked.

About a hundred fifty meters away, offered Nita, they could
visit a friend, a doctor. Her friend worked at a hospital, a slight
climb, through the trees and conveniently near the cemetery.

Soon Lainie could see a looming, depressed building strung

with molding moss. The day was at its most humid. She was convinced that her discomfort was witnessing blatant abundance among poverty, or the shoes, whatever. Hopefully, this hospital had a pharmacy or Tums. They entered a lobby with no receptionist. Nita led them without pause up the stairs, then down a very wide and long dorm-like space with empty beds made and unmade, lining the far walls. A close, heavy, old smell permeated the dank room. Oh, God, let's get out of here, too, thought Lainie, this reeks! A lone woman stood at the end of the room in a white smock and a stethoscope around her neck. Nurses, plain clothed, moved in and out of another room beyond the empty beds. The doctor, pitifully drawn and exhausted, turned, her hair thin and uncombed. She brightened when she saw Nita. After they hugged, Nita introduced everyone. Nita pushed her lip at Lainie, and doctor nodded. "I will get you something."

Patients moaned and howled from the nearby dark dorm-like room. Lainie inched forward to peek inside. The area's beds were crammed with writhing bodies. The bulk of nurses moved among them efficiently. Patients with their ailments packed the dank room. Lainie gauged distances to herself and to possible contagions. She backed away.

The doctor had returned holding out a small, plain envelope to Lainie. "Take a couple of these daytime and nighttime for two or three days. That should help you."

Lainie was puzzled. Nita, seeing her frown, explained, "Your hands hold your stomach."

Cock fights, Adidas, bowels, could she for one day NOT be so visible? Unlike the U.S., she did not blend in here like she thought she would. People judged her hair. People dismissed her ignorance and instead gave her status. People knew before she did that she ached, inside.

Exiting the hospital, Lainie asked how many doctors worked in that big hospital. Nita sighed. "This is not the best hospital. Staff is not paid much. They study in the States and return with their skills if they have family." So grim, Lainie thought, how could any-one heal here? Or work here?

At the cemetery, instead of Nate, Mike was waiting. Nita and Juan both uttered, "Oy."

"Good morning, good morning! I sent Nate home. The new school raises a flag today in town. I thought we should go. Get in." He pointed to his Jeep. Despite any protests, the women were whisked away and ended up at some brick school surrounded by men in matching red and white shirts. Parents and photographers stood focused on one woman, austere, and haughty.

Nita whispered, "Inez Serrañao, the mayor."

Mike prodded Reena and Lainie forward till they were be-hind the mayor. She did not acknowledge them. Festivities in-cluded the national anthem, an adolescent color guard, and the mayor's speech. Here, Lainie was the country cousin containing her stomach in a saggy cotton top, wearing ill-fitting Adidas. The photographer scrambled, squatted, and composed shots grouping Reena, Lainie, and the mayor. Lainie glared at Mike. Did he force "kin" to meet?

Reena poked Lainie, hissing, her lip at Inez. "Speak to her. Tell her who we are. Go on."

Lainie resisted but then took a step and held out her hand. "Ms. Mayor, thank you for your work." She blinked as the photog-rapher took a flash shot. "I-I we are, in town visiting, my mother, Reena Plebiña, Billina's daughter. I'm maybe your half-cousin, and . . ." But the mayor, looking anywhere but at Lainie shook three of Lainie's fingers mumbling, "Very good," and walked off. Reena had done it again: her mere suggestion put Lainie in a focal point. On her own, she had embarrassed herself. A flag was raised. Lainie headed for Mike's Jeep, commanding, "Take me home." Nita, Juan, and Reena hurried behind her and once in the Jeep, Mike said, "I thought you might like to see the old high school. Very historic."

Nita hedged. "Lainie has the runs." Lainie was aghast.

"I will take her to my house. It's modern." Mike cranked up the vehicle and took off.

Lainie tried again. "I really need to go home."

"We have TV." Mike replied. "We will watch and wait."

She wanted to scream, "Who cares about your stupid TV or your modern house or the high school! I'm so embarrassed!"

Mike's house was in town. They stepped down just as Horatio padded up to them. He hailed, "Ah, you found them, good!" He peered at her Adidas. "Do they fit?" Lainie smiled.

"Good, good. I almost thought they might be too small." He kissed Nita and bounded off. "See you at the house!" Nita's eyes were very wide as she looked at Reena.

XXV

Seeing the interior of Mike's house, Lainie almost forgot her anger. Five children slithered over floors, couches, and tables as the TV blared incredibly loud throughout the rooms. Mike, striding toward the kitchen, introduced the brood as "my children". Was Mike's whole family hard of hearing? He ushered Lainie to the C.R., which had an actual flush toilet and running water and ceramic tub and tile work and sinks with faucets, all mint green. Towels of all sorts hung on racks. A gold-leafed framed mirror hung over the sink area. This setup was like in the States, including the obnoxious TV. Obviously well paid, Mike was also well set up, furnishings, electronics, and gadgets and trophy wife? Where was she?

When Lainie joined everyone else in the main room, Juan was already playing with the children as if he were a child himself, smiling and poking. On the screen, a couple kissing moaned throughout a romantic soap opera. A girl seated near Lainie, her back to the TV, covered her eyes and ears. Lainie asked her, "Are you scared of something?" The girl pointed over her shoulder.

"We shouldn't see this," she whispered. "We're Catholic."

Mike, however, was deep into the long and overdramatic scene. In a utilitarian kitchen to Lainie's right, Nita and Reena talked with Mike's unintroduced wife, thin, pale and worn. Her dress was a sheening rayon print fashionable but limp on her thin frame. Her pursed smile flashed and receded like a Morse code, yes, no, no yes.

"Um, maybe we should go. I have to make a phone ca– . . ." Lainie realized her mistake, like the cockfight, like Adidas, one thing merely mentioned and quickly obtained.

"Use my phone. I get long distance." Mike pointed to the wall phone. She would have to stand and talk where most everybody was in the same room.

"It might be pretty expensive." Lainie tried to beg off, to which Mike just waved her off, glued to the TV. "*Way problema.*"

Who to call . . .she dialed, got an operator, who put the call through for her with additional numbers. After she hung up, she thought, why? Why did she call him, of all people?

Rick, former co-worker-turned-supervisor-turned-lover, had answered on the first ring and ho-ho'ed as was his style when he recognized her. "How's the trip, lady?"

She bantered. "Oh, um, fine. We're at a house right now, with a phone, but calls are really expensive, so I'll make this short."

"Whoa, wait a minute. How are you? You know I miss you." Rick was using that tone of voice, that wheedle-to-bed one. She felt her whole day so far was one cringe after another.

"Yeah, listen, I got to go. Um, lot of people here, and this is the only phone." Mike's whole family called out, "NO."

All seven of them held up pagers.

"Who's that?" Rick asked but added, "Hey, when are you back again?" She could feel his leer through the receiver. She deflected, "Can't say, gotta go. Bye. Take care. Have a good day." Then she had hung up.

Mike kept watching TV. "You could have talked longer."

Lainie, runs and all, was convinced no privacy would ever, ever again be hers. Soon, they were on the road.

Mike swung through town and alleyways so rapidly that even Juan gave his high-pitched alarm. For a jeepney driver, Lainie grimaced, that's telling.

The tourists now ended up at a very large multi-storied former high school with a center open-air courtyard to the skies. Reena exclaimed, "Oh, I went to school here, I think."

Nita corrected her. "No, the old one was bombed. This is rebuilt, 1948. You already left."

Cemented together with leftover bricks untouched by bombs, the building was still menacing. A few people milled about the interior courtyard, moving along the long walkways past former classrooms with discolored, uneven bamboo shades. Any active offices were on the first two floors. Mike had pointed up. "Condemned. Stairways are rusted. And Japanese . . ." Mike clucked his tongue, adding, "Bad memory, a bad place, haunted, *sigé*, ghosts."

His voice echoed lively even without booming, warbling against the inner walls. But what he said intrigued Lainie. She kept looking up. Nita continued the story. "Some school boys were fooling around. They dared one of them to stay a night on the third floor."

Reena interjected, "Oy, I told you that, or did I . . .?

Nita was a bit curt. "You are forgetful these days. *I* told you. I just said you weren't even here." She continued. "They found him the next day. His whole head of hair had turned white from fright."

Still staring at the floors above them, Lainie could construct the incident. She imagined a stern Japanese soldier marching on the walkways, his footsteps rhythmic and Gestapo like. She could almost see the building filling and multiplying with more and more soldiers, and bayonets, and bombs, and detonated shell casings.

"What are we doing here?" Nita sharply broke into Lainie's reverie.

"Did *you* say you wanted to see the high school?" Reena asked Lainie, who shook her head. Mike had disappeared. Nita remarked, "They keep official papers here, on land plots."

Peering over the edge, Lainie whistled. The echo ricocheted and pierced the air like a sharpshooter's bullet. Some spooked passersby glanced up, saw her, and scowled. Nita, glum, remarked, "We should've gotten our papers first." Reena nodded, a sanction for "*what you said*".

Finally, Mike returned.

Nita's question was insistent and not quiet. "Where did you go?"

"Oh, I just had some paperwork to check," Mike explained. "Tomorrow, Tacloban!"

They headed back to the Jeep, and only when they sat down did Nita continue her interrogation. "Did *we* need to come here with you?"

Mike looked straight ahead, his mouth set. Nita badgered him. "Because I didn't. This is your personal trip, without our permission. It's your car but our time."

"Well, maybe it IS a personal trip for you, and how would you know?" Mike turned on the ignition and revved the engine. "I can drop you off anytime if you do not need my services."

She retorted in her calm way. "We have few days left with our guests and sights to see."

"Then if you want to, you can tour yourself."

"We were, with Nate." Nita had the last word.

They drove in silence, Lainie's eyes ping-ponged between Nita and Mike. At the gate, he parked and idled. He swung his right elbow over the back of his seat and demanded, "So tomorrow, should I pick you up?" He swerved toward Lainie. "You're the guest. You say."

Lainie blushed as the tiebreaker, an awkward position. As the women descended from the jeep, Lainie stumbled but said, "We'll call." He bobbed his chin, pushed the gear into reverse and with a volcanic cloud of dust, executed a Y turn, screeched the wheels, and sped off.

Lainie hurried into the house, grabbed the bucket, pumped water into it, and disappeared into the C.R. Jun's incessant love song could have deflected the lingering tension, if it were playing. Lightning streaked across the eastern skies. Outside the C.R.'s opening, a fingered tropical wind combed the tree and brushed Lainie's face. She didn't care. She pulled off the ill-fitting shoes as she perched on the commode. Would she even get to eat anything at the Reunion only hours from then?

She dragged herself through the kitchen. The family had already set up Coleman lanterns and cigarettes. She entered the bedroom, plopped on the lower bunk, and curled up, groaning.

Not even fifteen minutes later, she would repeat the bucket routine and sit watching the sleeting rain and horizontal breezes outside the C.R. She was miserable. Her bowels taunted her. "Ha, ha, privileged American, deal with our Montezuma's Revenge! Serves you right!" She had exited but quickly headed back for the C.R. She was sure she had just beat Juan's record.

Unnoticed before, a sedate pile of hand-washed underwear from that morning lay on her upper bunk. Had someone taken the room key and re-washed Lainie's underwear, the stupid key on which Reena insisted because of her room-hogging *balikbayan* boxes? In her sac-like posture, Lainie joined the table group. Nita ventured, "Do you want some tea for your bowels?"

Lainie blared, "NO, thank you! Mom, did you give someone my CLEAN clothes? Ones I already washed?" She had just aired, like dirty laundry, the day's residual animosity.

Reena's eyes were wide. "No. Who could get in, hon?"

People looked off and away. Nita had been hush-hush about the key. The others had not made a big deal although they knew, like everyone knew every damn move they made.

Lainie wanted to just die, die, die. She groaned. Witnesses could go ahead and laugh or post some sensationalized headline: *Blasting bowels cause American's untimely death –last seen near a water buffalo.* Mourners, if any, would share that Lainie's last words were: *Sigé, she bitched about re-washed laundry.* Go ahead, chortle all you want. Go ahead.

After the coughs and shuffles subsided, she apologized to Nita, and everyone, again refused the tea, and continued to avoid the medicine she got from the hospital.

Without any preamble and given Mike's actions, the women re-enacted the same discussion that happened the night before as if Lainie, restless and ornery, had forgotten. Reena basked in the attention repeating everything word for word. They discussed the petition and declarations, and papers to be filed at the school. They were about to launch into the former night's mention about the local priest. But Lainie blurted. "Oh, Mom, either you want the land or you don't. That's not really why you came here. You came to . . . God, my feet ache!" she trailed off, disgusted with her short attempt to keep her mouth shut. She mentioned feet, but obviously, she was doubled over, holding her stomach.

"Are you sure you don't want some strong tea, to bind you?" Nita was very concerned. Dishes rattled in the kitchen.

"Thank you, salamat, no." Lainie was trying not to burst out crying. "I think I'll lay down awhile before dinner." She felt she required expiation for her grouchiness, for *kinabuhi* – her life.

"We'll wake you," added Nita. Lainie entered the bedroom. Pickle unblinking in its usual corner, looked sympathetic and twisted its neck. Lainie tossed a barb. "Some luck you are."

Dishes dinged. Winds lulled Lainie asleep till Reena patted her. "*Sss-sst.* Get up. Eat."

Stumbling out of the bunk and cradling her abdomen, Lainie

dragged herself into the main room. Coleman lanterns and candles illuminated three generations of family. Only the girls giggled at the storm surrounding them. For others this was just a normal brownout made abnormal by the presence of American guests. One was possibly a rich owner of very valuable property, and the other, with no privacy, was cursed with diarrhea.

After dishes were cleared away, Nita began again. "Oy, Father Smile, he scared me. And then the church was bombed." Lainie perked up. She spoke louder. "And then Geraldo in the rubble, projecting movies – you know all this, yes? Everything?" Everyone turned to Lainie.

Lainie wilted about elusive Ormoc, because so far, she felt she knew zip. Nita continued. "The church where the Japanese stored bombs? MacArthur returned. Americans took over the town. Your daddy was one of them. Say you know this."

"*Sigé*, say." Lainie's tone was anxious. "*Diri*, I-I don't . . . say for me." She turned to Juan.

Juan spoke, "*Diri, bawa unsa* – 'I don't know anything here.' *Talaga*?" She nodded.

Throughout Nita's talk-story, the room took on a different mood and even glowed with intermittent flashes of silent lightning. Thunder rolled like bowling balls and cracked like pins, again aligned and again sharply scattered.

"Reena and I heard about the movies in the church. Your daddy had already seen Reena. He asked a boy if he knew her name. The boy was a cousin." Nita smiled at Juan. "Yes, you."

In the lantern's subdued light, Juan covered his mouth but his eyes shone. Lainie intuited he recalled, too, that young boy that he was and felt a catch in her throat. That was how he fit in, her mother's go-between. She blinked. Without him, Lainie would not even be here.

"Girls had to be escorted anywhere publicly. And the church was dark at night. We would have to walk under a big banyan tree, the one where cigar-smoking *kaprés* and aswangs hung overhead to grab young girls. Big, bad giants and witches, oooh, we were scared. But your daddy told Juan to bring Reena, bring her friends, and see the movies for free. He ran the projector. He was in Entertainment, yes?" Reena nodded, oddly quiet. "So we saw the movies, and Juan introduced Reena, his cousin, to your daddy."

Reena interjected comments. "We promenaded with chaperones. But we found ways to be alone." She added, "To me, he was American Playboy, a soldier, and worse, divorced."

"He was here long time," Juan interjected. "He was staying in the church to protect the projector, *sigé*, things." Nita took over. "Government-issue. That was how Geraldo met Father Smile."

Just like when Lainie and her siblings heard this part as children, again she thrilled to the Tale of Father Smile. Nita went on. "They drank, you know, soldiers on their own. So late, after one long night of drinking, your daddy was alone, on guard and heard someone walking. He ignored the sound. But the pacing continued, back and forth, back and forth. So he called out."

Lainie and Nita both uttered, "*Halt! Who goes there?*"

Everyone listening smiled. The girls were gleeful.

"You have heard this." Nita was pleased. "Anyway, no one answered, then – footsteps. He took his M-1 rifle to the front and shouted." The girls hooted, "*Halt! Who goes there?*"

"But the steps continued, clop, clop, clop. He warned, '*Who goes there? If you don't stop, I will shoot!*' Footsteps go on. He aimed directly at the sound. '*Halt or I will shoot!*'"

"Stop, and then again, footsteps." Nita quickly barked, "Bang! He shoots!"

Everyone at the table was expectant. Everyone there had heard this story except for the women in the kitchen, which was very quiet. Still, the tension was thick. Nita continued.

"Nothing. No one is there. No one calls out in pain. But what your daddy still hears instead are, footsteps. The steps continue, unafraid, just a steady walking, like someone thinking, or praying. He shot at nothing. And whatever that nothing was, kept walking."

The room breathed. Nita finished. "Two years before, soldiers shot this Father Smile dead, yes. Talaga, no one could really get him to smile, very strict, devout, prayed morning to night. The townspeople always saw him pacing, late, during his Vespers around the church. Nothing would interrupt him, not even curfew, not even Japanese soldiers. He was killed in the front of the church."

She pushed her lip at Juan.

"The very next day that boy who introduced your parents, this man here, he had been poking at the church rubble. He held up and showed what he found to Geraldo: the priest's bones."

Juan, wide-eyed, nodded once. "I said, 'These are the bones of Father Smile.' And Geraldo, not blinking, he listens to me." Juan nodded to Nita to continue. She patted his arm and continued.

"Juan said, 'He was killed right here. People still hear his footsteps at night walking and silently praying. He ignored the soldiers who shot him because he did not halt. And now when anyone hears footsteps late at night around the church, they still think about the Tale of Father Smile.'"

Nita leaned back. "Is that how you remember it?"

"Exactly," said Lainie, amazed. As youngsters, she and her siblings wheedled Geraldo every night for the story as if hunched over a crowded fire. "Word for word." Lainie felt reverent. She searched for her own text. "This was our Talk-Story. You tell it well."

Nita shrugged with a small grin. "Ah, maybe you don't know, but I used to write."

A sudden battering of winds rattled the wooden sections of the cement house. The girls huddled close to Bonita. "Time for bed." Horatio spoke, "We should save on the gas." Juan wordlessly rose to turn off the lantern and crossed the room to lie on his banig in the corner. Reena retired. Lainie noted that Reena had not really talk-storied any part of the tale.

Almost hourly Lainie would step over many bodies strewn about the kitchen floor on her many trips to the C.R. She had to sit slanted away from the open window or be sprayed by the torrential rains battering Jun's long-legged nipa hut across the way. She left the C.R., tiptoe-ing gingerly among the slumbering hired maids not lucky to get a seat to sprawl on. Once in bed, Lainie was exhausted.

By sunrise, the tree outside was gone, torn from the ground but still green, a single root stubbornly clung to dirt.

After nights of cleansing rain and cleared sightlines, Lainie saw a different town.

XXVI

By the weekend, everyone counted another day without electricity.

Deling at Nita's door had returned and stood like a carabao after a quick, respectful *mano* technique from everyone. "'Allo, allo! *Maayong buntag*, so when's dinner, soon? We go today Saturday for Mass. Tch, tch, you chose the Lord's Day for your Reunion. 'Fredo, stand straight."

Holding her umbrella 'Fredo avoided any direct glance. He wore the familiar eggshell barong tagalog shirt, piña-stranded and pressed, contrasting the dark backside of his hands.

Nita and Reena discussed dates longer than expected. 'Fredo helped Deling sit on the far rattan couch. Deling, her thin top soaked, called out, "Go ahead, talk, talk. I will not leave until we have a date and time set."

Lainie had hurried over to help the boy and Deling who plopped onto the couch adjusting her knee-length skirt and mid-leg-high stockings. Grunting, she patted the boy's hand then pushed him away. The feisty woman leaned into Lainie.

"You write magazines?" she was very close to Lainie's face.

"Um, travel tips, stories."

"They sell pretty well?" Deling was direct. Her large, lined features filled Lainie's view.

"Well, the magazine does. I budgeted for this trip because I . . ." Deling interrupted her.

"This one," she tipped her head at the boy, "He should write. He writes very well. He is my prize pupil. I taught him all he knows. Now he lives with me."

"Oh, that's nice." Lainie was unsure what else to say.

Deling shifted, as she signaled the boy to fetch a doughy *pandesal* from the far-off table. She continued. "His mother can't care for him. His father deserted them. The boy's, what you say, needy of a break." This was one strong town *doyen* with a mission. Her next words set Lainie back. "His mother sells children, anyone's, her own. Sex, you know. I saved him." Lainie half-caught Deling's sequence how poor families find money for food, a shack, candy, sex toys, and porn clothes to lure more children to perform with others or with adults. 'Fredo headed back.

She stared at him too long. His innocence, why could he still wear it? How do braver people than her maintain after such abuse?

"So," Deling patted Lainie's hand. "You come for dinner, yes? You and your mother."

"Are they caught, the adults?" Lainie kept her eyes on Deling who replied, "Hmph, they are rich, foreign. They boost the economy." 'Fredo was implacable and looked elsewhere.

Nita and Reena approached them. "Monday. It's the only day. The Reunion's tomorrow, Sunday."

Deling stuffed the palm-sized *pandesal* in her bag as she motioned 'Fredo to help her up. "Good! All settled then. We break bread Monday, yes? Oy. Off to home. And take this."

Deling pushed some mimeographed brochures at Lainie, who later would read about the students matched with sponsors aka benefactors whose money paid for materials, books, clothes, and tuition. Oddly, her last parting shot was, "We see you and all your jungle family tomorrow. Tell them to behave, no shells."

Though Lainie signaled confusion, Bonita waved her off. No shellfish? Don't bring shells of crabs or shrimp? Lainie ducked into the bedroom to change after only two hours since daybreak. She was drenched with sweat. She noticed her Adidas had stretchers inside. Removing them, she sighed slipping into the Adidas now widened and fitting perfectly.

Minutes later Mike pulled up to the gates. Nita and Reena groaned. "He doesn't learn."

Mike was acting as if nothing had happened the day before. He sat beyond the gate, engine off, staring ahead. Nita sent Horatio to speak with him. As they watched, they saw Horatio palm an envelope to Mike. Instead of leaving, Mike followed Horatio to the house.

"*Ay 'sus*," Nita swore. Reena quipped, "He is like sticky rice, you can't shake him off."

"Good morning, *maayong buntag*." Mike boomed, remaining outside the door, even after Horatio entered. Mike was waiting for Nita's permission to enter. Everyone was waiting.

Horatio kept walking toward the kitchen, grumbling, grousing, till Nita asked, "Did you say something, Horatio? Go on, say." He returned to her. "Let the man in. Don't embarrass us!" He walked away again. Without rancor, Nita motioned to Mike. "*Maayong buntag*, come in, come in."

Gingerly, Mike stepped in the door and cleared his throat. "My pager never buzzed. But I was already out and about, so I came straight here. To Tacloban, *sigé*?"

"We did not call." Nita spoke evenly. Mike blanched, called on his bluff.

"But, you're here now." Nita was tactful. "Tacloban has

shopping. Yes, Lainie?"

Aiiee, Lainie withered, focus was back on her again. She stepped closer to Juan. "Juan, Tacloban? We only saw it flying over at night."

"Good!" Mike smashed his palms together. "We go."

With practiced regret, Bonita said her family would stay home. Nita and Juan sat in the Jeep's back. Lainie slithered next to them. "It's okay, Mom, sit up front. It'll be a long but comfy ride." Reena stink-eyed Lainie but quietly got in the front seat.

Nita leaned closer. "If you want to come back, you just say, okay?"

Throughout the day, Mike drove them across the San Juanico Bridge onto Samar Island just to come back and get a picture standing under the sign reading, "Welcome to Leyte." Then they viewed the seven gold-toned, over-sized figures commemorating MacArthur's 1944 Landing, his "fucking return", re-staged many times, as reported by Lainie's expat Manila students. She figured only insurrectos or communists would spread those facts, like MacArthur's affair. But that's another story.

Mike stopped at a pricey shopping center. "Imelda shops here." The Ormocanon women stood in a clump, unimpressed. Lainie coughed. Nita told Mike, "We shall return – to Ormoc."

No one spoke during the ride. Mike cranked up his radio full blast all the way to Nita's.

"You want to see anything else??" Mike startled them awake as they approached Ormoc.

Lainie cleared her throat. "Don Padre?"

Mike jumped. "What? Don Padre? But he's . . . "

"The first day, I promised myself I'd visit the hotel, the Don Padre. The bar overlooks the whole city. Talaga?"

Mike visibly relaxed. "O-h-h, THAT Don Padre, the hotel. Don Padre himself, though," he crossed himself and continued. "Oh, sure, I will buy. I will buy you all fancy cocktails!" Nita demurred. "Two o'clock? Cocktails?"

Reena added. "That hotel was not here when I left."

Nita quipped, "All of it is here *because* you left, all the War Brides with American husbands," she poked Reena. "Leaving, sending American dollars to us who stayed, *diba?*"

They all traveled to the Don Padre Hotel owned by none other than Luis Serrañao.

The ornate eight-story building dominated the town. The doorman bowed but slouched when he saw Mike. Only a trickling of tourists visited at this non-tourist time of year. Nita, Reena, Lainie, Juan and Mike rode the elevator to the top floor to overlook Ormoc Bay. Standing at the panoramic window, they saw the town itself was flat, the pier stretched into the sea, and Barangay 35 sat inland far to the right.

Here Lainie stood in a hotel with luxuries within an impoverished town. She scanned the large room. A lone piano was raked in a corner. Smoky mirrors covered both walls. The bar was empty, the most unpopulated space in all of Ormoc. Like a Majorcan-looking sea, an unearthly blue over an undulating horizon shimmered among hints of islands. Mike insisted escorting the elders to the restroom. Juan trailed after them laconically.

Lainie smarted at the varying and overly ornate eras clashing the décor. Recalling Reena's words, militia commanding this harbor in 1944 had witnessed the battle that changed the war in the Pacific and unlocked the linchpin to the Japanese stronghold. Chances were slim to live first-hand through a war. This hotel was nearly fifty years old. Reena was already stateside.

Lainie moved everyone's items to a window table and, hand under her chin, gazed out.

Someone moved a chair in the corner, a dark area. She peered into its recesses. A man sat alone, his white coat coming into focus. Was he watching her, in her lax, unsophisticated position in this relatively classy bar overlooking historic Ormoc Bay?

Someone else clinked a glass alerting her to look to her left. A bartender who must have just arrived was lining up highball glasses. Alerted, the efficient bartender approached her.

"Good afternoon, ma'am, may I take your order?"

"Um, yes, um, do you have Glen Livet?" Lainie actually expected a No.

"Scotch coming right up. On the rocks?"

Live dangerously, she advised herself. "Little rocks."

He remained. "Ma'am, a gentleman would like to buy you a drink."

Right: he was a gentleman who was the only guy in the whole bar. She had heard about scenes like this one. Had this gentleman, like Horatio, taken her for another "hospitality girl"? Decisions, decisions. Oh, hell, what could happen? After all, her mother was with her.

"Yes," cooed Lainie, "Thank him, please."

The bartender turned, made the drink but swept it out of sight and toward the man.

Movies, I'm IN one, she gulped.

Near the man, the bartender lifted the lure at her, tinkling the glass to come and get it.

He placed her drink right next to the man who looked like Marlon Brando *a la* Don Corleone. The bartender melted back to the bar. She realized here or stateside, joining a stranger, she'd be labeled easy. Whatever. She would just not right sit next to the man. Inelegantly carting bags and purses, she approached and moved her drink across from him.

Behind dark glasses, he smiled. "You have good taste in drinks. How are you, Miss?"

She replied. "I'm very well, thank you." He countered with, "Fine, thank you."

She wondered how long this repartee would have to play out, so unbelievably like a dated, sepia-toned film noir with double-entendre'd, not-so snappy dialog.

"May I ask your name?" He was truly gentlemanly, so debonair, his untouched dark Gauloises cigarette loosely held and his white shirt under his linen suit coat open at the neck. He was totally bald. What faded up as *The Godfather* movie poster cross-dissolved into *Now, Voyager* and then into *Orphan Annie*'s Daddy Warbucks. The setting screamed out so many movie titles.

"Lainie," she responded, adding, "Plebiña Cortez." She waited.

The man signaled the bartender for another drink. He tapped his Gauloises once, and ashes fell. "I am Luis Serrañao, son of Don Padre Serrañao. I own this hotel now. "

The skies brightened.

Acting cool but shaking in her not-so-cool Adidas, Lainie flashed a smile. "Thought so."

"You are in town alone or for, uh, family?" Luis prodded.

"Now I know you know my mother, your half-cousin. We're here together, at Nita's house, if you know where that is."

He smiled back. "Barangay 35."

"Exactly." They toasted, raising their chins simultaneously, not even rehearsed.

Mike and Juan ushered everyone in. Lainie waved. They approached. Nita recognized Luis. Juan joined Lainie. Mike was aloof. Reena asked, "Where's my things?"

"Hello, Reena," said Luis, and to Nita, "Nita. Greetings."

Dramatically, Reena ogled him and squeaked, "Luis? Oh, my God, is that you? Luis??"

"Yes, who else?"

"You know I'm at Nita's, Lainie and me, my daughter, one of my . . ."

"Yes, I do."

"Did Nita call you? Someone should've called you!"

"You, perhaps?" Not answering, Reena instead tinkled a laugh. His smile never left his face.

Lainie, Nita, and Mike graciously witnessed Luis's sedate smile and Reena's ostentatious, drawn-out reunion with him. Luis indicated for them all to sit and then remarked, "So, cuz, you are here after so many years because you miss Ormoc City after all."

Lainie tried to touch Reena's shoe with her Adidas.

Nita answered. "I asked her to come. Her husband died. She can travel. I miss her."

"Of course, of course. Drink? You? You, Reena?" he barely saw Juan, "You, sir?"

Luis did not address Mike. But Lainie did notice Mike position himself behind and left of Luis's back. He stood straight, hands clasped before him, staring ahead.

He was Luis's boy, a company man. Nita and Reena seemed smug and vindicated.

Lainie realized they had known, and she hadn't. Focused on Luis, Reena was now agog.

Luis turned fully to Nita. "So everything is good for you? Life's not too hard, is it?"

Nita smoothed her hem. "I have a store. We're fine."

Nita has a store, a sari-sari? Lainie blanched. How could she not know that? Where?

Luis focused on Reena. "My prayers for your husband and mother. I remember *Manang*."

Reena guffawed. "You should. We suckled from the same tit. Your mother had no milk, and mine did. We were both the same age."

"Well," he tapped his Galoises. "We still are."

A sudden change clouded Reena's face. "You cheated, poked me, and lied." Then she switched and teased him. "Kids, *ano*? We're all grown up now, Serrañao."

Lainie interjected, "Excuse me."

She pushed her Glen Livet away. Mike shifted. A glass clinked at the bar.

"You don't like it?"

"Stomach, you know," she twiddled her hand. Nita shifted, agreeing, her nod like a period capping Lainie's smart remark. Reena blunted the drama. "The runs."

Luis took back the reins. "Well, you must come have lunch at my house." He snapped his fingers. Mike fished in his pocket and placed a pen on the table near Luis. Unfazed, Luis glanced at Mike, lowing, "Thank you, you are, uh . . . ?"

"Mike," stated Mike. The bartender appeared with paper.

"Mike, yes, thank you," Luis smirked which Lainie caught and thought, "Come on."

The bartender turned on his heel and left. Reena snorted. Nita straightened slowly. Luis, with flair, wrote numbers on the sheet.

"Here is my address." Luis pushed the paper at Lainie instead of Reena. "And my phone. You will come for lunch on Monday." He twisted to view Mike. "Lunch! You drive, *sigé*? "

When *didn't* he drive? Everyone turned to her. Lainie calculated. "One?" Luis dictated and to Mike, said. "One, then. My guests will see my compound."

Lainie rose. Everyone did. She hugged Luis, who held on a bit longer. Pulling away, she led the group out. Once they were near Mike's jeep, she caught both Nita's and Reena's looks. Nita patted her chest, sweating. No one spoke as they rode. The papers, Lainie realized, that Mike had filed at the school's land office was for Luis. Mike did the legwork. Luis dictated which side trips to allow. Mike was his pawn. Luis had eyes all over town, watching Reena and Lainie.

And Mike was not only one set of eyes but also the ever-present tour guide. Perhaps Nita nearly firing Mike affected his spying during Lainie's last two days. But what was proven was: Lainie and Reena Plebiña had always been on Luis's radar. Mike's role had been verified.

XXVII

At the house, Nita headed straight into the house, past the throngs of men now in the throes of preparing for the Reunion. They got out of the jeep but Reena leaned back in, "So, Mike."

"Yes, ma'am," he anticipated something.

"The Reunion is tomorrow," she began, "About being a chauffeur Monday . . ."

Lainie blinked rapidly. Now Reena was actually firing him, a free chauffeur.

"So unless you probably work on Mondays, anyways – do you? Work?"

Lainie hung nearby, obviously eavesdropping, when her mother got to her point. "If you do work, we'll find our own way to Luis's house. Lainie? What do you think?"

If that exchange could have been handled in any worse a manner, Lainie couldn't think of any. Instead, she stuck out her hand. "Just in case, any more driving doesn't work out, thank you so much for putting up with us, ha, ha, showing us stuff, the cock fight, and all that, so, salamat."

Mike was still looking at the steering wheel. She hoped he wasn't hurt. But he bolted up and stepped out. The seething rage in his eyes made her back off. Reena, too, stepped back. Juan was too far to move in between them. In one movement, Mike swept up Lainie in a bear hug, almost cracking her back bending her so close to him. He pressed her breasts with his chest. He spoke low, rumbling, "I will miss you when you leave. You feel like a very nice woman." He looked fully at Reena. " Mr. Serrañao said, 'Drive', so, I drive. Monday. *Maayong gabii.*"

He got back into the jeep and not looking back, he drove off. Jun's CD player started low and then revved up, "*And even* (crackle) *I know how* (crackle) (crackle) *-part we are.*"

A cheer rose up from all over the barrio. Applause crackled from everywhere in the house. Electricity was back.

"*It helps to* (crackle) (crackle) (crackle) (crackle) - *bright star.*"

Lainie recovered from Mike's blatant fondling. She figured Mike answered to far too many employers, counting Reena. He'd always been working. Smashing her breasts was his tip.

Juan, mournful, ducked his head. Lainie patted his shoulder. "*Way problema*, Juan."

A flurry filled the house. Nate and Nita scurried to his Jeep and drove off. The kitchen help rattled over each other, clanging many ladles and pots. Men stumbled by woozy from drink. Others followed Dom's pig-roasting directions. Bonita fussed over the girls' hair and nails.

Lainie recalled Thursday night's petitions and declarations clipped from the *East Visayan News*. In their room, she looked in Reena's purse, with no apology. Reena had lain down on the lower bunk, her arm over her eyes, and seemed not to notice.

Whole pages in the paper listed announcements for changes of names, plot auctions, folding businesses, declarations of notices, repeated notices to change ownerships, and petitions. Most listings announced changes of sex, of all things. Hardly any petitions were for divorce.

Lainie compared the wording of Nita's clippings to the ones actually awarded any numbered plots of land, or petitions to acquire abandoned properties, or deaths locking up any pursuits for land. Too many years had passed. Without a deed, ownership was squarely in Luis's hands, yet someone gave notice that partial plots were up for sale. Was this a result of the faltering business, sugar, planted in land bombed forty-some years ago, or property abandoned by a blood relative because he or she preferred life in the mountains?

Could any original land grant negate any new paperwork since Reena's departure?

Lainie glanced at Reena pretending to nap.

"It would help to say out loud, at least, to Nita, that you want the land."

Lainie timed the silence. She jumped when seconds later, her wait was cut by a scream.

XXVIII

The ear-piercing scream startled Lainie. Her paper research was broken. Her suggestion hung in the space between herself and Reena. She dashed out, following Sari-Sari and Terri-Terri.

One of the piglets was being pulled with a rope to its doom. The pale white thing cried, agonizing, filled with terror. From afar, its companion, still corralled near the water buffalo, matched the pitiful howling. One of the girls stood with her fingers plugging her ears. Lainie found herself doing the same.

She kept turning away and turning back. She had to see the full sequence. No, she wanted to block each moment. She and Sari-Sari stood holding each other till Lainie's nails dug into the girl's arm, and she yelped. Before them, men straddled the pig or clasped its feet to prevent it from kicking. One man stretched its neck. Dom drew the pointed, sharpened blade across its throat. Steadily, he then pushed the tip into an artery. The piglet eeked once and lay still, not dead, just resigned. Blood streaming from its throat didn't even fill a gallon tub. The liquid would make *dinuguan*, blood soup. Sari-Sari and Lainie, squirming, finally entered the house and she ran to the crowded kitchen, stopping to pump water into the bucket for her C.R. visit.

Another world spun inside. Everyone took advantage of the available electricity.

More strange women filled the kitchen, practically tripping over each other dashing between the huge counter and the stove. Teri-Teri chattered to Lainie, pale, after her C.R. visit.

"It'll take all day to chop six dozen chickens for the Reunion, " Teri-Teri giggled. "Sixteen hours away. Manong Dom roasts the *lechon* first, and then times the chicken so everything's ready Sunday morning."

Having the runs hardly made Lainie expectant or excited.

Outside, the air filled with the roar of men's voices.

"Mama! Mama!" cried Sari-Sari, very excited. Lainie framed her view out the window.

A half-dozen rangy-looking men with headbands, dark-complected, draped with M-16 rifles strapped across their backs stood clapping the shoulders of Dom's helpers. Most of them were deceptively small with teenage builds. Dom nodded to their easy *mano*'s. Bonita mumbled, "They heard the radio notice. Early, *sigé*?" She clucked her tongue. "Ay, the Plebiña Reunion takes all kinds." She pawed the air at the girls. No one seemed alarmed.

The NPAs had arrived.

Horatio stood among them, casual, one knee bent, till one man enfolded him in a bear hug. That man turned to introduce a swarthier type who stoically shook Horatio's hand. Lainie glanced from one to another, about six of them, and took in all of their weapons: faces, rifles, clothes, guns, pistols, hands, bayonets, flip-flops, headbands, weapons, weapons, weapons. Such a visual contradiction, Horatio, trim, clean-shaven, in pressed, white designer, athletic gear nearby men in thin, t-shirts and worn, camou-colored war neck scarves, all munitioned and toughened. Juan stood outside Nita's door, guarding. He shifted. Just then Nate drove through the gates with Nita. They parked. Nate was star struck. Nita looked once at visitors and entered the house. Nate and Juan joined the females crowding the door, expectant, as Nita passed them.

"Will they stay?" Teri-Teri asked. Bonita tipped her head at her.

Nita held a briefcase and bags. Indicating Horatio, Juan said to Nita, "They'll use the patio one night. Horatio knows them but you know who is family. So, *Até*, whose choice do we go by?" Nita said little, heading to place her purse and case in her bedroom.

Lainie whirled on Reena. "Mom! Do you think some of the young NPAs right outside are . . . are family?" Reena followed Nita, coughing, not looking at Lainie.

But Nita moved away. "They stay in the jungle. Villagers join them and intermarry. They all come out a couple times a year."

Lainie frowned, not understanding the answer.

"Mom?"

Reena was ditzying at anything nearby. "Maybe some of them have familiar features."

Features: they all had the flatter noses, the varied skin tones, and other than the heaviest of them all, they all were about the same height. What particular features was she referring to? Lainie frowned. Not all of them could be related to her.

The family seemed content that any guests had arrived at all.

"*Até* Nita, are you going out to meet them?" Lainie was wrangling for a closer look.

"Horatio handled that. He's their host." Nita was blocking the kitchen ladies from approaching the window. They were poised, stretching their necks past her shoulders and chattering softly. Nita sighed, "*Tama na*." Workers reluctantly headed back to the kitchen. They had to serve meals. Soon, all helpers receded into their usual invisibility.

"So all the women huddle in the house and all the men hang outside trading war stories, huh?" Lainie quipped or thought she had, expecting a lightened mood or a grin.

Nita was curt. "Yes."

O-kay-y-y-y then, thought Lainie and inched toward the window to watch through the Venetian-type smoky glass slats. Her innards twanged. She ran to the C.R. again. When she returned, again Nita asked, "Tea? Strong tea?" And this time, Lainie accepted.

Reena, concentrated on her *balikbayan* boxes, had hardly looked up since the NPAs set up camp in the yard. Lainie sat watching till finally she convinced Reena to separate any unisex items. "The majority of guests are women, right?" Reena cleared her throat.

"Maybe. The count came in today." Lainie felt Reena might be disappointed.

"Filipino time," Lainie joked. "Mom, you don't have to cart back anything. If it's a low turnout, maybe they didn't hear the ad in time or even have a radio. Maybe this is too far or . . ."

"They think about five-hundred," Reena's eyes darting about, avoiding Lainie's gaze.

Lainie sat down. "What?"

"So we're low. I only brought four-hundred items."

"Excuse me, what?? Five hundred? You're feeding five-hundred guests?"

"Give or take." Reena tossed, and then retrieved items.

Lainie re-calculated: a dozen house relatives, kitchen and *lechon* helpers, Dom, the NPAs, any Barangay 35 who knew Nita, the town of Lunao, so, hey, why not throw in rest of Leyte?

She faltered. "How big is this pavilion? To hold that many people? What about chairs?"

"Then there's the priest and altar boys, and some city officials, if they accepted." Reena was still avoiding Lainie's eyes. Everyone, guests, pastors, politicians, and NPA would all be under one roof.

A cheer – Lainie peered out the bedroom window. Both butchered piglets, still white, were hoisted onto the swing set. A bamboo crank would vary heights and roasting times. Dom directed two younger boys to turn the spits and roast each speared pig evenly.

Dusk was settling in among huts and homes in the barrio, signaled by a rise of clucks, and moo's, and squawks, as if all of nature were calling out farewell to the sun and day. Five- hundred – Lainie marveled at the thought.

"I wonder if anyone might know your grandfather and tell more stories and . . ."

Lainie stopped long enough for Reena to look up. "And what?"

Lainie calculated once again: NPAs, jungle, family, Lunao, grandfather – family. She asked, "Mom, these guests, they're all NPAs, aren't they? The ones from the jungle, all families of NPAs, right? And the Lunao women, they're NPAs, too, villagers with families in the jungle. So, there are more NPAs than family here, right? Or are they both?"

Reena finally had stopped fidgeting.

Lainie posed, "Your grandfather was an NPA who hid in the jungles, right, until he died, the relative who lost the land *because* he was NPA. Am I right? Mom?"

Reena was silent. Finally she spoke. "Hon, they fought against Americans, and fifty years later, they fight along side and rebel again. From an early age, we're taught to report insurrectos. Since the war, they rebel again. They despise their protectors. Why can't they see it's better under U.S. rule? We just don't talk about them. So families today are ashamed of them."

"You mean you're ashamed."

Reena almost whispered. "That side fought Americans! Americans made the Philippines what it is. I brought you here to see what we are. Why rebels aren't grateful, I don't know. "

"Don't bite the hand, is that it? Mom: what I see is that you've lost what's us, too."

Reena shrugged. "Depends, hon. It depends."

Lainie gazed outside. Skies darkened. Men settled in for a long night ahead, drinking, talking, maybe some of them dozing, but not without an eye open or a rifle nearby.

"Could we meet them and talk to them, to that side of the family? Or do you deny them, too? Our ancestors, everyone who lived as rebels, are they wrong to be nationalists?"

Reena shook her head. "We women can't go out to the yard.

They will kidnap us, make them cook, and carry, and other things."

Lainie sounded a bit forceful. "Maybe all these women and children trekking cross the mountain, maybe want to cook, and other things." Lainie sounded a bit forceful. "How else would these men live without women in the jungles and in town? They do it for them!"

"Someone had to stay . . . and, and work the land." Reena said in a halting voice.

Lainie flipped. "So that is the land! Great-grandfather's land, the sugar plantations, the property that the Serrañaos took over – Luis has all of it because you . . . you left?"

"Well," Reena began, "Yes, some of it . . . most of it. I let Nita watch for me."

Lainie felt like crying and laughing at the same time. Her anguished howl might broadcast to the whole barrio, to Madawawing Mountains, and to all points on that one island: Plebiñas may not own a sugar plantation after all, Plebiñas of Ormoc who defined a large part of Leyte history.

Gathering her journal, a pen, Reena's camera, and a book of matches, Lainie got up and headed to the door. Using her mother's camera was the least she was entitled to at this point.

"Where are you going? It's dinner soon," Reena said.

Lainie just looked at her and exited.

In the main room, the aroma of roasting chickens permeated the house. Lainie's stomach no longer twanged. Strong tea worked after all. Discovery number – ah, why keep count?

Nita's whole family looked the same, but were they townies siding with the nationalists or just normal Ormocanons? Bonita's family had grown up in Nita's house; under Nita's care, Reena's mother had died of old age in this house. NPAs gathered here, at this house. Horatio was more than some mere philanderer, if he even was. But he was deferred to. Why?

"Where is your store, *Até*?" Lainie asked. Nita pointed with her lip. "Outside the gate. I just unlock the cover to the shop. I sell gum and sodas, little things, just for some extra income."

"It's never open. Still, money just flows in." Lainie waited. Nita was silent.

"I'll take pictures outside." Lainie moved to the door. "Maybe see what's sold."

Juan uttered his high-pitched warning. Still, she slipped out. "I'll be right back."

Outside, men smoked under the awning. At the smoking pit, one boy was swiping his long bangs away from his eyes, squatting at the end of the poles, one hand on the tip. He looked a bit suspicious, as if Lainie could grab the pole and dump a whole ninety-pound pig in some bag and boogie. She snapped a picture of the roasting pig and waited.

Then Dom was at her side, that perennial cigarette perched on the side of his mouth. In his flip-flops he had approached silently.

"I'm just taking pictures of the pigs at different stages." She composed a shot looking lengthwise at the pigs with the boy at the far end. "I won't take any of the men."

Dom kept staring at the pigs. "Enough of the boy," was all he said. The boy must be one of the men's sons. She switched off the camera and swung its strap around her shoulder.

Lainie smiled at the side of his face. "Thanks. Salamat."

"You know who they are?" Dom tapped his cigarette.

She swung her mother's camera over her other shoulder. "Family."

Dom gave a small smile. "Roasted *lechon* has crispy skin, farm raised. It's been cared for. Boars running in jungles live on the edge. They stay tough."

He glanced at the men yet pointed his lip at the pigs.

Lainie got it.

"Can anyone spare a San Miguel?" she asked.

Now Dom looked at her. He turned and headed back to the awning. Lainie looked at the boy. She gave a peace sign, corny, but better than bad Cebuano. The boy actually gave one back and brushed a lock from his face.

She followed Dom to the crowd of men. Juan, still nearer to the door, looked alarmed. Odd, she thought, he kept his distance when she was the nearest ever to danger on this trip.

Dom, in a low tone, requested anyone under the awning for a San Miguel beer. All the men shifted. She noticed they glanced at their rifles lined against the cement house. One of the men got up to fetch bottles from the plastic cooler. Dom stared at another man who wordlessly offered his seat to Lainie. She was in.

"Salamat," she offered, barely glancing at them. The one who fetched the beers called out. "Where are you from, Miss?"

Should she lie? But Lainie figured they already knew. "San Francisco. In California."

The men exchanged glances. One mumbled, "Berka-LEE, *ano*, Stanpord." Geez, thought Lainie, Jesus in heaven, is California a high-yield ransom? Are they insurrectos who kidnap? Would they haul her off, screeching, into a jeepney and whisk her into the jungle?

Could they wait till after the Reunion?

Dom spoke in Cebuano. The one with the beer bottles asked her, "Do you smoke?"

A slight laughter was heard from the group. She looked at the cigarette pack, "Marlboro." A shift, more glances. The man brought the pack and beers and strode toward her, shaking a cigarette out of the pack. Lainie took one. He glanced at Dom and then squatted. She was relieved when Dom moved toward Mr. Swarthy, as if he had sanctioned her presence – and eliminated her as a KFR (kidnap for ransom). Mr. Cigarette lit her cigarette and pausing, blew out the match and struck another match for his own cigarette.

"You are?" Lainie asked outright.

"A friend," he hedged, but then he held out his brown, sinewy hand. "I am Jose."

Jose's grip was firm and cool hand. He kept his gaze on her and gestured, "Stand a minute." When she did, Jose introduced her to Mr. Swarthy. "Our esteemed leader, 'Gundo."

The other men scratched their necks, smoked, or took a sip of beer. But 'Gundo straightened and did not move. She thought perhaps like others, he avoided English. Men coughed, ending the lukewarm introduction. Jose with his lip pointed to her chair to sit.

"Where is your husband?" Jose asked, blunt.

"He's no more." Lainie deflected.

"Dead?"

She explained. "He's no longer my husband."

Men mumbled. Jose's eyebrow twitched, inferring, "No wonder." Lainie steamed a bit.

Jose baited her. "You, uh, liberated, that kind? What means that, liberated?"

"Well," she knocked an ash. "Free, not restricted by expectations, or codes."

"If," Jose tapped his own cigarette, "You were not liberated, what would you be?" And he continued. "So no one to keep you huddled in the house, *sigé*?"

Lainie now really looked at him. Jose had a mess of very black, dull hair. He moved very easily, confidently. He had a very mischievous twinkle in his bottomless, pool-dark eyes. He was their comic relief, she gauged. He could, like a jester, bounce between the king and the court, evading any royal sentence for his blithe yet razor-sharp remarks.

"Should I be afraid to leave the company of women?" she asked. She took a long drink.

"*Mabuhi!*" he toasted and the men echoed. "*Mabuhi!*"

Again, Jose tossed a comment to the men. 'Gundo rumbled a short retort. Men grunted.

Lainie recognized this age-old game. Let's witness who get's the girl and how the getting's got. "It's easy to give a play-by-play in a language you know. Try it in English, one on one." She had already drunk half her beer. Juan shuffled nearby, anxious.

Jose blinked. From low octave C to middle C, men behind him sang, "Oh-h-h-h!"

"Another San Miguel, Miss?" he asked.

"Lainie," she corrected. "But you knew that, right?"

He smiled a winning smile. "*Sigé*. And your mother is Reena. *Manong* Dom told us." Eager-eared from afar, Dom eyeballed Jose and then ignored him.

"And Juan, too." Lainie pointed. Juan started to cross to them but she added, "My bodyguard. Well, my second cousin. My uncle. He looks out for me." Juan backed away again.

Lainie sighed. She had just committed the local sin, defining stations and class.

Jose grinned at Juan. "Good guard. Smart."

Hearing the compliment, Lainie noted, Juan slouched. He'd be nobody's fool.

Jose tipped a salute at Juan. What a charmer, Lainie decided. Well, she could charm, too.

"Are you interested in my mother?"

Men guffawed, prodding Jose on. He continued smiling. "If she's rich."

The banter continued. Without prompters, observers reacted like game show audiences.

She tipped the bottle up by her lips. "Do not disrespect my mother or your elder, Jose."

"Oh, you're older than me, eh?"

"Maybe I am. For sure I'm smarter."

"Oh-HO, a woman smarter than a man? HA."

"ALL women are smarter than men." Lainie's head spun a bit.

"American women would say that."

"American women who write." She drank her beer.

Jose's head swaggered. He said, "I write. And read."

"Newsletters, magazines, stories, poems? What?"

"Everything. Oy, 'Gundo. I write good letters, huh?" 'Jose

knew 'Gundo ignored him.

"Prove it. Write something."

"It does not make you smarter, Miss."

She corrected him. "Lainie. You're right. You do pretty well one-on-one, Jose. Bravo."

He just looked at her. The men were already bored and talking among themselves. He bent closer. "I will write for you. But first." Jose whistled for one of the two boys at the pit. He spoke quickly to him, and the boy ran off.

"Here." Lainie gave him a sheet from her journal and her pen. "Or should I go first?"

He took the paper and pen and began to write. "Anyone in town could see from your journal that you write." He lapsed into silence, writing, not stopping even once.

Lainie rose and went up to Juan, who looked like he would cower if she came closer. "Juan, I won't hurt you, what's the matter?"

He shook his head. Juan usually responded. His reticence was puzzling.

"What do I need to know? Should I go in?" Of them all, Juan usually answered.

Juan looked over her shoulder at the men. Again, he shook his head. Jose chortled.

Lainie returned to sit by Jose, who triumphantly handed her the piece of paper, on which letters were handwritten, small, with a European kind of flair. She read it. She read it again.

Then Lainie folded the sheet between pages of her journal. "Very good. Very astute."

"*Mabuhi*, me." Jose leaned back, resting his forearms on his stomach, his cigarette between his third and fourth fingers.

"Let me guess. Spain? Italy? Hong Kong? Where were you were educated?"

Poker-faced, Lainie in reality was somewhat rattled by what she had just read.

He waved her off. "No matter. I can just write, too." Then he added, "Go Cal."

The night was very warm. Lainie lifted her chin. Stars overhead winked and beckoned. Barrio residents ventured past the red gates to peek at the lechon. One boy turned the spit and, with his free hand, wiped sparkly drops of sweat lit by the flowing coals. Lainie heard kitchen workers issue urgent commands in Cebuano in time with gushing water on tin and aluminum pans. Teri-Teri opened the front door and whispered to the vigilant Juan. He remained at his post. Lainie watched shadows animate under the awning by the raking light of a Coleman lantern. Silhouetted caricatures of men drinking played sharply against the cement-block wall. Curious onlookers soon left.

All this, Lainie took in, just to recover from Jose's note. Her bottle felt like her neck, sweaty, slick, and sticky.

"Lunao," she said, defying the word to be a question.

Jose blew out smoke from both nostrils. He shrugged.

What Jose had written was, *Now is the time for all good men to come to the aid of their country,* exactly what Lainie had typed on Evie's typewriter on Thursday, in Lunao.

Maybe the typing phrase was common there, like in the States. Still, in that one line, Jose verified where were his many eyes and ears, even in that area, on that day, on her.

"You will be summoned soon for your evening meal," noted Jose. "You will have to say Grace, *sigé,* unless you don't remember."

Lainie, composed, said, "Once a Catholic, always an ex-Catholic, drilled on prayers every day. Hey, I ran into a rosary crowd one morning." She added, "You shoulda been there."

If he got the jab, he ignored it and snorted. "Aah, they pass themselves off as Catholics in name only. But in practice . . .? Ha. Then, I am the best Catholic in the world."

"You obey all the commandments? Can you recite all the commandments? Better yet, write them down." She was curious to see what he would write as his eleventh commandment.

"I know the important one. *Thou shalt not commit adultery.*" Jose gulped his beer.

Again, Lainie inwardly jumped. The commandment was the very same example Lainie had thrown at Horatio on their morning jog, Thursday morning, in Barangay 35.

But she took another breath. "Frankly, I think the coveting says the same thing, *Thou shalt not covet thy neighbor's wife.* Why are there two rules on adultery? Must have been a big thing back then," Lainie remarked, placing her last empty beer near the cooler.

"It's a big thing now," Jose announced, to which the men nearby toasted him as much as a drunken toast could be. "We should have divorce here, just like in America."

"Oh, I don't know. Things get lax, allowing more excuses, dismissing more vows." Lainie dug her hand into the cooler. "You want out of a marriage, poof, you're out."

"Like you." Jose was blunt.

She downed half a bottle and plowed on, "What does that do to a whole country, huh? Parents divorce, families bust up. And out the door goes the, the fiber of, of normalcy. Dissipated, a-a-adrift, asunder!"

"*Sigé!*" Jose bellowed. "Men should divorce, but not women, because of children. Keep the children with their mothers."

"Jose, if men divorce, they divorce women. How can one sex divorce and not another?"

"Oy!" The men boomed, most likely to the word spoken out loud, and by a woman: *sex.*

"Divorce is so men can have more women. But women cannot have more men." Jose stumbled a bit, as if he didn't quite believe the statement himself.

"That's absolutely silly." Lainie waved him off. The men grumbled. She veered. "You know, I saw a cock fight."

Jose blinked. "Ah, a change, okay, okay. And how was the cock fight, Miss?"

"It's the same subject: I saw very few women, maybe three of us altogether. But really, it's mostly men. Why is that?"

"Too much blood?" Jose popped another beer.

Lainie went on. "Women gamble, more than men, in America, or anywhere there's risk. They don't need to blow their own horns about it like men do."

"It's a rite," he said. "Didn't you know that?"

Lainie puffed. "Who determines who has that right?"

Jose explained, "No, a 'rite', like religion, like Catholic. Cockfights are more for men, to be, you know." he flexed his biceps.

Lainie laughed a little too readily. "Oh, to be strong?"

Jose was unflappable. "To be strong in all ways, *sigé*."

Lainie was straight-faced. "Okay-y-y, then."

"I will take you sometime," Jose pronounced. "I will explain to you why men betting on cock fights helps them."

By now, Juan hopped by the front door as if fire ants nipped at his soles. Men howled and hooted at their own drunkenness, derisively mocking the night's talk.

Lainie, quite loose now, posed a question in a voice louder than intended. "Tell me, truthfully, and I'm not joking now. I really want to know."

"What, what," Jose pretended boredom. "I just joke."

"Why do you fight? What's the fight all about, really? Land?"

Men uttered a warning. One muttered, "*Estoryahan* (too much talk)."

Jose coughed a bit and drew himself up. "Too serious."

"Please – why do you have to live in the jungle?"

"Aiee, two questions." Jose wiped his face and crossed to the cooler for another beer.

Teri-Teri had appeared again and whispered to Juan's ear. He nodded till she left.

Jose began, "We are rebels."

"Nationalists, patriots," Lainie added. He went on. "Terms, labels, means nothing. We resist corruption, elitism. The people lose so much here, because they do not have the money to pay anyone off. Everyone is paid off. So we fight."

Juan squeaked. Lainie patted the air. "*Talaga,* we're cool, everything's cool."

"Plebiñas have land but . . ." Lainie began, but Jose held up his hand.

"What is the phrase, small potatoes: land, property. The only problem is not who owns land, more like who owns who. We are not bought." He attempts singing. "*We who are happy and free.*" Men boo'ed him. He sung louder. "*Birds of same feather we flutter together Scout Rangers of fortune are we!*"

"Oh, my God, you've got an anthem?" Lainie exclaimed.

Jose almost fell over, holding his stomach. "Anthem, ha! We live in the jungle, Bye Bye Miss American Pie," he mocked, "because the towns are too limiting. We cannot do what we need to do for our Cause because they come looking for us all the time. What kind of living is that? What else can we do, where else, eh?"

"If you have your own land, that's where you live."

"How? Go to town, sign papers, wait twenty years, and they still hunt for us." Jose argued, the men urging him on. "You don't know the ways here or know how things are done."

Juan was pawing the air anxiously. "Oy. Eat. Eat!"

"So I've been told." Lainie ignoring Juan said dryly, "So give up."

"Oy." The response came from probably 'Gundo.

A cloud, unseen, covered the men under the awning, on this little corner of land, and on the whole barrio. One of the men stood. Jose caught 'Gundo's eye who just tipped his chin up and pointed his lower lip at Lainie.

Juan hid his alarm, badly. "Sss-Ssst. Lainie! Sss-ssst!"

The hefty M-16 rifles seemed to stand at attention against the cement brick wall. From indoors, women chattered. Shrill, accusing insects emitted siren-like, accusatory jabs in the heavy, dewy air.

Night was black not two meters off. In seconds, anyone could be dragged into darkness.

Again Juan hissed the familial island call at Lainie. He stood, half frantic behind Jose, his hand clawing at the air, mouthing to her to move off, cursing silently, "*Ay 'sus maryjosep!*"

Jose's eyes drew in the Coleman lantern's light. Smoky ribbons hung, static. While prepping for dinner, men lounged; women cleaned, a ritual set and secured.

Except for Lainie, the American.

As if hypnotized, the two squared off, Lainie's cigarette held lightly between her fingers, balancing her elbows on her knees, watching him.

Juan squirmed, frantic. Reena had knocked softly on the window, alerting him.

Lainie, instead, lounged back in the fold-up lawn chair, its plastic-woven seating nearly touching the ground. Still, she braced herself, her own defiant eyes never wavering from Jose's.

All this time Jose never moved.

To corrupt businessmen, politicians, the government, or even pastors, Jose and the others were the Enemy, the NPAs. Lainie raised her chin but saw, to her surprise, Reena, anxious, watching her. Panic scurried inside Lainie. Why was Reena so wide-eyed? In her face, Lainie could only read abject fear.

Lainie was courting danger again, of her own volition, dared by no one, and betting strange odds against herself that she'd emerge barely scarred but safe, bearing wounds she would forget. She added commandments for the future:

Never borrow a cigarette from a guy with a gun.

Never bet on odds six to two.

Never—ever—tell a somber, driven revolutionary to: Give. Up.

Jose breathed. Men shifted. "*Maayong udto*, tourist *bisita* lady. *Sigé*, have a nice day."

As Lainie turned, she saw Jose flick his cigarette at the house. Yellow embers fell like miniature sparkling fireworks. Hungry, mawwing shadows crawled the walls before darkness ate the last ash and any remnant of daylight.

Approaching the house, only Lainie knew her heart raced.

XXIX

Juan led. Lainie followed. Women avoided looking at her. The kitchen helpers were doling out dishes to the family. Were they also NPA, dedicated to live in town? They must be upset with her. Lainie glanced at everybody's bowed heads. Before one of the girls could speak, Lainie recited, "Bless us O Lord for these thy gifts which we are about to receive from thy bounty through Christ our Lord, Amen - and thank you for everyone here and bringing family together."

Tension subsided. Lainie earned back a few points. Like the men outside, inside the family took their cues from a dominant source, Nita, who had now relaxed.

Afar off, a soft guitar could be heard as night fell, inviting, velvet-toned, alluring, and accompanied by crickets. The air was a bit static, with or without real electricity, with the girls all giggly. Over dinner, Nita, Bonita, and Reena shared last-minute Reunion plans. Nate and Juan daydreamed, eyes on windows, set apart from freer men outside. They had remained in their same place near the Coleman lanterns, their poses content and languorous, echoing Rockwell's painting: Freedom From Want. But at this table, no knives were set, and amid bent heads over the ever-present *pandesal* basket, no turkey was placed central.

Needs attended, Reena, and characteristically, even Lainie

would still always want more.

Freedom From Want and Fear, Freedom Of Speech and Religion – Lainie smiled at the things she remembered from Art Appreciation. She now connected the four freedoms here, after the stare-down with Jose, and after only three days unraveling family mysteries.

Reena pawed the air. "Sst, Sari-Sari, kneel on pillows and look out. Tell us everything."

"Those men are laughing, loud, drunk. Oy, Até Vi just drove up. Yes, that's her."

Both the visitor and the musician had arrived at the same time as the Cebuano song.

Amazingly on cue, everyone inside stopped and looked at each other, wide-eyed, except Lainie. They all recognized at once what the tune was, except Lainie. During the flurry of motion, Teri-Teri was first to reach her sister at the window, then Bonita, Nita, and Reena. Lainie turned in her seat, clueless. The girls grinned, eeking, their cheeks held with closed fists.

"*Kundiman*," stated Nita. "And Vi."

"Oy, pushy," sighed Reena. "She'll run them over."

Finally, Lainie stood and took a step. But with a palm out and not looking at her, Nita willed her away from the window. "Not you, Lainie."

"*Ay, 'sus*," swore Reena. "The singer's here for, for *her*?" She swatted Lainie, missing.

Sari-Sari pointed. "Mama, the door."

Vi, who misplaced her passport in a barf bag, absent from her own merienda, burst in, all bright and boisterous and dimpled yet alternately dismayed.

Never starting with a hello from what Lainie could recall, *Até* Vi pushed the door shut behind her and blurted, " '*Tangina*, all these men all over your yard! And *kundiman*! Who are they serenading? Did you girls flirt with them? *Na-na-na-na-na*!"

Reena stood, arms akimbo, and fully swore. "Ay '*susmarjosep*, where have you been all this time? We show up at your house, and you're not there! We stood with strangers!"

Vi fended off the overly excited girls, like kittens crawling over her, and retorted. "I'm in town, all this time! I have family, too! Why is the house so noisy?"

"Guess," Reena quipped dryly and stood her ground. "You and your lechon stood us up!"

Whoever was singing had a beautiful voice. "The singer with his guitar is inside the gate," reported Sari-Sari. "Oh-oh, the boy is back, too, speaking to the man Lainie drank with."

"Ay, sigé, drinking?" Vi questioned. "Who? What? Who is he?"

"Jose?" Lainie was curious. He better not tell the musician to leave. That would be rude, shooing off someone just welcoming Reena and Lainie with a song the night before the big Reunion. Yes, Lainie deduced, that's what's going on.

"Everyone, sit, finish your meal." Nita ushered Vi to the table. The others reluctantly followed suit. "Sss-sst, Sari-Sari, you, too. Come sit."

"Awww." The girl drooped but left her lookout.

Lainie was confused. What was going on? Why was everyone ignoring the musician?

When everyone sat again, Lainie asked, innocently cutting food with her large spoon. "Should we invite the singer in?"

In one voice, the women all blared. "No-o-o-o–o!!!" Okay-y-y. Lainie receded.

Vi helped herself to a plate and some food, licked her fingers, and said glibly, "If you look out, or open the door, you'll encourage him. You know, I ate already, but this looks good."

"Encourage his singing?" Lainie felt this was all very odd.

"No – his courtship," Vi said. "Oy, ssst, Sari, Teri, either of you – my drink, please."

As Teri-Teri poured Vi a cup of soda, Lainie frowned. Did anyone even know the singer?

"Why would a stranger . . ." she stopped. Jose had sent the boy. "A boy is courting me?"

The girls groaned. Even the women shook their heads. Reena took center.

"The playboy." She looked defensive. "The one who sent for the singer."

The musician sang a *kundiman*, the Visayan love song to lure a female out of the house.

Vi badgered everyone for the latest live soap opera. All the while, she stuffed her face. Lainie sat numb. Nita left the plastic pitcher of juice right in front of Vi. Reena just ignored her. Lainie could now see, Reena was the ringleader. With a glance, she could orchestrate her clingy friends and relatives to do her bidding. Vi jumped hoops to maintain the venerated status as best friend. And Nita, the worker bee, implemented Reena's plans.

"Um, it's romantic, but can anyone tell me what he's singing?" Lainie asked.

"About love," Sari-Sari gave a shy smile. "With pain." she listened some more. "He '*will go away and not suffer being lonely*', something like that."

Vi gulped her drink. "Hmph, too much *soo-gar*."

"What did you do?" Reena faced Lainie directly. "Did you encourage him?"

"Sitting with him encourages him," Bonita commented.

Obviously, merely looking encouraged types like Jose. Still, she had flirted with this NPA. She groaned inwardly with the memory of Mykonos Island outside Greece. A fisherman had taken her and a friend to a local celebration on a dark hilltop. Dark-clothed women, with only their eyes visible, doled out a soupy portion to Lainie from a tub-sized iron tureen. After lots of *ouzo*, Lainie accepted a scarf dance with the fisherman. Unknown at the time to her, she had also accepted his hand in marriage – a whole other story.

Once alone with her, the fisherman had pounced, no longer just leering, but forceful and barking, the memory mirroring her escapes at age five scuttling backward into dark recesses, evading clawed fingers. She had screamed and wriggled free from the fisherman, and bolted. She had eluded close calls, frightful times, memories diluted with distance, and still she collected more, such as taunting a warrior.

"How often will I get a chance to talk to an NPA? All this time hearing, don't go in the jungle, like they're aliens. They're just like us, like, like the Panthers or Berkeley's Venceremos, the Symbionese!" Listeners' eyes glazed. "They're roused enough to do something, walk the walk, talk the talk, get angry." Lainie felt defensive. Juan clicked his tongue.

The room then was quiet except for Vi munching and the man outside singing.

"Sometimes," Nita picked up a dish near Vi, "it's better to be, you know, small, you know a word?"

Lainie was careful now. "But, *Até*, you have a yard full of NPAs. And you have Americans in your house. How small does that look?"

Reena's eyes bulged. "Be grateful that she lets us stay here! How else would we . . ."

Lainie pleaded. " I am grateful, but the jungle is here now. The jungle came to us."

The singer picked up the rhythm of the song outside the house. The girls giggled and poked each other. Nita was handing plates passed on by Bonita to the half-seen kitchen workers. When the table had been fully cleared off, Vi asked, "Dessert?"

Nita shook her head sadly. "Vi," she uttered and clucked her tongue.

"One word is invisible." Lainie answered Nita's question. "Many like that back home."

"I'll explain." Bonita now took over. "If anyone in the barrio tells authorities that NPAs are here, we all would know. That person would be labeled . . ."

"A patriot?" asked Lainie.

"An informer," Bonita corrected. "If the police come here, the NPAs run. And we are just women. Authorities expect more sense from a man to allow rebels in. But, no, we women cannot tell men to go away. We tell police, '*they came and took our food, and left. We cannot stop them.*' Ay, the police are corrupt and are paid to look the other way. They won't arrest anyone."

Lainie still wasn't quite matching things up. "By who, who pays them, the police?"

Bonita responded, "The rich, the rich relatives."

"They want the Reunion to happen. They allowed us." Vi licked her fingers and wiped off her face and hands. "That way they show their power."

Lainie's head was reeling.

Sari-Sari was translating the song, dipping her head, " '*A woman much like roses, with charm sprays the rose buds' potion: Here Rosas Pandan Down from mountains'*."

Here, there were a small barrio, a courtship, land, takeover, graft, and the people, playing small. None of this at all was invisible to Lainie.

Bonita was gathering the girls to head for bed, so Sari-Sari ended. "'*A legacy from, from ancestors the pride of our hills.*" Sari-Sari smiled. "I love that song. I feel so happy!"

Lainie asked anyone. "So we just don't acknowledge the singer at all?"

"If you look out or join him, you have said, yes," Nita explained. "Do you want to live in the jungle the rest of your life? How often were you warned, don't go in the jungle?"

"Ay, the one who courts is the one who pays the singer!" Reena was exasperated. "Turn out the lights so he knows he's rejected. Sari-Sari, Teri-Teri, night-night now."

"But what if she . . .?" Sari-Sari looked at Lainie, but Bonita moved the girl toward the opposite bedroom, interrupting. "She doesn't, do you? Or do you? Love him?"

Lainie protested throatily without saying either way. Reena

switched off the main room's light. A chorus of disappointed groans filled the patio area. The men had lost their bets on Jose.

"What about me?" Vi squeaked.

"*Maayong udto*, Vi." Nita kissed Vi briefly and headed to the kitchen area.

"Good. Your answer is clear. Everyone goes away," stated Reena to Lainie. Juan said to Vi, "*Sigé na*, I will escort you to your car." He headed out first. Some men believed Lainie had relented and cheered. Seeing only Juan with Vi, they groaned. Vi followed, head high, dispersing blithe greetings along the way. "*Maayong udto*, go home now." She drove off, Juan waving at the dust behind her. Lainie peeked out without being seen. "Wow, Vi sure likes food."

Reena walked away. "Hmph, she annoys me. She knew NPAs were here and the singer."

Seated on the rattan couch, Lainie could hear quiet laughter. The whole barrio knew NPAs had arrived. They knew a singer was paid to visit the May compound. She figured which rich relative had deep pockets. Police won't bother them. Lainie crawled onto her bunk. A movement on the wall – she reached to pet Pickle but missed as he slithered upward. "Go home," she said aloud and remembered. She had ignored Horatio's command: to go home.

"Mom, what's Horatio's job?"

In half-light, Reena snuffled. "Riding a fence."

Lainie twisted to look down at her. "Cheating?"

Reena sighed. "Who knows? Younger women are NPAs, too, and shoot guns, even kill."

Lainie gawked. "He's cheating on Nita with an NPA? That's why he's always off to meet someone? Is that why he brings gifts for guests to show he's a generous, attentive host?"

Lainie began to concoct whole scenes involving betrayal, jealousy, and revenge, to which she would allude discreetly for her article. Then again, why? This tack seemed trite, petty.

"Always writing but you don't pay attention." Reena sighed.

" Horatio *is* an NPA."

From under the patio, Jose's hearty laugh cut the night.

XXX

Alone, Reena recalled her many suitors, singing to her and then slouching off, unacknowledged by her. And then came Geraldo, singing *a capella* day or night, caring less who would hear, as long as she did. With him, she was that girl of seventeen again, before war changed her. Geraldo had chipped a small flake off her invisible wall. Yet still, after years of marriage, she had not whispered the words he had waited for years to hear.

If Reena stayed in Ormoc, even with needs attended, she'd always want more. She got Geraldo and Mukwonago. Life could only be right the minute hardened Reena would soften:

Early 1947

"Or do you . . .love him?" Vi peered at Reena's suitor, Geraldo, through the G.I. surplus camouflage netting, behind which he sat with the movie projector. "Because if you don't, hmm . . ."

Reena wondered but hadn't cared if movies in a church were sacrilegious.

Reena sat between Vi and Juan, who was in front of his sister, Nita. She had allowed Juan to repeat the message from Geraldo about movies at deconsecrated St. Peter and Paul Church.

No longer a church since 1944, the edifice was some battered cement wall with no roof. The sacristy served as the projection booth. Females of any age were not allowed into night events without a male escort. Juan, although nine years old, passed as their requirement.

Ever since the month-long bombing of Ormoc City by MacArthur's orders three years earlier, more and more companies of American soldiers poured onto the island of Leyte. And more and more mothers like Billina warned their hormonal daughters to beware. Beware of the cigar-smoking G.I.'s who may drop like heavy fronds from palm trees, like *kaprés*. Beware of golden-skinned enlisted men who would lure a teenage schoolgirl and "get her in trouble."

But Reena saw this soldier, when she had sat at the fountain with her gang in town. All he did, this very *gwapo* (handsome) Americanized Filipino soldier, was stare at her. And all she did was tip her head sideways and shrug because she knew she was cute.

Time, Reena determined, the time arrived to keep the promise at any cost no matter if he was Ilocano and not Visayan, or older, or if he smoked, or drank, both of which she knew this one did, heavily – or if he was married. She had already asked about him around the village. And she had decided, among the boys in the barrio or in all of Ormoc, none was her type. The short-lived War Brides Act cinched her plan. The word had spread that G.I.'s could marry Filipino women with no formal American citizenship and bring them to the United States. Reena would covet, and marry Geraldo, and desert her family, defy the heavens, and reinvent herself.

Planning, unmindful of any movie, Reena knew Vi would never have Geraldo. Vi didn't deserve him like Reena did. Reena learned English and office work so she could get a job anywhere. She budgeted for clothes, an outfit a week, because time would come when she'd have to spend their money on more important things, she and a husband.

When the movie ended, Reena smoothed out her crepe de chine dress, signaled her friends to wait outside, and walked to the sacristy. She would just thank him for the movie and introduce herself. She could only hope everything would work out.

She had The Eye. She could identify, in a crowded room, an ally. She knew Geraldo busied himself with the projector. He was pretending he didn't see her walk up to the camouflage left over from some gun batteries. She then gave her name, which he already knew, and tipped her head a lot, in that way. All he did was nod and gaze at her. She lit up his world at first glance.

She could make him vow that he would do anything for her, give up the playboy life, and drinking, and smoking, anything, just to see her radiant face every day. In reality as years passed, she realized he hadn't sacrificed much in most areas. Then again, she knew he believed she would eventually say she loved him. She suspected that he would chase her till she caught him.

She made herself elusive but in time, she might have to say she needed him.

Their first promenade, a date, was through town followed by her mother, aunts, curious, giggly town mates, and wistful adolescents. Reena knew Billina has had no rein on her for three years since the bombing. Reena wouldn't even go to church. Reena became a workaholic planning to take courses far away, not even anxious about separating from family. She ignored Ynez, her sister, the dark one, who also turned recalcitrant. She stopped kissing Billina good night. Reena had cried once in those three years, allowing herself to recall how her father died, perhaps looking for her between strafing, 1944 – or not.

Sighing, Billina had warned Reena. "Your hard- headedness will exasperate any husband. I will warn Geraldo. I will because him, I like."

The confident, saucy-eyed Americanized Filipino might tame Reena and become loving again. But Reena marrying someone divorced would insure a split from the church. She didn't care.

Reena had lost empathy from town mates since the bombing. Friends told Reena other fathers died. But their children grieved as if they had actually *loved* their parents.

Other survivors from the bombing like Reena seem to stand still next to her. Her drive and ambition and her lucrative sewing business sustained her. Although successful, she just didn't seem to care about people or their own tragedies.

She kept any sympathies short and swayed any attention in crowds back toward her. Reena knew what townspeople thought of her, even that hobo butcher, Dom.

Reena almost called off the engagement when Geraldo was quarantined and incommunicado on Angel Island in the San Francisco Bay. Without remorse, she instead contacted the officer whose laundry she washed. He had already returned to Texas.

"Why, yes, we still need a governess. You take care of paperwork in Manila, and I'll start proceedings here in the U.S.," the officer said. And of course, she did.

Word among Geraldo's friends, without access to phones, spread quickly. Geraldo returned and had to chase her in a jeep on Manila streets. When she haughtily agreed to sit with and make him explain, across the table she was dour and cold. No one would dare ask for her hand and then not write! She had sworn she would break up with Geraldo first. But he moved his hand near hers and looked deep into her Bette Davis eyes.

She balked. "I want to go to the States! I have a job, I have the chance to go!"

"The States? I'll take you. I'll bring you back there with me. No old officer would."

"He won't bother me. He's married." The words were dry in her mouth. Geraldo laughed.

"Oh, little girl, you don't know the ways of the world." Reena had flounced and moved away. Geraldo moved closer. He kissed her a long and passionate kiss, one she had never experienced before. My plan, she thought, and kissed him back.

Geraldo's flurry of logistics for her travels took sixteen months. He coordinated military permission to marry, then married her, added her to his benefits, moved her in with his parents, booked passage for the weeks-long travel on the S.S. Brewster, and saw out one tour. After their voyage, once stateside he had left Reena and their unborn child with a California relative while Geraldo finished his final tour. Even after that, Reena at twenty found herself in a foreign, cold-water flat with a newborn, another pregnancy, and a husband not ready to give up cigarettes, liquor, late nights, or life on the road. Reena reassessed the outcome to her plan.

She, unlike her many town mates, had made passage to the States. Could she tolerate brandy-soaked couplings resulting in more pregnancies or his continuous sexual needs? He demanded change; she defied him. She submitted to him woodenly. Saddled for years with three toddlers, in public she tolerated holding a hand of only one child and swiped away at the others.

She considered leaving them all. She could live with that self-imposed exile. She re-chinked the wall she had built. Because of lust, she chided herself, she had allowed Geraldo unguarded access. She filtered diluted affections to her kids who acclimated to her aloof manner.

She stayed. But distances and years built up between Reena and her children. A pang hit her this year to see "home". She made no promises to return. A place so far could pad other distances between her kids and herself. But she'd sidestepped telling them. No one needed to know what made Reena tick. She saw no reason to share why nothing moved her. With no effort, she remained as implacable as a statue, adamant, unrelenting, as if she were always this way.

The night before the Reunion, however, tripped her up. She had read the note Nita pushed under her door about the chickens. They had spoiled in the heat, useless for any Reunion.

On her lower bunk with Lainie above her, Reena squelched and gulped back tears.

XXXI

The dreams were chaotic. There were doors, lots of doors, none of them leading anywhere. Still, Lainie was obsessed opening as many as she could. One had Reena's face, close up, and something pushed her from behind, into her mother, who vanished. Lainie woke with a start, sweaty, and somewhat hung over. Groaning, she forced one eyelid to open and faced that ever-vigilant gecko, Pickle, who but for a glance, did not move. Lainie draped her head over the edge of the bunk.

Reena, very small, huddled on a chair behind the *balikbayan* boxes. She was baleful, sad, or numb. Lainie was puzzled. Reena was not easy to read on her day of days.

"The chickens went bad overnight." Reena announced, not even a good morning. Reena swiped at her cheeks. She was crying.

Lainie gave her a "pass", their unspoken creed allowing each other in vulnerable moments to pause their unwaged war, that cool exchange between parent and child that was seeded during adolescence and thin and weedy into adulthood. It would last an hour at most. Slipping off the bunk bed, Lainie sat on the lower bunk, waiting.

"Nita slipped a note under the door at three this morning. I had to pay for more chickens," Reena sniffed. "Oh-h-h, this is dumb."

Lainie ventured, "Well, that's not your fault there's no refrigeration."

"Why I'm doing this, hon, why am I here?" her mother began to spill. "I don't know these people here, they don't know me."

Hon, Lainie thought, she used that term when her guard is down.

Aloud, Lainie went on. "I haven't ever been here, but I wonder the same thing."

"I've been gone too long." Reena's admission hung in the air.

"You make fun of me," Reena blew her nose. "I see it. I see all of it, they laugh because I can't talk anymore. I forget our language.

They show me places I don't know. Nothing I know is here any-more." With impatience, Reena swiped at her eyes. "I laughed at my own mother. Ah, I'm too old to hang on to young ways."

Lainie let her fingers touch Reena's shoulder. "But you made good." She was careful. "You're your own proof. You made things happen. You came back."

"And brought nothing." Reena pitied herself. Lainie let her hand drop.

"So ashamed," Reena continued. "The Mayor didn't even look at me when we introduced ourselves. I live in the States! Mayor, hah! Of what? Stuck up, all of them."

"*Mapang.*" Lainie said. Reena blinked. She added, "Kind of like you."

"*Ay 'sus,* you know that word." Oblivious, Reena already by-passed her insult.

Lainie was silent. Reena kept the floor. Her eye started to drift sideways, the sign.

"I'm no 'shamed of NPA's." She growled as if Lainie had debated the subject. "Family or not, it's not my fault." Swift as a monsoon, she adds, "And you, taking off all the time!"

Lainie blurted back, "And you? You tell me nothing, but then I learn one thing at a time, and I'm embarrassed when I simper up to some mayor I don't know who ignores me. Me, not you. Whose idea is this to even reunite, piling these groups together under one roof? Do you *want* a war? And whatever you did when you lived here, they sure remember you now."

"They don't know me." Reena was defensive.

"And you didn't bring 'nothing', I'm not nothing. I'm here, we're both here, you know how that makes me feel?" Lainie stomped a distance away, breathing hard. "Jesus!"

"*Oy ssst,*" Reena hushed her. "They can hear you."

Lainie turned and just looked. "What? What can they hear?"

"The swearing, hon." She had turned the tables. "They're real Catholics."

Reena had just terminated her pass. Lainie checked a small clock. Half an hour had gone by. She scoured for her Reunion wear, a light, patterned pearl-button top and a cotton ankle-length skirt. At her side, she saw Reena reach for Lainie's hand. But she relinquished any hope that her mother would apologize when Reena herself swore, "Ay 'sus marjosep."

Lainie allowed Reena to rub her thumb on the back of Lainie's hand, her only show of affection. Like mother, like daughter, both held this penchant for skirting some truths. Mother and daughter were strangers – aliens – in their homeland. Pickle watched, keen and silent.

Lainie blinked. "Mom, was this grandma Billina's room?"

"You didn't know?" Reena, too, welcomed the change. "For her last ten years."

Lainie sighed. "How would I know?" She let this sink in. "Who but you would tell me?"

Reena shrugged, her practiced, calculated double-lift of her shoulders.

Lainie called above, "Grandma, if this gecko is your spirit, join us today. We're home." She turned. "Mom, is Horatio really NPA?" Reena only frowned. "What do I know?"

This day of days, Lainie sighed, Reena would not mar the mood by admitting anything.

In a sedate silence, Reena and Lainie dressed and applied makeup onto flaws and for a cheery facade, ruddied their cheeks and lips. As if royalty, Reena chose a bejeweled dark top and shiny skirt with low heels. She was again, Queen. And they emerged from the room.

Nita, Bonita, Sari-Sari, and Teri-Teri, already dressed and wearing corsages, gazed at Reena and Lainie. Kitchen ladies placed their palms on their cheeks, wistful. Bonita, crowded by them, moved with her elbow one eager woman, who flashed a toothy smile, eyes glistening.

In the C.R., Lainie stared outside. Whatever lighting that

shone that morning was mystic and unearthly. The lilting lyrics of Jun's CD song rode atop milk thistles in the air. She emerged. A tableau had formed in the main room. Commanding center stage, whatever force Reena bore was made even clearer. Helpers backed away as Reena strode by, majestic. Lainie thought, Billina's daughter did make good. Native and hybrid cultures would meet.

Nita prodded Lainie. "Come, people arrived already. They missed church to be here."

"Horatio?" Reena peeked around and above the throngs of kitchen people while Nita calmed and smoothed Reena's hair. "He went with Jun."

Lainie also peered around and asked, "Juan? Where's Juan?"

She had realized that she was now quite used to having him nearby, with his steady, soothing presence, his silence. Slightly impatient Nate pulled Juan out from his corner, his very white short-sleeve barong tagalog shone a silvery luster against his shiny chestnut-colored skin. Self-consciously, he swept a hand from his forehead to the back of his head, as if his short buzz cut would lie down. Lainie oohed. Juan blushed. Women hummed and aww'ed. He grinned shyly and waved them all off, half-turning away. He was delightful to watch.

As they all approached the red gate, Lainie thought she saw some women with large pots waddle down the road away from the house, one, then three, then more. A fourth carrier caught her eye and quickened her pace. Reena clicked her tongue. The women disappeared. From the bend careened cousin Vi who screeched her car to a halt and hurried to join them.

"Were you going to leave without me?" Vi puffed.

"The pavilion is around the corner," Bonita explained. "Nate will drive my mom, Até Reena, Lainie, and Juan. You can drive me and the girls."

Vi protested as the girls blanketed her but then shooed them into her car. Nate followed by Vi drove the dirt-packed bumpy road and arrived forty seconds later. Emerging from the jeep,

Lainie whispered, "We could've walked." Juan clicked his tongue.

Nate remarked, "Jeep or no, you arrive in style."

Like a blinder was removed, Lainie's view widened. Within the massive open-air roofed pavilion jammed against the outer perimeter were hundreds of kin, families with features, like hers, happy, elated strangers. Lainie stopped abruptly. "Too many — we're at the wrong place."

Nita urged her forward. "*Sigé sigé*: this is it. They're here for you."

At the entrance, both Reena and Lainie froze, and the room caught its collective breath. All together, the room faced the two women. And all at once, they cried, eyes glistening. With small wails that built to shouts and applause, the whole room exploded in an exuberant greeting.

"Mabuhi! Mabuhi!"

Lainie and Reena were projected forward toward the center. Lainie's tears flowed freely. She twirled to take in the whole pavilion. Her cheeks hurt from grinning. She began to shake the hand of each and every one of them, dressed in their best finery as they shed more tears when she touched them. Reena followed, hugging older women whom she recognized, and for others, timing each of her own handshakes to nanoseconds, inundated with brown, work-worn hands.

To Lainie's surprise, not all guests were relatives, though if they weren't, no one said. She saw the ladies on break from the market, wearing their same headscarves and aprons, each waving Lainie's small, stretchy hair bands, bawling. Splayed hands reached for hers. Lainie felt her wet cheeks stiff and ungiving. They looked so lovely, partial sets of teeth or none. Moving along the line, Lainie saw the postmistress who pushed free postcards at her. A beautiful, young woman with a child saddled on her hip waved, eyes shiny with tears. "*Até, Até* Reena." She was barely heard above the cacophony of voices. "Fausto, Missus, *asawa, esposa?*" Reena took her hand. "Lainie! Lainie, this is Fausto's wife and child!" Deling, seated with 'Fredo pawed the air. Lainie took and placed Deling's proffered hand to her own forehead. Jun, with the Night 1 window visitors huddled close, weeping and propelling their hands toward Lainie and Reena.

Jun bowed and cleared his throat reenacting his first greeting. "And how are you, ma'am, on this beautiful morning?" Jun's cohorts cheered and clapped him on his shoulders. Lainie straightened and responded, "*Maayong buntag*, Jun. *Kumusta ka?*" Guests howled in one big: "Ahhhh, *Maayo, salamat!*" They elbowed the tall Jun. Nearby, among other Lunao women, Evie thrust her latest newsletter, announcing, "*Sigé* na, celebrity ree-beww!"

Men howled in their awesome barong tagalog shirts. Wives wore stiff-edged sequined sleeve tops with light cotton bodices. Shy children pushed by parents held out tiny coconuts; kitchen helpers holding their forearms stood ill at ease. And then Reena and Lainie were heading toward a group set against the far perimeter of the pavilion. Reena and Lainie paused – NPA's.

Lainie did not recognize any of these men from the previous evening. Yet they stood straight, cradling their vintage M-1s and M-16 rifles. Undemonstrative, they only nodded. The two strongest, grimmest men flanked a seated older man. Hunchbacked, he straightened seeing them, wearing a somewhat ludicrous brimmed hat. He hugged a square thirty or thirty-five-inch flat item covered by floppy leather. As Lainie stepped forward, she noticed men flanking the elder close up ranks. In Lainie's ear, Nita whispered as if in church. "Marcelo, patriarch, Leyte's leader in the South." Lainie held out her hand. Marcelo extended his own rather thin, speckled hand toward her. His bodyguards relaxed. She performed the *mano*. The crowd was hushed. Reena pipped, "Oy," and turned to search for Nita for any special translation. As one bodyguard unwrapped the leather, Lainie gazed at the old man who was dark more in mood than in color, hunched like Sitting Bull had, in an old photo. Marcelo's stressed leather chaps looked very heavy. He met her gaze. His guard still struggled with the tough leather thong. The old man dispensed a judgment with a glance. He was bound to hold court with dignity and respect and still remain unreadable. The guard released the thong and revealed a picture frame.

Turning the frame, the elder held up the very old oil painting. Posed straight on was a man, somber, in dated clothes, turn of the century. The plain black background was marred by cracks in paint the shade of yellowed smoke, ashen from campfires, Rembrandt-like in mood.

Nita listened to the old man's words, intoning, cadenced, and turned to Reena and Lainie.

Nita began. "His name is Marcelo, leader and patriarch. He stood side by side next to your granduncle in many battles. Now, the Madawawing Mountains hold your grand-uncle. This is his portrait. He was a very brave man. He is called Fausto."

Reena's eyes widened. "Ay 'sus, Ynez's son is his namesake!"

Her blasphemous term halted everyone, everyone who knew Jovita and young Fausto, so everyone. Lainie cleared her throat. The crowd leaned forward.

"May I?" Lainie's question hung in the air. Marcelo nodded.

"Mom, show him your camera." Lainie urged and bent to inspect the delicate painting. The elder had glanced up at the guard who, in turn, shook his head no at Reena. Lainie memorized each lump in the buckling canvas, the centered composition, and like saving frosting on cake, she focused on the eyes. She almost reeled. Lainie saw pinpointed pupils mesmerizing and menacing. They broadcast her granduncle's legacy and venerated leadership. They held a ruthlessness taken and given at great costs. He had separated from family. That choice had earned him a dismissed existence. She stared a long time till Reena poked her. *Manong* Marcelo shoved forward and then pulled the frame away from Lainie, confusing her. Did he want her to have it?

Nita looked calm. "He does not want to just give."

Nita whispered to Reena, who hesitated and tipped her head, that way. Reena addressed Marcelo for Lainie. "No. No, thank you. *Salamat, manong*. No."

Reena pushed Lainie forward as Marcelo called to their backs. Nita hurriedly advised Lainie, "Don't look back. Think of *harana*, joining the man means yes – same thing."

Lainie and Reena shook hands while others in the crowd glanced warily at Marcelo and his entourage. Lainie spoke out the side of her mouth to Nita. "Is he watching?"

Not looking back, Nita replied, "He hasn't sent his sons after us – good sign."

They faced Dom with his clingy men folk, angling for any fumes of Dom's free lifestyle. With his lower lip, Dom pointed at Marcelo for Lainie and raised a warning eyebrow.

Throughout this drama, the crowd was amazingly patient.

She realized then, that she had not seen Jose.

They approached table with its crowning centerpiece, Dom's masterpiece – *lechon*. Behind the table were chairs for guests and hosts. Before sitting, Lainie and Reena hugged most warmly their hosts throughout the week, youngest to oldest: the girls blubbered and wiped their eyes; Bonita and Nate enveloped them both; Juan put his arm around Reena yet gave a longer, swingy hug to Lainie. Almost usurping the last honor meant for Nita and Horatio, Vi moved ahead of them. But Reena gave her stink eye, pointing to a far chair. Then tearfully, gratefully Nita, Horatio, Reena and Lainie hugged, signaling the start of festivities. No Serrañaos, or any city officials, or even Mike were present.

As Vi passed Lainie, she remarked, "Oy, jackfruit," referring to the goose-bumpy, bulbous, lime-green orb on the table. Lainie, tired of Vi's presumptions, spoke up.

"I asked what it was when I first saw it." Lainie added, "I'd say the jackfruit's mine."

"*Nangkà*," Vi hmphed. "Like Reena, so much attention," and started to sit next to Reena. But Nita also elbowed Vi to sit at the end. Someone thumped on the microphone.

"*Maayong buntag, Kummusta ka*, we will now hear Mass by Father Roddis. Father, if you please, and everyone, please rise."

Lainie hissed at Reena, "Really? High Mass or Low?" meaning, long or short.

Vi, pouting, straightened to assess some dishes that lay furthest away and then slouched.

"That's everything, isn't it?" Lainie murmured to which the priest, centered between two altar boys, glared pointedly at chatty Lainie before beginning his Call to his brethren. Lainie cringed. The congregation's response was in English. She squeaked to Nita, "Not in Latin?" Nita hid a grin, "Not since 1978." Lainie grimaced. She was a lapsed Catholic for over two decades.

Luckily, the priest conducted the Low Mass. Except for Reena and Lainie, most everyone else knelt on the bare floor. Lainie had already earned a stink-eye from Father Roddis. Finally Father Roddis spoke, "The peace of The Lord be with you." The room mumbled, "And also with you".

A flurry of activity began.

The kitchen women filed in with plates and platters of food, all different types of greens and gourds, much like the ones Lainie had collected from the market women. They pointed, *that's from us!* Next came mouth-watering pancit, lumpia, kare-kare, sotohan, fish soup, sinigang, pinakbet, and of course, adobo with pork, and roasted oddly chopped chickens, and rice, rice, rice. The controversial *balut* (fermented chicken embryos) were placed delicately toward the end of the table just next to the section of sweets including *babingka*. One plate was piled high with Lainie's breakfast fave, *pandesal* next to pans of sweet leche flan. Men from the barrio carried in cases of soda and beer and placed them near Father Roddis's chair. To the rumbling shouts and cheers of male guests, Jun wheeled in on a dolly full bottles of rum, again positioned near the beer and Father Roddis.

A queue line began to form. The delay was the priest intoning

Grace, changing into street clothes, and taking his place at the head of the line.

Guests leaned forward, their many bare toes in flip-flops braced as if on a starting block. Their children, many, many children, never flounced, unlike impatient, annoyingly privileged kids back home. Not even the babies cried. The travelers traveled out of respect for the family, out of curiosity, and then for the food. They had waited another hour through both the Mass and Grace. Theirs was a culture used to waiting.

The lineup included priest, the host family, Reena, Lainie, and altar boys. Vi was last.

Reena spoke low to Nita, "Oy, she will make me pay."

The group waddled slowly alongside the food, filling their plates. Lainie was selective figuring the jackfruit would fill plate two. Guests would use spoons to cut and scoop. They all sat except Horatio who announced to the whole room, "You may now join us." A stampede ensued.

XXXII

All the guests sprang into action, dashing pell-mell toward the food table, grabbing a paper plate, or two, and dishing onto them towering spoonfuls of lechon, pancit, lumpia and everything else. Lainie stared, open-mouthed. Lines of people surrounded all sides of the table. By the time everyone regained their floor space, earlier groups were back for seconds. The main table guests were already full and lounging. Still, Lainie chomped on her food watching the parade and was aware of Reena's eyes on her. Lainie felt she should somehow deflect attention away from herself to showcase Reena. She focused on the girls, eyes shiny with excitement.

Lainie tried to memorize as many varied faces and shapes as she could, from matte-like complexions and thin hair to unblemished faces and glowing manes. Everyone smiled. Lainie wondered if they could be swayed by this show of wealth, the food, the boxes, the radio ad?

Lainie noted that Nita had leaned close. "Some of these people have walked night and day over the mountains since Wednesday." Lainie counted: five days.

A lump rose to her throat. "Ohh . . . oh." She recovered. "Is there any more *lechon*?"

"Only another platter," Nita explained. "We kept some for us at the house." She saw Lainie's surprised look. "There's enough for forty or fifty more. When it's gone, it's gone."

Lainie felt small. "I had no idea. I should contribute something. How did you even . . ."

Nita patted her hand, as usual. "No questions. Go get some more before it's gone."

Lainie rose from her seat and headed back to the now depleted food table. She looked but could not find the jackfruit. Puzzled, she walked the length of the table before returning.

Bonita chewed, pacing herself. "Looking for your jackfruit? Go ask Vi."

Vi sat at the far end of the table, munching and discarding remnants of the jackfruit's rough shell. Vi was specifically ignoring Lainie. Then she finally spoke. "Oy, did you have any jackfruit? Mmm, very tasty, like pineapple, so sweet." Vi continued eating without apology.

When Lainie told her mother why the jackfruit disappeared, Reena's eyes became saucers, one eye leaning to the side. This signaled true volcanic anger. Nita shifted, coughing.

Reena fumed. "She does this all the time! This isn't her

Reunion! She's here every year!"

Lainie glanced at Nita. "Let me get you a soda, mom."

She strode past girls dancing to the deejay's American music and maneuvered by the case of rum manned by Horatio and Jun. If a guest had not yet claimed their full bottle of rum, Horatio would hand over a bottle or if a guest already claimed one, Horatio would eyeball Jun. The nearly foot taller Jun would urge that guest to return later. Free is free to a point.

Lainie picked out two sodas, chilled and drippy from the melting ice in the coolers and headed back. Sari-Sari, flushed and excited, pulled her into the group of pre-teen dancing girls. Lainie made a little attempt moving about with a bottle in each hand. She begged off to deliver the soda to her mother. The girls pouted but formed the circle again to dance with each other.

A man with black, curly tousled hair, rather well built in a short sleeve checkered shirt, long grey pants and wearing flip-flops stood in her way, a smile on his face. He was missing every other upper tooth. Lainie edged past him, though he continued to face her, grinning.

"Oy, he's still watching you," Bonita teased back at the table. "Talaga, another admirer. You will be married before you leave."

"Been there, done that," Lainie quipped, giving Reena her soda.

"You are . . .wild, like Até says?" Bonita took on a look like a soap-opera fan.

Lainie gauged her answer, to reveal or not reveal. She sighed. "Almost hitched in Taos, on Mykonos, San Francisco, Boulder, to *puté*, to not *puté*, to American, to not American . . ."

"Ay 'sus!" Bonita swore. "I had only two boyfriends by age 22! Can you count yours?"

"It's quality, not quantity." Lainie laughed like shattered glass on rocks. She turned to Nita. "Please, the painting – what was going on, why did Marcelo act that way?"

Nita sighed. "He does not just give. He trades." Reena

nodded, slurping balut, a delicacy, aka a fermented chick embryo.

"But I don't have anything. If I did, I would, Mom, for that painting of our grand-uncle, Fausto. What would you give? Our grandfather abandoned the land, and Fausto could've regained it. Wouldn't the portrait be a good option to that, as a family legacy? Mom?"

Reena stared at a point above her. Nita poked her.

"Your grandfather did want the land," Reena answered. "It wasn't really his turn. He wasn't actually the oldest."

Lainie squinted. She needed to force some focus. "Okay, so Fausto was the oldest. It was always Fausto's land, the oldest grand-uncle, never our actual grandfather's, is that it?"

"Sort of." Reena was cryptic. Nita sighed. Reena added, "A good part was."

Nita swore: "Rinang, cuz, ay *nagumpisana naman*," surprisingly, a Tagalog phrase.

"Yes, all right, maybe most of the land. I can't talk here."

"Synopsize!" Lainie was adamant, meaning, pissed.

"Yes!" prodded Nita. "How she says."

Girls eeked while dancing to music that switched to a lively rock and roll tune.

" 'Synopsize', '*sus*." Reena clicked her tongue and took a breath. "It's Fausto's land to the 1900's, but he gave it up once he rebelled."

"He did not," corrected Nita.

"He became an insurrecto! The Spanish were leaving, Americans come in, and instead of surrendering, he resists them, too, after all those years we're under Spain. You'd think he had given in to a worse power, with the States, tch, tch. But family can't hold his land for him."

Nita interrupted. "They did until the 1950s during Billina's last years. She . . ."

"My mother could not do anything." Reena blustered, "Against the City? Against Luis?"

"Assessors post abandoned lots to auction if the taxes have not been paid." Nita took over. "If no one pays or extends their rights because someone is in hiding, they auction to the highest bidder." To Reena she said, "You're the oldest. You could've done something."

"I was just married, I couldn't come right back, I had a baby, I traveled alone coming here, I mean, going, leaving, ay, you're mixing me up," Reena sputtered. Nita just regarded her.

"*Até.*" Nita pointedly used the formal term. "You were never mixed up. You always knew what you were doing. Geraldo – did you ever tell him you had land? Ever?"

Their silence now was louder than the girls shouting for Lainie to come join them again. Nita, forbearing cousin, faced off Reena, their relationship more defined now in Lainie's eyes. Reena had made a lifetime of maneuvering people to her will. Reena left the islands and her mother. For many decades, Nita cared for Billina who, alone, had held onto Leyte land for a future Plebiña. Reena married Geraldo, riding his U.S. citizenship so one foot was in Ormoc. She took over forty years to return. Eventually, she tagged Lainie as the means to reclaim the land that Reena had abandoned, land battled for by Nita years after Fausto left, then Fausto's brother, and then Reena's mother. Since then, hundreds of hectares had been land waiting for Reena.

Lainie felt hollow realizing that Reena had painted her wild, the least likely type to take on town magnates. She felt worse that Reena used, even abused Nita, expecting her to defer and to kowtow and to do the dirty work. That was how she could keep planning for the trip. Lainie blinked. If anyone could, Nita connected former and current Reena and knew her true intentions.

"Did I ever tell him? What good would that do?" Reena blazed a hole through Nita's reserve. "Yes, I know what I'm doing. I even know Marcelo would give me a painting and protection *if* I pursued the land. I knew what I'd lose, too." Ever so slightly she glanced at Lainie. Changing her tone, she added, "Let's empty the balikbayan boxes and get rid of this junk."

185

Nita held fast. "Oh, Call it junk now." Reena blurted. "This was for you! All for you!"

Guests drifted elsewhere, away from the table and leftovers. Lainie sank a bit.

In one move, Reena blocked a tradeoff: her daughter for a painting aka, Lainie's life with NPAs. Exchanging the painting for Lainie may have placed the contested land back in Reena's hands. Would family really do that to family, Lainie wondered, for a Cause? Would she?

After a moment, during which music filled the space and girls danced, men swallowed rum, mountain life paused, and generations touched, Lainie spoke. "The *balikbayans*?"

Again festive, Reena waved them both toward the boxes that had been propped up behind their head table. Those boxes had mesmerized and enticed anyone who had not spent nights among them in a small, locked room. Lainie frowned, seeing the tattered boxes from all sides.

Vi sauntered by and looked sideways into both boxes gnawing on a succulent, crisp pigskin morsel. Reena *sss-sst*'ed. Vi disdainfully ignored her. As feasters picked at the food table and the deejay lowered the music, Nate thumped on the microphone by the podium.

"Everyone, *kadiyot lang. Maayong buntag. Kumusta ka! Ako si* Nate." At ease, Nate radiated confidence. Lainie, impressed, Bonita toss her head. "He's good, eh? Salesman!"

"MABUHI!" The crowd, tipsy, issued a short, noisy toast at the head table, Nate continued. "We thank Father Roddis for the Mass and for all the help on the food, and now what you've been waiting for, some words from both our guests of honor, Reena, and her daughter, Lainie, from Mukwonago, Wisconsin in the United States! Let's have some applause!"

The crowd's encouragement was exuberant. Lainie was shell-shocked. "Huh?"

Reena assumed that face of total wonderment. Coy, she

smoothed down her bejeweled top. Nate guided her on the three stairs toward the podium.

Lainie entreated Nita. "Please, I don't know how to speak, how could I . . .?"

But Juan had joined them and whispered into Lainie's ear. She stood stock still listening while Reena and Nate adjusted the height and volume of the mike. Juan patted Lainie's back.

"Salamat, Juan, salamat," said Lainie. Now Reena spoke.

The huge banner behind Reena with her name, her city, Lainie's name, and "Welcome" had been stitched with ready-made letters onto purple felt, faux velvet for faux dynastic royalty.

"Um, everybody, um, *kadiyot lang. Maayong buntag. Kumusta ka! Ako si* Reena," Reena began. Lainie vowed that she would not be the third to repeat Nate's sequence or Reena's.

"Are you enjoying yourselves?" Reena echoed Nate's introduction nearly verbatim.

Reena continued. "I, uh, was here forty-two years ago. You kids wouldn't know that so thank you for coming, uh, *ay, 'su–,*" she caught herself. "Um, we've been staying with my cousin, Nita, oh, and Horatio, you know them, uh, sorry, this is English, 'cause people tell me my Cebuano is not so good anymore, heh-heh. *Dili ko makasulti'g Cebuano. Oy,* my daughter's with me, she should be married now, oy, she's single now."

Lainie dipped her head. Reena went on. "No, she's good, she writes, all the time, writing, about this, about me, I think. But we come here, to see you, to show you, I mean, her, my town where I lived. So different now, and I miss it, I miss you all. *Ay 'sus,* I gonna cry now. Um, I brought some things, we do a what-you-call lottery, maybe you see the things we have back home, I mean, this is home, too, well, you know, all the same, here, there, except for you – you're not there. So-o-o, I come back to visit. I have not changed, not in how I miss you, a lot."

By now, listeners have quieted down. And I follow that, thought Lainie.

"Okay, okay, enough, so now the boxes," Reena switched the mood. "You all got two numbers, then . . ." Nate whispered to her. "Oh-oh, so get a ticket from Nate, and, and Nate will call them out, so then you come up, *sigé na*." Reena moved away from the mike but pushed past Nate again to grab the stem. "Again, thank you. Listen to my daughter now, she's good. Bye."

Jesus God in heaven help me, prayed Lainie as the applause, a good part of it, sounded somewhat half-hearted and confused. Reena pawed the air at Lainie to *come, come up here*. Lainie found herself onstage. Nate encouraged her. "Just follow your mother. Just smile."

Lainie stood facing the crowd split into various groups throughout the pavilion. She spoke softly. "*Salamat maraming po.*" She was greeted with polite applause. "My name is Lainie." she began. From the head table, she could hear her mother burst out. "Oy, I didn't give my name!" Nita, shushing her, pointed with her lower lip at the banner behind Lainie's head.

Okay, Lainie bit her lip. Speak. Smile. Synopsize.

"Both my parents left the Philippines to be a young, newly married couple in the U.S. We, none of us, were born here, but I always wondered what living here would be like. I still don't really know." Her pause heightened the already perfectly still response. She barreled on. "I didn't study like I should have before coming here. People tell me, I don't know the ways, and that's true, but – I want to. The ways are fuzzy to me. I keep using this American lens of mine, I mean . . . I'm just too American at times. I apologize. I'm sorry. But a few very helpful people make me see more, and I thank them. I know I ask a whole lot of questions. But, that's just one way for me to, to know. To know you, all of you."

Lainie heard sniffles. "Like why yes means No; or what's the taste of jackfruit which I still don't know. But mostly, what parts of me are so much like you, and vice versa. So as short as this visit is I just want to thank you for showing me – me. And you. Everyone I've met, or passed on the street, please just know: I will always remember you. Salamat, salamat."

Lainie moved back from the podium and only heard the echo of the room's single claps, which built into continuous applause. Nita poked her. "Get up. Get up. Lanita Plebiña Cortez."

Lainie blinked. *Ay 'sus marjosep*, She just got it: "Lainie" was Lanita's namesake.

Eyes glistening, Lainie reviewed the clues given and ignored. Reena had honored Nita naming one daughter not after her mother, Billina, or her sister, Ynez, but after *this* Plebiña, her real best friend. The noise died down, and music cranked up. Nate signaled. "Not now, later."

He shushed everyone vigorously. "*Sigé na*, lottery! Oy, ssssst, lottery, lottery!"

A record scratched to a stop. Reena, amazed, said, "What you say, hon, you made good."

"I got good titchers." She pointed her lip at Juan. "Our private glossary of terms."

She and Juan had, for a few minutes during every day, had been practicing terms to repeat before dropping off to sleep. This paid off with her improvised Reunion day speech.

Some men carried the rapidly dissembling *balikbayan* boxes center. Some women, one Lainie recognized from the kitchen, bagged some leftovers. Nate called out, and half the room inched up their hands. Nita translated that they admitted they spoke English! "They just don't use it."

Lainie thought, "Well, I'll be damned."

"So please tell the others that I call a number, that person gives me his number and then picks from either box. And thank *Até* Reena." He trilled. "Three, nine, eight. Three, nine, eight."

People manning the lottery were distracted from manning cases of Tondena Manila Rum Gold. First, three men pilfered bottles. This affected festivities. Drunken scenes erupted.

A short woman with a blocky, Dutch boy cut of her silver-flecked hair politely held out her square paper, sedately chose an item, bowed to Reena, and nearly ran back to her seat.

Each successive winner displayed more and more bravado as the lottery continued. Children looked back to their families and held up three or four items till an authority-type grunted and nodded. One had scampered to his seat but returned and *mano*'ed Reena quickly. Men sauntered, drawing up their full four-foot-ten height, scoured the box, and with a slight bow turned away. People scrambled faster, lingering in boxes, bowed, and tripped off. Nate hinted that they should "please know that *Até* Reena brought these gifts many miles across the ocean, i.e., so pay your respects." Seeing that little would change, Nate called a timeout. Reena sweated, and Nita spoke. "Let them dance now."

Vi swore, "*Ay 'sus*, nothing in there, just junk."

Lainie couldn't help herself and shot back, "You do know you owe me a jackfruit, right?"

Vi recoiled, wide-eyed, and turned to Reena. "How she talks to me!"

Reena eyeballed Vi. "You're junk! Call my things junk. You told me to buy these!"

A deejay blared the latest popular pop tune. One little boy danced among many teen girls. In a corner men hoisted rum bottles. The coterie of girls on the dance floor had doubled. Lainie turned at a touch on her back. 'Fredo indicated Deling afar off pawing at the air toward her.

Lainie thought quickly. "Ay, 'Fredo, tell *Até* we'll have a quiet visit tomorrow, *sigé*?"

Like a Fellini movie, scenes spun by Lainie depicting all these types at home in their barrio. Men lounging near the case of rum men hailed her, "Missus, ma'am, rum? Good rum!"

She hesitated. Drinks till then had been San Miguel beer and a Scotch. A shot of rum wouldn't hurt. She approached. They cheered. Someone launched across the sea of bodies to snatch an unused plastic cup, wipe the rim with a napkin and hold it aloft for a pour. He then gave Lainie the cup, the same man with curly hair and missing teeth. She thanked him, took the cup, and toasted them all. The men began chanting. Lainie recognized it: "Down the Hatch".

Demurely shaking her head, Lainie sipped but then downed the shot. Aiee, that went down harsh, but she maintained. Toasted again, she announced, *"I shall return."*

She could hear the guffaws directed at her back. She then allowed Sari-Sari to pull her toward the flush-faced girls. Another cheer went up. Lainie saw again, the applause was for her.

Reminded that this was Reena's shining hour, she saw her mom holding her own court. Women stroked her bejeweled sleeve. Vi stood separate from this newest, adoring public.

The girls were trying to get Lainie to show them some American steps. Lainie demonstrated a simple scoot, with attitude and then a back beat, syncopated move. The girls screamed and followed suit. Some querulous tones from the peanut gallery inferred that the American is showing off. Someone tapped Lainie, a man in his twenties. His buddies hooted. She guessed they dared him to dance with a guest of honor. Another partner cut in. Other boys now tagged their secret crushes. The crushes had achieved their original goals – meeting guys.

A screeching feedback from the microphone – Nate cupped the wand. "Lottery!"

The deejay cut the music. The girls play-acted their utter sorrow separating from their conquests and then immediately retrieved their numbers.

Back at the table, Reena half-whispered, "Well, you're popular. Look, these women want me to write to them." She showed all the little sheets with names and addresses on them. "They think I'm coming back next year and will stay with them. That means, send money first."

Nate's calm demeanor was tested. Two people approached with the same number. Another winner brought a bag to stuff. Nate called three numbers at a time to speed things up; it took nearly forty minutes to get rid of nearly one hundred items. Some guests compared what they chose to what others chose, a prettier top or a larger scarf. Toys, too obscure to figure out, were already broken. People depleted the rum case; boredom and testosterone reared up. Jun loomed over one obnoxious, tottering rum thief; men backed off. Horatio's closest friends carried in a couple dozen more Tondena Manila Gold. Lainie, just nursing her rum, got woozy. The girls pulled her center to dance; men urged her to drink. Lainie's line of dancers blocked Mr. Curly, hovering. Nate barked, "Lottery!" She felt the whole room watched their soap opera laying bets: Will or won't Mr. Curly dance with Leyte's version of *Dynasty*'s daughter?

By the next lottery, winners chose their winnings first and barely acknowledged Reena.

"Aiee," sighed Nita. "People, people."

Lainie hid a grin. Even afar, people behaved like those in the States. Obsessed, they, too, had expectations that Reena's samples of consumerism would also improve their lives.

Music blasted. Mr. Curly dashed forward. To cheers, Lainie danced with him. She saw a stately, white-haired man bow to Reena. She rose to dance with him, employing her deprecating shrug, implying no-no with yes-yes in her eyes.

Mr. Curly had no rhythm. Bent, he swung his arms back and forth as if pumping in one place at a foot race. The audience sighed soft, but sympathetic chuckles. Lainie realized they all knew he couldn't dance a lick.

"So what's your name?" Lainie attempted conversation. The English threw him. He gyrated wildly, panicked. She attempted, "Um, *unsay imu 'an?*" He brightened. " 'Jandro. Alejandro," He tried, too. "Lainie? Lainie is *maanyag*. Beautiful." She melted.

By now, all the girls had partners, teasing, eyes cast down. Mountain parents hailed their sons or daughters. Mothers and families with bags strapped to their backs were anxious to trek back up the mountains before nightfall. They were hearty souls not overstaying their welcome.

Nate must have detected the change as well and signaled the deejay to stop mid-song. "Lottery! Last of lottery! More items than people now! Last of the lottery!"

Some travelers put their packs on the floor. Lainie, who had graced 'Jandro with an extra dance, finalized their public, soap-opera episode. She shook 'Jandro's hand, thanking him. They both knew they would not dance again. To full applause, he headed toward his buddies who clapped him on the back. They seemed very proud of his diligence and his attempt at dancing.

Reena, however, was taking a much longer time saying farewell to Mr. Stately White. He bent forward patting her hand, his face close to hers, till he departed. Like a girl again, she pulled her shoulders up in glee at the grinning Nita and truculent Vi. Lainie teased her. "Gwapo."

Nate called out numbers but revelers glanced inside the box and walked away, giftless. Reena waved her hand. "Aah, give the junk to whoever wants them." Lainie sighed. Months of collecting clothes, toys, radios, small electronics, packing, repacking, traveling with and now dispensing items from the balikbayan boxes led to this: Reena would throw them to the crowds.

Nate nodded and was about to speak into the mike when a lone woman walked toward the center past the two boxes. How she walked struck Lainie, austere and majestically regal. Her white-streaked hair was pulled back. On her clear, gleaming neck she wore a huge brooch. Its cuts caught the sun's lowering rays throughout the pavilion. She wore silver earrings and a bracelet and glided by in her long, slithering skirt. She was like a proud mare, nostrils flared. Ragged clothes did not look ragged on her. Bare-foot, she did not move as if she was shoeless.

She bowed first to Nate and then to the head table. She bowed the longest to Reena. She spoke quietly and directly. Reena leaned toward Nita, who took the cue to translate into her ear. The woman remained prominently center within the pavilion.

Whatever she said transfixed all who could hear and understand her. She implored with dignity, her inflections posing rhetorical questions. Some listeners gasped. There was no mockery or impatience. Then, bowing again, the woman turned and walked away, holding up a dismissive hand at the box. She continued out the building, the guests' eyes lowered as she passed. No one was with her. No one followed.

Nate broke the silence. "Everyone, the numbers are over. Take whatever's inside." There was a slight pause, and then people pounced.

XXXIII

"Do we clean up?" Lainie yawned, already knowing the answer, which Nita verified. "No, others will do it. Let's go home."

The horde that decimated the remaining *balikbayan* box was thorough. Anyone who thought to have a chance at leftovers had given up, shell-shocked at the destruction and altercations over certain items. Retrieving their packed bags for the journey over Madawawing Mountains, some people shook their heads, gathered their kin, and traipsed out of the pavilion.

Lainie watched Horatio searching the room. Someone pointed outside, and at a jogger's gait, he left. She had been wrong about him because she favored Nita. She guessed the whole barrio knew what he represented, the town counterpart for the jungle NPAs. Still, perhaps there might be a female in town whose role matched his. Meeting constantly with him, she, too, might bear the Catholic shame breaking Commandments Number Six and

Nine, the coveting issues. But supporting a cause, like Lainie's exiled students, he should be forgiven, right? Lainie hooked her arm into Nita's and got in return reassuring pats. *Way problema.* Nita would be just fine.

Jun's standoff with the short rum thief flared again before the festivities died down. Unknown to Lainie, the shorter man was a kind of NPA wanna-be, hanging around but not associated with them. He had issues salved by rum. Reena's forty-second year Reunion went off with so far only a few hitches. Island relatives collected new memories. Lainie breathed deeply.

She hoped the whole event was worth the baggage fee. Reena claimed to bring what she could to her countrymen. Lainie concluded, what Reena had was an elusive life and a culmination of needless things. A rhinestone bracelet sparkles but will not brand the owner entitled. Buffed shoes will not guarantee privilege. Reena was still one of them in that way. She was not a mayor or one with power or status. She was not even anyone with land. She bought wholesale her own forty-some-year-old dream, symbols of abundance, the flexibility to buy what she wanted for show, even junk, trinkets, breakable toys, or polyester passed off as silk.

Reena herself had dismissed the boxes too readily. She met her goal, returning like MacArthur. Like Rockwell's painted family, she herself had been delivered from Want. For those left holding the bag —Nita — barrio life waxed and waned between the best and the worst of times. Family, mindful or not about their own subsistence living, still held their own.

Back at the house, a slew of men again occupied the yard under the awning. All traces of a pig roast were gone except for a slight aroma mingled with that of the chicken batch number two. Night sounds already commandeered the air around them. Even crickets sounded free of restrictions, resounding loudly. The women passed the men posturing in the yard, simmering in some undecipherable argument. In the Plebiña house, the family moved to their rooms to change. Although tired, they all still regrouped around the main room's table, like all the nights before. Horatio disappeared but returned with a bottle of a popular rum which Lainie could see close up. This was Don Papa rum, with a gecko on a man's head and a bug-eyed *tarsier* tucked in his scarf. The label was imprinted Bleeding Heart Rum Company, Mt. Canlaon – *The Spirit of Don Papa Lives On In Us All, 40% Alcohol*. Good enough. Lainie would like to drink to that.

To her surprise, Horatio held up the bottle to her. "Try? Yes?" She nodded. He poured again for Nate as well. Juan and all women demurred, settling for sodas instead.

"But you would," Horatio remarked, tipping the glass toward Lainie. "You try anything."

She bristled and felt her eye travel sideways.

Nita spoke up. "What if she did? Maybe she's not so invisible that way."

Before anyone could comment, she spoke directly to Lainie. "Your speech was very nice. You are brave admitting anything like that. Americans don't admit to much."

Lainie cooled off. Pointedly, she toasted Reena, never admitting anything. "Hear, hear."

Her mother just shrugged and then blurted, "Vi owes you another jackfruit."

They all laughed seated around the table. From their room, the girls were on their stomachs on the bed, listening sleepily. Lainie bet her lone piña bag she'd never see "jack" from Vi.

Everyone sighed in unison. Lainie asked, "So what did that shiny woman say to you, Mom, the one who ignored the box?"

The cousins shifted, shaking their heads.

Nate was curious. "She was shiny, wasn't she?"

"She radiated like she was kind of ethereal, not quite really here," Lainie explained.

"She is a descendant of Fausto," Nita began. "Direct line to the land, oldest child."

Lainie blinked, exclaiming, "Well, that fixes everything,

doesn't it? She's the one to file, I mean, if she's Fausto's direct line instead of from Fausto's brother's line, what about that?"

"She doesn't want the land, either," Reena said.

All Lainie could muster was, "Huh."

First, everyone felt they deserved this unattainable land, and now, no one wanted to touch the land. Around the table, the women were calm. The men remained distant.

Reena swallowed. "Her name is Ikapati. When she heard the radio ad, she wondered, '*will we contest the land? Will we again own it, as the right side of the family, with what is our legacy?*' She asked if without doubt could we be one bloodline that is truly of Leyte?"

The men, Horatio, Nate, and Juan, were respectfully quiet. Here in this setting, the position of matriarch re-gained its status – the purer blood ran in these women's families.

"The right side," Lainie echoed.

Nita was blunt. "Luis's Spanish father, Don Padre, married in but spawned a bastard. Luis was always the most ambitious. Ambition runs in his line. He favored his father who gave him the other siblings' inheritances – to a, a . . ."

"Bastard," Lainie again echoed. Only the remote lineage, the bastard, wanted the land. Lainie took a sip of rum. "I need a score card, but go on."

"She said . . ." Reena glanced at Nita. "She said I should let the land go. She said, I had already let go, not when I left but when I married out."

Out meant, out of the race, foreign.

"Out?" asked Lainie, "But dad's a Filipino."

"He's American," Nita emphasized. "He's the reason Reena would never return in body or soul. You abandoned land, and for your love, we lose a legacy." Nita turned to Reena. "Does that sound like you, sacrificing anything for love?" The question seemed harsh. Lainie detected that Nita's patience, at this moment, had worn thin with this talk and with Ikapati's appearance.

Lainie had to ask. "Did you blame Mom all these years, *Até*, for leaving?"

A bass rumble outside grew to a mild roar. Juan tipped his head to see past Lainie. Nita composed her reply. "Ikapati says Reena should let go. Well, I must, too."

Lainie willed Reena to respond. Tension hung like a coconut poised to fall.

Finally Reena said, "I know what you do for us, for me, and what you still do. I do."

The mild roar outside had now evolved into an outright brawl. Men were shouting in different dialects. In a flash, Juan was at the window. Yet, as if poked, he stepped back and looked at Horatio. Lainie figured this was a head of household standoff: should Juan or Horatio intercede? Horatio sighed. Nita touched his arm and pointed her lower lip toward Juan: let him.

Horatio pushed his lower lip and lifted his chin. "*Sigé sigé!*" He signaled Juan, who whipped open the door and dashed out, amazing Lainie. Juan was sprite and had already wormed his way to the center of the altercation just as Horatio and the women came to the door to watch.

In the clearing, *Manong* Marcelo's clan faced off with 'Gundo's unit. The most vocal, Jose, spat English at the pugnacious rum thief wanna-be: "No manners born in a sty." The groupie swayed, drunk, but glanced at the house. Lainie stared. Jose was proving Mr. rum thief wanna-be could not retaliate in English.

Jose needled him. "Igorot."

Lainie gasped. She knew the term. Reena had called her Igorot, a lot.

Mr. rum thief wanna-be was rankled. He understood that epithet. Igorots were at the St. Louis Fair 1904, displayed like monkeys, thought to be too stupid to resist white men relocating their whole village for months. They died in their first winter, their tribal tattoos sliced from their bodies still on display at the Smithsonian. Inebriated and swaying, Marcelo's men did not jump to defend Mr. rum thief wanna-be.

"Oy, here, take this, *sigé na*, go, go." Juan held a bottle of rum. Silence countered the combination of rum, reunions, and hormones. Juan uncorked the bottle and lifted it to each mouth timing their swigs, still with a calm tone in English, following Jose's lead.

"The men already here last night, these NPA are local, for the people. Marcelo and his six sons are also are NPA. Oy, save some, *tawo*. They're with Abu Sayyaf in Mindanao. Radical. They move everywhere. I believe this is what both groups do, *sigé*, for all of us. At the Reunion, you, small man, why be small in so many ways?" Some men laughed, as one guzzled rum.

Mr. rum thief slurred, "*Kinsa nakadawat sa rum?* Who gets? *Sigé*, me, I do! For them!"

Juan was unflappable, moving among the men with the bottle.

"Ay, you? The reunion is over, the *family gets the rum*, are you *gago*, stupid? You were not right." Juan clicks his tongue. "'*Manong Marcelo sent me to get rum.*' Why would he do that, send you when he has six large sons at his side? Here, drink. And then go."

Nita was petting Lainie's arm. "We go inside. It's over. We stop watching."

Lainie pouted. "But I wanna see what happens." Nita herded Bonita inside, sighing.

Juan took the bottle from Mr. rum thief but stepped to the cooler and brought beer to the group, handing them to men on both sides. He spoke, "We have leaders here, with history. They make nice, but only so long, so long. Small ways ruin our Reunion, why make trouble, eh? Oy, I don't even live here, and I see what is the trouble." He clicked his tongue again.

"Today family met family, nice family. They fed everyone who is family and not family, *sigé*? And we all know who the families really are." At this, Mr. rum thief receded a step. "Don't ruin a nice day, nice that we do not fight each other, over things like land, and, and such. You go, please, go. Take your shells back to the mountains. I share with you, you share space. Go sleep outside the gate. Last night's group was here first. OR, or you take the cooler and go. Go now."

Lainie just "got" Deling's warning: not shrimp, not crab, but gun shells – those shells.

Marcelo's sons had already gathered their gear when Nita left. None of them looked at Lainie. They would not suffer any more embarrassment than they had to. The lecture was for Mr. rum thief.

The Reunion's wrap up, though, seemed directed at Lainie, about family . . . and space. The tirade was not about what was leftover but more like who was due what. Soggy, Lainie reviewed Juan's words, delivered so anyone – she, specifically knowing English – would understand.

Juan grew in stature, Lainie saw, judging by the saucer like eyes and soft glances by listeners. Lainie believed all the loose ends had been tied up. But now there was this house.

Beyond the gate, silhouetted bodies broke subdued light pacing left and right. Marcelo's group passed a bottle among them and appeared to settle in to camp. Perhaps, like shadow people, these groups were meant for fleeting glimpses. Someone like Lainie then could claim they do exist, these gods of the jungle with passions and frailties. Then she would swear there was definitely more to detect in caverns of darkness behind three or more trees.

"So," Reena began, "*Salamat*, Juan. You did good." He paused but then spoke:

"*Até*, and Lainie: we are not like that, not for family, and not for our guests. What you don't see are other facts, about this house. I never knew this house. Nita could only build a place like this because of you, Reena, and Nita's own store, and Horatio's pension, so everyone would have a place to live, everyone, even Manang Billina, and you, and your daughter, and one day, her daughter."

"Yes," Lainie segueway'ed, tipsy. "So how much gum and candy and soda can cover cement and glass and the stove and the jeep?" She jutted her lip directed at some items.

"We provide more than gum," Nita stated but turned to Reena. "And you have still not told your daughter how this house came to be."

Reena mutely nodded, so Nita continued. "Your mother sent us money every month to cover Billina's costs, not your daddy's money, no. He would be mad, feeling he could not afford feeding seven of you and buy a house and car, medicine, clothes. Our cuz worked for us selling trinkets and sewing dresses for customers to wear at your daddy's music and when he died, working at her Dollar Store job. So little by little, she sends what she can since 1949. What is left after Billina's costs, I put into this house, years and years, five, ten, twenty, fifty a month in American dollars starting years after Reena left. You do the math."

But Lainie would not be distracted. "But Billina died in 1965. You still send money?"

Reena shrugged. Lainie was blunt. "All to not be here – guilt is expensive, eh, mom."

As if cued, everyone at the table came to Reena's defense. "She helped us all, what goes to Nita comes to us, too, Americans do that, Filipinos who leave for America do that, so many send money to family, to home," and the definitive comeback, "You don't know the ways here."

Lainie had been calculating during everyone's tirade.

"About twenty thousand," she stated. "That's rounded off."

The number startled all of them, even Reena in an exaggerated way.

"Ay 'sus. That's over nine hundred thousand pesos. No wonder they think I'm moneybags. That's nearly twenty-four thousand dollars. *Putang ina mo.*"

Reena did not realize her slip, though Lainie had: this figure was no surprise to Reena.

"I knew you'd have the real number." Lainie smiled oddly.

The whole room was quiet, except for the girls snoring. So young, Lainie thought, their brains don't need this now. Maybe later, at Lainie's age, they'll vaguely recall a talk over a Van Gogh-like dinner table, and legacies, and land, and payback. One day, blurred dreams may be stark truths.

"Moneybags," Lainie repeated. "That money could've bought back your land, but . . ."

Protests again reared up. "This is better, right? This home was always the better choice."

Lainie bet no one could read her face. But she was content. Let the land go. Or keep it. Whatever. This singular space in time would last and these names, all of them in themselves would be legacies.

Lainie held out her glass to Horatio who poured again. "Ikapati, who called dad just American. Is she a *doyen*?"

With relief, everyone latched on, changing the subject. Bonita gasped, and Nita blurted, "Is she? *Talaga*, maybe she is! You know that word, like a high priestess?"

Reena was deep in thought, for good reasons. Everyone else talked or refilled sodas or snacked on *pandesal*. They swerved from Reena's years-long secrets. She could duck any unwanted attention. Lainie saw Nita touch Reena's shoulder. Perhaps, she thought, their subterranean resentments would, like the plantations, again lie fallow. Nita spoke.

"What Ikapati said was, she did not blame Reena's husband, your daddy, no more than, how did she say it, '*No more than a bee blames a blossom its allure. What attracts, attracts.*' All family at this Reunion, she said, has expectations. I say to them, too, let them all go. This Ormocanon is a woman who wanted more, and for that, she pays a price. '*Have you paid fully,*' she asked, and aiiee, she recites Reena's whole name and surnames that go back three, four generations! She asks, '*Do you think that you have redeemed your departure by bringing back trinkets, because, anak,'* and she addresses the whole room and we're all silent − '*because your blood is not yet diluted, soon, though, on foreign earth Plebiña blood will thin, just not yet.'* She ended with, '*Your daughters carry redemption.'* Oh-oh, and she knew, she knew when she said, '*You, Reena, hid in our mountains and bombs dropped, and you vowed something. Did you sell your soul, when you promised a lifelong task? Did you really think you sacrificed more than you gained? Come out from hiding. Reena. This is not it, not what you really do here today.'* And that was when the woman left and ignored the box."

By now, Reena was weeping quietly, her shoulders heaved with little squeaks sounding in her throat. Like Lainie, everyone knew not to comfort or touch her. No one then would ask what her vow had been, during a cold, long night on November 27, 1944. Lainie felt, though, that in various ways, all of them had dealt with her solitary cage keeping them at bay. She banned intimacy with spotty separations then patch-worked the holes in relationships as if that would bind agéd silk, thinning and fragile. Perhaps she believed family, re-woven over the years, could still hold a center without her. She'd add, *God permits.*

Bonita signaled Nate to retire to their room. Juan lay out his banig, unrolling and rolling.

Reena waited. Lainie briefly touched her neck, and Reena wilted. Nita whispered to her. Both cousins entered their room with the bunk bed. They talked for nearly an hour before separating. Lainie sat at the table and passed another hour listening to the silence.

Lainie got a bit drunk. Juan's head dipped and jerked. Soon he fell deep into sleep. She had the interior to herself, despite the snoring. The girls were the loudest. They all carried that family trait, sleep apnea, predominant in the females, perhaps a sign of held breaths, begging for release. Lainie snickered, but tremulous snores like corrugated roars and birdlike, chattering whistles drowned her guffaws. She headed to the C.R., pumped water into the bucket on her way and realized no bodies were strewn about the kitchen floor. After flushing the commode, she remained seated, gazing out at the night. Jun's CD played low, barely undetectable.

She heard a rustling. Maybe she might see a *tarsier,* like on the rum label, its big ol' eyes and funny little body with long, knuckled toes and finger pads like Pickle's. She kept envisioning the mammal when, beneath the C.R. opening for a window, the dried palm frond cracked and split from something heavy. Lainie froze.

"Oy."

What the hell.

"Oy, *ssst,* is that you?" a male voice – Jose's.

Jesus Christ on a cracker, thought Lainie.

"Jose?" she hissed. "What are you doing?"

"*Kundiman,* "he quipped. "The lovesick song – it didn't work on you. So here I am."

Was that only last night when Jose paid for the singer to perform because he himself couldn't sing? Briefly, she now marveled at her father's bravery courting her mother.

"And this *does* work? Crawling up to a window of a C.R.?" Lainie shot back, embarrassed. What if she were actually using the C.R. instead of frittering her time away, imagining tarsiers?

"Come out, Lainie. I have a surprise," Jose whispered.

"I'm sure. Good night."

"No, no, *oy, ssst,* I do, really: *tupada* only happens this time of the night, two times a year. *E-speshul!* You should see it." Jose sounded like he was scrambling up the side of the house.

"Jose, go away, you'll wake somebody."

"You should be thanking me. They're gone, the troublemakers." Jose was puffing, so Lainie leaned over to peek out. Their heads bumped together. She failed prying his fingers off the window ledge. Jose just grinned, hanging on tight. He so-o frustrated her.

"Let go," ordered Lainie. "I figured you were involved. We heard what happened."

"Not all of it." Jose perched his elbows on the sill. "But I can tell you on the way. Come."

Lainie hesitated. What *was* a *tupada*? She'd ask Juan, but not Jose, ever. She sighed.

"I can't use the front door. But there's a main window. Once I climb down, though . . ." Lainie recalled the window-climbing *manang* and decided: If she can climb out, so could Lainie.

"I know where it is," Jose said. "Listen for me. Noise travels."

That main window, however, was right next to Bonita and Nate's room. The front door, she knew, meant passing Juan. He, too, would just think she was *gago*.

Seeing her pause, Jose urged, "You – you write what, huh? This is a lifetime experience. This is beyond words. Be that kind of writer. Get out from behind the words."

She waited, a nanosecond. "Call me when you see me," she stated. " Call me 'it'."

"*Sigé na* – 'it'."

And with that, Lainie watched Jose drop out of sight.

What was Jose's type that drew *her* type like a stud finder to nails? This foolhardy move would prove Reena and Geraldo only traipsed to the land of opportunity so Lainie could drop like a sack of potatoes out a window in the dead of night in their foreign birth country and dodge amorous arms and cavernous jungles.

She moved stealthily from the C.R., through the kitchen, sidled against the main room's wall right next to Bonita's bedroom door. Taking a deep breath, she peered out the window, checked again for the cacophony of household snores, and eased herself out the window. Chanting in her head, she repeated: "If she can, if she can, if she can . . ." She stepped down into the humidity and finished. "I can."

From the darkness came a soft call: " 'It' – this way."

XXXIV

"It." Jose yanked his jeep's gears into third as he drove Lainie away from Barangay 35. "What kind of code name is that? Why not Mata Hari or Tokyo Rose? It."

Lainie's heart was pumping, flushing from either too much rum, or from the thrill. Once again, she had snuck out of the house without a guard, to experience the unknown. Jose and a *tupada* were as unknown to her as directness was to Reena. Hmm, she thought, a shot at mom.

"I don't know." She puffed taking in all the scenery she could, collecting hints on how to get back. "Somehow some woman came to mind who kept saying, 'This ain't it, this ain't it.' Well, at this moment, or at least today, I'm *It*. And don't call me *gago*."

Jose laughed and glanced in the rear view mirror. "Why would I do that? You saw the drunken man looking up at Jun like a lizard to an eagle? That's *gago*."

"Okay, so tell me your version of what happened in the yard." Twisting in her seat, Lainie checked out the scenery. She saw one set of headlights not far behind them, then a couple more behind that vehicle. Popular, she thought, this *tupada*. Jose seemed to read her mind.

"First, a *tupada*, you don't know what that is, I can tell." He waited and with her silence, continued. "A *tupada* is a cock fight! *E-speshul* only for you. Didn't I promise I'd take you to one?"

In her own passenger side mirror, Lainie now saw three cars behind them closing in. Distracted, she replied, "Well, uh, why at night, what's so different about this one?"

"Authentic! We Filipinos make good, you know, this for that, you give, we give. Do not think we are all just takers, take, and take, like some people at the Reunion." Jose drove fast.

Lainie turned fully toward him. "Wait, Juan said . . . I didn't see you at the Reunion."

"Oy, you were looking for me, eh? *Kundiman worked*!" he

chortled. " '*To* know, you said, all of you.' " Jose smiled, recalling Lainie's speech. "I saw parts, I saw the devastation! Not 'de bus station –devastation!' Of the balikbayans? Do you know that joke?"

"No. What are you talking about?" Lainie was checking her mirror every few seconds.

Jose continued blithely. "Your guests tore into that box, devastation. Ay, *joke lang*. "

Lainie wasn't tracking him. "I think we're being followed ever since we left Nita's."

"Those are our men." Jose was now on the dark road leading north from Ormoc.

Lainie's stomach lurched.

"And where is this *tupada*? Near Lunao?"

Jose clicked his tongue. "Ay, no, it's a secret place. A *tupada* is more for animism, our old religion – sometimes. Oh, and it's illegal, banned."

She gulped. "So only a few people know where or when this *tupada* is, *sigé*?

He nodded, looking straight ahead. "*Sigé na.*"

He'd have to take her back. He'd have to. He could not just head for the mountains. She should have awakened Juan, which would have meant borrowing the jeep. Hmm. No.

"The yard fight was not my fault." Jose's voice broke her train of thought. "Expectations, like the shiny woman said, *let them go*, I said. That's all I said. But Marcelo is stubborn, his sons don't care, they already have wives. Marcelo sees a strong one, wants her, even a shiny one, that's how he is."

Again, Lainie blinked rapidly. "Wives? Marcelo wanted a wife?? But he's, he's . . ."

"Ancient!" Jose blurted to the air. "That's what I said. Maybe that's why he was mad."

Lainie's knees wobbled, oh my God, oh my God, oh my God. If she had taken the painting, she'd have given her hand in marriage to one of Marcelo's sons or to Marcelo himself. She had dodged the marriage bullet in Mykonos and Boulder – getting to be a habit, she thought.

"But, but they can't just do that. Can they?" Lainie had averted another danger.

In that humid dampness of darkness, she shivered.

"I told you, you should thank me." Jose repeated. "Oy, ten kilometers or more now."

"Yeah, so," she was barely audible. "Juan with rum saved me from a forced union?"

Jose guffawed. "Oy, *way problema*. His sons already talked Marcelo out of it. They can't just shop for another wife just 'cause they're in town! They must let their own wives know first about anyone new in bed. And Marcelo? After he gets somebody, he forgets her name, anyway."

Jose saw a very small Lainie next to him. "*Joke lang, talaga*, how you take a joke!"

"Right," she mumbled. "Joke, funny." She wasn't laughing. Something in her rummy brain nagged at her. "Um, the shiny woman – I'm learning things I, well, none of us kids knew before. And the shiny woman told everyone in the room to shape up 'cause the box 'ain't it.'"

"Maybe, I don't know, I was bored. I already left." Jose inexplicably lied, and turned off another dirt path he had been following. Lainie had stopped memorizing directions.

Lainie continued. "The land, those boxes, none of it, she said, was '*it*'. She knew about my mother hiding in the mountains in 1944." Jose dismissed that.

"Many people hid, even my father." He pronounced, "Ikapati is a *Diwata*, a *doyen*, a priestess named after a deity, for prosperity. So for the Reunion, she sneered at what she represents and at what everyone wants."

"I wish you'd seen her at the end. She was very commanding in that golden light." Lainie watched as Jose parked near a lone tree trunk and the wood-structure quasi-hidden *tupada*. Still, that whole canopied section of the jungle lit up with a soft glow and winked through loose slats. She touched his arm. "I only used that term, shiny, tonight. Where did you hear it?"

"The goddess of fertility," Jose turned off the engine and pocketed the keys. "The cockfight also gives tribute to abundance in offspring, things like that. Ready?"

Alarmed, Lainie recoiled. "For what?"

Jose sighed. "The *tupada*, the ultimate cockfight."

"Well, okay, but, I don't have much money."

He waved her off but remarked, "Money, money, not everything's about money. *Sigé na*, your family was just blessed by a *diwata*! You will all be showered with abundance."

"One relative is a priestess, and even more are . . . like you?" Lainie had paused at NPA.

"No daughter of Fausto or grand-daughter or anyone is named Ikapati in your family. We all heard over bonfires the names of the oh-so great family of Fausto, and we know our deities." Jose was a bit irate but he quickly settled down. "You would know, too, if you were here."

Lainie fell silent. By now, men from the other vehicles had filed into the *tupada*.

"Because of that, that visit by Ikapati, you, all of you, are marked. *E-speshul*, but marked like Cain. You have the protection of the Fertility Goddess. Make a cross," Jose instructed, though it seemed odd to Lainie to dictate a Catholic gesture for something not Catholic.

But she did. Lainie completed the full sign of the Catholic cross, finger to the forehead, chest, left shoulder, right shoulder, as if she had performed the move only yesterday.

Jose pulled a half-bottle of rum out of the car, slugged some down, and gave Lainie the bottle. He was off, like that, with Lainie, of the undiluted bloodline of a once-prominent family on the island of Leyte, who ran after him toward the welcoming lights of the *tupada*.

A cock crowed.

Inside this open-air multi-tented cockpit, they were blasted by the noise and frenetic action as they entered, followed by the rest of the men in the other jeep. The shouting consisted of a repeated: "*Ta-da-di-da-di-da-di-da*" welcoming bets from all comers. Jose swept through like a prince, signaling for a beer and tossing a couple bets at some kristos that he passed. He couldn't have known which cockerels were even pitted against each other. By this time Jose's buddies were planted drinking beer at the entrances. Jose and Lainie were seated, trying to peer over the heads of the bettors who would not sit. Some boys, barefoot, wore luxurious clothes with matching headscarves, blousy tops with intricate complications and pantaloon bottoms.

She looked around the jungle opening. Here, quite a few more women were present. Actually, with men nearby, they looked like couples. She poked Jose. "Did you know women would be here, more than usual?"

"That is how fertility works, man, woman, hen, cock." Jose took a swig. "That second bet is for you."

All Lainie could see, swallowing a large gulp of rum, were people near an indeterminate ring moving around, most of them in flip-flops. Some men with not quite official vests strutted freely within the ring. She figured the barrio version with Mike conducted less formal cockfights.

"So *tupada* is when the bet is won, the couple is assured to be fertile, is that it? Um, in the States the analogy we use is 'birds and bees'." Lainie swigged.

"In the States, they would." Jose had a bit of an attitude in his voice.

Lainie chugged and regarded his faraway look. "The States aren't high on your list of faves, I take it."

He checked back in, smiling briefly, "Aah, they're not so bad. They bring tourists like you, the ones who ask so many questions."

"Okay, so what's so different from cock fights at

Nadongholan?" Lainie, a bit blurry, could sense now that an hour or so of this constant din would soon get on her nerves. And she might turn shurr-ly, slurry, surly.

"Look. You see the difference." Jose lifted his chin.

Other than the roosters were bigger, Lainie couldn't quite get what set this 'lil ol' fight apart from the other. Was it the colors, maybe, the snow-white breasts and backs of the proudest birds or the dancerly sweep of tail feathers? Or was the swell of the downy collar like the fluffy mane of a cat? With the back of his hand, Jose tapped under his chin.

"Right!" she slurred. "The-the wattle, under the chinny-chin-chin, and the comb, *whoosh*. Right, they just looked like regular fuckin' chickens at the, the legal place they kill roosters."

Jose hid a smile.

"They have a special diet. After they're dead, they're eaten like usual, no e-speshul burial like racing horses. So *gago*, Americans, capitalizing on horses, imperialists." Jose sneered.

"You radical, man," she commented and just as the crowds lowered their volume, she asked, "How long have you been, you know, NPA, militant?"

"Ah, NPA," he replied. "Early seventies. I almost graduated – but militant? All my life, I'm in the provinces. City people order my family about, you know the term, *bourgeoisie?*"

"Well, obviously, you do." Lainie was impressed, eyeballs twitching. "Shit."

"I had as scholarship, 'cause I'm, guess what: smart. By the late sixties, I gave up my studies. I went back to my people, the farmers. I learned with them."

"I-I don't really know about the shitty political atmosphere." Lainie waved him off, "Sorry, *tah-lah-gah*." She was feeling somewhat ornery, mocking him in his language.

Jose turned fully in his seat to face her. "You want to know. I tell you. I give you the, the what you call, the Cliff's Notes version, or better yet, you can stay another week."

A blast of cheers boomed through the jungle, all emanating from the congregation around them. A full-on brawl between a couple of foghorn-leghorn type of roosters flared for a whole thirty seconds in a cloud of feathers, and hops, and jumps. Lainie almost saw the razor on one of the legs slash his opponent in an upper cut mid-air. She was convinced the receiving rooster was wounded when it staggered a bit. Lainie tipped up the rum bottle. Drinking numbed her to all this bird violence, the flailing, unprovoked except by the mere glare of another cock.

"Hokay, a good example." Jose leaned on both knees, his hand out for the rum bottle. "Each year of these cocks is ten years of mine. They fight best at year one or two, like me. Early 1980's, 1983, I almost left, again. Benigno Aquino, you know him? Hokay, he's killed, you know, right on the tarmac in Manila. And I thought then, that's it. Aquino comes back because Marcos – do you know *him*? Oh, right: you just know his wife Imelda's shoes. Anyway, Marcos ends martial law, after thirteen years, and exiled Aquino returns, gone since 1971, since the Miranda bombing. Look it up. Marcos is blamed, but that's another story at another *tupada*.

"So by 1983, Aquino is a marked man. He's shot dead descending from the plane. But his death insured the end of Marcos's reign. Martial law actually increased the numbers of NPAs against the government. Good, huh? Then his wife, Cory Aquino, takes over, supported by CPP and its leader, Jose Sison. CPP, the Communist Party of the Philippines, supports Cory, Aquino's widow. And then, by association we, the NPA, back her, too, *sigé?* But, *talaga,* on January 22, 1987, yes, I remember the date, four years after she's safely sworn in, Cory *slaughters* my comrades in Manila, farm workers, peasants, some of the thousands at a peaceful rally attacked by district and regional police, a task force, the Marines, water cannons, tear gas, nearly fifty injured, four of the 18 killed – I remember because I knew them, all of them, NPA, backing Cory, *who kills them*. A counter-attack would guarantee a civil war, minutes, well, four years after already thirteen years of martial law! I will say this again *to keep in your brain* like I keep in mine. Farmers went on strike. Anything for farming is taken from landlords and given to cronies – a grab for land. Cory declares the CPP leader a terrorist, her flip-flop supporter. He flees to the Netherlands."

Jose took a swig. This kept him from slicing the air, missing both Lainie and nearby viewers. "So many politicians the CPP support, and then oppose, and then support again. And we, the NPA, the militant force, the strong-arm of CPP, we go along with that for years. I almost left again. But we go back to the people, and stay local, build battalions, and fight their fights, against local corruption, and the elite, and say fuck the *bourgeoisie*. We are not your attack dogs at the cost of nationalism! Maoist, Stalinist, *we go back to the people*! They are kept in slums, their hospitals are shams, they drink polluted water, and they eat moldy food. So we defy authority our way, or I would've quit a long time ago."

The din of bettors and losers, a *sentensyador,* and *kristos* served as a background throughout Jose's rant right up to the time he stopped.

"Before martial law, we had support from China, if you heard of that country," Jose was getting caustic. "Two thousand M-14s from Mao himself. Remember him, once a man in charge of a country called China? That's spelled: cee-aitch-eye . . ."

"Oh, screw you," Lainie muttered. "I know Mao Tse Tung and China and Trotsky and Russia and Cuba and Castro and Che Guevara and the Bay of Pigs, okay? I even heard about Sukarno! Do YOU know Venceremos in the Bay Area, Mr. Go Cal? Or the radical Grapevine newspaper – I worked for them, I wrote for them, I just, I just . . ."

"Don't know the Philippines," Jose finished. "Or that Cory even gave us NPA's in Manila her family's sugar plantation and even Hacienda Luisita in Manila, elitist-owned. And bam! The next minute the AFP, Cory's Yellow Army – Armed Forces of the Philippines – attacked us. Nearly five thousand killed in the two

years after her husband died. Our numbers fell. Leaders were cap-
tured. I was still here, but I heard. We all heard," Jose began to
laugh, a brittle laugh. "We are like Mexico's Che Guevara, teach-
ing in rural mountains. Ask me how we live. We penalize can-
didates for their campaign rights and for opponents we charge
"Revolutionary taxes". And then we are like your Mafia, what you
call, Cosa Nostra, Black Hand for our Black Thursday."

He became morose. He imitated Marlon Brando with, "We
make offers they can't refuse. Nineteen Eighty-Three, the Miranda
Massacre."

He stared ahead, with a thin smile. He would not, at this moment, look at her.

She flounced, "So why is this a good example? This cockerel
fight?"

On his own, he brought himself back. "Ah, good, you remember." he put a chummy arm around her shoulder and pointed his
finger an inch from her eye. "See, that big cockerel, Imperialism,
or U.S. intervention, or Capitalism, Elitism, whatever you think,
rears up, then flattens out, and waits, watching for an opening.
That mid-size one there, he is matched in weight but not height,
a disadvantage for this round. Theirs is a pretend-fight, defiant,
but no jabs, no connections, no BET because they are really on
the same side – the CPP-NPA. One of them may lose, or maybe
it's a draw, but battered as they may be, they will still live to fight
as one AND," Jose emphasized, " 'to render service to the Filipino
people'. FYI: that's our slogan.

"Maybe you still do not see, *way problema*. We are still on
the defensive. To this day we wonder who is our real enemy. The
ones in our slogan? Or the ones who oppose the government le-
gitimately or non-violently, unlike us? Because we NPAs armed
as we are, still re-affirm CPP, on our terms, but we are always
for the rural masses. Ha! So civilized we are, *talaga*, no matter
whose blood, any response, violent or not, redeems us sinners.
But what god is this who forgives us for breaking only selected

commandments? Our weak spot: we align with the ones who sell us out every time, a Judas. The difference is, our Judas has kept every. Dirty. Coin."

Lainie's head was woozy. She could hear Jose's words. She could see, fuzzily, the *sentsyador* count down roosters, defenders of the weak, who paused too long before a blow. Kristos became the CPP, backing whoever was winning. The undeclared remained detached. These roosters, heroes in the oddest package, crowed a mantra like one Lainie read in a book:

"In every motion of these animals, not given Reason, they posed nothing ungraceful. Another Higher Reason guided every-thing they did."

In a slurry speech with Jose weaving nearby, she bobbed. "Y'know, y'know, I know some radical League of Philippine Students. They're part of the large mi- . . ." she burped, "-gration at the tail-ass end of the Marcuzz Regime. 'Zwus a project about travel for, like, roots."

By now, she had an arm around his neck and could smell rum and tobacco. She muffled a phrase as if lips covered hers. She sang to him, "Hail hero, full of grace," and dubbed him a foghorn leghorn hero, and they laughed and maybe Jose kissed her again, or not, as she eventually slouched, open-mouthed and snored against his chest.

XXXV

Crunching – dry fronds, long, crackling, like fire, inky black, damp – is that piss?? Lainie spat out some bits of leaves and focused. She was lying on some woven yarn like bag, its nubbiness pressing behind her upper arm. Jose stood, his back to her, smoking and facing the coliseum. The sweet-ish tang of marijuana suspended in the air. He tongued two of his fingers and doused the joint. He was zoned, in another frame of mind.

"Oy." She giggled at the term and sat up.

He turned. "We're leaving."

"Um," was all she could manage. She wondered, the we we, or that general we?

"Do you know how much hostages are?"

His abrupt question sobered her up quickly. "Am I a hostage?"

Jose reverted to his easy attitude. "Who would know, eh? Anyone in the States? You're not married. You're not rich. Your mother brought money, not much, not enough. Are you famous, in politics, own a business? Are you in the movies? Do you know your own worth?"

In her head, Lainie felt she could burst into tears. Defiant, she retorted, "Do you?"

Jose shrugged but grinned. "You are like a child. What bargain can you make, huh?"

Lainie began, "Well, I am American, that could be enough for some peo- . . ."

In two steps, Jose advanced and shook her by her arms. "What is this, what is this, huh? What is this between us?" The kiss was so quick and hard against her mouth, she could not retort with anything sharp or effective. He went on. "I am a rebel. You are a rebel's prize." Gradually, he released her, the taint of his smoky breath still on her lips.

He had vaulted any boundary for that kiss and to grab her

like that. She really did want to cry but didn't. He had just called her a pawn, between conquerors and the conquered, plugging the space between his ideology, strong and focused, and hers, undefined. What a weak and arbitrary place for her to be, she thought. How alike were her and Reena's stance, on anything.

"That would be the only thing people would think, that I forced you, that I forced myself *on* you. None of the reasons why kidnaps take place will excuse that, you agree? Do you understand? And you wouldn't tell them, would you, to save yourself from any embarrassment, that *you* took that step out the window. You wanted to leave that life behind. And for that, I am a pawn. You played me like a trinket over words, for me to surrender. And I almost did." He ran a hand through his hair. "Ay, *gago*, this place, and you, and me, in it."

Lainie smarted at her presumption. He was poetic, Berkeley. Go Cal.

"Let me go." She spoke in a clear voice. Inside, she was weaving.

Jose looked off. She hoped he was gauging an alternate ending to this joyride.

She tried again. "I won't say anything. We just had fun, and you can let me go."

"*Claro, diba*: you don't get it, do you? I can't let you go."

Lainie froze. She listed people who might wail but do nothing, or strangers who might rail at such a world, or Reena, howling at Geraldo's wake, an act less likely that she'd do for her own daughter.

Lainie flashed on a life as a ward of the jungle, one of the many willing women who were insurrectos themselves but who must bypass the needs of men to hoard energy for *their* needs.

Lainie had gotten through similar mishaps. She would get through this as well. *Way problema.*

"I can't let you go if I never had you to begin with."

She was bobbing, a ball of nausea rising from her center. Had she heard right? Something like regret tripped his voice. For her choices, her stands, he would never give up his, not for a mess like her. His words swirled too fast, like her stomach. Oh God, what sin is this, an eleventh commandment: Thou shalt not Give Up.

Temptress that she pretended to be swayed Jose, sardonic, laconic Jose. Could he consider surrender for one brief moment to the American he would never really have or to that America most dreamers could never have? That was a regret and a sin, his and hers. Lainie could never forgive herself if, under a drunken moon, a spirit like Jose ever gave in to one like her.

Lainie managed to say, "*Now is the time.*" Jose gave a mirthless laugh: "*Ay sigé*, maybe now you get it. You know, eh, the choice that will change everything for us both?"

She needed to steady her nerves. Lainie longed for a cigarette but reaching for one would show her hand shaking. The muffled, loping tones of the t*upada* crowd waxed and waned indicating wins and losses. She could only detect furtiveness by twigs snapping behind the darkest foliage, or flight by breezes swooshing through the softest fronds. She thought she heard paws scuttling on bark or under day-baked brush. For sure, someone cooked with fishy *bagoong*.

She squelched her nausea. "I know . . .you watched us in Lunao where I typed, and the pier where I wrote, and probably even at the Don Padre. You've been everywhere. *Sigé?*"

Jose grinned. " '*Tangina*, no one can be everywhere. Only the invisible, *sigé na*."

Invisible: Nita's term. "I passed 'the invisible' every day, didn't I? Were they . . .?"

"Someone selling fruit, or up a tree, or cleaning pools?" Jose seemed amused and added, "How about a host whose mistress is *Pilipinas*? I name nobody, of course, just give examples."

Lainie felt a mid-chest gag rising. Jose announced, "*Pilipinas* is the one we do anything for, our ageless, timeless Philippines. Miss Travel Writer, what would you do at any cost for something you cannot even touch, something beyond money or even land, hah? You are marked. You have so much, and still you wring us dry wheedling for assurances, justifying your escape to Paradise. Well, this . . ." he spread his arms wide, "is It."

He tapped her forefinger and then lifted her hand to his lips, again emphasizing, "Now is the time."

If Lainie were a mistress at all, she, too, took a backseat to *Pilipinas*, the Philippines. She was local drama. She was the town's television, a living soap opera, the faux version of *Dynasty*.

"I'm gonna be sick," she slurred. Jose's call could not retrieve her from the vortex.

XXXVI

Lainie laid her wet head, babe-like, in someone's arms. Muffled, roaring baritones flooded the air, then guttural, frantic barks – all voices of men, women, and saviors. She could distinguish soothing "*sssshhhhh,*" from the person holding her. His small, rough, calloused fingers stroked her arm, as if that one spot were a tiny pet.

Not far off, Jun, fronting one group, barked and waved his arms making him appear larger. Lainie's captors were unimpressed, sardonic, and unblinking. Jun was agitated. Another neighbor splayed his arm downward between the two crowds. Lainie felt a prod. Someone helped to her feet.

"Come, we go now, quick, get up, *sigé na!*" He was Juan, uncharacteristically demanding and pushy yet, Lainie knew, making the right call. She searched the crowd for Jose. After all, he had brought her here to . . . where was she? She whirled when cheers and boo's exploded near the tent. But the crowd squawked at them instead of at any roosters, her retrieval from the sin of a gamble. Juan saw her searching.

"He's gone." Juan knew Lainie was looking for bad boy Jose. She blushed. Could Juan know, self-deprecating, insecure Lainie had bought the myth that a rebel's life on the run is romantic or free? Juan pulled on Lainie a bit aggressively till she whimpered, really hung over.

"I-I thought we'd just talk, Jose and me." Lainie slurred and even to her, the lame excuse sounded – lame. Juan pointed his lower lip. They joined his fellow rescuers. The gawking crowd cued Lainie, who backed off measuring the menace between the two groups. One of them threw an empty San Miguel beer bottle between the men, purposefully missing anyone. Juan prodded her forward. A flareup from both sides quickly subsided when Juan called, *"Tama na."*

Somehow, Lainie was piled into a jeep with six or seven other neighbors. She counted two more clutching fearlessly onto the back. Everyone was grim, reflective.

Lainie, sobered by cool air, spoke. "Are you angry?"

The silence was thick. After about ten seconds, Juan spoke. "Missus, we warned you. We protect our own. Some of those men are family and should know better. They were wrong. We right the wrong. You don't know the ways here."

"Okay, okay, sorry." Lainie pouted. "Sorry I don't know the language or the ways, sorry I took off, how many times do I apologize for being American."

The men were mumbling among themselves, confused and grousing. How ungrateful she sounded for their efforts. Lainie was embarrassed. She turned in her seat between the driver and Juan. *"Salamat,* 'scusa, I mean, *maraming salamat po."*

Some of them nodded or lifted their chins. Her attempt to

speak was enough.

"Did he?" Juan asked. "Take you?"

Lainie hedged. "Well, he took me to that place only a few know about."

Jun snorted. "Everyone knows that place, *diba*." Lainie felt sheepish.

Was this *tupada* planned beforehand? Was it – instead of a secret cockfight – just a meet up? Both the renegade group and her rescuers knew where to go. They know. Always, they know.

"Someone like him knows better how not to be found," Juan stared ahead. "Especially if he didn't want to be." Some of the men behind throughout the jeep agreed gutturally.

Juan's hand shook slightly. Lainie wanted to turn and plead with them to talk to her, someone, please, say in English what was not being said. The tension was unbearable.

"Nita will explain." Juan turned to look out his side of the jeep away from Lainie.

"Will anyone . . .does anyone . . .?" but Lainie stopped.

She did not know the ways here. But she felt safe in this crowded jeep. So why did she not even know their names? She was sure they knew hers and her mother's, the Americans, the foreigners, or, God forbid: someone born like her – not an alien – but into a family of sellouts. Jose was right. She was marked, labeled: sellouts mistook real Paradise. Lainie realized that Reena with some skill had attained the American lifestyle. Geraldo had also made good signing up with P.I's colonizers. Was it possible that Paradise was not ahead but behind them? What had they forsaken? "Home" to her parents was not Paradise. Those who never returned committed the sin of coveting the trinkets that surrounded them, enslaving them, usurping them.

"Oy," she said, and the men grumbled till they were silent. Lainie was twisting something in her hands. "Pop," she squeaked and lifted an imaginary bottle toward them. "Mabuhay, heroes *naman. Salamat.*" She continued to hold up the bottle till they, too, held their imaginary bottles.

"OY!" they all said and drank their imaginary beers. The roar repeated. Juan, eyes ahead, quickly brushed at wetness, and his frown gave way to relief.

#

Very late, very dark – they bumped their way toward Ormoc City, swung north past other barrios to Barangay 35 onto more potholed roads, and took the blocky turn along the wood-hewn corral, fencing in the lone water buffalo. Instinctively, Lainie leaned forward, her heart pumping. She had to see home again, this home, her mother.

"Where is it? Where is it?" she asked though only Juan could hear her. Only she, Jun, and Juan were awake. Her stomach contracted with dread. What if mom thought Lainie abandoned her? Would Reena even believe Lainie would choose a self-exile like that?

The deep crater in the road forced Juan to swing wide out and back again, his headlights directed at the corral. And Lainie saw him, her carabao, its oxen head low and its gaze steady, as if another night would turn into just another day. Oh, he was beautiful. Lainie caught the lump in her throat. She never thought she would be so glad to see him, or a day, again.

Jun's radio was silent.

All the lights were on at Nita's house. A Coleman lantern on the outdoor table backlit Nita. Hesitant figures approached and blocked more of the beam's focus. Men descended from the jeep stoically passing their women. One wife swiped at her man and fell into his arms. Another watched her man pass and stooped to inspect a weedy blossom. Juan ushered Lainie off the jeep as if she were a princess then patted Nita's hand as he passed. Nita enfolded Lainie quietly in her arms, uttering a brief litany. Her mother, Lainie was puzzled, where was she? After all Lainie had been through, damn it, where was her own mother? A light shone.

A tiny woman emerged into its rays. In her mother's voice all the tiny woman said was, "So."

Lainie knew she would have to make the cross toward her. She did and hugged her a long time. The tiny figure that was Reena then straightened and swiped at her own cheeks. Reena characteristically pushed at Lainie with a final swat across Lainie's stomach.

"Always something," she managed to add but then kept her hand on Lainie's arm as they joined the others hovering outside Nita's house. Juan settled the crowd and their din of questions.

He turned to Lainie. Nita gestured. "She'll talk later." Heads swiveled toward Juan.

"Hokay, so I just wake up. An engine, vroom, wakes me parked beyond Jun's. I feel something, you know, not good. So I wake Nita to say, knock on their door, and she knocks, and Nita asks Reena, 'Are you both okay, can you check?' And she says, Lainie is gone. So I wake the boy on the floor. 'Go jump the fences to take the shortcut to the main road and see which way the vehicle turns, south to Baybay or north to Tacloban.' And I run to Jun's house 'Please, drive the rest of us in your jeep.' And women wake their men folk from the barrio. The boy is at the crossroads and jumps in when we drive up in Jun's jeep. Two, two cars ahead of us, and when the first one turns left, I knew. I had a feeling. I say, 'Go, go follow.' I jump out to wait for more *silingans* in the next jeep. So many help us. It's so dark, but we have moonlight. We'll find her. I got in the neighbor's jeep and we drove further. I could smell the dust and the gas. I had to ask where to go. I thought I knew the way. We could hear the voices, so we got out of the jeep just when the other jeep arrived, eight of us. Inside the *tupada* is so noisy. Outside, Lainie is propped up. I thought she was asleep. She could not sit up on her own. I could see that. Someone would have to lift her. We covered all the exits. Everyone was alert, but NPA, they block the way. I ask, 'May we now escort her back?' No one says. They scratch their necks. I said, 'Please, for our family, not this way, not this one, Family, I say again.' One of them signals to come closer. I see he has no bolo. He waits but he almost pushes her at me. She wakes up. And Jun, Jun, where are you? Jun starts talking how wrong this is, on Reunion Day. On and on he goes till he finally knows when to stop, *talaga*, like a priest sermonizing." Laughter punctuated an ending.

The dawn's light tinged the sky. Lainie regarded Juan, at her side for the whole trip, waiting as she toured the mausoleum, checking moneychangers, and saving her. He had more than paid for his flight and had committed fully to his role as a bodyguard.

At some invisible signal, people turned to Lainie. To her surprise, Reena stood up. "I can tell them what you say." Still, Nita stood nearby Reena to interpret, and Lainie began.

"Um, hello, uh, *maayong buntag*. I-I'm sorry you're up so early after a late night because of my thoughtlessness. I apologize. You found me. You were all scared. I-I don't know the ways like I should."

Listeners just stared. She felt small. To lighten the mood, she dodged. "I should've just gone to sleep. You know, my first night, some of you came in through that window. I-I tried it, and slipped out and kept going. I didn't want to wake anyone, like Juan, anyone." People were zoning. She sidestepped. "I didn't win any bets. Too much rum, so I fell asleep. Someone splashed water in my face . . ."

A few women pulled at their men to leave. Lainie blurted, "You saved me."

Stillness set in the room. "Thank you for helping me." Her words cracked, and a thumping wracked her chest. Only sheer will kept tears back.

"*Salamat*, for . . .for my life."

Someone gave a single sob, very near her. Reena's palm smoothed Lainie's forearm.

XXXVII

For neighbors wanting more details, Lainie mentioned Jose's *harana*. She blushed, remembering. But people frowned: Who was she talking about? "Jose? Who's Jose? *Kinsa?*"

Not everyone had been privy to the *harana* serenade.

"Jose!" Lainie tried again. How could they miss the cavalier rebel who emerged from the jungle half a dozen times a year to eat decent food by Coleman lantern with *silingans*? Some men avoided her gaze. In an instant, she figured something out. They knew.

They knew all along where she and Jose were. They knew who he was. The farmers, fishermen at the docks – oh my God, she thought. She had wondered even then how could they only farm and fish when warriors backed their rights. They, when called, would join NPAs.

On this trip, she had bandied with danger all along.

But this time she trivialized her own adventure, like Reena fabricating old aerograms.

Realistically for an insignificant tourist like her, no American embassy would initiate a rescue on the spot or bump up her case in a queue. Her Fil students told her cases they knew where Filipino Americans, vocal against the country's corruption, were detained. Without speed, they finally had been released after Marcos fell. Their detainment did not even make headlines in the U.S. What more would aid Lainie, a KFR, who never stated her own stand, on anything?

Once the stragglers cleared out, beyond Nita's compound, Lainie saw Juan watching the sunrise. Lainie stood beside him looking east and spoke low. "*Salamat*, Juan – really."

Juan continued to watch the sun rise. She detected chants in the distance, the rosary crowd. She imagined their busy fingers trailing across rosary beads, and mantilla-draped matrons and men in crisp linen tops, a foot-high crucifix, the Call, and the Response. She could even envision Horatio jogging past them in his LaCoste two-button shirt, cotton shorts, pure white tennis shoes, and athletic, color-trimmed socks.

When the sunlight touched Juan's head, Lainie maneuvered to block the rays.

"So, who is Jose? Is that just what you call him, a nickname?"

"No, like ali-, alien," Juan said. " No, no, like . . ."

"Alias," Lainie said. She added, "I'm the alien."

"Jose goes by Kommander." Juan patted her arm, "Ikapati, the diwata, saved you."

She believed him.

"*Oy, sss-sst*! Come eat. Breakfast is late already," called Nita pawing the air. "Horatio's here, too, come, come!" Juan waved Lainie forward. "Go."

The rising sun painted him. His head shone, as if helmeted, and as if on a different body.

In the house, Horatio prodded Nita for the event that he had missed. Still waiting for Juan, Lainie searched and saw him past the tree-lined jungle encroaching the dirt road. Juan shook a man's hand, the Kommander's, she decided. They had concluded some transaction.

"*Somewhere* (crackle) *true.*" Jun's CD player again blasted the air. The barrio cheered.

Nita called out. " 'Hear ye, hear ye, seven o'clock, and all is well.' Come now. Eat."

Lainie got it. When Lainie disappeared, Jun had switched off the radio, like a monsoon when it cuts power. He was the town crier. His songs placated the whole barrio. He switched on the player when Lainie returned, safe. The barrio and all anxious residents could again rest easy.

"Hear ye" verified that life could flourish unabated, instilling values and righting wrongs with a dreamy song and its simple quests. "*out there, out where dreams come true.*"

Core values did not need to be written. They were givens. Two men transacted for normalcy – for NPAs, a meal, kinship, and a respite from war and for Lainie, safety. Juan with the Kommander, orchestrated that, balancing give and take. She was family. That's their way.

A lone kitchen helper with her own pot dashed past Lainie, her face drained and guilty. Lainie flashed on Reena crying in their room: no chickens had spoiled. The helpers had been securing their portions before the Reunion happened by claiming spoilage. Cook the food. Take any excess. She shook her head. That was another way, Lainie figured, of some other neighbors.

"There were leftover gifts in the boxes." Reena ate a fried egg. "I can't take them back."

Nita said, "*Way problema*, I'll give them homes."

Lainie scooped out one egg and more bacon. "Is this okay? Did I take too much?"

Everyone shushed her. "Take, take, we have food, take some!" Nate remarked. "To have enough food for everyone is good, to have even more for family after the Reunion is better."

"Were they really all family?" Lainie asked. Was she inappropriate, again?

People dinged their spoons on their dishes as if eating. Finally, Teri-Teri her spoon in her mouth, garbled out, "We're all family, right, Mommy? Can I have another bacon?"

Right then, Lainie puddled right up, her throat caught the bit of bacon, so she gulped down her cup of ade, hiding her eyes. A child uttered one simple truth, and Lainie cried.

"All of them," Juan re-emphasized. "All of them, you feed if they're hungry. They give back somehow. No one says how. You just give; they give back, like that. *Sigé*?"

The way Juan emphasized words made Lainie glance up. He jutted his lip, indicating outside. Of course. For championing the town's needs, "Jose" made good and was served food and company. Lainie's clandestine adventure was a risky trip for warriors, men on the lam.

But the experience benefitted her, too, with a life outside

words, compliments of unsung heroes. *Reason guided their magnificent resistance, like fighters in the ring, unconquered, full of grace, and sublime.*

Reena, for no reason, patted Lainie's arm, then retreated, shrugging.

Nita was grinning, Mona-Lisa like. Bonita and Nate cuddled their two girls, as if they were younger again, when closeness meant assurance. Horatio was checking his Omega watch. Juan, unblinking, was watching Horatio. In his way he, like Horatio, was poised for flight.

"Forgot something in town," Horatio mumbled, pushing his chair back.

Juan jumped up. "I'll drive you."

Horatio looked shocked. "Oh, no, I-I can just go."

"And come right back, with me. I'll drive you." Juan avoided Nita's look. "It's Lainie's last day. Hosts need to spend last times with guests, *diba.*" He was quietly forceful.

Lainie gauged the room again. Nita was allowing her brother to keep her husband home while Juan was still around. Juan's scepter was still in place. Lainie detected this couple's bond, however broken, still had connections. For Nita, Juan would make those bonds more evident.

Another puzzle piece clicked solidly into place for Lainie. Here, women accommodated indiscretions. For NPAs, higher motives ruled. Juan determined that for this day, Horatio, openly supporting NPA for one night, would not need to be in town.

Juan positioned himself like a linebacker, ready to pounce either left or right of Horatio. A slight pause, and he relented. "Yes, I-I forgot, I thought Lainie was leaving in two days."

Horatio sat back down, and Juan relaxed. *No more disrespect for my sister*, Lainie could almost hear Juan thinking, *you will be a family while I am here.*

Mabuhi, Juan, thought Lainie.

Nita, championed, leaned back, the resilient matron.

Sari-Sari chirped, "Oy."

A man and a boy, both thin beyond lean, stood outside, beat. Nate summed it up. "More guests. I bet they heard the radio ad late. They've been walking ever since, maybe four days."

Nita brought them each a dish. Lainie had confused the boy who reacted with alarm when she, among his elders, bypassed his *mano*. The father and son were very tired, road-dusty, and jungle-dark. The boy was barefoot. Not even an hour later, the man urged his boy to rise. Juan entreated them to stay and rest. The man insisted that they would not impose themselves any more, addressing all of them with, "You coming back and staying, you have given so much."

Reena hugged them and stroked their heads and cheeks, choked, silent, and grateful.

"Were they our cousins or an uncle? Or just Ormocanons, countrymen?" Lainie asked watching them trudge down the road toward the water buffalo's corral.

Juan with a familiar gesture, jutting his lower lip at the receding figures, made his point, clear and final: We are all Family. *Sigé*.

XXXVIII

Lainie slept.

Hers were a jumble of dreams, none of them set in California or the U.S. Scenes of green, green, a lot of green and teeth – she faced white even teeth, and bizarre, toothless or haphazard teeth, yet all smiling or versions of smiles, all right up in her face. She could see not only into their grins but also beyond them, the utterly innocent, and unarguable, joyful happiness. She scanned areas past their heads into a lush, thick, verdant wall, stretching far up and far left and right of her, till she woke, sweaty.

Lainie had not moved the whole time while she slept, so the covers were as wet as her body. Her dead sleep bled the hangover out of her, and she was thirsty. Next to her on the wall was bulging-eyed Pickle, his back, emerald with ruby-red splatter-brush marks. He hung upside down, splaying his suctioned toes gripping the cement wall. Pickle licked its own eyeball once.

Lainie didn't move. They maintained eye contact till she shifted, and the lizard shuttled away toward the light. She forgot to ask Billina's gecko about any fun beyond the Reunion.

"Hmph, you finally up?" Reena was on her bunk bed. "You really snore loud."

After stretching, Lainie lounged a few seconds and then slid down the side of the bunk, bracing her fall by bending her knees, and then popped up. 'Ta da."

"Everyone's sleeping," Reena said. "You kept them all up a long time last night."

"I've got to change, whew!" Lainie dug into her backpack and drew out the single, shapeless dress. She would have to hand-wash her last-day clothes in a pot by the C.R. – and her underarms. Soon, though, she would linger under running shower water – Wednesday.

"You should wear a padded bra," Reena commented as Lainie slipped the dress over her head. "Remember, lunch." Lainie nodded. Reena's remarks ran off her like coconut juice.

"Did you give him anything?" Reena asked.

Lainie peered at her mother as she dropped the dress in place and shook herself free from its cling. "Give who what?"

"Jose, or whoever he was. He showed you a good time. What did you give him?"

One-eyed, gauging Reena's real intentions, Lainie sat by her mother's feet on the lower bunk. "I did not sleep with him."

Reena stammered, "I did not say, sleep! Ay, 'sus, I just wondered what you gave him."

"Not sex, Mom, in any way or form. A good time, we talked, and drank, and laughed, flirted, maybe one kiss. That's all."

"Well, you gave something then, if he wanted to take you away. They take Americans, all kinds. To them, it's all about ransom, and . . ."

"No, it's not. He didn't take you," Lainie stated simply.

"Me?? I'm an old woman!"

"A rich, old woman. A rich, old American woman."

"I'm not rich!" She did not deny being American.

"Mom, you flashed money around like the *grande dame*. Unlike me, you could really afford this trip. You came back to show off your money."

Reena was struck silent. Her eyes seemed to look at the day at the bank with Nita.

"No-o-o," was all she said.

Lainie continued. "You gave your money to Nita and said, *ayy, too much, count my money for me*, like she was a servant–embarrassing, mom. She's your hostess, your friend."

Reena looked shamed.

Lainie wanted to stop but the inference about Jose fueled her. "So don't judge me on what never happened. We had fun. He was smart and, irreverent, and he saw, he saw things."

"He saw through you," Reena stated. "They all do. They see what we are, the Americans, slumming. *Ay 'susmarjosep, summabich*, all this scheming."

Reena was scrunching up her mouth. Oh, no, not the tears, Lainie thought. Here comes the self-loathing and all that crap.

"Oh, mo-o-m," Lainie sighed. "Americans just . . . mime privilege and pretend to be entitled. Filipinos scheme here, too, like Luis, they manipulate. Opportunists scuttle everywhere. The helpers? Spoiled chicken, my ass, and now these women now want you to visit them, and hold *lechons* at their places, like a room under a roof will buy them an American favor."

Reena said, "It might, instead of a hotel in town. And any peso is better than none."

"It's still not enough, though, is it? You came back with stuff, but guests wanted more. You want more. Nita is probably in debt putting us up, feeding us, paying Mike's gasoline."

"She what? She paid for his gas?" Reena spouted as Lainie went on.

"You think I don't watch but I do. I pretend I'm not affected, by the poverty or disease, or lack of shoes, the hair or teeth, the grab for things, the desperation. People here have no money for their dental care or their education. I have things but they're never enough. I have a sagging roof, a rusty car, it's more than them, and still it's not enough. How can they believe I have so much more than they do, and they smile and give, and I still bellyache."

A long, quiet period followed while Lainie's eyes darted to points in the air, her head too full of the last few days. Though the focus was, thankfully, not on her for a change, Reena broke the silence. "What you see, Lainie, what you see."

"What do you mean?"

"I saw you looking up at a tree once, in that arboretum in Golden Gate Park. You stared for such a long time, till I asked what did you see, you remember that?"

"Sort of," Lainie hedged. Of course, she remembered.

"You said, you were imagining a person unseen, lying crosswise on the largest branch and so, so invisible because the branch hides him. Why would you think that, why would anyone want to see what's hidden behind big things, things covered up in plain sight. Somehow you would, pointing to things other people want hidden. I don't know where you got that. Where?"

"*Sa'an?* I don't know," Lainie sighed. "Maybe you? Like everything else? *Sa'an.*"

Here they were their last night in Reena's home town, in

232

grandma Billina's last room, and only now did the dialog flow between them. All this time, they could have talked a bit deeper, a bit more personally instead of one-upping each other, or calling each other on dumb crap, traits immutably passed on. They were made more evident by the family, Nate, Bonita, Juan, and Nita, all of them, mirroring back and through each other to Lainie herself.

"Can we stop, mom," Lainie said finally. "Can we just let all the bull crap lie fallow, even for just a little while? I'm tired. Aren't you?"

"Oh, hon," Reena used the term so infrequently. "You don't know – you don't know."

"Then, please. Please tell me."

"No," Reena went on. "You don't know me, how I was before. I . . . I built walls, these walls for my mother," she patted them and the gecko dashed upward. "Around me, hon, I have walls. Ah, you don't understand what am I saying, you wouldn't, ever."

"Okay, let me try," Lainie began. "In a theater community, some actors are big fish in a little pond." Reena barked a laugh.

Lainie continued. "You don't know me, either, what my life is like. Don't you see we both do the same things? In that little pond, we get so small to each other, because nothing we do was ever enough; no one around us gives us our due. And the fear that Time or chances passed us up, it drives us. We promise the moon, let us make one mark, let us bask in light just once, but what we aim for is still never enough. The flash of a moment, and then it's nothing again. Gone."

Reena was shaking her head, fingering the hem on her day dress.

"Stop me anytime. Stop me at the war."

Reena froze a bit then uttered, "It was – it was so scary, hon."

"What," Lainie paused but forged ahead. "What promise on the edge of that mountain up there – what did you say to whatever god you knew then and ignore now? The one you call on in practically every phrase? Did you know that? *Jesus Mary Joseph*, it's not a curse. It's a cry."

Her mother opened her mouth, paused, and then closed it, pursed. A moment passed.

"Okay then, okay," Lainie sighed, but she tried one more time. "The so-called 'bullets' I dodged, to see if I could, I was pushing it, seeing how far I could go and still come out beating the odds. Sometimes I just wanted any bargain to fall through, so I wouldn't need to keep the promise I made. I wouldn't have to. But I do come through. I'm charged to keep the promises."

Reena grunted. "Well, I did not hold to my promise to, to never give anything. This world takes and takes, why not me? I say, God ignores me, so damn me for a reason! I will take, so help me, I will. And," she added, "Never love, anyone, no, no, no."

"No love?" Lainie was shocked. "Who gains from that? It's spiteful. Why dare the heavens to damn you or and stay loveless or god-less or be worse, why? Why make a vow?"

At that, Reena jerked a bit, as if she had an epiphany and blurted, "I loved him, I didn't want to, but our life, our – you kids."

"You mean dad, he was always waiting. I wondered, did you ever really love him?" Lainie treaded lightly. "Or us, because you know it was never enough. We waited, too."

Reena wrung her hands. She had not wanted to think about this, ever again, and the armored Reena flared again. "You want me to say it? You want me to say, I love . . ."

"No," Lainie was exasperated. "No, too easy, Mom, when it's harder to do, that's the wall coming down. So stop it, okay? Who are you trying to convince that you're so untouchable? I'm untouchable. Ask me where I learned that. I'm that way, from you. We're not so different."

Reena's eyes filled and blurred. "The ones here who stayed, they were braver than me."

Lainie remained quiet.

"They wanted to live, and I did not, not that way. They are so brave, living like this." Reena gestured at the house. "So little to

234

spare, why should anything like love be so free?"

"So that's what you promised, for a piece of you, we had to bargain, all of us?"

Reena spat. "I vowed to love even less!"

"But why?"

"Because the world hated so much. It doesn't deserve my love."

"Then you're right: you didn't hold to it."

"I tried."

"Badly. You didn't keep your own vow."

Reena blinked. Lainie was shaking, but from more than disagreement.

"You couldn't hide that so you kicked yourself and pushed us away. I saw. You raged at us. You thought your secret was out, for all of us to see. God, Mom, please. Don't kid anymore."

Lainie's tone became slashing, wanting to hack at the space so solid between them. But she had to temper the blows, just let them land. As always, her lashings glanced off Reena's steel surface – zing, resound, and like a super ball bound away.

Reena stared. "You pushed, too, so young, pushing, pushing at others kids, ooh, I could've slapped you for that. I always asked the heavens what made you that way."

"The heavens?" Lainie let that cut, and then blurted, "Dad made you kiss us one night, remember that? *Ask the heavens* why! Dad made you say it, remember? I do."

Her mother looked drained. After a moment, she just shook her head and kept shaking it. Reena would never admit anything more. No secret was out. No night of kisses ever happened.

Lainie's throat constricted. She could force an admission and deserved one. Instead, she let Reena off the hook. "Okay. Okay, enough."

She missed the opportunity. Lainie denied her secrets as well.

Love, its remnants, was what Lainie herself parceled out to

ones like Jose, just crumbs, scattered like the bounty of a mouse. He, and others, saw that. And until she saw what strength she had and what she really escaped – the darkness of her past blocking her future – *now might be the time* for a heart like hers to journey out a window toward *It*, her own shiny Paradise.

"Do you want to take my pesos and divvy them up among the family? Say they're from you?" asked Lainie. The words were simple, a tinny noise to fill an awkward space.

The moment had passed. Reena, at first distracted, quickly shook her head.

"No, no, we'll account for our own. They should know the money is from you, hon."

What felt odd? Reena called her "hon" more than once this morning. The gecko, unusually active, darted along the west corner and disappeared through a gap in the window.

Reena again busied herself. "Luis's lunch. Don't wear that. Be better. It's the Serrañaos."

Again the day pass expired between them, Lainie flounced out of the room with her wallet and a hat. Be better, Lainie steamed. Why promise to aim for that any more than to promise withholding love? One is indisputable, the other, just implausible.

She now vowed she would show this Luis the better, unbeatable side of the Plebiñas.

No one was in the main room. She stepped outside. Next door, Jun's song played even louder on his CD player as he stood buffing his cherry-red jeep, showing no signs of fatigue from her rescue from the jungle. Jun got into his vehicle as Lainie walked up. Greeting him, again she thanked him for retrieving her, and please – would he drop her off in town?

XXXIX

Reena stands, her tear-stained face still defiant, as she faces Geraldo. He is speaking full Tagalog, incensed and very agitated. Now and then, he raises his hand as if to strike her, but she whimpers, like when the blows actually land. Moments earlier, frustrated, she blasts him with her real thoughts she harbors over the past seven years. Their family is grown, all very close in age, and all very active, underfoot, and to her, disrupting Reena's young life. She does not count on this scenario. This derails her planning, all she maneuvers to get here, to live a better, and more indulgent, unaccountable lifestyle. Children are in the picture, of course. Any married couple has to endure that burden, but just not so early, not while she is still so young herself.

However, that is not how the words come out.

Maybe the weather irks her. Humid, relentless, the summer's air-sucking heat seeps into the usually drafty house of two bedrooms overrun by children. Or perhaps her outburst stems from the weight of bills that Geraldo refuses to acknowledge, leaving the minuses and plusses to Reena, letting her adjust and carry them all over into her sleepless nights. Then again, just the children themselves existing was enough, the fact of them, the sex she tolerates to have them. Sex lacks details, gleaned from hushed inferences. She just doesn't know about any of nuances, otherwise she would have planned better, between births, between Geraldo's hungers.

So sleep-deprived, and for want of privileges and privacy, Reena lashes out when Geraldo again presses her for that sex, the kind she abhors, and knows the least about. He is a maniac, she blurts, pulling away, he gets what he wants, and she gets another nine months of pain adding to regrets collected over the past years.

"You think I love this? You think I love them? Or you?? I didn't want this! I don't want you!" and that is when the first blow hit, not hard, just surprising. Geraldo has, for the most part, been patient, for a man with needs, constant needs. He works more than one job. His is a routine shared by most immigrants, *walang problema*. But that day, that moment, two outwardly, well-oiled ratcheted wheels working a marriage already complicated by dialects, age, and "needs", screech against each other and grind to a halt.

"You say that? You don't love your children? Our children?" his voice splinters like icicles on Wisconsin walkways, his words forced, though breaking, "I-I knew you didn't love me. But what kind of mother are you? Huh? Huh?" and Geraldo strikes softly, open-handed on each question. Oh my God, Reena thinks frantically. *'Susmaryosep,* oh my God, oh God, oh Jesus, she exposes the vow. She reveals what she masks behind that coy, angelic alabaster face she tips making plans happen, shielding her stone-gate heart.

She does not love anyone.

Years earlier she masters another language, gains an office education, snags the right man, and births the requisite number of children. She does not need to love anyone to accomplish this goal. She bypasses any step that means giving herself to anyone totally. Her nonexistent god will see, personified by her, one product of his that neither loves nor hates but still gains on earth with no regard to gain any heaven.

One shaken, frightful episode alone on a mountainside and Reena lives as an unloving creature. She will not miss opportunities. She will indulge. She deserves accumulations. She will not be invisible. Some god allows her life, despite war. Why recede, why give more than get? Dreamers talk. The Devoted dream. They prattle about illusionary love. She, without it, will act. Who needs love to get what they want?

"I vow – should I live – to leave what I love, and miss nothing, no one, now or ever. And I will give up anything to make that happen. I give up love. I will never lose myself. This world can't love. I want none of it, not this jungle, not parents, family, just me, me. Make bullets miss me. I vow to keep up this wall. I vow I will not be god's instrument to love or hate. Love will not reduce me, so help me god."

The U.S. bombing campaign seems like years but halts on a dime with her vow. Massive shelling cover her last scream of that defiant vow only meant for ears in heaven. To hell with dreaming that love saves them. She starts that day, to live beyond words.

Reena finally cries, beginning as a low whimper, then a groan, to an outright howl, longer and louder. Hers is only one of many in Ormoc that day, beneath rubbles, behind barriers, and like her, among the mountain ranges. All the earth, the trees, the animals, the spirits hear them, the wounded souls surviving bombs, the stricken voices vowing for betterment. One voice differed, vowing the worst: Reena's. When bombs stop, the vow begins.

Then, years later Geraldo demonstrates his own boiling hurt. He drags Reena across the carpet to the children's room holding her hair by their roots. He forces her to apologize to the children deep in dreams. He shoves her. "Kiss them with real love," he commands. She sobs. One child hears, one with many questions. A cycle continues. Another gate closes.

Reena lingers on that memory on the mountain less often. She varies the moment, even some words, but justifies them all. By Reunion Day, she forgets her original vow. But the *diwata* Ikapati intones her secret publicly. And Lainie gets to peer past Reena's fence.

In her world, Reena keeps her vow. Love she hoards is parceled out hard.

In her own way, she does relent and shells out crumbs at a time.

For her, that is enough.

XXXX

The last lone ride to town with Jun, the neighbor, was again, without Juan. Lainie just needed to try finding, one last time, that special item, one that would sum up the memory that could only be of Ormoc. Sticking to small shops, she wore dark glasses and a floppy hat to hide her shiny hair and not stick out. But the souvenir could not be found. So she flagged a jeepney to take her back to Nita's house, She got lost. She had the driver head back and forth between two particular roads before she recognized the path. The driver mumbled *gago*. She agreed. Would she ever know the right way?

"I know: the one standing there, steady," she said. "At that water buffalo, turn here."

He turned. Lainie was home.

Everyone at Nita's just looked up when she entered the house a few minutes later. They looked and returned to their own lives. The Reunion had passed. Guests lived to tell it all.

About twelve thirty, Mike stood at the door, neatly dressed, hair combed, even closely shaven, for a change. Lainie, too, wore her best, only twice-worn outfit. Only Reena and Lainie would lunch with Luis, in reality, a business lunch. The land case, which Nita had opened, Reena would close. During the drive, Reena kept fingering Lainie's hand. This display of affection stopped sometime before arrival.

Mike jabbered non-stop catching them up with his weekend as if they were long-lost friends, citing names whom neither Reena nor Lainie knew. He never asked about the Reunion.

Perhaps he drove around to show them sights they had missed the previous five days. But Lainie felt Mike purposely zigzagged to confuse them about any directions to the "compound."

They drove through open gilded gates about fifteen feet high and breezed past hundreds of orchid bushes, plants, birds of paradise, freesias, roses, ferns, jasmine, coleus, daisies, marigolds, bougainvillea, wisteria, and oleander. Reena's eyes even lined up. They also passed at least three gardeners, an emptied Olympic-sized swimming pool, and a handful of thin women in light-colored uniforms. Mike parked behind the humongous latest model jeep set in front of the carriage-high covered portico with Chinese motifs. He opened the jeep's door, offering his hand to escort first Reena and then Lainie. Mother and daughter exchanged looks.

Flanking the open double entranceway were planters, two ceramic elephants a quarter of their usual size, Chinese style, in brilliant jewel tones like rubies, emeralds, amber, and lapis lazuli, wondrously enameled and lustrous. Their forelegs were the same width as Lainie's waist. Luis's impressive Chinese art collection far outshone the local Filipino art in local stores. A set of authentic, polished carabao horns hung over an interior door.

Lainie was too aware that, again, she had carried her garbage-bag purse that hung on her right arm. An elaborately coiffed woman greeted them inside the door. Lainie noticed that Mike stood at attention at the entrance, hands over his belt, and staring straight ahead. He wore shades.

Soon Don Corleone aka Luis swept into the reception area, or whatever the room was. Lainie could see ahead yet another spacious room with black-enameled chairs along the walls.

"Welcome, welcome to my abode."

Bastard son of Don Padre Serrañao, Luis Serrañao bowed, dressed in white except for his colorful ascot. Lainie almost laughed imagining the frightful eyes of the tarsier on the rum bottle, possibly hidden near his neck. Luis graciously indicated to a coiffed helper to relieve both Reena and Lainie of their purses. Lainie demurred. Reena cradled her oversize purse and rattled, "Oh-oh, I need my nose drops and Kleenex for my sinuses. You have them, too, you know, sinuses." Luis flipped a hand, dismissing the help and Reena's remark.

Luis then ushered them into the parlor – yes, parlor, Lainie decided – and they sat across from each other on white washed, cushion-pillowed rattan chairs.

"So, Reena," began Luis. "*Mi casa, su casa*, eh? You like?" Reena bobbed her head.

"And you, Lainie? Lainie, is that right?" he purred. "A familiar name . . .beautiful."

"Thank you, salamat, for remembering." Lainie said. "Since Saturday."

He laughed. "So have you seen all the sights? Ah, you had a Reunion since then, yes? Oh, look up the stairs here. Forty-nine rooms, can you believe it?"

Lainie felt a growing annoyance. He had already negated their big Reunion by not attending and now glossing over it. He was pushing her buttons. He must be family.

"Now that was beautiful, wasn't it, Mom, the Reunion?" Lainie turned to Reena, who was like a hummingbird, her eyes darting all around, even at the ceiling, ooh'ing softly to herself. She barely nodded at Lainie.

"Mom figured on about five-hundred guests, from all over the island, right, mom?" Lainie gently elbowed Reena to join the conversation. "Mom-m-m?"

Reena came to briefly.

"Oh, yes, Luis, you should've come, you and your mayor. I did send word that you were all invited, but you're probably so busy, with your Serrañao name on everything, on stores and hotels." She drifted off, seeing a Japanese bonsai tree on a side table. "Ooh, I like that."

Luis kept smiling. "I was busy." He added, "I sent a contribution."

Both Lainie and Reena simultaneously bit their lips.

Luis continued. "Nita sent the money back. Ah, well. I used it, elsewhere."

Lainie ran the tape in her head. Horatio had returned Luis's money via Mike sitting in his jeep two mornings earlier. She was glad she didn't know how much was Luis's donation.

Luis crossed one leg in his crisp, pressed slacks over the other leg. "After that, I got very, very busy. Sorry. And tell Nita sorry for, uh, assuming anything like a contribution."

Making some point, he wagged his finger, a thinly disguised scolding and leaned back. "Would you like a Scotch before lunch? Reena? Lainie?" He lingered on her beautiful name.

She could still taste the rum, so Lainie refused. So did Reena. And so did Luis.

"Gout, you know." He tapped his ribcage with his wrist. Gout, Lainie knew, is in joints.

"So what do you do back in the States?" Luis, so debonair, came off like the cartoon character, Pepe LePeu. Lainie sighed. For God's sake, they weren't like the household help, grateful for any glances levied on them by the massah. Seated, Lainie kept her spine straight.

Reena, on cue, gushed, "Lainie writes, Lainie has articles, she even types. You should hear her!"

Lainie interrupted. "And mom still works, even retired." She darted a stink-eye at Reena.

"Where is this Mukwonago? Wisconsin?" Luis obviously knew the Reunion's banner.

Reena described where in Middle America was this Wisconsin. Lainie inspected the very tasteful statues and table ceramics positioned artfully, some in doorways, or ones close to windows, against huge mirrors. A crystal glass display cube dissected a room. Luis really did up the décor and still, he was base, acting like he was better than they were.

He remarked, "Ah, just trinkets that relatives can share, depending on, you know."

"Yes," echoed Reena. "Depending." Lainie added, "The operative word." Luis laughed.

"Well, no cocktails. Let's lunch." Luis gestured just enough to alert half-hidden maids.

Reena, Luis, and Lainie moved to another room farther

inside, taking in *objets d'art* and paintings they passed. An oblong glass table in a dining area was rather common, and the view, nonexistent. Window washers blocked the panorama of the spacious grounds. To Lainie, Luis had bare-assed his disdain for his guests and their class, his faux hospitality.

Plain melmac dinnerware, nondescript, sat squat, lowly, even for guests. Lunch was not in a main dining room. Vistas had no pristine views. Luis would not release the window washers even for an hour. To Reena, everything looked stupendous. Lainie felt heat rise to her neck.

Two clingy house helpers entered and stood, waiting. Luis announced that they may serve lunch. They nodded, eyes wide, their bare arms touching. Lainie thought they were so close to each other, that they *were* each other. They took in both Reena and Lainie between lowered glances, like young does awaiting signals to run. Lainie bet this was their first day, hired to embellish the aesthetic interior of the forty-nine-room mansion. Luis was showing impatience.

"Ask them what they want to drink." He instructed them curtly, flashing a quick, uneasy smile at Lainie who figured they didn't really know what were their jobs.

"Oh-oh, *sigé*, ma'am, miss, any, uh, drinks?" One asked. The other huddled behind her.

"Oh, I don't know, " Reena looked at Lainie. "A high ball, Lainie, or your Scotch?"

Lainie slowly closed her eyes and then opened them, pursing her lips. "Um, no, mom, Luis already asked earlier, so no alcohol or cocktail right now. Ask for soda." She sounded bold.

The helpers looked panicked. "Soda? Ade?" They looked at Luis and nodded. "No."

"I apologize, we don't have any soda. How about milk?" Luis's eyes drilled the two helpers thoroughly. Again they nodded. "Um, no."

"What actually is lunch?" Lainie asked outright. "That might match any liquids, maybe."

Luis twirled a finger in the air, and the helpers disappeared. The uncomfortable wait was torturous. When they re-appeared, spaced apart, each carrying plates on platters, Reena stared at chicken salad sandwich triangles with white bread, a few celery sticks, black olives, and potato salad. Two smaller plates had each a slice of rolled sweet bread with some white cream filling.

Lainie had promised herself not to pig out especially after the Reunion. Still, she was furious, thinking, "Sure, show off forty-nine rooms, miss the Reunion, soap up the windows, and this is why I have to be better? Go ahead, steal the land, and then serve us leftovers, you class-less bastard!" But Lainie calmed herself down and spoke evenly.

"Oh, we almost forgot. Mom, bring out your pictures. Show them to Luis over lunch."

Reena paused. "Now, with food right here?"

"No, now don't be shy." Lainie urged. "Show him your flowers, and the old Christmas pictures, when we were all young. It's just to get you caught up with our American family, Luis, if that's okay. I know you don't have much time for us. Mom, the pictures?"

Luis was a bit confused. "Should they set aside lunch? And the drinks?"

Lainie helped Reena open the album she had sequestered away in her huge purse. "No, no, just leave it. Bread won't get any drier, and for a drink, mom? Milk's not good for you, lactose-intolerant, you know. Coffee? Tea, iced tea, maybe?" Lainie looked directly at the helpers clutching the empty platters to their chests. They looked from Luis to Lainie and back.

"Iced tea, of course, two of them." Luis took back the reins, but Lainie corrected. "No tea for me. How about pineapple juice? Oh, good, mom, these pictures are perfect."

No one moved. Lainie would not look up from the album. Finally, she heard Luis echo, "Pineapple juice, of course." The women scurried off. Pineapple juice, though not yet Luis's cash crop, meant canned juice, from stores, in town, a trip, by car.

Reena described pictures and made no eye contact with Luis. Lainie tipped her head.

"Thanks for having pineapples 'cause I know I usually pass on soda and milk myself. In fact, I pass on most sugary foods. So-o-o much food every day, and the *pandesal*, I just can't pass that up. Oh, here's a good photo of us all – that's my sisters and brothers. Mom, you name them off." Still, Lainie continued to rattle away allowing neither Reena nor Luis much to say and not even picking at her own soggy sandwiches. She did take one olive. "Oh-oh, and here's one of mom's garden. That's why she's really impressed with all your flowers. Wouldn't it be nice to see your pool? Too bad it's empty, though." She paused.

"They're cleaning it, the sides are a bit green." Luis began but Lainie forged on. "Wow, lucky us, we got here on your cleaning day, no swim, no view, but no biggie. They found a swimsuit for me the other day, but I have to admit, that sugar does a number on the waistline. Oh, thanks, not mentioning my breasts, by the way. You have a good waistline, not saggy."

"Thank you, I work ou- . . ." Luis started again.

"I bet you don't eat as much sugary stuff as the rest of us do, I mean, you got people to meet, no Sugary Serrañaos want to meet up with anyone important all heavy from power lunches, right? Here's a picture of the yard with all mom's friends listening to my dad perform, he sang to her, you know, when they courted. He's full Ilocano, not half-Spanish, like you."

Luis, by now, had leaned back in his chair, poking at his dish and dipping his head occasionally as Lainie ranted on. And by now, the helpers had dashed back into the room, a bit sweaty, and steadied their hands to place the drippy glasses of pineapple juice from the local store on the oblong table. They puffed. Lainie asked, "My mom's iced tea? *Salamat*."

"Take my dish." Luis ordered briskly. They did and left.

"So that's about it, right, mom?" Lainie flipped through the remaining pages of the album but Reena placed her hand on one page. "This, hon, this one is of my mother, Billina."

Reena moved the book directly in front of Luis now that his dish was gone. "Remember, Luis, she gave us both milk, usually at the same time. And look how big you are now. She would be proud that her milk made such a big man like you."

Lainie compared them to playing solitaire with the flash win of poker. Mom won the pot.

Luis pointed to their plates. "You must eat."

"*Sigé*." Lainie daintily took one bite, smiled, drank down her pineapple juice, and pushed the plate away. "Big Reunion yesterday. Now, *that* was food."

Luis tapped on the glass tabletop, his right knee over his left. "Would you like to see the pool?" He pawed his hand toward one helper and whispered. She exited. Reena and Lainie rose.

The three of them strolled outside between the empty pool and a staging area for about six workers. Looking deep into the chipped, sky blue-painted bottom of the kidney-shaped depression, they could see two men with wide brushes scraping away lime-green algae as another man hosed down the scrapings. Reena dawdled behind Luis and Lainie who, a bit suspicious, turned to see Reena handling a leaf for far too long. She was known to take cuttings from arboretums and hothouses, grow them in her own yard, and grow them even bigger.

"Mom," Lainie warned. Reena shrugged and dawdled less obviously.

"I want you to have the phones and addresses of my children in the States," Luis announced out of the blue. "I think you would have a lot to talk about. You make points, talking like you do, probably writing, too, *sigé*?"

They were passing the largest profusion of orchids. Lainie sounded blithe.

"Words just make bigger points out loud. So where in the States are they?"

"North of Los Angeles: Westborough," Luis answered. Yeah, by four hundred miles, thought Lainie. Aloud, she commented, "We'd say that's south of San Francisco, slightly closer than L.A. by three-hundred eighty miles," said Lainie. "I'll leave my information, too."

"You know," Luis slowed down. "The land is long gone – worn out."

Lainie stopped and looked for Reena. She was too far back to hear this part.

He continued. "Nature beat it. Typhoons, floods, bombs." He quoted a familiar phrase. *"The money won't flow when the sugar's not sweet."* He plucked a perfect bloom and crushed it.

"Maybe *diwatas* punish insurrectos as well as us landowners, for sins we commit or even for sins a father commits." Luis sighed. "But God forgives all the time, *talaga*. I say, everyone should let sleeping dogs lie. Let the land lie easy."

Lainie waited, then re-quoted, "Fallow – lie fallow. Flowing all along, though, is always the money. *Talaga*?" She mentally added, Luis, son of bastard Don Padre, half-cousin to Reena.

Luis smiled and hawked into a nearby pot, a move again revealing his peasantry versus true gentry. Let him lie, Lainie grimaced, lie fallow, lie bald-faced, lie like a rug.

They had traveled around to the front entrance again. Mike still stood, waiting. Luis signaled him to follow them all. They traveled the same route through the massive house to the same room with the glass table. The windows were clear, and his estate was visible and nearly heavenly. Another lunch was served, thinly sliced roast beef, baby red potatoes, a spritely green salad, and glass of red wine. Reena had scarfed down the earlier offering. From a potted coleus, Luis had bent off and gave Reena cutting, signaling a maid to wrap it. Mike now stood at attention behind Luis's chair.

"I thought maybe the short walk would improve our appetites," Luis said, spreading a fresh linen napkin on his lap. "We add knives here, by the way. Eat everything. Please."

Lainie peered into the food. "Well, not everything – just what's on the plate."

Whatever the reason was for the upgrade, the food was delicious. Lainie ate the whole lunch and drank half her wine. Reena kept checking her big purse.

They made the motions to end the visit, wisely, in the long run. Luis pointed up at Mike and asked, "So this Mike has shown you what you wanted to see on this trip? He's a good driver? *Ano*, he took you on roads that were safe and fast, yes? How did he do?"

Reena smiled, shrugged a bit. "He's a good driver, lots of turns and roads here. I don't know about his working your fields, though, if he ever works at all." Mike heaved a big sigh.

Luis laughed out loud. Reena added, "Maybe not as an overseer, always driving us, but he did, you know, good."

Very slowly, Mike, behind his Foster Grants, swung in Luis's direction and then cranked himself back, inscrutable.

Luis had his garden help hand to Reena a bouquet of flowers from his garden. She was elated and leaning up, rubbed noses with Don Luis Serrañao. Talk about sugary, Lainie grinned. Luis gave Lainie a long hug and reminded her to contact his children.

"You are headstrong. You are Reena's daughter." Luis looked relaxed and added to Reena, "Enjoy the flowers and the like."

His final remark was, "Land, in this economy, is a crutch. Anyone is better off without it, especially living so far away. Lainie, enjoy your last day, yes?"

Luis knew Lainie's schedule from Mike.

"Oh, yes, my last day. Last thoughts, however," Lainie pushed her lower lip at Reena.

On cue, Reena quipped, "I love gardens. I know how earth works, Luis. And you."

As Mike drove them off the grounds, the formerly focused pool and garden workers and even the house helpers straightened and waved. Riding back, Reena and Lainie spoke very little.

But they regaled Nita and her whole family on their return.

Mike, who had left after finishing his job, this time shook Lainie's hand and bowed to the rest of the family. He cranked the music way up as he barreled through Barangay 35 a last time. His job was done.

Reena then emptied her arms full of bouquets, Luis's cutting and also the two cuttings she had confiscated during the walk through his garden.

"For the kids." Seeing their looks, she exclaimed, "It's all for you kids."

"You will be ready in a couple hours?" asked Nate. "Deling's for dinner, remember?"

"But we just ate." Lainie added, hoping to nap. "And I have to pack."

"You did pack," Reena said. "I saw all you have."

"I'll drive them," Juan offered. "Draw me a map."

Lainie knew she had, and wanted, to attend. Still, just a half hour of sleep would help.

However, a motorcycle revved outside.

Fannie, Fausto's wife, was just as beautiful as the first time they had seen her with her daughter at the Reunion. His family of three arrived during the brief break before Deling's dinner. They perched outside the gate, a National Geographic photo depicting a third-world family unit. They sat on Fausto's motorcycle, the girl between her parents. Facing the camera, all three had the same expression, one of meditative patience and somber smiles. The composition declared, this is us. This is our life for the moment. Catch us this way. Catch the same later.

"*Hatagi siya og* bike ride," Fannie directed at Fausto. Lainie caught two words. His features were implacable, that passive-aggressive response Lainie recognized in her own family.

Hoisting the girl from the motorcycle, Fannie would not

speak English. And Lainie could only half-translate Fannie's minimal Cebuano.

"*Ikaw nagsaad, talaga?*" Fannie seemed to wheedle, descending off the bike.

Lainie spoke, "He doesn't have to give me a ride. It's okay."

Everyone looked at her, amazed. Nita hadn't even translated. Fausto cleared his throat and indicated that Lainie should sit on the bike. She did. He switched on the ignition and took off, a bewildered Lainie waving at the receding figures, even at the water buffalo, past the pavilion, the market, even the first cock fight arena, and then at the people squatting near the road catching wayward breezes. Other than Tacloban and Lunao, she saw in reverse the places the family had sped her by over the last five astounding days.

By day, the same route as the night before was totally different. No way could Lainie have found her way back on her own after the *tupada*. Fausto didn't talk, which was a relief. They'd be yelling at each above the relentless nasal buzz of the motorcycle.

She reviewed her arrival days earlier to this final day. She had ignored warnings to move around the island alone. Why fear solitary travel, why cripple her confidence in another area? Reena had made her own very long and very lonely journey, years' worth. Arms heavenward on the bike, Lainie reviewed a list. She, like Reena, should give more of herself, loner that she was, and keep some reserves in check, and, to be truly better, and un-chink what loner hearts guard.

Since her arrival, each new revelation buffeted and awakened Lainie. She recalled that throughout their early lives, her parents endured daily conflicts of class and culture. By withholding that history, Reena had buffered that unpleasantness for her children, pointedly, Lainie, but misled them, believing treatment in the U.S. would never descend into classism like in the Philippines. Five days was all it took for Lainie to immerse herself in Reena's drama-laden saga. Other than the visual background of bald and utter poverty, sentiments and governance were the same there as in the States for the have's and the have-nots.

The night with Jose was her way to gain some insight about Reena's culture through her own means and not by some chance remark. The discovery: their cultures had always been the same. What Reena experienced, her children absorbed in their genes, as had all the Plebiñas.

Fausto revved his engine. He, too, must be absorbing a discovery: his real mother had abandoned him. Like Lainie, though, road lust lured him. Through it, he juggled a smattering of cultures, so unlike his own. Like Geraldo and Reena and the growing number of overseas workers, he left home for the money. Reena had dodged her obligation and only now returned. Fausto kept his: to keep returning. Like so many who had left their homes, Reena had hoped, God willing, that both the compensation and sacrifice would pay off. Her sacrifice cost her a lot.

Her years stateside, Reena did live a better life but raised children deficient in their own culture and language and sadly resigned to her indifference. To her, that was a small price, one that would pay off, till Reena heard one grandson ask her, "What's a grandma? What are you?"

Startled, Lainie nearly fell off when Fausto hit a bump, biking at its worst. She hooted.

Through gritted teeth, he barked, "You must like to live like this, on the edge."

She understood.

Fausto settled his own family obligation by offering Lainie a ride. She felt his remoteness, familiar because it mirrored hers and in a sense, Reena's. Or was his frustration like Lainie's: why cater to strangers who had never acknowledged his, or her, existence before? Why should he share anything of himself, to anyone, when results are abandonment and betrayal?

"I live worse," Lainie shouted. "I thought on the edge meant I didn't need a family."

Why had she said that? Fausto slowed down and then idled at a jungle intersection.

"*Gago*, eh?" His voice softened. "Better to know we have them than not, *talaga*?"

At a loss, Lainie could only shrug and mumble, "*Sigé*, then." He laughed.

He drove them past the carabao. The work beast lazily stared back. His steadiness reflected the hardened and placid looks distinguishing Fausto's and Nita's family, and vendors, town mates, town crier, and butcher. And they matched the admirable traits of carabaos. Their kin hoisted aloft defiance and serenity like a torch – that flame of Plebiña audacity. A hybrid line seeded and made good in new soil for both Cortezes and Plebiñas but at a cost: missing out on any knowledge passed on from previous generations. Still, like Reena's confiscated cuttings, there were advantages for hybrids stemming from other influences, perhaps simple bravado.

The young couple, Fausto and Fannie and child took off, their time together, precious. A nephew had met his aunt and cousin; the old world touched the new. It was enough.

XXXXI

Deling was late.

Insistent on a dinner, she was not at her hut when Juan, Reena, and Lainie arrived.

" 'S okay, we wait!" her jolly housemate, Remy, had swung open the door to the two-room dwelling and took upon herself the task to entertain them with her lively talk. 'Come in, come in, come in!" Remy gestured, her broad, flushed cheeks like plums flanking her nose.

Lainie was by now tired and getting a bit cranky. Now because of an even later dinner, she would not get enough sleep before the drive early in the morning back to the Tacloban airstrip with Juan.

Looking into the interior, she was struck by Deling's spare walls, floors, and open cabinets. Walking from the car, they again passed barrio huts like those in Manila and in Bgy. 35 with its twisting, indistinguishable, claustrophobic walkways. Days earlier wending their way to Vi's place along the Anilao the day Vi missed her own merienda, Lainie had only watched her feet tiptoeing over litter. She had avoided staring at the rippled tin siding with thin rags covering windowless openings and propped-up corrugated roofs. She gawked now and wondered what had she feared then, that the mere proximity of these dwellings would block any opportunity to taste the opulence they had just witnessed at the Serrañao mansion, that barrio life existing at all would only hinder their escape from poverty? Is that what challenged locals, like her mother once was? Juan, Reena, and Lainie stepped onto the two slats serving as stairs. Suddenly, the boy, 'Fredo, burst through the door, kissed Remy, and dropped a paper bag onto a monkey pod wood platter. Excusing himself again, he dashed out. Remy shook her head.

"Such a good boy," she hugged herself. "He helps Deling so much. I do what I can here, but he runs here, everywhere."

Remy with short hair was about as tall as Deling but younger. In cut-off jeans and a thin flimsy top that in no way hid her very large bust. Remy unabashedly showed off her attributes.

"What do you do in Ormoc?" asked Reena.

"Oh, I don't work, I'm on disability," Remy explained. "I'm Deling's girl friend."

Ah.

Both Reena and Lainie smiled and said nothing. The hut was now more noticeably smaller, with three residents in two rooms. Still, just their co-habitation could not prove any sexual relationship. Nothing flaunted anything gay, just a décor of devout Catholicism. Noticeably, plastic-covered holy cards were pinned to various areas with a crucifix in each room. Lainie noted threadbare towels, and blankets, a number of banigs on the raw bamboo wood floor, simple furniture, and many plastic bags. A bucket and a commode took up an open-aired side space.

Rustling crinkled 'Fredo's paper bag. Lainie was startled. Juan was speaking in Cebuano to Remy. Reena was trying to keep up. None of them paid any attention to the moving bag.

Juan and Remy were young schoolmates together. Remy was "*bayot*" (gay), and Juan was posing many questions, curiously. In fact, he was deeply interested.

Lainie asked, "Um, does anyone hear the bag?"

"*Way problema*, it's just the chicken," Remy said. The bird was still alive.

"Well, maybe we should, um, get it ready." Lainie reconsidered.

As if she would kill and pluck her first chicken – that was unlikely.

"No, we'll wait for Deling. She has a method," Remy said, making Lainie wonder what Remy did at all to help.

"Maybe I'll take a walk along the Anilao River," said Lainie. Very loud protestations stopped her. Juan looked the most worried. No doubt in his mind, she had probably gone off on her own a bit too many times. She flashed a grin. "Or not."

She sat and almost dozed while the others talked. Eventually, both 'Fredo and Deling, puffing, entered. He aided her at every step, helping her to sit, removing her shawl, placing her ever-present umbrella by the door, used not for spotty rain, but for the sun. She was beaded with sweat, and her thin, gray hair was mottled.

"Sorree-ah, sorree, sorree," Deling chanted between puffs,

unwinding her cotton scarf from around her hand. She dabbed at her face. Sweat poured from her brow and neck. Lainie marveled at the woman's stamina, given her weight and probable medical condition.

"Hokay, hokay, dinner, hah? We hungry?" Deling had entered her own world much as she breezed into others, with more fanfare than any greeting. She smiled broadly once she was settled. "Oy, you are here. Welcome to my humble abode."

Each day Lainie had been thrown and awed by every situation that she and Reena experienced. Each one had topped the next bits of daily drama and spots of *tsismis*. Here, the last night of her visit, she sighed, a simple, quiet dinner would be totally welcome.

'Fredo said very little and went about his duties like clockwork, with no corrections or additions from Deling. Remy just watched. If Deling, in a softer tone, demanded anything, Remy cheerfully accommodated her, but never offered on her own to do anything.

Deling directed, "Set five plates, forks, spoons, and pineapple cans."

No mid-meal store run was needed.

Deling waddled with the paper bag and a bolo knife toward the hut's side space.

Lainie followed. "Do you mind if I watch?"

Deling looked sideways but with a single stroke and no ceremony, she hacked off the chicken's head. The body fluttered as she held its neck. Blood jerked and flowed onto the dirt.

"Like that," Deling stated, wiping the blade on a long, green grassy leaf. "Do you pluck? Never mind, 'Fredo will pluck the feathers."

Lainie guessed that she herself must have looked somewhat green. 'Fredo joined them in work clothes, best for plucking chickens. Deling tottered behind, pushing Lainie ahead of her back into the hut.

As she plopped herself spread-legged under her long dress in front of Reena and Lainie, Deling blared, "So what are you doing here?"

They were surprised. "Um, we're here for dinner?" Reena added, "You invited us?"

Deling snorted. "No, really, why did you come back? What do you want with us?"

This was in Reena's ballpark. Lainie leaned back.

"Well, *Manang* Deling," Reena was faltering. Reena never faltered. She sidestepped. She diverted, but never faltered. Deling waited, drawing a finger under her nose. Reena breathed.

"I-I missed my town mates. I miss Ormoc."

"You said that, at the Reunion, you tried to cry."

Ay-yah, thought Lainie who braced for Deling to slash her to ribbons, too.

"Well, I don't, I only wanted . . ." Reena is at a loss.

"Oh, ignore me!" Deling suddenly swiped and missed Reena's leg. "Let's get this chicken cooked, eh? *Merienda!*"

Lainie then noticed that both Remy and Juan were gone. 'Fredo re-entered with the plucked chicken, appearing more stringy than it had with feathers. Deling dictated to 'Fredo to prepare small potatoes and carrots. He used the same bolo knife that killed the chicken.

"Come sit while I cook," Deling commanded Reena, who scurried closer like a scolded adolescent.

"I knew Billina, your mother. She was a quiet woman, except when it came to you. Oh-oh, *salamat* – thank you for the big feast. Many people did your bidding, just like before."

"I wasn't, I was helping," Reena protested.

"Yesterday was one of the biggest events we had in Ormoc, with all its drama-drama, *sigé na*. The woman, all showy and shiny, she 'tell it like it is,' *talaga*? Pass me that salt."

Lainie paused. Shiny –Deling also used the term, shiny. Rising, she reached for the salt and handed it to Deling, who nearly poured the contents on the chicken. Lainie envisioned returning home with high blood pressure, and adding that week's carbs, probably with diabetes.

"Is it true? You agree with that woman?" Deling licked her thumb, eyeballing Reena.

Remy and Juan had returned. Deling asked, "Everything co-pasetic?" Remy grinned. Lainie now saw one of Remy's purposes – to take up the slack. 'Fredo was so quiet they forgot he was there.

"Pretend napkins?" Remy tore off paper towels from a small roll. "'*Da Da the Nightlife*'!" She poked Juan who looked pensive. Whatever they discussed affected him.

Deling checked on 'Fredo's vegetables and loudly announced, "Hokay, dinner is ready!"

Lainie saw the still bloody carcass parts, mysteriously cut in haphazard sections, sizzling in the black iron skillet. To her, the chicken was visually raw and not at all cooked.

But they all sat around the tiny three-by-five table, and held hands, and 'Fredo said Grace. Once he was done, Deling added some words in Cebuano. Reena hmphed and nodded.

" 'God is good, God is great, Good God almighty, let's all eat'!" Remy joked and dove into the skillet that held the semi-cooked chicken. Lainie knew a spoon would not cut it.

Deling asked Juan short, polite questions. They passed small potatoes and chomped on raw carrots. Lainie still full from Luis's second lunch and could not chew stringy chicken, ate small portions. Plus she was anxious. Deling might ream her out any minute now.

Reena munched staring at her food, one eye gravitating to its outer corner on her face.

When the meal was over, Remy gathered dishes and washed them in the side space area. 'Fredo wiped off the table and double burner, swept a bit, and for a while glued himself to a corner table to study. Remy and Juan left again. Deling led Reena and Lainie to the couch.

"He's a good student. I taught him all he knows." Deling repeated herself from before.

"So-o-o," Reena was poised to square off again. "What do

you need, *manang*? Did you train that woman? Was she also your friend, that one who 'tells it like it is'?"

"Ay, no." Deling settled back filling her small couch. "I do not need to know her, but you? What redemption is due she spoke of for you? After this visit, will you come back? If you don't, what do you leave here this time? 'Fredo, go study next door. Go, go."

Obediently, 'Fredo picked up his books and left.

"What did you promise, in the mountains?" pressed Deling, leaning forward.

Lainie wished she could leave, too, and maybe join Juan and Remy.

Reena stared, her lips moving, but said nothing.

"Was your man your one true love?" Deling's question startled Lainie. "Or was he a stepping stone out of here, to the States?"

Who? Was Deling mixing up Lainie's father with – the Texas Captain?

Deling prodded, "Or was it Antonio? Vi said he was the one not interested in the States."

Lainie sat quite still. Tonight, her last, was not one destined to be a simple, quiet dinner.

"Vi," was all Reena said. "Queen of nothing but *tsismis*."

"Aah, we all knew. She verified it. Say now: what bargain did you make with the devil?"

Reena narrowed her eyes. "I don't think I want to tell you," she answered calmly.

"Oy."

"I don't think I have to tell you. What do you want from me? Money?"

Deling scoffed. "Money."

"Money!" Reena challenged. " 'Moneybags' they call me because I hold a Reunion. So what do you want? Bonita told us. She said, 'she wants something, that one.' What is it?"

Bingo. Reena just topped Reena. Again.

Deling didn't quite go on the offensive. "If you flaunt it,

people notice. Give me money. Give us money. You give it to Nita all this time. Why not the rest of us?"

"She took care of my mother. Did you?" Reena's eye wandered like a klieg light. "'*Sus*, you all want money, this town got two batches of chicken out of me, none of it was spoiled. I know. Go ask Luis for money, big man. I saw his house today. Big spender's right here in town. He 'makes contributions'. Ask him."

"Nita barely dressed Billina. I heard." Deling was now on shaky ground. "Nita cheated you, no one told you, hah, and she gets more and more for her house, and her kids and grandkids. All from you, every month, every year."

"Enough, *putang ina mo.*" Reena rose and started pacing the floor. Oh, God, I got to get her out of here, thought Lainie. This was a true display of full-on, barrio *tsismis*.

"Oy." Deling reared back.

"You wait to get me alone to talk behind Nita's back? Why didn't you 'tattle' to me? Any one of you could've written me! You want my money so bad, but you don't know what Nita did! She gave me all her receipts. I know what she spent! Even my mother wrote me, you think my mother would lie? Billina Plebiña had more worth in her little finger than this whole barrio! You know my mother, ha!" Reena clenched her fists. "Oooh, I'm glad I left this place!"

Reena was on a roll and in the best English Lainie had ever heard her speak.

Suddenly, Reena pulled open her large purse. "Here. You want money? Here, and here!" She slapped some paper bills on the table. "That's all I want to share. I share the big things with my friend, the one who took good care of my family when I couldn't. Could you?"

By now, Deling was holding out her hands, splayed out toward Reena, shushing her and actually apologizing. Reena evaded her arms and kept pacing. Deling could not easily, or more dramatically, rise from the couch without 'Fredo's assistance. And

Lainie would only watch.

This was not her battle.

Reena puffed, and then slowed down, puffing less. Finally, hesitantly, she admitted, "I got to go to the C.R."

Deling pointed to the back area, and then *sss-sst'*ed to remind Reena to take a full bucket of water with her.

So much for yet another discovery, Lainie blinked and receded into her seat.

Since receiving aerograms, ones like Lainie had retrieved from the mail, Reena had been, and always was, in touch with grandma Billina. She had paid guilty coins for her redemption and to have Nita care for Billina, the mother she had waved off like a fly in 1947.

Deling pointed at the bills on the table. "Bring it to me. Go, please, bring me that."

Lainie sighed and got up to gather the money. She handed the bills to Deling who counted them efficiently. After sectioning some for herself, Deling held out the paper pesos. "Give this back to her. I don't need it."

"Give it back yourself, *manang.*" Lainie kept her hands at her side. "Please. Or keep it. Because she will take it back. And you should apologize to Nita, for your *tsismis.*"

Deling bunched all the money together. Lainie doubted she heard the last few words.

"What about you?" Deling looked up at her.

Lainie gulped.

"Me?"

"You say yesterday you want to know us? How well?"

"I'm not sure I know what you . . ."

"If you want to know us, help this boy. Help 'Fredo."

Lainie sucked her lip. "Ah. So now you want money, from me."

"You have some, too. You came here."

Lainie sighed. "You know, just because I flew here doesn't mean I'm rich. And you know, you don't know me, either. Did anyone ever ask me how I live, what little I have?"

By now Reena had returned and stood by the door, listening. Lainie's tone sharpened.

"This is my life. I work at least three jobs a day and teach every week. Somehow I have time to write. I pay rent and bills and budget only for food. I have no real car. I do this all on less than forty dollars a day. I will have no money when I return. I'm not sure I'll have one of my jobs. I don't have a Remy or a 'Fredo. No family lives near me. It's all on me. You think I'm flush enough to help anybody?"

"Have 'Fredo stay with you. Send him to school." Deling was blunt and very determined. "Bring him to America."

"*Ay 'sus*," Reena uttered from her corner.

Lainie thought to just plop down a bunch of bucks and imitate her mother.

But she saw the look of desperation in Deling's eyes. She saw her as someone just like Nita, carrying the load for so many years but for so many others like 'Fredo. Lainie had read Deling's articles where many students had moved on to higher education because of her. She was a broker of sorts, a promoter, and a go-between. Children, with defeated parents like 'Fredo's, would live in her minute hut. Minds, hungry for knowledge, endured the nearly slave like conditions, fetching, carrying, carting Deling. They knew, and Lainie could now understand, that Deling gave her all to them. The least they could do was serve her, hold her umbrella, catch a chicken, and share the space with her and her probable lover.

For Reena, redemption cost money. Those like her had left, shirking obligations to family and community. Those like Deling stayed and cared for town mates. Deling served them.

Guilt weighted Reena's cross for leaving and for returning. Poor mom, thought Lainie.

Lainie wished she could help Deling and 'Fredo. She knew money could aid them only for a short while. Would another route do more, when she'd be better equipped, when she had real worth herself, thought Lainie. Sorry, Deling, sorry, 'Fredo, sorry, sorry, Ormoc – sorry.

"I can't bring 'Fredo to the States, *Manang* Deling. I can't. But here . . ." Lainie pulled out her hoarded mad money, fifty pesos. "This would've been a snack on the flight home or a watered-down Scotch when I arrive. But it can't be both. That's how little I have. So this little bit, this is the better choice, *diba*?" She offered the coins and let them roll onto the table, a plaintive move.

Deling listened. She drummed her fingers near the coins, thinking, and stared at Lainie.

"I'll take it." With a hand, she swept the coins into the other. "Because you need me to."

Reena hoisted her purse just as Juan, Remy, and 'Fredo returned. Remy, seeing the coins, joked.

"I thank us for you, eh? Save you the trouble: *'Thank you for the chicken, so goo-ood, so juicy!'*"

Ah, a sendoff, Lainie felt. Remy shook their hands and whispered loudly to Juan.

"You try that, eh? *Sigé*, try them all! Give her much pleasure, eh? You know?"

Like a nautilus, Juan started and blushed. His ruddiness took on a deeper plum color.

Deling directed 'Fredo. "Walk them to Nita's jeep."

Regarding her briefly, she swiped at Lainie's arm then pulled her to her chest.

Pushing her back, Deling then wrapped her arms around Reena, whispered a bit, and held her at a distance, both unwavering in their final looks.

'Fredo bounded away, rather gleefully, thought Lainie. Was he aware that Deling again lobbied for him either to study in Ormoc or to escape it? She imagined a young Reena at his age. He, too, was set apart, wanting just a bit more. Lainie bet as much.

She glanced back, her own last view of the ragtag section near the Anilao River. Remy had scooped Deling in a big hug.

Neither of the affectionate women were couture'd or svelte, costumed or mascara'ed. Lainie believed that for each other, they had all they needed.

Something gnawed at Lainie: Nita's role. Nita's jeep, Nita's house, her compound, and her store were not called Horatio's but hers. Even the town, Lainie realized, seemed to downplay Horatio's NPA role. Lainie felt her own rapid blinks. The town scrutinized whatever Nita did. She was under the town's microscope: patient, somewhat resigned Nita.

Lainie had been the sideshow, a minor character. Everyone watched Nita to see how she would serve the benefactress who subsidized her for years, of the faux dynasty of Barangay 35.

The ride home was quiet. Lainie joked, "So-o-o juicy, huh, that raw, scrawny chicken."

Juan spoke up. "They have chicken so few times, and they share it with you! Sometimes just be gracious, Lainie. Pick up what people do that you don't see, *sigé?*"

The mood during the drive home was subdued. Night hid the usually present carabao. With a start, she blinked: Juan's tone. His was like her brother, Adam's, in the voice Juan used when Nita scolded him, probably about being a better bodyguard for errant Lainie. Still, this ride was smoother, calmer, devoid of curiosity or dread of the drive ahead. Like her San Francisco, Lainie felt she knew: routes. Lainie had been reviewing the whole week and not gawking out the window composing clever snippets for curious travelers. She had swung full circle from where she had felt adrift among strangers to being strangely comforted, enfolded – accepted, though perhaps in reality, considered an oddity. In that case to a town, she was at least, their oddity.

They sounded like family, the squabbles among each other, the ease to lay out to each other their complaints, or their misgivings, or their truths. Juan called Lainie on her snarkiness.

And she had bore the reprimand. His rebuke had been justified, much like ... at *home*.

At the house, the girls were already asleep. Bonita assured Lainie. "They'll be awake with us to say goodbye at 4am." It seemed this departure involved less participation.

To Reena, Nita added, "They stay with me while Nate drives you, Lainie, and Juan to Tacloban Airport. We still have you, cuz, for awhile."

She patted Reena's shoulder. But then, Nita – Lanita, Lainie's namesake, cried. Her eyes flooded. Lainie's last night, and Lainie felt Nita's tears, and even her own, would wash this drama clean. "Até, "Lainie cooed, "Salamat, don't cry. For all you've done, Salamat."

Nearby, a lyrical harana floated in the night air for another expectant yet aloof lover. Contrasting that, Jun's radio signaled a night of all's well. *"Somewhere (crackle) there . . ."*

Perched near the lower bunk, Lainie noted how immense the room was without those humongous *balikbayan* boxes. Lainie's backpack was neat and ready. Pickle was nowhere to be seen. Lainie had marked envelopes with Sari-Sari and Teri-Teri's names. They held pesos to be left in its home country, a rule dictating money exchanges. Reena lounged on her lower bunk.

Perched on the top bunk, Lainie cleared her throat. "Mom, I got a question."

"You always have questions."

"The vow, what the shiny woman said you made in the mountains. Was there one?"

She was at first, silent. "What about it."

"Did you leave grandma Billina to Nita? Like she would stand in for you, with her?"

Silence.

"Was Dad a stand in for someone else you left?"

Lainie heard a small laugh.

"What was it, Mom? What was it about? Please?" Reena sighed.

"About? You, hon. All of you. How without me being me, you could not be you. I don't have you depend on me. When I'm gone, you know you've helped yourself. I'd make you learn that sooner than I had. You all did. You're all too much like me." She tipped her head, that way. "In bad times, don't believe a god will come through for you, or a parent. No one will." She paused. "Are all your questioned answered? You got your article now? Don't answer."

Reena's rhetorical questions lay between them. No boxes served as distractions.

Why did they all, her whole family, operate this way. Lainie leaned on Pickle's wall.

Lainie never asked about Reena's love again. Their own hot-cold relationship was simply frenetic because she was so much like Reena. But Reena's cage was a type of post-traumatic syndrome. Imagining a haphazard map of strings, Lainie connected the dots:

Reena had had a soul-shaking moment topping anything Lainie herself experienced. She bargained a loveless life against imminent death. However, Reena had not planned thoroughly. She could not know that she could not keep that vow. She'd ache, recognizing her children's loss of innocence, like the one she had. And then she read an aerogram.

She missed family, like arms cut from shoulders, like hearts pulled from chests.

Lainie decided that no god had gifted Reena; no god would rescue her from Want; and no god would secure her a Norman Rockwell-like tableau. Reena made things happen. Always refer-ring to a god, Reena voiced another vow on Lainie's last night:

"Never mind what the shiny woman said. God forbid you ever hold to a vow like I did. Ay, dear God in your wisdom, let all mean-ingless dares be the ones you will ignore." With that, Reena shut off. In the distance, neighbors toasted beer. A carabao bellowed.

Lainie's dreams that night were ironically a checklist: Make it, make it to the plane. Offer Juan the window seat. Keep the passport nearby. Hide the jackfruit. Open red gates.

XXXXII

Nate drove solemnly; Reena waved her byes. Lainie and Juan, reflective, boarded their flight. Juan, prodigal jeepney driver, had no welcome at Manila Airport, which puzzled even Juan. He hailed a jeepney for Lainie and himself, clicking his tongue all the way back to his house, to a mid-size apartment above a store in Metro Manila. When they arrived, Juan confronted the fellow jeepney driver. "You took a roundabout way so the meter would be high, *'tangina!*" Juan shorted him. The driver protested weakly. Juan ignored him. He carried their bags up the stairs.

Lainie and Juan had decided she would wait the six-hour layover at his house with his wife, Anndeliza. She was inscrutable upon their arrival, as if Juan had just returned from the store and not from his home island, far, far away. She had only rose to take his duffel bag. He took the lead and pulled her close.

"Anndeliza, I am home," he zoomed in for a kiss. Lainie turned away and saw a smooth looking woman with a pair of scissors, a surface nearby strewn with brushes and hairspray.

"So you both had a good trip?" The woman tipped a cup in Lainie's direction, "Ade?" Lainie realized the hairdresser was actually a man, dressed appropriately for his/her business. Lainie nodded.

"Kummusta, I am Cher." The porcelain-faced man's voice lilted on his nom de plume. He had been trimming Anndeliza's hair and reached for a Pepsi bottle. Not easily won over, Anndeliza moved from Juan's embrace, retrieved two glasses nearby and poured their drinks. Theirs was a tiny place. Lainie geared up.

"Thank you for letting my mom borrow Juan to guard me," Lainie said, to which Anndeliza glanced at Lainie and moved to her hairdresser. He raised his eyebrows.

"Guard, eh," Anndeliza echoed. "Yes, many skills."

Juan, Lainie guessed was employing Remy's "advice" on courting and in time, on intimate techniques. The setting was a challenge: the hairdresser's proximity was too close; Juan should be nearer to his wife. She now would make Juan wonder how she spent his time away.

"Cher." Lainie toasted him. "You hab her new CD? Did you see her bee-dee-oh? Sex-ee, no?"

Cher turned wide-eyed and wondrous. "Ay, *talaga*! Were you on the S.S. Missouri for Cher's show? Oh, to be a fly, to be a FLY!"

Lainie moved closer, detecting a rum odor. Juan had not taken his eyes of Anndeliza.

"Oh-oh, that's in L.A. I'm from San Pranceesco, *diba*." Lainie found herself lapsing into a type of vernacular, the low monotone of *tsismis*. Juan was reaching for Anndeliza's hand. She was not quite pulling away. The air smelled a bit like warmed liquor.

"Oy, C.R.? Long trip by plane and from the airport." Lainie pushed her lip toward a back area. Cher led Lainie, obviously knowing the layout, and gushed, "You must tell me, what it's like, Calipornia *talaga*, all singers and dancers."

"*Sigé na*, and you, e-spike spike?" Lainie mimed pouring into her Pepsi. "Hooch." She giggled when Cher looked perplexed. Lainie wheedled. "You share rum; I tell you all, *talaga*?"

Cher dug out the surreptitious pint of rum from his back pocket. "OY, and all the liberties! In 'Prisco!"

Lainie peered back at Juan and Anndeliza, missing each other, now connected. As he hugged her closer, he caught Lainie's eye. She thought, a small payback, Juan, for her life.

Cher, for three hours, happily shared rum and Pepsi with Lainie in the back room. After both couples passed time in their different pursuits, Juan finally appeared. "Airport," he said.

Before returning to Aquino Airport, Lainie presented an envelope with more bills to Juan.

"No, no," he pushed back. She plied him with more envelopes. "And Primo's family."

Juan looked woebegone. She felt she must stand on protocol and dismiss any *faux pas*.

"I would have spent it on something to bring back and show

any of this really happened. But I couldn't think of anything. Nothing quite hit the mark, nothing was just right to the point and memorable, if you know what I mean," she explained to Juan. He nodded sympathetically.

At the airport, Lainie watched him get out of his customized jeepney. As he hugged her, he chanted, "You always found your way home, *sa karaba, liko sa tuo.*" He wiped away his tears and swept his hand over his buzz cut. "*Adunay usa ka maayong biyahe.*"

"Something about the carabao, a trip, a journey. A good journey, *diba*?" Lainie saw through her watery veil. "*Biyahe*, cuz. *Sigé*: sublime." He smoothed his buzz cut, sniffling.

And Juan, jeepney driver, bodyguard, her unsung hero, was gone, and Lainie flew home.

Within the month, Lainie and Reena, both having returned, inundated the family with photos and anecdotes of Lainie's one week in Ormoc to Reena's three. Neither of them mentioned the vow, though, neither to siblings, daughters, sons or their children, nor ever again to each other.

A cycle paused.

XXXXIII

Reena lay in bed during her last week in the residential re-hab center. Her small hospital room now had only favorite albums and pictures of grandchildren. Lainie had just flown in from Hawai'i, selected aerograms clutched in one hand, pulling them from pocket areas with the other. Nearly thirty years since Ormoc, and Lainie found herself still asking questions. She had googled

Ormoc and had read about their land listings and now read them to ailing Reena.

In 1989, while they both were in Ormoc, Nita had filed the papers relinquishing, in Reena's name, the plots of which Luis had no need. For thirty years the squatter tenants raised the money to pay the land taxes till Luis died. His loss on sugar plus two typhoons and the hotel renovation took up his valuable time and money, besides what was left from "insurance" that was paid to the encroaching drug cartels. His surviving offspring signed off on more adjoining plots.

They had little to lose given their lucrative pineapple crop. The squatters, thanks to their own U.S.-based children, retained their own family lawyer. Though post-2016 legal challenges from Luis Serrañao's offspring were heavy, the tenants prevailed.

"Ah, well." Reena shifted stiffly in place, addressing her visitors. "Momma, grand-uncle, we Plebiñas all had our day already. My fruits and Luis's flowers from across the sea still bloom at home here."

"Why didn't you tell me Nita wrote this to you?" Lainie led with the damning question.

Adam and Calista lived miles from Tina and Anne-Marie, and Lainie more miles from all of them. "Life's been good," Reena's sighed to her visitors. "The kids, well, they're as far as . . ." The group at her bed waited. "As I kept them." A hum nearby behind a curtain now sounded louder.

"At least none of them broke more commandments than me!" Reena laughed. Her roommate humming behind the track-pulley curtain paused at Reena's laugh and then, as if vague, started humming again.

Both adult care residents would never go home again. Lainie took in the small room.

That one year was the only time Reena had visited Ormoc, 1989. What could she return to now, with property scattered, and with more layers separating old family holdings from new.

Reena chimed, "I dated Mr. White and even kissed him. My last day in Ormoc."

Lainie was used to the random subjects brought up in phone calls to Reena, events from the week before swirled around incidents decades old. She tucked her own questions aside and listened.

"But I told him," Reena kept confessing, "I still love someone else."

Nita's store, hardly ever open during their visit, had taken off. In guarded words through the letters Lainie had deciphered, Horatio and Nate, who still visited every year, had cleaned the path of "business-donated" funds for NPA activities, which doubled when Presidents changed hands.

Corruption filtered more into the provinces, and KFRs, kidnaps for ransom, occurred more often. Dangerous but lucrative, they increased with tourism. Earning 5,000 pesos one month, Nita had returned Reena's monthly money. Beyond her debt, Nita still paid. And Reena returned the excess. Both stopped sending simultaneously.

The barrio had been abuzz. Tsismis ran like blood from a wound among the *silingans* who reveled at the Reunion, the prime event of 1989. Once Reena and her American dollars had left, the town began snubbing Nita. Nita's efforts to please Reena had earned envy from soured local relatives.

"I don't remember when Nita wrote me." Reena picked at the thin coverlet on her bed.

"Well, then, I'll read it to you," stated Lainie, scouring one aerogram. "Nita shut herself off even from you. Ah, here: Horatio wrote – amazingly upbeat, by the way – that now that she's officially blind, he had been passed on the torch to care solely for her.'"

"Her clouded eyes never cleared. Give me that water." Reena held her hand aloft.

"I never knew, why didn't you tell me? How could Barangay 35 treat her that way?"

Reena sipped the water. She seemed coherent, saying, "The

night you left, ay, Nita, she cried all night. Her eyes became cloudy and stayed that way through the rest of my trip."

The subject then changed. "Vi was mad. Brags about her many grandchildren, I said, yeah, but who remembers *your* visit, hah?"

Lainie kept extracting from aerograms. "Two years later, the Flood of '91, 4,000 died, Deling moved. The Anilao River covered everything. She died from double pneumonia."

"Billina, *nanay*," Reena nodded to some unheard comment. Lainie flipped aerograms with yellow stickers.

"This one says Fausto was telling everybody he had no family. Sad. That's sad."

"Yes, Reena laughed. Lainie frowned. Reena pushed her lower lip toward the foot of the bed. "Nanay's funny: '*Plebiñas do not grant gods time off.*' "

"When did she say that?"

Reena lifted her chin as a pointer. "Just now, see her? With all the others?"

Lainie stood looking at Reena a long moment. She took out another aerogram.

"Luis's crop drowned in the Flood. He switched from rotten sugar stalks to pineapple. Man, mom, what bad luck. And pouring money into his hotel and the drug trade, and another typhoon . . ." Reena interrupted Lainie.

"Ah, shiny lady. Predicted by you, aah, yes, you!"

This was becoming a challenge for Lainie, bringing up news reminding Reena and realizing more and more that her foot was in an alternate reality speaking to dead relatives.

She tested Reena. "Remember the NPA's? They're still active. There's a Visayan, outside Leyte, coming up the ranks: Duterte. Did you keep up with that, Mom?"

" '*Susmaryjosep*, you're all over the place. Of course, he's a Mayor. Why are you talking about politics? I thought this was about the letters."

Convinced that she had Reena's ear for a precious minute, Lainie sighed. "Well, it is, and this ain't. No, I don't want to talk about politics."

Reena started to rattle on. "There's no more land, the squatters own it, they tilled it a hundred years, so forget the deed. Let them raise their kids there. I raised you here."

Lainie was speechless. How did she know that was the very point, sore as it had been before 1989, which Lainie wanted to clear up? Reena continued to lecture the wall next to her as Lainie found and re-read the letter in Horatio's slanted handwriting:

"Bonita and Nate . . . in Christchurch with their daughters. They married Kiwis. Teresa who had been called Teri-Teri, at age 21 learned that the Abu Sayyaf leader Marcelo's rotted canvas painting held a deed written in Spanish, a land grant to Reena's great-great grandfather for his loyalty to Spain . . . the deed nearly disintegrated when it was pulled from the frame . . . now stored somewhere in the Madawawing Mountains."

Lainie stopped reading. Reena nodded.

"The place where the cockfight's a game, and the water buffalo, constant. Yes, yes, poetic, eh? And God willing, He laughs last . . . Lainie: cross yourself."

But Lainie shook her head. She felt around inside her straw bag for a tissue. She would not cry, not here.

Within a month after her return in 1989, Lainie had received from Juan, paid with money in the envelopes, a shipment of six simple rattan bags with "Ormoc City" sewn on them. Inside, were dates and words Lainie had learned every day from Juan and which she had memorized each evening. The inflections stayed; pronunciations faded. Now, though, instead of a packet of tissues, her hand stopped on a rolled piece of paper. She pulled at the hidden sheet and read the word by the fading light of Reena's nightlight: *home*. Cebuano for

Home.

"The same, hon, see? The word anywhere, for us, is the

same. Tell her," Reena insisted to her invisible tribe. "No, you, you should titch her, *among balay,* language! *Ay, 'susmaryjosep . . ."*

Reena had reverted to her first language, preaching to the converted seen only by her at the end of her bed, lola Billina and aunts, uncles, and people who passed on.

"It's okay, mom. You can leave now."

Reena's eyes lit up in joyous recognition. Family was like a cutting she fostered. Lineage and land, root-bound or re-potted, she nurtured stalks and seeds near and far, despite holding ground to a vow yet straying from it. She laughed.

How ironic that a clarion call resounds over time as simply a sigh – one, sublime.

GLOSSARY

Abbu Sayyaf militant nationalists based in Mindanao+

AFP Armed Forces Philippines/60k volunteer police 2014

Aguinaldo first president of the Philippiness 1899

ako si my name is

anak child

Anilao river in Ormoc

ano what

ano, naa bay makasulti ingles diri? do you speak English

asawa/esposa wife

Ate' term for elder female (vs eldest)

bagoong fish-based sauce

balikbayan shipping box

banig a slat-made rug to roll up, some floor covering

barong tagalog men's shirt made of pineapple leaf fibers

barrangay [35 is fictitious] neighborhood barrio;
  historically, boat with a full clan

barrio neighborhood (Spanish)

baryo barrio/barangay

Baybay town south of Ormoc along Ormoc Bay

Benigno Aquino, Cory activist assassinated in 1983, wife
  Cory is elected President

Biliran, Panoan islands north and south of Leyte

bolo wide-bladed knives for everyday use

bugok stupid

C.R. comfort room

camarones jumbo shrimp

carabao water buffalo, beast of burden

Cebuano dialect among Visayan islands

cockerel full term for cock

CPP Communist Party of Philippines, Marxist/Leninist values

diki ko makasulti'g cebuano I can talk/understand
    Cebuano

diwata priestess, female spiritual guides

Don Corleone Marlon Brando's character in GODFATHER

doyen termed women of stature in any field

Duterte Philippines president since 2017

Dynasty TV series rich family soap opera

gago stupid

Galois dark French clove cigarette

Gold Mountain term by Asian countries of the U.S

gwapo handsome

hamon bacon

harana suitor's love song, major chords

hectare equivalent to .3 mile

Ilocano dialect of the Ilocos area, Luzon island

Imelda first name of P.I.'s First Lady till 1986

insurrecto term for a rebel by foreign usurpers

jackfruit / nangka large bulbous fruit, hangs in bunches

jeepney aka jitney as pronounced, abandoned WWII U.S. jeep
    aka taxi

joke lang that was a joke

Jose Rizal poet, illustrado, novelist; incited rebellion;
    executed 1896

kababayan neighbor

kadiyot lang excuse me

kapre demon spirit in trees smoking cigars

KFR kidnap for ransom

kin family

kinsa who

kristos man who takes bets for cock fights

kumusta ca? how are you?

kundiman suitor's pining love song, minor **chords**

kuya term for younger male

lechon roast pig

Loma Prieta identifies SF's 1989 5.7 earthquake

Lunao fictitious town

Maayong buntag good morning good night

maayong udto good night

Madawawing mountain range east of Ormoc, Leyte

Maka istorya ka ug Binisaya? Can you speak Visayan?

Makati area within Manila

manang, manong terms for female and male elders

Manila capital of the Philippines, island of Luzon

mano act of respect for an elder, hand to forehead

mantilla material to cover female heads in church

maot ugly

mapang stuck up, snooty, haughty

Marcos dictator 1965-1986; wife Imelda was First Lady

merienda party, a gathering with food

Metro Manila Manila's city center

Mindanao southern Muslim island of Philippines

Miranda massacre 1971 fire bombing of nationalists
including NPA

Mukwonago town south of Milwaukee, WI

nagumpisana naman goes on and on (Tagalog)

narthex lobby of church

Ninoy Aquino, Cory anti-Marcos activist assassinated in
   1983; wife Cory elected pres.

NPA New People's Army, branch under CPP

Ormocanon a resident of Ormoc, harbor city

ouzo anise drink in Greece

P.I. acronym for Philippine Islands

pan de sal bread roll

pasayan shrimp

peso 8 pesos to a dollar in 1989-90

piña material made from pineapple leaf veins

Putang ina mo son of a whore

Rosas Pandan upbeat Cebuano Balitaw folk song-Prof.
   Manuel Velez folk 1974

sa'an where

sabong cock fight, unofficial, the barangay version

salamat thank you

salamat maraming po thank you all

Samar island east of Leyte

sentesyador main ring master

sige' sige' na okay, go on

Siligong thick bacon

silingan neighbor (C.)

Sitting Bull Sioux medicine man, predicted Little Bighorn
   1876, activist

Smokey Mountain Manila's garbage dump

sus marjosep Jesus Mary Joseph, revered names as curses

Tacloban capital of Leyte

Tagalog official Filipino language, prevalent on Luzon

Taglish half Tagalog half English

talaga really, isn't that right

Talk-Story oral story; actual Barroga play title, 1992

tama na stop

Tita term for aunt or similar female elder

Tito term for uncle or similar male elder

Toko / gecko Tokay lizard

tsismis gossip

tupada unofficial cock fight

unsay ngalan mo? What's your name?

Visayan dialect of the Leyte/Visayan islands

W.C. water closet; rest room

Walled City 16th century Fort Santiago Manila

Waray-Waray dialect of Samar/Visayan island area

way problema no problem (Cebuano);

walay problema no problem (Tagalog)

welcome sa welcome

ABOUT THE AUTHOR

Per her website, JEANNIE BARROGA has been called "a prototype of a new American playwright writing from the hub of a hundred cultural intersections" particularly championing Filipino-American theatre. Her papers are archived at Stanford University Special Collections. She is published by Amherst Press, Routledge Press, and more; and is compiling *Katatagan: Endurance* about Bay Area Filipino-American theater artists.

Buffalo'ed, (the play) about Black U.S. Buffalo Soldiers in 1899, the Philippines, is a recipient of the W.A. Gerbode and The William and Flora Hewlett Foundations grants, produced by both San Jose Stage and Kumu Kahua Theatre. The latter also had mounted *Talk-Story* after TheatreWorks' premiere. *Walls* was awarded the National Endowment for the Arts Access to Artistic Excellence Grant and has had multiple productions. *Banyan* was awarded the Arty Award for Best Original Production and Best Actress (11 of 37 nominations). She has directed at LaMama's New York, Brava Theater Center, and more. Barroga's plays have been produced locally and nationally at Bindlestiff Studio, Brava for Women in the Arts, El Teatro Campesino, Mark Taper Forum, New World Theatre Amherst, Pan Asian New York, Warehouse Repertory, etc. Initiating the Playwright Forum, she served as the first literary managers for both TheatreWorks and for the Oakland Ensemble Theater. Based in the Bay Area since 1972 and writing plays since 1981, she is a Lifetime Member of the Dramatists Guild and had been Artistic Director for both Teatro ng Tanan and the Asian American Theater Company. Her subjects focus on social justice, art and women. www.jeanniebarroga.com

This book is typeset in Georgia. The title is set in Wide Latin.

CPSIA information can be obtained
at www.ICGtesting.com
Printed in the USA
FSHW020408281221